THE
AMIRAH
DIAMOND

TINA L. HENDRICKS

ISBN: 978-1-7368816-0-6 (print)
ISBN: 978-1-7368816-1-3 (ebook)

*Dedicated to my daughter, Shea Lynn Hendricks—my
inspiration and the love of my life.*

PART ONE

◆

GUARDIAN

OF

ENEMIES

$$\blacklozenge$$

Chapter One

The doorbell rings. A deep orchestra echoes through Locket Manor. Gaillynn smiles at the melody; however, her heart thumps. She pulls her attention away from her book and glances up at the crystal chandelier. She points her toes in rhythm with the doorbell's organ keystrokes, right, left, right. She recalls pirouetting across the marbled floor as a child—long ago when she was eager to answer the door.

Gaillynn settles back to her book. While she reads, she also basks in the silent display of affection from an object she considers to be her life force—a stone radiating a pulsing glow that caresses Gaillynn's skin with warmth and love. This magical ore is confined in chains and attached to a thick, lengthy steel pendulum in the tall case clock across from her. Its presence in her life is a blanket of security and love ensuring her survival.

The doorbell rings again. Gaillynn's brows squeeze together, and invisible daggers prick the back of her neck. The sound of the chimes is lovely, but the caller reminds her that there is a world outside her home, Locket Manor. A world that on occasion threatens to revoke her withdrawal from it.

She listens to the full melody a second time, holding her breath and waiting for her mother to answer the door. It chimes again. Gaillynn's heart rate quickens. "Just answer the door, Mom," she says to herself.

Another persistent calling of the rhythmic pitch announces a disruption to her fourteen-year hibernation within the confines of her home. Gaillynn, now thirty-two years old, longs for her mother's help. "Mom?" There is no answer. Gaillynn raises her voice, "Gia Amirah?" Gaillynn holds her breath. "Mom, are you in here?" Silence.

◆

Gaillynn's mother is outside. She sits on the floor of the garden behind Locket Manor in her daily meditation pose. Her eyes are closed, her arms are open and resting on her crisscrossed knees. She inhales the air around her through her nose then exhales through her mouth repeating the words, "In and out," in silence. Bouquets of pine, saltwater, and fragrant blooms fill her nose. A soft smile curves the corners of her mouth, and she is unaware of her adult daughter's current turmoil.

Gia, short for Georgia, hums. Her happiness evokes swirls of wind around her. Whirlpools of dancing air pull delicate dandelion seeds up and over her head. The seeds parachute into a return journey landing weightlessly in her long brown hair. Dark-green grass and honeysuckle clover show their affection by pressing themselves against her legs. The sweet nectar of the clover's white flowers invites busy bumblebees.

Gia's meditation allows her mind to travel to places beyond her reality. Today her vision is of a male lion approaching a lioness. His mane is broad, and his head is dropped low, with protruding fanglike incisors. His shoulders tense with each step toward the lioness.

Her back is to him, but her cub sees him. The lion cub stiffens her petite body in his direction. The lioness turns to the male lion, who does not belong to her pride. The lioness raises her head and roars. She leaps upon him and wraps her jaws around his neck. Gia's eyes open.

"Gaillynn. My lioness. My Leo." A vortex of Earth's breath swirls around Gia—she smiles.

Gia relaxes her shoulders. "Gaillynn is fierce," she whispers. Pride expands her chest. For a moment, she has forgotten her regretful secret. But, not for long. Her smile disappears, her bottom lip turns down, and her gut fills with shame. "Robbie would still be alive if it weren't for me, and because of his death, Gaillynn has recoiled from the world for the past fourteen years."

◆

Inside the living room, Gaillynn also breathes deeply intending to calm herself. She presses a crocheted bookmark between two pages. The bookmark was a Mother's Day gift from her fourteen-year-old daughter, Gisela, who prefers to be called Ella. Ella crocheted her mother's name in lime green, Gaillynn Shea Amirah, surrounded by hundreds of tiny flowers on a piece of old lace. Ella glued the lace over a cardboard cutout, and she braided a matching tassel that Gaillynn now flips aside. Gaillynn closes her book and presses it to the yellow settee.

The stone's rhythm changes. Gaillynn's body jumps to standing. She tilts her head to the side. "What?" she asks the stone. Gaillynn peers outside through the window—the air has darkened, and the wind shakes the trees. "Something's up."

Gaillynn studies the stone in its resting place—secured in chains at the end of metal rods in the clock. Her eyes trace the almost round shape of the coveted family ore. The stone is translucent blue, with rough gold edges like a giant uncut gem. She recalls the story of Glinda, the clockmaker—Glinda, drawn to the stone by dreams and destiny, discovered the stone and built the clock over two hundred years ago.

"Why are you linked to me? To us? Why do you love me so? Why do our moods affect the weather? What is it that you are trying to tell me?"

As she anticipates, the stone deviates from its purpose of keeping time. Its sway within the clock becomes heavy and wide. A whisper of air moves over Gaillynn's skin. She hasn't experienced this feeling since Robbie's murder fourteen years ago—beaten to death by Cooper, who claimed he thought Robbie was rapping Gaillynn. Nine months later, Ella was born.

"Mom?" Gaillynn says. Again, Gia doesn't answer. "Shit." Gaillynn is resistant to move from the settee. "The only person who ever visits Locket Manor is Andie, and she just walks in. Plus, it's been over two years since Andie visited. I'm sure she's mad at me. God, I'm a terrible friend. No, it can't be Andie." Gaillynn bites her lip.

Gaillynn's protective instincts perk up along with the hair on the back of her neck. She cups her hands around her flat abdomen, where Ella grew fourteen years ago. She spent her pregnancy mourning Robbie and blaming the stone for his death. But as soon as her baby girl was born, her love for Ella medicated her grief. Ella became the love of her life and has blossomed into an intelligent and wise young woman.

Just moments before the caller at the door, Ella walked the length of the cobblestone driveway to the yellow bus waiting to take her to school—eighth grade.

Gaillynn moves toward the front door on her toes. Through the thick glass, she eyes the large shape standing on the other side of the hand-carved, Brazilian mahogany. It's Cooper.

Her green eyes darken, and her trembling hand reaches for the wide door handle. She studies Cooper's tall frame, protruding chest, and firmly planted feet. Those boots. He is wearing the same boots he wore when he kicked Robbie to death fourteen years ago. Cooper smashed Robbie's temple with his fist, rendering him unconscious. Robbie went limp and fell into Cooper's kick to the face. A sting of rage reddens Gaillynn's cheeks.

Her eyes travel from Cooper's feet to his face. Sadness and anger begin to press against her chest—she growls. Cooper's shaved hair is the style of a recently released convict. His eyes are the same—an empty dark brown so cold that Gaillynn shivers.

Gaillynn's fury causes the air around him to become aroused. The giant pine trees sway and bustle into an excited frenzy. Fallen leaves from the Golden Oak that stands guard outside Ella's window blow toward him and skip over his black, steel-toed boots. A summoning whistle rattles the door between them. He crosses his arms and turns away from Locket Manor to study the sudden change in the weather.

Gaillynn raises her oversized platinum wristwatch. The diamond hour markers and mother-of-pearl dial indicate six hours until school is out and Ella comes home. Her eyes dart from hour to hour on her wristwatch, negotiating her next move.

She wraps her fingers around the door handle—her rising temperature warms the cold metal. Gaillynn is far too furious at Cooper to ignore his visit. Her head turns toward the chest containing the handgun. She hesitates and wipes the wetness building in her eyes. Gaillynn visualizes herself pointing the pistol at Cooper's face and shooting him—his skull explodes. *Oh, Jesus, then there would be a mess to clean.* She pushes a breath from her chest, intended to incite patience. There is no reason to kill him. Ella is safe.

Gaillynn opens the door a few inches and uses her bare left foot to secure the door in its place. Brave snowflakes accompany the brisk air rushing inside Locket Manor to their death.

Gaillynn hasn't dressed for the day yet and still wears her dark blue pajamas buttoned all the way to the top, the collar hugging her thin neck. The outside air caresses her skin, which is always too warm to feel the cold.

"I'm not letting you in." She crosses her arms. "You have some nerve coming here." The familiar haze of anger blurs her vision.

Cooper becomes shadowed with black fog, and rage antagonizes her ability to remain calm. Her breathing deepens. She presses her forehead toward him. The hostile blackness that outlines his frame imitates the furious black fog Gaillynn saw when he killed Robbie.

"Gail, that night went all wrong." Cooper rubs his forehead as he speaks. His hand and knuckles bulge through thick and callused skin. A scar remains from his assault on Robbie. "We were seniors in high school, Gail. I was young and stupid."

"That night went all wrong?" His words are insincere. Gaillynn outlines the features of his face. Fourteen years have barely aged him, though jail has nurtured a hardness in his expression and added multiple scars to his face.

"Are you here to apologize?"

Cooper ignores Gaillynn's question He peers over her; his eyes searching into Locket Manor.

She inhales a dose of cool air. "Arguing with you, Cooper, will not make me feel better." *But killing you would.* He continues to search behind Gaillynn. "So, you're not here to say you're sorry?" Gaillynn's limbs tingle. *He's up to something,* she thinks.

◆

The sky continues to darken above them. A violent storm swirls into a cyclone of deepening gray. However, behind the house, Gia's skin absorbs the warm sun. Gia continues to not fear for Gaillynn even after her vision of an intruder in the figure of a male lion appeared. Gaillynn is capable of anything and more persistent and fierce than any other person I know. "Hmmm…"

◆

Regret now ravages Gaillynn's entire being. The memories of Robbie's death, customarily hidden where they can't harm her, have come into view. Cooper ambushed her today. Now, without warning, sadness and anger spans her chest and travel down to her stomach. "Cooper, I don't care what you have to say. Get the hell off of my property before I do something I will regret."

Opposite of her mother's current state of mind, Gaillynn has become agitated. She fears losing control. She has a daughter now and cannot act on her impulse to kill to silence a threat. She attempts to close the door, but Cooper wedges his hand between the door and its jamb and holds it open. His eyes hurdle past her, searching the large entry room and the living room beyond.

"What's wrong with you, Cooper?"

"Gail. Let me in."

"No, you fucking fuck. Get out of here." She pushes against the door. He resists.

"Do you still have that clock with the stone?"

Her body stiffens. "What did you say?"

"That clock? You still have it?"

A blast of icy wind whips past Cooper and strikes Gaillynn's face. Her hair flies away from her body. Her toes steady the door as the wind increases.

"What? Why?" she whispers. A new kind of panic comes over her. Her limbs engorge with physical strength, and her eyes widen. Adrenaline pumps through her veins and pounds in her ears.

Gaillynn slams the door with force, right on Cooper's fingers. He jumps back in surprise and shakes his hand.

Gaillynn locks the door. Cooper attempts to open it by pressing his shoulder into the door. She furrows her eyebrows and tucks her chin to her chest, leaning her body against the door. Gaillynn wrestles through the images of Robbie's death. *What is Cooper's interest in the clock? And why?* she wonders.

Fourteen years of stillness within the chaos of her grief comes to an abrupt halt. "I should have known," she whispers.

Cooper gives the door one last shake. Thunder claps in the sky above him and Gaillynn.

◆

Outback in the sunny garden, Gia's eyes pop open at the noise. Sunshine blinds her. She squints against the light and sees the storm cloud over the front of Locket Manor. Vines of ivy and bittersweet wrap around her legs and arms, harnessing her to the garden soil. "What's going on, Gail?"

◆

Gaillynn recalls Cooper's words the night he beat Robbie to death: "There will always be bad in your life."

"What would make him say such a thing? No one knows about the stone. No one knows about its power and the devastation of the family's happiness with pain, except, oh no." Her voice drops low and airy. "Could he be a Chandler descendent?"

Gaillynn says his name as she knows it to be: "Cooper Blethen."

A winter typhoon surrounds Locket Manor. Gusts of wind circle the estate, rattling everything. The air becomes fridged, turning

Cooper's skin white and his lips blue. He presses against the wind and returns to his car.

Gaillynn's knees give out, and her body buckles to the floor. She pulls a deep breath to the bottom of her lungs and pushes it out through puckered lips. Her cheeks flush with redness that spreads down her neck. A sob escapes her throat, followed by another growl. Anger swirls throughout her body causing her to shake, and tears pour from her eyes.

"He wants the stone. If he wants the stone, that means Ella is not safe." Gaillynn tries to make sense of his interest in the clock. "Blethen is his mother's surname. Only one person could have known our secret," she whispers with forced articulation.

Gaillynn looks toward the ceiling with a raised eyebrow. She seeks to make eye contact with a space within Locket Manor where the imagined ghosts of Amirah women rest. Her eyes focus on the nothingness below the roof and above where the living dwell.

Gaillynn speaks to her dead grandmother from four generations ago. "Christopher, fucking, Chandler. It's true, isn't it, Grammy Ginny? The family rumor that your true love, Christopher Chandler, overheard the family secret is true? And you refused his love?" She scolds the imagined spirit of her ancestor Ginny.

Gaillynn paces the house. "What do I do?" Her heels pound into the floor on her way back to the living room. She checks the clock. The stone no longer swings. Instead, it has become fixed far to the right. This position indicates something good is happening. The horror comes when the stone's quest to equilibrate its easily unbalanced energy fixes itself in the opposite place—left.

"What the hell? How can this be good?" she asks the stone. "Are you happy right now?" Gaillynn crosses her arms and sticks out one of her hips. She lets out a huff and shakes her head. "I don't understand. What does this mean?"

◆

The stone appears a beautiful ornament fixed inside a towering tall-case clock. Time is its virtue; however, the movement of the stone is primarily a measurement of the Amirah women's commanding moments. The potent energy within the stone moves the heavy pendulum from right to left—North to South.

A current of ardor pulls the angelic stone North at the onset of euphoria within an Amirah woman. The women have a connection to their family stone and all earthly elements, causing moods and emotions to reflect themselves by the weather. Its link is most vibrant with the newest born. A hormonal excitement, maybe. A dynamic and golden glow radiates love and adoration. In its quest to reconcile an exotic moment, an equally horrific event must ensue. The stone makes sure of it. Just like it did the night it took Robbie from Gaillynn.

After the inciting moment of joy when Gaillynn gave up her virginity to Robbie, the weight of the stone heavied, its color darkened to a cold, ocean blue, and its pull to the South indicated the necessary onset of the correcting event to balance the overabundance of verve. And none of the women know why.

◆

Today the stone's movement appears void of a connection to Gaillynn, Gia, or Ella. Today it is a measurement of its euphoria—the women have no idea that this is a message from Earth. Gaillynn exhales a defeated huff.

She rechecks the time. *Okay, I've got five hours and fifty-four minutes until school's out*, she thinks.

Gaillynn hurries through the house and searches for her cell phone. She mutters questions to herself. "His mother's surname is Blethen, but that's not his father's surname. What is his father's last name? This moment is the one time I wish the wife had taken the damn husband's name. If it's Chandler, we are in danger."

She halts in front of one of the two libraries in Locket Manor.

"I need to find my yearbooks—a weak contribution to the Hendrick Wing library. Let's see; I hid you." Her eyes dart from cover to cover in search of the books.

"Years of accumulating thousands of rare first editions and series of scholarly manuscripts topped with my yearbooks. Ha."

Gaillynn scans the bookcases for their location, climbs the rolling library ladder to a shelf near the top, and finds her senior yearbook. She wipes the dust from the cover with her forearm.

At the bottom of the ladder, she fans through the pages searching for Cooper's senior photo. The caption below his photo reads, 'Cooper Andrew C-Blethen.'

"What the hell does capital C dash Blethen mean?"

She carries the book through the house and buries her face through the pages trying to find more—nothing. She spots her cell phone on the pale-yellow settee where she had been reading. She tosses her yearbook to the floor and sits down with a huff. She wraps her hands around her phone, presses her feet up to relevé, and bounces her knees together.

Gaillynn presses a hand to her chest. The familiar punch of loneliness thumps its repeating injury. The stone, like a drug, satisfies her and ensures her survival but isolates her from everyone else.

"This moment is like so many others when I can't ask for help.

Again, our past forces me to deal with this awful family secret alone. On most days, I would sooner confide in imagined apparitions of ascendants past; if only the ghosts could help me now. Locket Manor—my sanctum, prison, home, and shelter. The stone—my phoenix. None enough today."

"Who can I trust without putting them in danger?" Gaillynn asks herself.

Andie.

Chapter Two

Gaillynn's mind flashes back to the first time she and Andie spoke so many years ago—second grade, on the playground, on the Monday before Gaillynn's seventh birthday.

"Gaillynn, my mom called you the rich, unlucky girl." Gaillynn's cheeks redden. She pushes her feet back under the seat of her swing and presses her chest forward. The swing responds and pulls her higher into the air. The breeze clears her hair out of her face, then tangles it in front of her eyes on the return swing backward.

"She said your boys always die. But she told me that I shouldn't say anything 'cause it's just horrible bad luck and that you're just the sweetest little girl." Andie's voice comes in and out of range as Gaillynn swings past her. Andie sits on her swing and leans forward with her elbows wrapped around the chains. She digs her sneakers into the dirt below her.

Gaillynn thrusts one more time forward to a frightening height above the metal bar of the swing set. At the peak of her forward swing, she leaps off the seat, flies through the air, and lands firmly on her feet. She turns to face Andie, crosses her arms, and sticks out one of her hips.

"Andie, if your mother told you not to talk about it, then why are you talking about it?" Gaillynn steps toward the girl and fists the cold chains just above Andie's shoulders. She steps in very close to Andie, and Gaillynn's chest heaves breaths so forceful that they move Andie's yellow bangs.

"I'm sorry, Gaillynn, I didn't mean anything. I'm so sorry." Gaillynn knows that most people in town believe her family has a curse with bad luck in love. But Gaillynn knows it is much worse than that. She knows there is a much more vital force to blame for the deaths surrounding her ancestors. A potent and adored evil terrorizes and sustains her family.

Other kids on the school playground take notice of the two girls and begin gathering around them.

"You should just keep your mouth shut, Andie."

"Gail, I'm sorry. I don't want anything to happen to your dad. I'm so stupid. I'm sure your dad will be fine. Believe me. I'm sure."

"My family is just like everyone else's family. There is nothing wrong with my family, and you should just shut your mouth..." Gaillynn huffs. She doesn't know what else to say. She turns and pushes through the onlooking crowd. Tears well in her eyes. Many of the kids, including Andie, follow her. Some pat her shoulders and attempt to calm her with words of apology and encouragement.

All of her classmates adore her and worry now that she is upset. Gaillynn appreciates their show of support and comes out of her angered state. She is relieved that she doesn't have to talk about it anymore and relieved that the stone is still a secret. What upsets her the most is that she is so different from her friends, that her family has such a shocking secret, and that her survival depends on keeping it.

The kids return, arm in arm, back inside the classroom. Gaillynn and a classmate start up a game of desk football with a triangular folded note. They flick it back and forth, giggle, and whisper behind the back of their teacher, who is writing on the chalkboard. In large letters, the teacher writes: Quebec Trip—Four days, and three nights, beginning May 15th.

"I would like a show of hands of who is interested in the four-day Quebec trip this year." Everyone but Gaillynn raises their hand. "Now, I have sent an email with permission slips to your parents, and I am hopeful that you can all go," says the teacher.

Gaillynn sinks in her seat. Another stinging reminder that she is not like her friends. A four-day trip away from the stone would make her very sick. She knows she can't go. Though they had just quarreled outside in their first-ever words to each other, Andie recognizes that Gaillynn's hand is not raised and drops hers down too. Gaillynn smiles at Andie.

"Gail, we can have a sleepover instead."

Gaillynn nods her head; a half-smile lifts her cheek. She leans toward Andie and whispers, "I'm having a birthday party next weekend. Do you want to come?"

"Oh my God, yes. Are you turning seven?"

"Yes," Gaillynn replies. The beautiful feeling of finding a friend fills Gaillynn with happiness. Incredibly a friend clever enough to figure out, and guess correctly, how old she would soon be.

◆

As the childhood memory fades, Gaillynn dials Andie's phone number, then taps her toes while she counts how many rings it takes Andie to pick up. One. Two. Three.

"Gaillynn?"

"Hey, Andie. Yes, it's Gaillynn. You remember Cooper, right?"

"Of course. Do you think I could forget? Gail, how is Ella? How are you? Is everything okay?"

"I can't chit-chat, Andie..."

"I hear he is getting out of jail soon."

"He is definitely out of jail. Andie, listen. Do you know what his father's last name is?"

"You mean was? He's dead, Gail. He committed suicide."

"I know he did. I need to know what his last name was. Please, Andie. Now!"

"Jesus, calm down. I don't know why I keep trying; you are the worst friend, Gaillynn. You call me out of the blue after like two years, and this is all you want?"

Gaillynn remains silent. *No, she wants so much more. She wants her friend's love, but at this moment, she is terrified. She is constantly pushing Andie away and out of her life so she can withdraw and bury her pain.* Gaillynn's throat tightens, and her eyes close—she begins to hyperventilate.

Andie hear's her best friend's erratic breathing. "Okay, Gail honey, calm down. His father took his wife's name, Blethen, but my dad was friends with him growing up. My dad always called him Chandler. Do you remember him? He was always at my house when we were little. That was his last name before he took Blethen. Cooper's name is Cooper Chandler Blethen. You know, Cooper Andrew C-Blethen? Get it? That is what the C is for in the yearbook. They ran out of room—it looked so stupid like that."

Gaillynn drops the phone and covers her mouth with her hands. Andie's voice rises through the air as she continues talking. "I'm still so mad at myself for ever having a crush on Cooper..." But Gaillynn had stopped listening.

"Jesus fucking Christ, Grammy Ginny." Gaillynn looks to the sky as she whispers to the air through her teeth. "I knew that story was true. I just fucking knew it. So much for the safety of our family secrets. What were you thinking?" Gaillynn paces in front of the clock.

She seethes a monologue whisper. "Yes, your refused love, Christopher Chandler, heard the story, and somehow Cooper knows too." Gaillynn punches the air. "It's the stone he has wanted all along. He didn't want me in high school, he wanted the frigging stone, and he killed Robbie because of it."

Gaillynn bends down to her phone, taps the end call button, and hangs up on Andie, who is still talking. "Shit," Gaillynn mutters. "Yet again, I have behaved unforgivably rude to the only person, outside of myself, that I can trust."

Gaillynn holds the phone in front of her face and speaks to it as if Andie can still hear her. "Andie, I'm sorry, but there is nothing I can do. And you must trust me that you are safer this way." Gaillynn's body begins to shake even harder, and she punches her fist into her thigh.

"So it wasn't our curse that took Robbie. It wasn't the stone's need for an equal awful after I lost my virginity to him. It was Cooper all along."

Gaillynn kneels in front of the clock. She clasps her fingers together and presses them to her lips. She drops her head and closes her eyes—she prays to the stone. Tears drip from her trembling cheeks and off the tip of her nose. The wind outside becomes slow, like the rolling highs and lows of the deep ocean. The tall pine trees sway, and their piney scent spirals through the calm the air surrounding Locket Manor.

"Why did Robbie have to die?" Gaillynn's chest heaves. The tightness in her throat rips pain down the length of her neck. "I'm trying to understand. If you love us so much, why would you let this happen? Ella is no longer safe." The stone's light brightens.

The heat radiating from its core wraps Gaillynn in an embrace, transmitting love and stimulation to the neurotransmitters that link them. Inclusions of gold within the blue-stone glow and swirl.

Oxytocin courses from the stone, through the space between them, and into Gaillynn's body. Gaillynn and the stone's nerve synapses are firing and receiving the same messages of calmness and love.

A surge of epinephrine jolts her back to the moment. "Cooper is out of prison. He killed Ella's father, and now he wants the stone. What would he do with it should he have it? It is not connected to him like it is us." *It doesn't matter,* she thinks. *All that matters is that Ella is no longer safe. And perhaps it wasn't the stone's doing after all.*

Gaillynn drops her head back and points her chin to the faraway ceiling. She takes a deep breath and lowers her voice to a deep, controlled, and rhythmic pitch. She delivers a command to herself that as a child, she said to her mother often: "You are stronger than him."

She tucks her chin to her chest and glares at the stone, now returned to floating in its breathtaking tall-case clock like an innocent bystander. Her head drops to the side, and she lets out a frustrated huff.

"So now you want something bad? I'll give you something bad, you son-of-a-bitch." She caresses the glass on the door of the clock with affection over the stone, flares her nostrils, and furrows her eyebrows. Gaillynn takes a deep breath and lets it out with a muffled roar.

◆

Outside, Gia walks toward the house humming a high-pitched melody while plucking petals from a daisy. She climbs the stone steps to the patio on the backside of Locket Manor—a lengthy wooden porch without a railing lined with clay pots filled with ferns and flowers. Situated in the middle of the porch are three lone wicker chairs surrounding a metal fire tub.

Gia turns the brass doorknob to the right and plunges her shoulder into the stubborn door—it doesn't budge. She drops the flower, grasps the knob with both hands, then thrusts her shoulder and upper arm against the door. It comes unstuck from its jamb and drags across the marble floor. Gia's bare feet slap across the floor and her humming echoes through the halls toward the living room.

"Gail, what's going on in here? I saw the sky."

"Nothing I can't handle, Mom."

"I know you can handle whatever it is, but what is it?"

"Cooper's out of prison," says Gaillynn.

Gia's face goes white.

◆

Cooper sits in his car, rubbing his injured hand, and scanning the enormous estate. He studies the windows and edges, looking for vulnerabilities in the anatomy of the colossal structure. He presses his eyebrows together and snarls up one side of his top lip. He breathes open-mouthed, and his chest heaves. "Okay, bitch," Cooper spits and drives away. "I've waited this long—I can wait a little longer."

Chapter Three

Four Hours after Cooper's Visit

Gaillynn taps the arrow key on her laptop. With each arrow tap, a video perspective change of Locket Manor. Live footage streams from the newly installed home surveillance system. Dozens of wireless cameras placed today throughout the grounds display various views of Locket Manor, inside and out, and assemble themselves on her screen.

"I can give you a demo before I go," chirps the technician. Gaillynn can smell the man's sweat and old work boots.

"No. Thank you. I'm all set. I'll walk you out." She folds her laptop closed and motions for him to exit.

"But I should tell you,"

"Nope, you can go." Gaillynn leads him out of Locket Manor.

"You can find instructions on how to configure and sync the app on your phone and watch through our website." She doesn't respond. They step outside, and Gaillynn locks the front door behind them.

His truck, parked at the bottom of Locket Manor's stone steps so broad they are reminiscent of an early English Baroque Perron, appears a toy. He takes wide, slow steps, keeping an eye on his feet while balancing himself with spread arms. The other technicians gather around the aged square vehicle to load up their equipment.

◆

Locket Manor is the most significant security contract Davis Security has ever landed, and the family-owned business will have a profitable year because of it. Davis Security did not refuse Gaillynn's request for an immediate installation, and they used their entire inventory to accommodate her request for a same-day setup. They even met her demands for a complete installation within five hours.

◆

Gaillynn stands on the porch with her arms crossed. The air has calmed, and she can hear birds singing from the trees around her. She checks her watch—one hour until school is out. The last worker, carrying a long ladder, joins the group at the company vehicle. Gaillynn gives her foot one final tap, then pushes a deep impatient growl toward them. She gives up waiting and heads to the six-car garage attached to the left of the mansion.

She raises her platinum wristwatch into view and taps the sizable round face with her pointer finger. The digitalized image of the diamond hour markers and mother-of-pearl dial set disappears and becomes a list of command options. She taps an icon that resembles a garage door, which expands into six additional options—one for each garage door. She taps the number one, and the first bay begins to open. She ducks under the rising door and gets into her car.

Gaillynn presses the gas pedal with force. The car is quick to respond and moves backward, causing a high-pitched squeal from her tires. She pulls the steering wheel all the way around to the left and pushes her foot to the floor. Gaillynn speeds by the crew of workers in her red Mercedes. Small pebbles bounce off the white van. The Mercedes' convertible top is down, but she is unfazed by the cold air. The wind blows her long hair back from her face.

With only a short time left until Ella is out of school for the day, even the brief commute through the quaint town, where there is no such thing as being in a hurry, to the Stonington Town Library agitates her. Every delay, stop sign, pedestrian, bicycle, and the rusted minivan in front of her cause her to honk and pass dangerously.

Finally, she arrives, takes the first parking spot she finds, jumps out of the car, and leaps up the steps to the library two at a time. She pushes the thick wooden door open with so much force it bounces off the inside wall of the quiet building. A woman behind the desk looks up over her glasses.

Gaillynn asks, "Does the library keep the town newspapers? The Gazette? I'm looking for copies of the ones from October, November, and December 2008."

"Yes, we have a space for archived documents in the basement; if you give me a minute, I can find that whole year for you," offers the friendly, gray-haired woman. Her voice is soft and caring. The woman smiles at Gaillynn, stands, and walks out from behind the desk. She removes her glasses and places them on her chest to dangle from a beaded chain, hoisting them around her neck. Her too-tight skirt keep her steps short and her flat black shoes create quick clicks across the floor toward the back of the library. Gaillynn follows.

"I remember October 2008. That was the year Hank Blethen took his own life; God rest his soul. This town has had so much bad luck and so much sadness. Not to mention those Amirah widows. I think they have had the worst luck of all, always losing their husbands. Oh, but thank goodness for all those life insurance policies. I think they are the richest family in Stonington. And they stay so young-looking." The librarian puts a cupped hand to the side of her mouth, then whispers, "I'd love to know who their plastic surgeon is, honestly."

Gaillynn watches the quick back-and-forth twitch of the librarian's hips in front of her. The woman continues talking. "All of the Amirah women's first names begin with a G. I find it fitting. The G sound is firm and strong, like goddess. After all that they have been through yet, they go on. You know what I mean?" The librarian turns her head to Gaillynn whose eyes are rolled up under their lids.

Gaillynn's irritated expression prompts the librarian to freeze and cover her mouth with her hand. The woman studies Gaillynn's green eyes, long eyelashes, bare feet, and tight black leggings covered with a black trench coat tied at the waist. She eyes the layered jewelry that barely sparkles with age and values the librarian cannot fathom.

The librarian inhales so quickly a squeak escapes her throat. The librarian wrinkles her face and tightens her shoulders. Her eyes widen, and she returns her glasses to her face. Gaillynn's beauty is unmistakably Amirah—curly, rich mahogany hair covering her entire back; her skin is as light as white porcelain, with glowing radiance, and her green eyes glare impatiently from her watch to the librarian. *An Amirah, for sure.*

"Oh dear, I shouldn't speak of things that I know nothing about. Let me go get those papers." The woman hurries away and jiggles the keys in her hand as she heads down the spiral wooden staircase to the library's basement.

Gaillynn looks down at herself. She realizes that she doesn't remember what she put on for clothes before the security company arrived. She exhales, "Phew," when she sees that she isn't still wearing her pajamas.

She lifts her bare toes from the floor—Gaillynn has given up trying to remember to wear shoes so other people don't freak out. Having her feet skin to skin with what's below her has always felt more normal. When the earth touches her, she feels like she can draw sustenance from it, like a magnetic pull, the need to breathe, or the desire for her heart to beat without being told to do so.

She fingers the large diamond studs in her ears and tries to remember when she last took them out or wore a different pair. The tight platinum bangles around her wrist clink together against her platinum watch band, and the diamonds, so coated with years of wearing, appear dulled. Here she is, out of Locket Manor at the town library. "This is not how I expected my day to go."

Gaillynn is used to hearing about how unlucky her family is and how life insurance policies have made them rich. She has grown numb to the comment and can't decide if it's an insult or jealousy. "Here you are, Ms. Librarian blabbing about my family's wealth as a result of death, and I wonder why you don't do the same? Everyone dies. Stupid," she whispers.

The woman returns with a cardboard box. She is glistening with sweat and breathing hard. "Whoa, those stairs are narrow. Here you go, my dear," she says without making eye contact.

Gaillynn takes the box. "Thank you. How come these newspapers aren't online? I tried the internet, and there is nothing."

"I've been told that the Gazette's owner just never wanted to give in to the internet revolution. Her parents started the paper, and she grew up with it and didn't want to lose the act of"—she holds up her fingers and crunches them into quotation marks—"'reading the paper.' She wanted her hometown to keep one small shred of the way it used to be by not going online. It's charming, I think."

"Charming? It's not very convenient. I had to leave my house." Gaillynn chuckles at herself and turns before the librarian can respond or apologize.

Eager to read the article she never read in October of 2008, Gaillynn finds an empty table with a small desk lamp. She pulls each paper out of its dusty casket and searches for the date in the upper right-hand corner. She flips through the months in chronological order to October, November, and December of 2008.

She remembers looking at this paper as a kid. She feels a slight trace of happy nostalgia for just a brief moment, a feeling she hasn't felt since Robbie died. There were always people from town featured in the headlines. The stories chronicled the successes of the town's residents on the front page. The featured article was always about something happening—a new business, a winning football game, or this year's cost for baby bantam chicks at Sanford's Farm. That's how they got to know each other; local family stories that brought everyone in town a little closer.

Until the October 2008 edition, Gaillynn reads the headline out loud. "Husband of Attorney Jessica Anne Blethen, Father of Alleged Murderer, Cooper Andrew Chandler Blethen, Found Dead on the Cliffs at Rockefeller Bay." A bitter headline was announcing a suicide caused by the same incident that began Gaillynn's pronounced hatred of life outside of Locket Manor. Gaillynn fixes her eyes on his name. She reads, "Chandler" out loud. "I knew it."

Below it, the subtitle, "Hank Andrew Chandler Blethen, found dead of self-inflicted strangulation and blunt force trauma," she whispers.

"How the hell does self-inflicted strangulation work? He couldn't have hung himself out there. What the hell? I never cared to learn the details about the death of Cooper's father back when it happened, nor did I want to talk or ask about it. I was too busy grieving the loss of Robbie.

"So you committed suicide? God, I was happy Cooper lost you. Cooper deserved it." Under the headline was a photo of a large cliff, stained with dark-red blood, overlooking the Atlantic Ocean. "Jesus, if it weren't for your damn blood, that photo would have been quite beautiful. I love that spot."

And then she realizes something too odd to be a coincidence. "Holy shit," she whispers. "Rockefeller Bay borders our property."

Her eyes scan the library to make sure no one heard her. Gaillynn's heart speeds up—it pounds in her throat. "There is a path from my house to those very cliffs. A course that I made traveling barefooted hundreds of times back and forth over the years of my childhood. Through the red beach roses, back and forth to jump off of the high cliffs into the icy cold water."

She would carry a rose petal with her and press it to her nose. Gaillynn inhaled the rose's sweet scent as she walked. Once she reached the edge, she would leap from the cliff at least fifteen feet above the water at low tide and watch the rose petal float beside her. And not just for the danger or thrill of it, but because the ocean called to her. It wanted to wrap her up in its waves and drench her skin with its salty water.

"Why did you commit suicide so close to our house, Hank? Were you after the stone too? No. Wouldn't I have known? Maybe not. Cooper fooled me." She flips to the November issue in search of more. She reads another article.

'As the authorities uncover details of the death of Hank C. Blethen, it becomes more of a mystery to those who knew him. His autopsy revealed that Hank wrapped a rope around his neck in what the officials call a modified noose. Instead of hanging himself, he strangled himself with the strength of his own hands. Mr. Blethen crushed his throat by wounding the ends of a rope around his fists and pulling the rope tight. As he began to suffocate, Mr. Blethen fell forward, cracked his skull, and bled to death.'

"Jesus Hank, this was not a quick or easy way to suffocate yourself. It seems more like a form of self-torture, something the stone would cause you to do," Gaillynn says. "It was the stone. That's why you did it there. The stone called to you. Then today, it seemed happy Cooper had returned. But why?" She shakes her head and continues to read.

'A suicide note left for his widowed wife, Attorney Jessica Anne Blethen, has been turned over to the police. At the request of Attorney Blethen, it is published here today in hopes anyone who has any information will come forward. In this time of overwhelming grief, the family asks if anyone understands these words of the late Hank Andrew Chandler Blethen that they please come forward. We hope to understand this tragic event soon and provide answers for the people who cared for him most.'

"Oh no. Please, don't be about us," Gaillynn mouths without sound.

'Dear Jessica,

I was reckless with a secret I swore to keep. It was a bedtime story between father and son passed down from generation to generation of Chandler men. It was the folklore of love, magic, and immortality, with hidden identities that I revealed. I have been punished for it every day since. It threatened me, it spoke to me, it suffocated me. But now I will be free. Do not blame Cooper for what he has done. Destiny played us both. I could have been a better father; I could see who he was becoming, but I never stopped it—and I told him anyway. I never corrected him; I let him have his obsession like it was a game—it's not a game. You cannot trust

Cooper because Cooper and I share the same purpose—a plan. I should have told you, but I was too ashamed. I am so sorry, my lovely Jessica. This day has been coming for me from the first day I betrayed my oath and shared the deadly truth within a secret. My mistake will haunt me no more; instead, I will finally be free of its menacing voice. My death is my forgiveness.

I genuinely love you.

Hank'

Gaillynn's chin falls to her chest, and her forehead lands on her palm. She closes her eyes and whispers, "My fucking God," then releases her frustrations with a loud and rumbled growl—a proclamation of battle. Her roar startles the librarian, who shakes in her chair, causing her glasses to drop down her nose.

Reading Hank's suicide note is the proof she was seeking. Cooper knows her family secret, and Cooper is a Chandler—a descendant of the refused love of her ancestor, Ginny Amirah. Earlier that day, Gaillynn decided that she didn't need to kill Cooper. Revenge for Robbie's death was not enough. Now, Gaillynn has a larger purpose—their lives for his.

"I will be clever."

Chapter Four

That night, sleep has come for Gia. It squeezes her chest and pulls at her consciousness, nagging her with relentless want. "Come with me," whispers nightly slumber. The arousal of the tiny hairs on the back of her neck sends a shiver over her skin. Her kitten, Dondy, trots across the oversized bed to Gia's neck. He wraps himself into a circle, purring as he presses his back to her chin and his face to her shoulder.

Gia slips inside the waiting dream and opens her eyes to face an exaggerated shadow who's beckoning her. The figure, imposed by light from the fireplace against the feathered quill that's quivering in her hand, appears alive. She fixes her gaze on the shadow. Emerging from its obscure shape is the black umbra of a ghost. In her dreaming state, she says to the shadow, "You are a messenger. What do you have to say?"

Gia's chest rises against the downy comforter. Dondy raises his head in response then Gia exhales. Dondy closes his eyes and continues to purr.

Gia bestows all of her attention on the shadow. She studies the shape on the wall. It resembles a storm cloud—symbolic of the stone's destruction of her happiness and its promise to provide serenity in return. The shadow blurs and seeks a new form.

For a moment, nostalgia comes over her. The shadow is a white bulbous cloud against a blue sky. Her mind has traveled to a warm summer day, where her younger self lies on a blanket in the field behind her home, Locket Manor. She is with Toby, Gaillynn's father. They are identifying shapes within the clouds. "I see a horse." Gia points at the sky.

"That's not a horse, Gia. I see an angel," says Toby. His face hovers over hers; desire softens his eyes, and he leans toward her mouth and kisses her. Toby isn't looking at the sky at all. He looks at her. Toby unbuttons her blouse and pushes it open to reveal her breasts. He eyes them with love. His fingers pull at the belt around her waist and release her trousers. His hands roam her body. Gia welcomes his touch and moans with satisfaction as his fingers find the inside of her panties. Dondy readjusts.

The shadow of her feather quill becomes Toby. She inhales a sharp breath and swallows a cry. Shadow Toby falls to his death.

A single tear escapes her eye and rolls to Dondy's silver fur. "I loved him, and I lost him because of the stone's curse. In life, the stone transformed him into a beast—his evil shown in this shadow within a hunched, muscular figure. His horned head lifts against the wall, and then his body becomes erect." Gia growls a warning at the shadow's manifestation, and the growl escapes her sleeping body. Dondy opens his eyes.

Gia glares with hatred at the vision of evil. Her pierced eyes press toward it, and her nostrils flare, pulling her upper lip into a snarl. "I am not afraid of you." She pulls the words from her throat. The shadow retreats and transforms again—this time into a woman. A harmonic humming replaces the growl within her. Dondy twists his head under his paw.

The female shadow's wild hair blows in a nonexistent wind.

The woman holds a shadow replica of the stone. Tears overflow to Gia's cheeks. Sadness punches her chest.

"Egos of power-hungry men," the shadow says. "are abundant and infectious among them. My charge is finding a cure for their illness caused by fear. Its symptoms have caused rot among people—hate, violence, and greed. Alas, I will be a queen."

Gia tilts her head toward the shadow figure on her wall. The voice she hears has familiarity, but she can't identify it. "If the stone were a person, it would be this shadow. A shifting outline, exposing indecency, and with time becomes a trusted warrior and companion of survival. Our stone is a killer of dreams, a thief, yet a giver of love. As hypocritical as it sounds, it makes perfect sense—if you understand the stone. Its true purpose is to heal, and with the potency of its goodness and love, it will heal us."

She dips the feather quill into a vat of ink and writes.

"The shadow of my writing quill blurs the fabric of my home. The knots of an innocent wooden wall turn into a ghostly shapeshifter. It is frightening, and then it is love. These trades have been the way of our lives with the stone. Fear for happiness and an unwritten list of instructions that I dare not refuse.

"I dream that I am a warrior. I am wholly unsure in real life, though I have physical strength, a long life, and un-aged skin. I am the eldest in the current hierarchy of three, as it has always been at Locket Manor. My daughter, cunning and wise, Gaillynn, forgive me.

"My granddaughter, Ella—our salvation rests with you."

Gia's vision dissipates. Dondy's purr vibrates her neck then goes silent. He raises his head and focuses on the darkness. His ears twitch. He leaps out of Gia's bed, races out of Kendal's wing, across the first-floor kitchen, up the stairs to Hendrick's wing, and into Gaillynn's bedroom.

With her new security system in place but set on silent mode, Gaillynn's sleep is interrupted by the sound of a deep purr. Her mother's new kitten, Dondy, taps her nose with its white-and-gray paw. Gaillynn squints one of her eyes open at the cat. She identifies a blurry outline of his perky ears and long whiskers. Dondy's face is so close to hers's she can smell his fishy breath. Gaillynn puts her hand to his head and scratches. The kitten is not satisfied, so he voices a loud meow.

"What, Dondy? I'm trying to sleep." Gaillynn opens both of her eyes to give the kitten her full attention. He turns and struts away from her to the edge of her bed. He points his tail straight at the ceiling and directs his nose toward the window. He prances in place, then turns to Gaillynn and lets out another loud meow.

Gaillynn cocks her head to the side. She sits up and continues to watch him. He jumps to the floor, prances across the room then leaps up onto the window sill. Dondy crouches into an alert attack pose and fixes his face toward something below, outside. He hisses, showing all of his tiny teeth.

Gaillynn jumps to her feet and leaps to the window. Outside she sees a dark figure moving toward the house. Dondy growled again. Her cell phone and wristwatch, both on a white charging platform the size of an average cutting board on her bedside table, vibrate. In bright red, a repeating sequence of one-word streams across both screens—ALARM.

Gaillynn dashes out of her room and down the stairs into the library and opens her laptop. The same bright red repeating sequence of the word ALARM streams across the blocked pattern of eight different views of Locket Manor. None of them reveal the shadowy figure.

She taps the arrow key. The current camera vantage points

change with eight different ones. This time she sees the prowler in a frame on the top right corner of her computer screen. It's the Northside garden with a view into the family living room in the Hendrick wing. The room where the clock is—where the stone is.

The prowlers profile nears in the camera's view. He is standing outside of the living room, looking into one of the large windows that face the clock. He pulls the black hood from his head. It's Cooper.

An increasing brightness illuminates his face. "Is that the stone?" She gets up from her desk and tiptoes toward the living room with Dondy at her heels. She peers in toward the window where Cooper stands. She can see his face through the glass. The stone is pulsing, and its golden glow is revealing him to Gaillynn. The stone has hypnotized him.

"You are the reason I had this surveillance system installed, you piece of shit. And if you try anything, you'll regret it." Gaillynn turns her face from Cooper to the stone and back and forth again. She lets out a quiet huff. Dondy circles Gaillynn's legs and rubs against her. *You've got to be kidding me.* She drops her arms and turns her back on Cooper and the stone.

"Thanks a lot," she whispers to the stone. She returns to the library and plants herself in the chair at her desk. Dondy jumps onto her lap and curls himself into a ball. A message from the police station stating that they are on their way appears on her laptop. Gaillynn taps the false-alarm option informing them not to come.

Gaillynn doesn't want Cooper to share his knowledge of the stone, but she doesn't trust him, so she types 9-1-1 into her cell phone but doesn't send the call. Instead, she sets her phone aside and watches him. "One wrong move, asshole, and I'm hitting send."

Gaillynn moves her cursor to the view of Cooper and double

clicks—the entire screen becomes him. His fingertips, resting on the windowpane, steady him—he is motionless. Seconds turn to minutes. Minutes turn to hours.

Gaillynn wakes early the following morning to the sound of her mother and Ella making coffee in the kitchen. She lifts her head from her numbed arm that pillowed her face on the desk; she focuses on her computer. Cooper is gone. She clicks through all of the views of the house and sees nothing out of the ordinary.

Gaillynn opens the recording of the last twenty-four hours and scrolls through the footage until she finds Cooper. She presses and holds the arrow key to speed through the recording of his time at Locket Manor. She witnesses the darkness in the footage slowly brighten as morning approached. Cooper was motionless, steady, obsessed, and didn't move from the window once. After standing there for four hours, he regained some sort of consciousness and walked away. "Jesus," she whispers, and she lets out a long breath.

She deletes 9-1-1 from standby on her cell phone, closes the screen, and joins Ella and Gia in the kitchen.

Chapter Five

Seven Hours Earlier

Cooper peers out over the dashboard and through the windshield to the ocean at Rockefeller Bay. Hot air blows from the heat vents, and his engine's idle rumbles and vibrates. "So this is where you did it, Dad?" He scans the edge of the cliff through the window. "Huh." Cooper smoothes the creases out of a crumpled piece of paper to the center of his steering wheel and sketches a likeness of Locket Manor. He adds: three floors of windows, the front door, and a large arrow pointing to the location of the tall case clock.

Debris plummets across his windshield. The wind has picked up, however, the moon over the ocean across from him remains bright, and the sky is clear. He turns the metal knob and rolls down the window. A whisper of wind brushes his face and into his ear—a voice. He whips his head to the left, and studies the woods and the edge of the cliff where he is parked—where his father committed suicide fourteen years ago.

Again, a whisper. Then a hum—the voice of a woman. It hooks him into a trance. He turns off the car's motor and exits the warm interior. The whisper travels down a path. He follows.

Cooper locks his eyes onto the face of the full moon hanging low in the sky. "What is happening to me?" he asks the moon. The moon doesn't respond. Instead, it offers its brightness to light the worn path he is forced to travel. Dense blooms of beach rose crowd his journey, and their thorns pull with resistance against his clothing.

His eyes widen and the corners of his mouth drop toward his chin—eerie shadows cast before him like spirit victims coercing him on in their direction. He flails his elbows, trying to regain control of his body—he is forced to walk against his will. Cooper leans back—a failed attempt to refuse. His body trembles with anger, yet his legs, unwilling, continue forward. He shakes his head and cries out to the woman's voice, "I'm not your puppet."

The prickling rose bushes bludgeon Cooper like a hostile mob as they tear holes in his clothing and gash his skin. The leaves, covered in cool ocean mist and recent rain, bounce against his body. His faded blue jeans, black-hooded sweatshirt, and black steel-toed boots absorb their water and slosh around his legs and feet. He looks down at his limbs—stilts under someone else's control. The cold water sucking his pants to his legs offers the only proof that they are part of him.

He eyes the roses and focuses on their redness. The delicate red rose petals appear soft yet out of reach. "Please," he begs. "Help me. Something has me." His body walks past with mechanical awkwardness. He is unable to pause, and the roses' noiselessness offers no pity.

Now I'm talking to roses, he thinks. He laughs at himself and concedes. "Jesus, just let their soft, delicate, and fragrant likenesses distract me. Their aroma is so alluring and such an extreme contrast to the salty spice of the ocean that I'm so used to smelling. Oh, Jesus, who am I kidding? I'm not sorry for what I've done," he calls to the woods.

He closes his eyes and breaths in—a distraction from his loss of bodily control. "I do not like feeling powerless." He sees a vision of the stone—its ghost here with him in the forest—a golden-blue glow that pulses with heat and brightness. He can hear the humming. There are voices of many women now, and they are calling his name.

"I will take you from Locket Manor, and you will be mine. I will control you," he says to the stone.

The smell of the roses reminds him of a woman's perfume. He smiles broadly. "Maybe Gaillynn's perfume." He laughs—it echoes back at him.

A jagged pin-prick jolts his heart—a vicious and intentional stabbing from many thorns. "Jesus. Stop. Fuck." He squeezes his eyebrows together and offers a futile fight against the power of the stone drawing him toward it. The rose bushes lash at him with arrogant beauty and continue their aggression toward him.

Cooper grunts a throaty laugh. "The curse dooms me. It's true, isn't it?" He looks to the shadows of the stalking pine trees for a reply. "I'm going to die. I'm next, aren't I? Hell, I don't care. I'm not afraid of you." He attempts a failed punch into the air. "Gaillynn, you bitch. I just want the gem."

The weight of his greed pushes his wet shoes deeper into the mud. His body becomes heavy; he struggles to keep his knees from buckling under the pressure. A painful knot forms in his throat, and his airway tightens. He gasps.

"Jesus."

Cooper summons every ounce of strength and forces his moving body to come to an abrupt stop. He wobbles in the darkness against the force that pulls at him. His chest heaves. He closes his eyes and reaches his hands into the bushes to feel the thick plants around him. He drops his back, and with his nose to the sky, he sucks in the beautiful bouquet in the air. With every chest raising inhalation of the cold and fragrant air, he feels more invigorated. This power the stone has over him only makes him want it more.

"I will have this power you cast over me, and it will be mine."

He fists the prickled bushes and squeezes their thorns into his palms to assist in his refusal to move forward. The roses become a powerful reminder of what he's taken away from Gaillynn and her daughter. He imagines that the water leaching into his clothing from their leaves is their tears. "Ah, ah, ah," he laughs. Each rip of the vicious thorns against his skin is yet another loss her family has endured. His laughs intensify. He wipes his running nose on his wet sleeve and succumbs to a power stronger than he. His body lunges forward.

The cool air chills through his soaked clothing to his skin, and a ghostly shape of breath exits his lungs. It lingers in front of his face, staring back at him with judgment and disgust.

An owl hoots its magnificent and masterful vibrato, a warning from deep within the woods that imprison him. Again it calls—an exquisite mosaic of sound. A symphony executed with perfection. The owl—an elusive resident of a brutal forest—and Cooper—an intruder, an infected splinter. Cooper's body stiffens at its sound. Fear threatens to overpower him.

He wraps his arms around his waist in search of warmth. He shivers, and a forced lurch forward is so sudden that it jerks his head backward, causing him to suck in a quick breath.

He spreads his arms for balance. His attempt to regain control is hopeless. He drops his arms and withdraws his fight. He forfeits all resistance and allows the pull of a force he can't explain, but somehow he knows it is from the power of Gaillynn's stone.

His shoulders relax, and his body becomes limp. The weight of gluttony clenches his heart. "If I am what you want, I will obey.

Soon you will be mine. I will find a way." His feet drag. "Take me. I'm yours. For now." He smiles.

The force thrusts his body into a sudden diversion to the edge of the earth. He levitates over the edge and faces a threat to his life. "Ahhhh," he screams. Cooper waves his arms in a failed attempt to return himself to stable ground. The ocean pounds the rocks far below him. Should this power that controls his body let go, he will plummet to his death. "Okay, okay. I fear you. What do you want?"

His body is righted and forced to walk on. He takes a deep and thankful breath.

Finally, Cooper arrives at the edge of the beach rose patch, and the worn trail ends. Anger and pride ravage his chest. With one final fight for the return of free will over his body, he forces himself to stop against the forward momentum. Cooper bends forward and plants his hands on the ground.

"No," rattles through his throat. "Stop this." The stone's power forces him to stand up; he scans the field of grass before him to Locket Manor. Cooper's body lurches forward as if pulled by an invisible rope. His feet, reluctant but steady, continue to move forward under a power other than his own. He pants like a stressed dog.

The coolness of more water soaking through his shoes as he strides through the expansive lawn of lush green grass wakens his goosebumps. The brightness of the moon casts his unsteady shadow beside him. His reflection is small and cowering, a shameful portrait painted by the moon. He peers up at Locket Manor and into the spotlight of the moon. He drops his head away from it. "What will come of me?" He holds his breath.

A tall, gurgling fountain with four large tiers overflowing with water stands before him. "Jesus, more tears," he whispers through a smile. "You bitches deserve it."

He locks eyes with a cherub child made of stone pouring water from a large cement pot at the top of the fountain—the keeper of the exquisite centerpiece of the long, cobblestone driveway. He squints at the child. "Don't fucking stare at me, you son-of-a-bitch."

He bends forward to dry heave as he paces through the lawn. The dizzying back and forth from fear and panic to greed and anger rise in his stomach. A pain in his chest pulls his hand over it.

"What the fuck," he says. Cooper winces with pain. He strains to remain in his feet as his legs lunge toward Locket Manor. Tears now roll down his cheeks. The pain in his chest intensifies. "I am a puppet strung and powerless to a force which moves me against my will closer and closer to Locket Manor. How is this happening?" he whispers, too exhausted for anything louder.

"It's the stone, I know it. That damn stone—it will be mine. I will have the power over death for love and the strength unknown to other men. I will live longer than any others, and its riches will bathe me in wealth."

He trips through a garden. He eyes the colorful plants untouched by the normal cycle of browning in preparation for their winter hibernation. "Ah-ha." He points to them. "The death of summer's flowers succumbing to autumn eluded this garden. See? Do you see?" he asks himself.

Cooper's trek ends at a final destination—the North wall of Locket Manor.

A firm and invisible push against his back press him to a tall window on the first floor and his face to the glass. He scans a spacious living room. He exhales, painting the window in front of him with a white cloud. "I'm here," he whispers. "What the hell do you want?"

The stone receives him with love. "I'm here," he says again. The stone embraces Cooper warming his skin, and a soft kindness wraps him with gratitude and forgiveness. He no longer shivers. He peers through the glass, past the fog from his breath and his stern reflection and shaved head.

A prodigious tall-case clock, the guardsman of the exquisite ore, gazes back at him from inside—its golden face and shining dark wood appear to be the silhouette of a giant in the darkness. Its gaze is loving and kind—the blue-stone swirls with gold and shares an intoxicating dose of calming Oxytocin with Cooper.

His breathing slows. The glow of the gem at the end of a long pendulum within the clock brightens. Cooper pulls his shoulders back, and the stone radiates warmth throughout his body. The stone, a beacon of beauty and pure love, is gold and blue, metallic and iridescent light. It hangs eye level to his stare, out of reach but small enough to fit in his hands. The clock's pendulum begins to swing back and forth.

Cooper relaxes. His eyes become fixed with its rhythm and follow the stone; his eyebrows release their furrow, and his pierced lips soften. The pain in his chest subsides. He pulls the hood of his sweatshirt off of his head.

Deep within him rises the hum of thousands of women. Not just the Amirah women or the apparitions of those remaining to appease the curse, but more, many more. His ears numb to the most calming sound he has ever experienced. So many voices in vibration and a wave of fluid unity. Their words are unclear, an unfamiliar language, hymn, or spell, he isn't sure, but their message is beautiful. Their gratitude fills his heart, and their hum lullabies his anger. He is connected and within a trance with this beautiful gem glowing and communicating with him. Cooper breathes in and out and listens.

"A worthy sacrifice." Cooper's words are so airy and light he barely makes a whisper. His body is like a statue, enraptured with pleasure. Seconds turn to minutes; minutes turn to hours.

The delight in releasing anger and greed captivates him as if under the influence of the most glorious, amatory drug. Now, after years of tortured seeking and want, he understands—this has all been as it should be.

The stone's brilliance dims. Cooper backs away from the window; calmness continues to embrace him. He stands up straight, wipes the tears, snot, and water from his face, and turns away from the stone. His brown eyes are changed and now reflect the blue and gold glow of the stone.

His augmented vision pierces the dark and the invisible world around him. He breathes in the stillness then lifts his left hand to check his watch unaware of how much time passed while spellbound by the stone's love. It is now so late into the night that the next day begins its rise.

The silence of the sleeping world has intensified. The idleness of the sleeping town around Cooper fills his ears with such an empty sound it seems roaring.

His feet move forward, retracing his steps through the winding garden trail to the soft, wet grass. The whisper of his footsteps against the soft ground is the most prominent noise around him. His feet drag through the damp grass and carry him out of Locket Manor's sight. He inserts himself into the woods with a crunch against the ground. He rolls his shoulders back and presses his chest forward. He flexes his biceps and welcomes a newfound strength. Determination pounds out of his heels as he travels through the oceanside forest.

Cooper reaches for the door handle of his parked car. He examines the hundreds of bleeding cuts on his hands, and the blood mixing with the water. The redness spreads across his skin like a storm cloud forming in the sky. He lifts his head to the sparkling black sky behind the moon.

The blue-and-gold spark in his eyes fizzles out. Cooper shakes his head. He inhales the salty ocean air through his nose. Control over his body has returned. He gazes down at his feet. He stares at his steel-toed boots. He recalls the sound and feel of Robbie's skull against his foot. The power he felt, after taking Robbie's life, returns. He looks past his shoes and focuses on the stone of the cliff's edge under his feet. He is standing in the exact spot where his father committed suicide. He spits a single huff. "Idiot," and slumps into the driver's seat of his car and falls asleep.

‹◆›

Chapter Six

The following Friday morning, Gaillynn, in her dark blue, button-up, business suit style, pajamas and holding a steaming cup of hot, black coffee, leans against the kitchen sink. Gia stands at the island counter, removing the empty candy wrappers from her handbag. A pile develops on the counter. Her mother's long wavy hair is pulled back, away from her face in a loose ponytail. A wave of love for her mother thumps Gaillynn's chest—she lifts one side of her mouth to smile. Her mother's porcelain white skin, long dark eyelashes, and beautiful green eyes are also an inherited gift given to herself and Ella.

Gia wears a light brown wool blazer over a bright white turtleneck and black, pleated cargo pants. Her rarely worn hiking boots strung up tightly and tucked underneath the crisp ironed hem.

"Mom, you'll be back Sunday, right?" Gaillynn asks.

"Yes. I can't be away from the stone any longer than that, honey. I'll get too weak. Wow, fourteen is a big deal. Ella is becoming a woman, you know? Are you sure you want to stay home this year, honey? Ella will be disappointed and…"

"Mom. You'll be there until Sunday. No sooner and no later? Right?" Gaillynn repeats.

"Gail, yes. I promise." Gia continues to organize the contents of her purse. "Don't forget to feed Dondy for me. Twice a day."

Dondy, a twelve-week-old, long-haired rescue kitten, swats at a shoelace dangling from under Gia's pant leg. He rears up into the air and pounces fully attacking her leather shoe. He digs claws of all four of his feet into the innocent boot, kicks Gia's heel with his hind legs, and bites the reinforced leather toe.

"Oh, and if you can't find him, he's probably up on the third floor in Kendal library. He loves that room. He sleeps on the floor by the big bookcase every day," Gia says. She crumples the candy wrappers into her fists and pitches them into the trash.

"Okay, Mom. Got it."

Ella bounces down the wide spiraling stairs with a blue and white flower-pattern weekender bag strung over her shoulder. She carries her ever-present computer pad and writing stylus in her free hand. Her bouncing curls of deep mahogany settle onto her shoulders and spread out like a shawl over the large hood of a butter-yellow sweatshirt. She wears bright white sneakers and loose-fitting, faded blue jeans rolled up, revealing her ankles. She approaches her mother and grandmother in the kitchen.

Ella regards her mother's pajamas—an obvious clue that her mother's decision not to travel with them has not changed. Ella kneels to Dondy and pats his back. He responds with an attack on her wrist. Ella giggles.

"There's my Libra. Happy birthday, Ella, my dear," says her grandmother.

"Thanks, Grammy Gia. So you're not coming, Mom?" asks Ella with stiffness.

"Dondy is too young to be left alone already, honey."

"Well then, I'll stay home," says Gia. "He's my kitten."

"No, no, no, Mom. You love Eden's Garden as much as Ella does. You two go."

"Andie would watch him, Mom. I can't believe you're going to miss my birthday."

"Dondy doesn't know Andie yet. I'll be too worried about him, sweet girl. Just have fun, don't worry. I'll go next year when you turn fifteen."

"Okay, Mom. Whatever. You never leave this darn house. I won't try to change your mind. It's, like, impossible, anyway."

"Ella, I'm sorry to disappoint you, honey. I know you'll have a great time, and Grammy Gia has promised me you will be back on Sunday. Not a minute longer. I want to hear all about what they whip up in the kitchen for your birthday this year, okay? And please give Marguerite and Jack a hug for me."

Ella stands up with the kitten in her arms and kisses his head. "Of course," says Ella with a twist of poor sportsmanship. "It's only two nights, and if you came with us, you could hug them yourself. You could use this trip, Mom."

"Ella…"

Ella huffs and turns on her heels. "Are you ready, Grammy Gia?" Ella interrupts.

"Yes, ma'am. Let's hit the road." Gia takes Dondy from Ella, kisses him, and returns him to the floor. He dashes out of the kitchen with a spirited run.

Gaillynn wraps Ella in a tight hug and breathes in her smell. "I love you, Ella. I hope you have a wonderful birthday getaway at Eden's Garden again this year. I'll keep an eye on you with the locator app on my watch, but stay with Grammy at all times, okay?"

"Where else would I go, Mom? But if you're so worried, you can change your mind about not coming." Ella waits for her mother's argument—Gaillynn doesn't respond. Ella drops her shoulders and huffs. "I love you too, Mom. Bye."

Gaillynn accompanies them to the garage and taps her wristwatch. A list of commands populates its wide round face. She taps the icon that controls the six garage doors, then number two of the six choices and the garage door behind her mother's car begins to open. As the wooden door glides overhead, lights flicker on from above. The garage brightens. The sun is on the other side of the house, and the dusky morning air clouds any attempt from the light fixtures to brighten the cold garage much.

Ella and her grandmother load their luggage into the trunk of the white Mercedes sedan and unplug the vehicle from its charging cord next to the cable attached to the red Mercedes. They settle themselves into the front seats, wave at Gaillynn through the windshield, and back out of the garage.

Gaillynn's eyes pierce, and her heart thumps with eagerness as she watches them prepare to leave for two whole nights; she waves back. Her foot taps the wooden floor. She watches them circle the fountain, water splashing down its tiers. The women in the car make their way along the lengthy cobblestone driveway. Gaillynn studies the vehicle. The blinker flashes on; the car sits longer than necessary for not one single vehicle to pass, then exits the driveway.

Gaillynn lets out a quick breath. "Finally!" She closes the garage door and heads for her computer. Her solution to Cooper begins—a careful plan is laid out in her mind, and it requires Ella and Gia to be out of Locket Manor. "Check," she says while drawing an invisible checkmark in the air with her finger.

She replays the recorded video of Cooper's face haunting her surveillance cameras over the last week. The silent footage reveals his dark, shadowy figure and his obsessive hours of staring into the living room window—hypnotized by the stone. Every single night over the last week, Dondy woke Gaillynn at his arrival. "Here is all the evidence I need to know that you, Cooper are a threat to this family and the stone.

"You are one brave, stupid mother-fucker," Gaillynn says to his face on her computer screen. "What the hell are you planning? Whatever it is, it ends tonight. Reprisal, my sweet friend, I have missed you." Gaillynn recalls the last time she plotted to protect her family. "God, I was seven. Yup, it's been a long time." She deletes the history of Cooper in the surveillance system, powers off all of the cameras and house alarms, and deletes the security system's app from her cell phone.

◆

Gia and Ella begin their annual trip to Eden's Garden for Ella's birthday in the white Mercedes.

"Hot chocolate?" Gia clicks on the blinker and pulls the car to a stop at the end of the driveway exiting Locket Manor.

"Grammy!" exclaims Ella.

"What?" Gia jumps. "You scared me; why did you yell?"

"I haven't had hot chocolate since I was ten. You know that. It's so full of sugar." Ella opens Twitter on her phone and scrolls through Earth Science Weekly's posts.

"Oh geez, honey. That's all? Black coffee then?"

"Yes, Grammy Gia. Please."

"For the birthday girl? Anything you want, my dear. Forrest's Coffee Forest, here we come."

"Tradition dictates, Grammy. Did you know they are the only coffee bar in Stonington committed to not using any single-use items? Every cup, coffee filter, percolator, and napkin is washable and reusable."

"Haven't they grown into other cities?" Asks Gia.

"Portland, I think."

Gia slows the car as they approach the coffee shop's drive-through. A familiar female voice with a thick Maine accent comes through the speaker. "Welcome to Forrest's Coffee Forest. Did you bring your reusable mug, or do you need a returnable loaner for five dollars?"

"We have mugs, thank you; we'll have two large black coffees, please."

"Is this Miss Gia Amirah?"

"Yes, ma'am, it is."

"Well, I thought so. No lettuce fruit cup this morning for little Ella, bean?"

Giselle leans over her grandmother. "Yes, I'll have one. Thank you."

"That's more like it. Pull-on up to the next window, dear," says the drive-through service agent.

"It's Irene, isn't it?" Ella smiles.

Gia nods and drives her car around the cement building painted emerald green to the next window. The face of an energetic, elderly woman wearing a name tag that reads "Irene" appears.

"Hello, dears, are you heading up North for your yearly trip?"

"Good morning, Irene. Yes, we certainly are," Gia says as she passes two tall silver coffee mugs to Irene. Irene smiles and takes a cup in each gloved hand, and gives them to the barista behind her. Irene has fewer teeth since last year, and the remaining ones are a bit browner, but that does not keep her from smiling her widest smile.

"Where the heck is Gaillynn?" Irene passes Gia a round ball of lettuce tied with a braided rope of beet-greens with a two-foot stainless-steel food thong. Ella reaches in and catches the lettuce ball over her grandmother's lap.

"Gail's staying home this year. We have a new kitten so she is babysitting. But we're going to miss her," says Gia.

"Hell, not as much as she's gonna miss you." Irene winks at Ella and returns their cups to Gia each filled with hot coffee.

Ella takes the mugs from her grandmother and presses the lids to make sure they are tight. Gia pays Irene with two twenty-dollar bills, "Keep the change. Thank you, Irene."

"You ladies have a safe trip, you hear?"

Ella waves goodbye to Irene. She lifts the lettuce fruit cup to her mouth and bites the beet-green rope. She sucks it into her mouth like a slippery piece of spaghetti. Ella chews with a smile. Three large leaves of dark-green lettuce fall open to reveal a bright combination of berries, chopped apple, and banana.

Gia drives out of the lot and heads North on Route One. Ella crunches away until she eats the entire contents and lettuce packaging of the lettuce fruit cup.

"You should come over to my wing at home and play with Dondy when we get back, Ella. He will make you laugh so hard; he is crazy."

"He comes over to my wing, Grammy."

"Oh, good. Your mother would kill me if she knew, but he climbs the curtains." They laugh. "He runs around like he's crazy, as fast as he can all over all of the furniture. He digs his claws right in." They both giggle between sips of coffee.

Ella fixes a thoughtful stare out of the car's window beside her; the beautiful colors of the changing leaves blur past as her grandmother drives toward the place that they love as much as their own home and have been visiting for Ella's birthday since she was born.

"I love that we do this every year, Grammy."

"Me too, sweetie. It's a much-needed break for all of us. I know you have been busy getting the school year started, so it's nice to spend some time with you, honey. One more year until high school. I cannot keep up with how fast you are growing up." Gia flicks a glance at Ella. "Are things going okay for your mom?"

"She is fine. I guess. She seems stressed out a lot, you know, like, I'm not sure what is going on right now. She doesn't tell me anything, but something is up with her. This trip makes her so happy she shouldn't have stayed home. She needs more happiness in her life. Eden's Garden the only thing she does outside of the house."

"I know. But, I'm sure things are fine, honey. Gail probably doesn't want you to worry, especially on your birthday. She is a powerful woman, as you know, and she wants the best for you." Gia removes one of her hands from the steering wheel and pats Ella's knee. "Gaillynn takes care of so much at home and tries hard to make everything perfect. That has always been very important to her. Just remember, you don't have to worry about her, ever. She is one of the most capable people there is."

"I know, but I wish she knew she doesn't have to make things perfect—things aren't perfect all of the time. Do you know? And she thinks she can hide things from me, Grammy. She lies when I ask what is wrong, and she always says: 'nothing, sweet girl.' And when she says that, I know something is wrong." Ella drops her eyes to her hands.

"I think Mom and I are alike, you know, somewhat, but she is so impulsive sometimes, Grammy Gia. She never thinks things out; she wants things done, like now," Ella says.

"Yes, you two are similar in some ways and others the complete opposite. You are more conscientious, wary of your powerful emotions, even anger, and do not become fixated on your desire to set things right. But boy, your mother does."

"I know, Grammy; she is so reactive."

Gia pulls a plastic baggie out of her purse filled with granola.

"Grammy!"

"What? Stop yelling like that. You scared me again."

"Where did you get that plastic bag? You're not supposed to use single-use plastics. I thought we stopped buying those?"

Gia chuckles. With a smile, she says, "Stop scolding me, honey. I found this in the drawer, and I've used it twice so far."

Ella laughs. "Sorry, Grammy, it's okay. The real problem is that companies still manufacture plastic bags. Not using them or buying them is only a small gesture. We need to reconfigure the industries that are polluting our globe. They need a solution, an alternative." Ella taps her computer. The twelve-by-twelve screen brightens to her touch. Ella opens a notepad icon in the corner, and the screen takes on the appearance of a yellow, legal-sized notepad. She presses her hair behind her ears and writes notes to herself with her bright yellow stylus pen that resembles a number two pencil. They drive in silence for a few miles.

"You know what, Ella? I can see you're writing, probably something genius like your solution to Earth's pollution problem, but do you want to hear a story?"

"Um, yes. I love your stories."

"Okay good, because I've been waiting to tell you this one. I was waiting for you to get older. Since you're a teenager now, it's time I told you a love story. I read your great-great-grammy Ginny's diary. And even though we know that through the years she never let herself love anyone, she did."

"What? Grammy Ginny did love someone? Oh my God, I want to hear every little detail," squeals Ella as she folds the cover over her notebook laptop closed. "I thought she wouldn't love anyone because of the stone's curse?" Ella takes a sip of her coffee, licks her top lip, and wiggles in her seat.

Gia begins, "First of all, the stone surrounds itself with three generations of Amirah women at all times."

"I know; Mom told me about that."

"Of the three women, there is always a mother, a daughter, and a granddaughter."

"Ah-ha, I know."

"Ginny lived with her mother and grandmother and was very afraid of the stone's condemnation of happiness with a demand for sadness. And because of that, she refused to allow herself to love any man too much. But she did love someone, and she forbid herself to show or act on it. She wrote her story in a diary that I found hidden in the clock before you were born."

"You found a diary in the clock? Really?"

"Yes, I did. It's hand-written stories from many Amirah women before us, beginning with our ancestor who brought the clock and the stone from England to Maine."

"The story you used to tell me at bedtime about Glinda, the clockmaker?"

"Yes. But, I only told you the good parts. Glinda was a warrior, and she survived some ruthless times. Glinda was the grandmother of the woman who brought the stone to Maine; well, Maine wasn't its name back then, but you know what I mean."

"I get it. A diary. Wow. I would love to read it, Grammy."

"Someday, honey. I haven't even told your mother about the diary yet." A pang of regret settles in Gia's stomach—she wasn't ready to tell Ella about the diary. Gia wrote the secret of Robbie's murder in the journal.

"So, what was his name?" Ella asks.

"His name was Christopher Chandler, and she wrote that she loved him more than she could describe. Reading Grammy Ginny's story was like reading a romance novel. Her story was passionate and painful; I wept the first time I read it. She spoke of Christopher with such sweetness that I began to feel like I knew him. Plus, I reread the story about twelve times."

Ella giggles.

"It began when they were in high school. Their eyes would meet, and Ginny's heart would pound so hard it made the ruffle on her dress tremble in his presence. The world around her disappeared and blurred into a slow-motion."

Gia takes a sip of her coffee, and Ella chimes in, "What did he look like, Grammy? My God, I can't believe this. I am so happy that she felt love and was loved this way," exclaims the giddy teenager. "I've always thought her life must have been so sad. Refusing love because of fear must be horrible."

"Well, it is good and bad all at the same time. You see, Ginny wouldn't allow it to happen. She spent her entire life fighting the power of the stone. Can you imagine how hard that must have been?"

"Crazy-hard."

"When she was very young, she learned how to measure when something too good for her to handle the stone's return swing. She calculated the stone's energy by putting tape on the glass.

"When she felt something great happening, and the stone glowed gold and swung right, she would stick a piece of tape on the glass and then also a piece when it would turn a cold ocean-blue color and swing back with the correcting, reciprocal pain to balance its unstable energy. So she learned how to measure the good and the equal amount of pain that she could tolerate. If any happiness went near or beyond her tape, she would pull back immediately to stop the cycle. She was afraid to suffer and probably for Christopher's life."

"Wow." Ella frowns and sticks out her bottom lip.

"She wrote that Christopher was wonderful and Ginny was the only girl he wanted to be. He saved himself for her and dated no one in high school. And he made certain that his love for her was undeniable," Gia says.

"So he committed himself to the woman he loved, even though she wouldn't allow the romance to happen," Ella says. "Wow."

"Right? Christopher dated no one in high school. He waited for her and was patient but pursued Ginny her entire high school career. Each time he would ask her to dinner, a dance, a school event, anything, she would say no. She was too scared of how strong her feelings were for him. But," Gia emphasizes.

Ella raises her eyebrows. "But what?"

"Finally, she said yes, to the last high school dance before graduation. Grammy Ginny wanted her final high school dance to be remarkable. She vowed that she would make sure nothing too good would happen, but she couldn't imagine leaving high school without her date being Christopher.

"Her heart ached for him; she wanted to let herself go and be with him, but her fear of what might happen as the pendulum in the clock drew back was too great. He would die, and it would be her fault. She lived in fear of the pain losing him would cause."

"Oh, that is so sad," Ella says, her eyes tear up, and her hand presses against her heart. Again, she frowns and sticks out her lower lip.

"So—the dance. Christopher's tuxedo was black, and his shoes were shined. He gave Ginny a delicate corsage that she wore around her wrist.

"He divulged all of his feelings for her. He told her that he couldn't hold it in, and she needed to know how strong his feelings were for her. He was so happy that she'd said yes to the dance, and he hoped this was finally his chance to be with her—the girl he wants to be with forever.

"Christopher told her that he found her beauty to be vivid and unmatched, and his heart pounded when she was around. He loved her curly dark hair, her porcelain skin, her determination, and her hardheadedness. He loved that she was so bright and committed to school and that she dressed so neatly.

"Ginny wrote that this moment made her very sad because she felt the same way but couldn't tell him. She was so scared she would lose Christopher and that he would die if she did. Ginny loved him, and her desire for him was painful. She wanted Christopher to wrap her up in his love, but she would never give him a chance. She would only agree to the dance."

Ella presses her hand to her heart.

"They danced with their bodies touching, and she wrote that at the end of the night when he brought her home, she let him kiss her."

Ella's frown turns into a smile. "What? Oh my God. That's so romantic that they finally kissed." She wipes away tears that have pooled in her eyes.

"But then, she pulled away again and kept her love for him a secret. After high school, he repeatedly asked her to marry him, and he got the same answer every time. No."

"Grammy, did she ever tell him why?" Ella's frown returns. "Why would she deny herself such love?"

"I don't think she deliberately told him, but she wrote in the diary that he might have overheard the story."

"The story of our stone?" asks Ella with her palm over her mouth. "Oh no," she says through her fingers. "How? How is that possible?"

"Ginny forced herself to withhold her love. She declined his final request during the last phone call she ever had with him. Her fortitude was failing, and her heart was so joyless without him that Ginny was careless with the telephone receiver. You see, she tried to hang up on him. Back in the 1920s, the phones were different—there was a handset and a receiver. To end a call, you had to replace the handset within the receiver securely."

"Oh, yes. We have a phone like that at our school's technology museum. I've seen one; I know what you mean."

"Christopher's repeated requests for her hand in marriage wore her thin; she wasn't paying attention, and her attempt to put the handset back in the cradle of the rotary phone was unsuccessful, and she didn't know it until it was too late. She never hung up on him. And if that is true, what he overheard was the entire story."

"No way. That is not good, Grammy. Someone could know about us."

"Yes, I know, but honey, this was a long time ago. We would know by now if someone knew," Gia responds.

Gia explains how it happened, with drama and feeling as if acting out the diary entry. "Ginny wrote that what he overheard went something like:

" 'Marry him, Ginny. Don't punish yourself this way,' Ginny's mother said.

" 'No, Mom, I can't. We're cursed. We can never be truly happy. If I let myself love him or marry him, he will die, the stone will kill him. So that means I would be to blame for his death. The stone is what is punishing me, not me. Why does this stone have such a connection to us? Why can't it just leave us alone?'

" 'Ginny, the stone does not cause you pain; it measures your happiness and your sadness,' explained her mother."

"Oh," says Ella. "I've never considered that is measures instead of instigates."

"I think Ginny's mom was trying to make her feel better. I think the stone causes discomfort, but I'm not sure why."

"Huh," says Ella. "What else did he hear, Grammy?"

"Ginny argued, 'That is not true, Mom. I will never believe that. It needs equal bad to good, and it must cause the bad because it balances itself every time. It's horrible and evil. It demands that our happiness shatters with grief. Like it wants to kill me from heartbreak.'

"Ginny's mother hugged and proceeded to tell Ginny the heartwarming story of Glinda the clockmaker and how she discovered the stone. The same story I have told you and Gaillynn over and over again."

Ella cups both of her hands around the warm coffee mug and says, "I love that story. You know, that story makes me so proud to be an Amirah woman, and it fills me with confidence and power. But Grammy Ginny felt the exact opposite. She felt fear and restriction. So much that she starved herself of happiness—oh, he overheard that story? That story explains everything." Ella flashes her eyes at her grandmother. "Oh no, this is getting worse."

"Ginny wrote that after the entire Glinda the clockmaker story, she and her mother heard an unexpected click. Ginny had never hung up their phone all the way, and it sounded like Christopher just hung up on his end," explains Gia.

Ella almost spits out her coffee. "Oh my God. He totally heard then."

"She suspected Christopher listened on the other end of the phone until the story was complete and that he realized the rumors were accurate but truly much worse than anyone knew—that our family is more than cursed with bad luck in love. And that a powerful stone causes the deaths of our true loves in order to remain balanced," says Gia.

"But at least Christopher would have known that she loved him, right, Grammy?"

"Yes, that is what Ginny thought too. Ginny hoped that would be enough for him."

"Grammy, that is crazy. Grammy Ginny caused her pain by trying to avoid pain. Like, that seriously makes no sense. Why didn't she understand that? Life is good and bad for everyone. The clock cycles our intense good and bad experiences like a schedule, and its swing does more than tell time; everyone still has good and bad. Maybe more unexpectedly than us and not in such equal measure of good to bad, and maybe not such horrible and tragic deaths, or dying as young and quickly after marriage as us, but they still have it."

"It sounds horrible when you say it like that, Ella." Gia looks back and forth from the road to Ella's face. "We are cursed, aren't we?"

Ella doesn't answer. Instead, she says, "So she refused happiness, and that was her counterpoise. Ginny gave the stone its rebound. She caused her parallel pain to her happiness. I mean, like, that proves how strong she was and all, but that is just crazy, you know?" Ella says.

"Wow. I have never thought of it that way before. You, my dear, are so right." Gia spits a dumbfounded "Huh," and drives on in silence while Ella's wise words sink in.

Gia's mind returns to her dreadful secret. One she is so ashamed of that she has kept it buried inside herself all of these years. *Cooper killed Ella's father, and it was all my fault*, she thinks. *Why have I trusted only the hidden diary with the truth?*

"All of the terrible events in our lives are lessons. Lessons we can all learn from," Gia says. Ella smiles at her.

"As long as the stories are shared," Gia says. "But what are these lessons trying to teach us? There is something I can't put her finger on. Yes, something the stone has been trying to tell us. I can feel it. It has always been there, a nagging presence in the pit of my stomach—a feeling I continually push away.

"It reminds me of living life based on a script. I know what is coming, and even when it makes no sense at all, the stone's energy assures me that whatever it is, it has a purpose. We are missing something important, and I vow to find answers upon our return to Locket Manor."

"Me too. And I think you're right, Grammy Gia. It seems like we would be aware if anyone knew about the stone," says Ella in an insecure tone. Gia smiles at her. "So, Grammy, when did Grammy Ginny marry Grampy Hendrick?"

"Oh, right. So after high school, after that last marriage proposal from Christopher Chandler, Ginny began dating your great-great-grandfather, Hendrick. They were married in 1935, and Christopher moved on as well. He and his wife had two sons. Living in the same town was very hard for Ginny.

"If their children's children had children, they would be about the same age as your mother. Maybe she knows them?" Gia says.

"They still live in town?" Ella asks. Her eyes are wide and frozen with fear. "My God, what if they still live in town?" Ella opens her notebook and writes: Chandler's children the same age as Mom?

"I don't know; maybe they still do, Ella. It is possible. Let's search for Chandler families and see if we can find out who they are when we get back. But, don't let it worry you."

"I can't help it. I'm worried. We have to solve this mystery, Grammy." Ella says.

"Don't be scared, honey. Nothing bad will happen. Your mother would never allow it."

Ella and her grandmother travel the last few miles of their trip.

Ella continues to write in her notebook, and the warm car carries them toward Eden's Garden. Gia sips her cooling coffee; she makes a promise to herself—a promise to sit with the stone in silence and open her mind to listen to what it has been trying to tell her.

All of these deaths of lovers and husbands have to be for a reason. The senseless way they all die at such young ages, and always shortly after an Amirah woman gives in to her desires for their love and affection. Why?

"Are the chains that bind the stone in the clock and to the Amirah women just a metaphor for the stone's enslavement of our horrors? Gia says." Is the stone fulfilled?"

"Grammy, have you written our stories in the diary?"

"Oh, I have written one," Gia says with hesitation. The sting of guilt pierces her stomach. Could she ever let Ella read the story of her terrible secret?

"Hasn't anyone ever tried to figure out how or why the stone has such a power over us? I don't understand why every single husband or boyfriend has gets killed?" asks Ella.

"I'm sure many Amirah women have tried in the past, honey. But the stone has such a hold over us, and we need to be near it, or we die, so it has become an unquestionable part of our lives. We need it. That's why we all live together."

"I know." Ella is not satisfied. "It's not normal, though. There has to be a reason or at least a cause. There is no science on what happens to us. There are no documented occurrences of similar families with superior strength, your ability to heal, and see things. Our ability to feel the living earth around us and under our feet. Grammy, it just doesn't exist."

"That's exactly why it's our secret, honey. No one can know about the stone and our abilities. Let's hope Christopher Chandler is a myth."

"What do we do, Grammy, if someone knows the truth about us? That scares me."

Gia shrugs her shoulders. "Don't worry, honey. Your mother will know what to do."

◆

Chapter Seven

Born an instinctual protector, Gaillynn is the newest defender in a long line of the Amirah women since the stone's discovery. Generations of Amirah women's lovers settle a debt with an assumed bargain of loss of life for love, all the while not knowing how or who wagered it. The stone is their most potent and precious life force—a force they will sacrifice anything or anyone to protect.

Gaillynn's duty as the warden of their safety has never been a conscious one, nor has she questioned its oddity. She simply acts as necessary to ensure their safety and survival. Threat to their lives, home, or the stone requires swift consequences, and with Ella out of the house and on her way to a safe place, Gaillynn embraces her alter ego of magnificent evil and prepares for the newest fight for their lives.

Her charge, her mission in life, is to be the guardian of all she loves and hates. It's part of her design and her genetic makeup. She's dutiful, fierce, and determined, with the ability to act without a conscious decision to do so—a mother. The stone's secrets and all of the times evil has come their way, all lay buried within the Amirah women and the walls of Locket Manor, and she is the guardswoman.

◆

Gaillynn taps the sparkling watch display, and a list of commands appears. She taps the friend-finder app, and Ella's face chimes into focus, moving slowly along a tiny map—this confirms Gia and Ella are traveling North, away from Locket Manor. Gaillynn is clear to move forward with her plan.

She begins preparing the house for Locket Manor's next secret by covering the clock with a dark blanket. After a few tries, she is successful at swinging the blanket over the top. She hurries around the house, clicking off dozens of chandeliers and sconces.

She lunges up the stairs two at a time to her bedroom and begins the task of emptying the enormous floor-to-ceiling safe of all of the valuable contents locked inside.

The safe, equivalent to the size of a vault in a bank, is one of two in Locket Manor and a family heirloom passed down from her grandfather, Hendrick. Not only an exquisite piece of history but also moisture, fire, and water-resistant. The gold markings from the maker on the front side, Dread Nought London, are now scratched and worn and have become almost unreadable. The rust is beginning to take over and has aged the painted metal with an acquired beauty.

She clears all four shelves of their pearls, diamond rings, gold coins, bonds, and insurance policies. All jewelry, numerous and valuable, is tossed in a tangled mess into boxes. She heaves five heavy fur coats onto her bed, then pulls a dozen original Andrew Wyeth paintings, too rare and valuable to hang on the walls, across the floor, and leans them against her bed. She releases the wooden shelves from inside the safe. Dust collected around the jewels maps out the location of the now missing items. She spits a puff of air blowing the dust into the air and sets the shelving aside.

Gaillynn retrieves the heavy wooden chair from her desk in the

Hendrick library and places it in the vault's center. She sits down in the chair and inspects the inside of the metal box. It appears adequately large, but to be sure, she kicks up her feet to see how far they will reach. There is ample space inside. She pulls the heavy door closed, careful not to engage the lock, and sees no evidence of light leaks. Satisfied, she pushes the door open and steps outside.

The fur coats, sealed in clear, airtight garment bags, lie on her bed. Gaillynn removes two from their bags. She places the empty, open garment containers over the chair inside the safe. She closes the door and turns the gold wheel enough to secure the door without locking it.

She loads her arms full of the family heirlooms to move them to a different safe. She travels back and forth from her bedroom, a total of twelve times, to the Southside of the basement and locks the priceless valuables in the twin vault.

Now finished with relocating the contents previously stored in her bedroom's safe Gaillynn stops in the kitchen for water. She fills a tall glass from the dispenser on the front of the refrigerator; she gulps large mouthfuls of the cold liquid and checks her wristwatch—three o'clock pm. She then taps the face of her watch. The silver and diamond jewelry disguise disappears and replaces itself with the friends-finder app. Ella's smiling face blinks open with a wind-chime sound alert. It reads, "Eden's Garden, Mount Desert, ninety-seven miles away." "Perfect," Gaillynn says. She taps the clock icon and the watch profile re-appears in its gorgeous glory.

Gaillynn fists a red Macintosh apple from the basket of fruit on the counter and takes a large bite while she heads back to her bedroom. She steps inside her spacious walk-in closet and begins pawing through the layers of vertical hanging items while she finishes eating her apple.

There are two considerably large glass chandeliers illuminating the room full of clothes. The room's centerpiece is a sturdy white metal vanity situated on the far wall and a pale-blue, floral, circular French provincial-style couch. A wide floor-to-ceiling mirror leans against its metal footings in the back right corner.

Gaillynn's toes wiggle into the deep white carpet as she makes her way around, inspecting all of her options. She fishes out the slinkiest red dress she can find and slips it on.

Gaillynn stares at her reflection in the closet's tall mirror. It has been so long since she has looked at her body. To her surprise, it is the same. How could that be? She feels so changed over the last fourteen years. Angry and ugly changed. But her appearance remains beautiful and intact. "Huh," she says as she eyes herself. Maybe it is the lens with which she admires herself today that is different.

After all, she has mothered a child and grown older. There are subtle changes, but there. Today she embraces them with respect and adoration.

Gaillynn moves to her elaborate vanity and sits down in front of the mirror. She hasn't worn makeup in fourteen years. Andie's Christmas gift to Gaillynn this past year, left outside at the front door wrapped in sparkling snowflake paper and a giant red ribbon, was the newest KKW line of eye and lip pigments with a pair of mint-green flannel pajamas. The pajamas, unused, still have their tags, and she is opening the makeup for the first time, almost a full year later.

Gaillynn accepts Andie's gifts without response or reciprocation and looks forward to them every year. She sees them as tokens of a promise of friendship, and they ensure Gaillynn that the love of her only friend remains. No matter how long it has been since Gaillynn's last act of genuine friendliness. Gaillynn has convinced herself that Andie knows her well enough to know that there are demons Gaillynn just cannot share. Therefore, Andie still loves her and will always be her best friend. She hopes.

Today is a perfect day to try new cosmetic products. She piles her hair on top of her head into a messy bun, pins the mound of tangles into place, and begins.

The makeup's compact is mirrored chrome as if developed by the most brilliant minds of the cosmetics industry. In contrasting matte-chrome, Gaillynn reads, "War Paint." She chuckles. "Perfect."

Gaillynn opens the eye palette and lifts the silver brush applicator. First, she smudges an almost black-brown color called *Vindicate* into the outside corners of her eyelids. She then blends a shimmery gold color named *Spiteful* into the inside corners. She goes for a frosty mocha color until she sees its name: "Forgiveness?" Gaillynn changes her mind and avoids *Forgiveness* with a huff. She coats her long eyelashes with black mascara, then checks her artistry for imperfections—none. Gaillynn finishes with pressing a deep red lipstick to her mouth and locks eyes with her reflection in her vanity mirror.

She thinks of Robbie, and their daughter, Ella. "What will Ella think of me? Maybe I shouldn't do this." The night Cooper beat Robbie to death flashes into her mind like a bolt of lightning zapping her back into focus.

She doesn't push it away like she usually does. Instead, she lets herself replay the horrific events of fourteen years ago. She needs fuel for her anger—she needs to solidify that there is no other way and must move forward with her scheme—tonight.

She taps her wristwatch, chooses the music symbol, then a voice from the speaker in the ceiling asks, "What do you want to hear?"

"Sorry, from my favorites playlist." Madonna's voice hums out of the speakers in the ceiling.

"Je suis désolé, Lo siento, Ik ben droevig, Sono spiacente, Perdóname."

The rhythm inspires her readiness. The lyrics resonate with her current lack of apologetic intentions. She sings with a whisper:

"You're not half the man you think you are. Save your words because you've gone too far. I've listened to your lies and all your stories (I've listened to your stories). You're not half the man you'd like to be."

◆

The memories come back, flooding her mind with sensations: the smell of the school corridor, the sounds of hundreds of students busying their way through the halls, the harsh fluorescent lighting blurs her sight, and then it became clear, and she is there—the Thursday before Homecoming weekend of high school senior year.

Cooper approaches Gaillynn's locker. She collects her morning class load of books filtering through the stack piled in her locker, finds the flyer announcing senior class trip: "Class of 2008, Rafting the Dead River," and wedges it between two class schedules taped to the inside of her locker door. Gaillynn would love to go rafting. The idea of jumping out of the raft to float through the rapids alone sounded so fun. Although, the reality is: she can't go. And it gives her the sick feeling of envy.

Gaillynn pulls the books she needs out from the pile and wraps her arm under their weight. Cooper approaches her; he leans an assuming shoulder on the locker next to Gaillynn's and flips his hair out of his face.

"Hi, Gaillynn."

Gaillynn tips her head to her right shoulder, lowers her chin to her chest, and takes a deep breath. "Hello, Cooper." She eyes his dark, steel-toed shoes—the must-have shoes most worn by the popular crowd—the only color variations—brown or black. And they must be steel-toed. She rolls her eyes.

"The Homecoming dance is Friday."

"I know. Thanks for reminding me, Cooper. Have a great day." Gaillynn is flustered and wise to where this conversation is going; she neglects to shut her locker and attempts to walk away. Cooper stops her with a firm hand on her shoulder.

Gaillynn growls.

"You're coming with me, Gail," he announces as if she has won the grand prize for Homecoming.

"Sorry, Cooper, I already have a date. I'm sure one of your many followers would be happy to accept your invitation. And please, Cooper, ask her properly. Don't command her." Gaillynn knew his next choice would be Andie.

"Are you going with Robbie? That lowlife lumberjack."

"Yes, I am going with Robbie. I'd pick a lumberjack like him over a jackass like you any day." She pulls her shoulder from his clutch.

As she walks away, she passes Cooper's entourage of friends that have lined up to watch. The first one she sees is Lenny. His adorable face relieves her mood. Lenny tries to make her laugh with a clever joke; however, Cooper's yelling drowns out his attempt.

"That's bullshit, and you know it, Gail." Gaillynn doesn't respond. "Okay, bitch. Shit. You are walking away from me. Have fun with the loser, Gaillynn." Humiliated and angry, Cooper slams her locker shut and struts away to a group of girls giggling in a circle. The girls quiet their conversation at the arrival of the school's most attractive bachelor. They shoot quick looks toward him then back to their feet.

"Andie, you're going to the dance with me," he orders.

"Okay," says Gaillynn's best friend, Andie. Andie's blond hair is in a high and tight ponytail. She wears a denim skirt that reveals almost all of her muscular, long legs. A pink V-neck cotton t-shirt drops low on her chest, and a gold necklace drapes her collar bone.

She snaps her bubble gum and giggles with her girlfriends. Andie and Gaillynn make eye contact. Gaillynn rolls her eyes and gives Andie the peace sign with her fingers.

"I'll pick you up at seven," Cooper yells back at Andie from further down the hallway.

◆

Gaillynn lifts the blood-red lipstick in front of her face, and she winds the tube up. The red shaft of lip color is exposed and points erectly toward the ceiling. "Oh, Andie," Gaillynn whispers. She rewinds the tube of lipstick and as she does, the brand's letters: KKW and the color's name, O+, pressed in its side disappear. She remembers that night—Homecoming.

◆

Gaillynn lies to her mother and claims she is going to the dance with Andie and their girlfriends. She kisses Gia goodbye, then dances her way down the cobblestone driveway in high heels. She wears a tan wool coat that she doesn't need over a strapless, full-length, ballet-pink dress with a lace bodice and dainty, matching high heels.

Robbie's car, an old family suburban, waits just around the corner from Gaillynn's driveway. Its low rumble puffs white exhaust into the cool air. As soon as he sees her heading toward him, he jumps out to meet Gaillynn. Robbie kisses her, "Hello," and they spend a moment staring into each other's eyes. His wavy, light brown hair moves in the wind. His dark gray suit and matching ballet-pink tie exude the intoxicating smell of pine and cologne.

"I missed you, Gaillynn," Robbie whispers. "You should've let me pick you up at your door."

"No, Robbie, I haven't told my mother about us yet." She kisses him. "I missed you too."

"Are you sure you want to go to the dance?"

She punches his arm. "Yes, Robbie! Of course, I do."

"You look so beautiful. I just want to look at you all night," he admits.

"Well, thank you. You look pretty beautiful yourself. We can look at each other at the dance."

He opens the passenger door, lifts Gaillynn's dress from the ground, and she sits down. He bends into the car to kiss her. He closes her door and rushes over to the driver's side, and jumps in.

◆

Staring into the vanity mirror, Gaillynn pulls the loose strap of her red dress back up onto her shoulder. She wipes the tears forming in her eyes. The lipstick looks too perfect on her full, pouting lips. She rubs her fingers across her mouth, and the ruby color of revenge smears across her face. She tilts her head to her right shoulder, tucks her chin to her chest, takes a deep breath, and smiles at the memory of Robbie that night. Her cheeks blush with heat, and her skin becomes blotched with adrenaline, and she remembers the dance.

◆

They danced slow and close even during the fast songs. They were deliriously in love and completely absorbed into each other, but Gaillynn can feel Cooper watching them from across the gymnasium. Hatred burns in his eyes. He studies their every move and is never too far away. He leads Andie to dance close to Gaillynn and Robbie. Gaillynn feels uneasy—his nearness causes her chest to tighten.

"Robbie, I think I'm ready to leave," Gaillynn whispers into Robbie's ear. He takes her hand and leads her off the dance floor. They retrieve their jackets from the coatroom manned by an underclassman taking tips. Robbie wraps his coat around Gaillynn's shoulders and carries her's over his arm. They say goodbye to their friends, and they exit the school. They descend the school's stairs to the parking lot and the suburban. He opens the passenger door for Gaillynn, and he lifts her dress off the ground as she climbs in.

Robbie and Gaillynn drive away from the high school; Gaillynn leans across the front seat and rests her head on his shoulder.

Unbeknownst to them, Cooper follows.

Their destination is the closed wood mill owned by Robbie's family. Robbie reduces his speed through the mill, abiding by the five-mile-per-hour speed signs. Gaillynn watches him drive with such slow intension, and she doesn't care how long it takes to arrive. Gaillynn smiles.

Robbie turns to her, "What?"

"I love you."

He parks the suburban and leaps out. Robbie races around to Gaillynn's side to open the door. He reaches his hand toward hers, and he guides her out of her seat. "I love you too." He cups her face with his palms and kisses her. They walk shoulder to shoulder and hands intertwined to the wood mill; Robbie carries a rolled-up blanket.

A sudden and spirited wind whips dirt and dust around the two young lovers. Gaillynn raises an eyebrow and looks in the directions of her home, three miles away. She sends a silent warning to the stone. "Don't you even think about it."

◆

Looking at herself in the mirror in her closet inside Locket Manor, and now fourteen years later, Gaillynn remembers how happy and excited she felt that night long ago to be alone with Robbie. It was the memorable night she had been anticipating for weeks. Nothing else in the world but each other mattered at that moment.

Their euphoria drenched their skin. The night was all theirs. Gaillynn decided weeks ago that it would be the night she would give herself to Robbie. She wanted him to be her first, and only, so she ignored what she knew about the stone—that its energy would become unbalanced with this act of love and that the stone would require and cause a correcting horrific event. She ignored it all, and she let her passion take over.

◆

Neither turn on the lights. The brightness of the clear night and a half-moon illuminating through the windows allow Gaillynn and Robbie to see everything they need to see—each other. They stand in the center of the room and kiss. Robbie is in love with her; Gaillynn feels it; she can tell by the slowness and depth of his breathing. As he kisses her, he inhales her scent and wraps his arms around her waist. He pulls her close to him.

Gaillynn's heart flutters, and heat rises in her body. Robbie inhales her sweet smell of maple and sugar; it draws him in. It is more potent than usual at this moment; like perfume, it is the smell of her beauty and exquisite energy. Her scent is like an endorphin he craves. He wipes the sweat from her forehead.

Gaillynn wants more.

They gaze with love into each other's eyes, pull away, and each takes one side of the blanket. They fluff it up into the air, and presses it down to the ground. They kick off their shoes and settle to center of the blanket on the floor. They ignore the tiny fragments of wood pieces and dirt poking up through the fibers.

"Oh, I almost forgot," says Robbie. He jumps up and dashes

into a dark room and returns with a bottle of champagne and two plastic cups.

"How did you know we would come here, Robbie?"

"I hoped." He pops the cork and fills the plastic cups half full. Robbie raises his drink into the air. "Cheers to Homecoming, you, and senior year."

"Cheers," Gaillynn says before she takes a drink. "Cheers to the only boy in town who clipped playing cards to the rim of his bicycle frame so the spokes would flip the cards and sound like a motorcycle." They laugh.

"You remember that?"

"Oh my God, yes, and your bright blue Nike windbreaker. You wore that thing every day that summer. You were so damn cute," says Gaillynn. "You still are." She kisses him.

"Well, what about you? You climbed, like, every tree in town barefoot. You were always in a tree and always barefoot. What is up with that anyway? And your body is always so warm."

"It runs in my family. We're all hot-blooded, and we like to feel the earth under our feet."

"Gaillynn, I have always had a crush on you. Even in kindergarten."

"Oh yeah, well, I have always loved the pine smell that has become part of you from working at the mill." They kiss again.

"I will build our home out of the lumber from our family mill, and it will smell just like me."

Gaillynn laughs. "Do you promise?"

"I promise." He kisses her, then stops, pulls away, and stares at Gaillynn.

"What, Robbie?"

"I know this is a crazy question but, Gaillynn, can we get married at your house, outside near the ocean?"

"Okay." Gaillynn pauses. "Was that a proposal?" Robbie takes her hand, and they stand up.

"Yes," Robbie says.

Gaillynn's chin falls to her chest, she tilts her head to her right shoulder curling her eyes up at him, "Yes," she answers. Their last words committed themselves to each other and in the center of their blanket, they dance to no music and the rhythm of their passion.

Their faces press close—they kiss and breathe in each other's scent. Their bodies sway, and Robbie pulls Gaillynn's waist tighter toward his. Neither have been with anyone else before. Still, with the power of their love and the feverish passion growing between them tonight, they would consummate their unbreakable commitment to each other. Their first time, this night of Homecoming, senior year, in the deserted saw house littered with wood, dust, and smelling of pine and the outdoors.

Gaillynn pushes Robbie's suit coat off his shoulders, steps behind him, pulls his jacket from his arms, and drops it to the floor. She wraps her arms around him from behind and begins unbuttoning his white shirt. Robbie faces Gaillynn and takes her hands in his.

"Gaillynn, are you sure?" Robbie asks. She kisses him.

"Yes." Gaillynn turns and presents him with the ribbons crisscrossed down her back. He unties each one. They take their time undressing each other, and then their bodies move to the floor. Robbie leans his weight onto Gaillynn with his elbows on each side of her on the floor. He caresses her hair out of her face, he kisses her cheek, and then her neck. Gaillynn opens herself up to him, and she pulls his hips into hers. They become one.

Gaillynn lets go of her fears and reaches her arms up over her head. Robbie caresses her breasts. Gaillynn moans. He runs his hands up to hers over her head. They wrap their fingers together and squeeze. Their bodies shine from the heat between them. Gaillynn's life force beams with happiness, and their love envelopes them.

◆

Gaillynn returns the chrome cover to the red lipstick, and her hands fall to her lap. "I still love you, Robbie." She cries, pulls a tissue from the box at her vanity and presses it to the corners of her eyes. The music from above stokes her anger increasing her desire for retribution. *"I've heard it all before, I've heard it all before."* She forces herself to replay the horror that came next.

◆

Their lovemaking comes to a glorious end, followed by an abrupt surprise when Cooper and a force of wind breaks through the door. Cooper flips on the lights. The first thing he sees is Gaillynn and Robbie naked on the floor. Robbie is on top of Gaillynn, and he has her hands pinned over her head with her knees pressed open around him.

"Get off her, Robbie." Cooper rushes to Robbie and drags him off of Gaillynn. "What the hell do you think you're doing to her?" Cooper raises his fist and smashes it to Robbie's face, and then the other, an ambidextrous madman. Robbie is surprised by the attack, and he can't react quick enough, nor can Gaillynn.

"Stop," Gaillynn screams.

A gust of wind slams the door, and Cooper continues to pound Robbie. Robbie is shocked and lovestruck, all at the same time, and unable to get his footing. Cooper's punches have made him dizzy, and the bright lights blur and confuse his eyesight. He begins to fall.

"Stop, Cooper. Stop it," Gaillynn shouts. She jumps on Cooper's back, wraps her arms around his neck, and claws at his face with her hands and fingernails. She digs at his eyes, rips at his nose and lips, but her naked, slippery body cannot hold on. She falls off.

Robbie drops toward the floor and Cooper. Cooper rears back and gives him a powerful kick to the center of Robbie's face. Cooper repeats the insult four more times. Robbie's head bounces back from the blows, and his body becomes still. The shape of his face is lost. Blood paints his features with grotesque evidence of Cooper's attack—Robbie is unrecognizable.

"No," Gaillynn cries. "No. Leave him alone. Cooper, leave us alone." Gaillynn pulls herself up from the floor. She doesn't bother to cover herself and kneels beside Robbie. "Robbie. Please. Robbie, speak to me. Wake up, Robbie. Oh God, please. Cooper, what is wrong with you? What the hell is wrong with you?"

"He was raping you, Gaillynn. What did you expect me to do?"

"He was not raping me, Cooper. I love him. We were making love." Gaillynn cries into Robbie's chest. The man she loves, the man she has just given her virginity to, is unresponsive.

"What? No. He was raping you. I saw him restraining your arms." Cooper acts confused. "He wasn't raping you?" He pretends to become dizzy and sits down on a nearby workbench. He presses his forearm to the cuts on his face from Gaillynn's fingernails and absorbs the blood. He sniffs his reddened nose and dabs his sleeve to it carefully. He winces.

"He was NOT raping me. I love him. We left the dance to come here, to be alone. He was not raping me." It had all happened so fast; her time with Robbie went from intimate to tragic in a matter of seconds. Gaillynn thinks of the clock and the stone, and she imagines the sequence of predictable swings to the right when they made love to the inevitable swing left for his death. *This balancing is the natural order of my life—the stone will torment me in equal comparison to my bliss.*

◆

Gaillynn asks her smeared lipstick reflection in the vanity mirror, "How could I have been so stupid? How could I have thought it would end any other way?" She sniffs her running nose and wipes the tears from her cheeks. "Frigging fairytales."

Downstairs, the stone's gold swirls in a slow and sad pattern; the stone shares Gaillynn's heartbreak.

◆

She remembers hugging Robbie and pressing her forehead to his chest. He doesn't respond. Gaillynn closes her eyes and takes long, deep breaths pulling in his smell through her nose. She kisses his chest then his still mouth.

She raises her head and glares at Cooper; Gaillynn releases a loud, defeated huff. She wants to kill him. She tries to calm herself and thinks of the stone. Robbie will die, and it is all out of her control—the stone's power will always win. Gaillynn holds Robbie's hand and covers his body with the blanket that had only seconds before cradled them in the most beautiful moment of her life.

"Don't take him from me. Please. I beg you. Don't take him from me. He did nothing wrong," Gaillynn says to the stone, assuming it can hear her. The door to the mill flicks open just a few inches. Rain spits inside. Gaillynn feels a gentle breath of humid air pass over hers and Robbie's naked bodies. She breaks down into loud sobs. She is angry not only with Cooper but herself. The stone had become unbalanced because of her energetic connection to it. The stone warned her on her way into the mill. It tried to remind her what would happen. The stone must always seek its stabilizing event. "Never again will I be so stupid," she promises herself.

"Let me help you, Gaillynn," Cooper whispers. "I can be here for you and help you through this. There will always be bad in your life. I was just trying to help. I am so sorry." He wraps his arm around her bare-back.

She slaps it away. "Get away from me. Don't touch me. I hate you. Just get away from me."

◆

Gaillynn stares at the mirror image of the vein pulsing in her neck. She removes the diamond studs from her ears and fastens a pair of tear-drop-shaped ruby earrings in their place. The light reflects a red sparkle. It reminds her of the flashing lights, the sirens, and the pouring rain that erupted next.

◆

The wood mill fills with police cars and ambulances. Robbie is rushed into an ambulance and taken to the hospital. There is bleeding in his brain from his head and facial trauma.

Robbie died two hours later.

◆

Gaillynn's heart quivers and an erratic inhale shakes her chest. She recalls the light sentence Cooper received—her nostrils flair. His plea of not guilty, supported by his misunderstanding of the situation for rape, was a lie—Gaillynn draws a deep breath in through her nose. Cooper, and the upstanding reputation of his family, convinced the jury of his regret—Gaillynn slams the eye palette's lid closed.

The entire courtroom was swayed and very sympathetic to his

claim—Gaillynn stands. Madonna sings above her: *"I've heard it all before, I've heard it all before."*

Cooper was found guilty of manslaughter, not murder, and served only fourteen years of his original twenty-two-year sentence. His parole hearing ended with his release due to good behavior and without parole—Gaillynn sits down and slams her fist on the vanity. *"I've heard it all before, I've heard it all before."*

Nausea rises in her stomach, and the foul taste of revenge makes her mouth water. She craves its flavor and ingests its demands with a loud swallow. Gaillynn's anger implores her to avenge Robbie's death and to protect their child. She is absolute in her decision to move forward with her plan. Anticipation flutters in her chest like the propellers of a stealth helicopter.

Gaillynn locks eyes at her own in the mirror. Her eyebrows press together, and her lips quiver. She applies a fresh coat of the red lipstick, leaves the previous smudged application, and completes her outfit with a pair of shining black stilettos.

She clicks her way through the house with a confident swagger and into the kitchen for one last detail. She withdraws a medicine bottle from her purse and shakes its contents. The sound of pills in plastic pierces her ears. Adrenaline travels from her chest to her fingertips.

She twists open a bottleneck beer and pours the contents of the medicine bottle into it. She turns the cap back on the beer with force and tears the label. She swirls the bubbly liquid then hides the bottle in the back of the refrigerator.

Gaillynn sprinkles dry cat food into Dondy's dish. "Here kitty, kitty, kitty." He is nowhere in sight, but Gaillynn has no time to look for him.

Gaillynn does not set the alarm system; the surveillance cameras remain turned off, and she doesn't lock the front door. She clicks her high heels and swings her hips to the garage. Gaillynn opens the first bay with a tap on her wristwatch.

Inside the red Mercedes, she inspects herself in the rearview mirror. She focuses back at her own eyes with a fierce glare. "Stupid asshole. Are you ready for me?" Satisfied with the warrior gaze returned by her very own eyes, she speeds away from Locket Manor, leaving the garage door wide open.

After a short drive along the ocean, she reaches the boat landing of Burnt Cove and the town bar, Union Station, where she hopes Cooper will be—a Stonington Friday night hangout. She suspected he would join locals since his short jail sentence ended, along with all of the others who still relish reliving their glory days from high school.

Union Station, an old railway station turned pub, is a mason's masterpiece, the town's most beautiful of its many antique brick buildings, and is surrounded by retired train tracks and dilapidated cable cars.

Gaillynn's car bounces over a pair of rusted and worn railroad tracks that pass in front of the bar. The rails are now a walking path with grass growing between the metal. She blocks the trail with her car, parking it as crooked as possible.

Gaillynn exits her car and approaches the entrance. She hesitates outside and studies the crowd through the window. She spots Cooper tapping beer cans with a comrade; Cooper slips his cell phone into his pocket, and they shake hands. She steps to the door and focuses on the peeling paint separating her from her prey. Gaillynn takes a deep breath, shakes her arms and legs, and rolls her head from shoulder to shoulder.

＊

CHAPTER EIGHT

Gia's white Mercedes crunches over the crushed rock driveway of Eden's Garden. The white antique home welcomes them with its brightness.

"We're here." Ella opens the car door and jumps out. A short, fuzzy-haired woman rushes out of the inn to greet her. "Auntie Marguerite," says Ella.

"You're here, Ella. We are so excited to see you again," says the woman hugging Ella's waist. She wears a faded flower-print apron over a short-sleeved white t-shirt. Her khaki pants and tiny white sneakers adorn their usual splattered grease stains.

"Did you bring your momma, Ella? Where is your momma?"

"No, sorry, Marguerite. It's just Grammy and me this year."

"Oh, dear. Well, that's okay, you come inside where it's warm. You can help me in the kitchen. We're getting ready for tomorrow's breakfast."

Ella peers over marguerite's head at her smiling grandmother and Ella is ushered in with a push by Marguerite. Ella smells the kitchen on Marguerite—the scent rises from the top of the short woman's head. The wrinkles in Marguerite's face deepen each year, and her curly, frizzy hair has thinned and grayed. Marguerite's hands are stocky and muscular, with thick fingernails and deep lines from age and hard work around her knuckles. When she smiles, her eyes disappear, and the deep furrows around her lips from years of smoking cigarettes smooth.

"I'm so happy to be here. I love this place and the people here, Auntie Marguerite. Since I was born, we have come here one weekend a year; and how is it that your staff is still the same?"

"I pay the staff well. They'd be dumb to leave."

"Well, they treat me like part of a family that Locket Manor is missing. I think it's more than what you pay them, Auntie." Marguerite squeezes Ella's waist and tilts her head up at the tall girl. "I wish Mom had come along too. I always love seeing how happy Eden's Garden makes her. Happiness is something Mom lacks. There is something about you and Jack and the caring and welcoming vibe of Eden's Garden that makes her different, somehow. But she insisted on babysitting Grammy's new kitten."

"I know, dear. Don't you worry about that right now." Marguerite leads Ella away from the main entrance to the left side of the inn to a secret door that leads directly to the kitchen. A white box truck has parked near the kitchen's hidden entry; the sign on the vehicle reads "Christine's Fresh Catch." A youthful, tan-skinned, muscular woman carries bushels of freshly dug clams to the inn. Her green rubber boots, covered with a dark-gray, velvety, clay-like muck, are folded down to her ankles—evidence of her hoeing through the soft and salty odoriferous clam-flats herself harvesting their dinner.

The woman salutes Marguerite and Ella as she passes. The wind blows the woman's yellow hair into her face, so she presses it back behind her ear. She retrieves a large box of live lobsters from her truck and carries them into the kitchen's walk-in cooler.

Marguerite pulls a thick roll of cash that's held together with a rubber band from her pocket. Ella steps up to the bulletin board on the wall near the entry and finds the picture of herself as a baby on Jack's lap, Marguerite's husband. Jack's round belly leaves little room for Ella, but his smile proves he doesn't care. Ella scans the pictures. She focuses on one of Marguerite holding out her hands to Ella's newly walking toddler self. Ella wears footy pajamas that are a bit too short with the feet cut off. She clutches a banana. Ella smiles and touches the photos with her fingers.

Marguerite pulls a few green bills from her unique rubber band wallet and passes them to the woman who brought the day's freshest catch. "Thank you, Christine," Marguerite says. She pats the girl on the shoulder.

"It smells so good in here," Ella remarks and turns from the memory wall to the crowd of chefs hard at work in the kitchen. They welcome Ella with hearty hellos and the clanging of pots and pans. "Happy Birthday," they all say over each other. Ella appreciates their warm welcome and blushes at their attention.

"What's on tomorrow's breakfast menu?" Ella asks.

"Peach cobbler-stuffed French toast, dear," answers Marguerite.

"Can you teach me, Auntie Marguerite?"

Marguerite reaches up and pinches Ella's cheek with her wrinkled fingers and smiles at her; her eyes disappear. "Of course. Go get your apron, dear."

◆

Gia taps the Mercedes emblem on the back of the car, and the trunk pops open with a beep. She scans the land surrounding Eden's Garden. She embraces the quiet ocean and still air. A seagull trumpets a long "huah, huah." Another echoes back a more elaborate "keow," disputing the first's claim on the pristine seaside territory.

The coast is much less jagged here, and the line where the land melts into the sea feels much kinder than at Locket Manor. There is an elegant and gradual sloping to the hillside at Eden's Garden that turns into the soft sand as it meets the calm sea.

Eden's Garden sets on a bay secluded from winds and waves by rolling hills and mountains. The ocean here is most often calm and serene, unlike Locket Manor, where the waves are fierce and accompanied by a constant wind force. Gia appreciates the break.

She retrieves their small bags from the car and enters the inn through the main entrance. The first room that greats her is a foyer with a fresh coat of paint in a warm cream color that reminds her of a buttery cup of coffee with rich milk. Another new addition to the foyer: framed photos filling the entire wall. There are dozens of old black-and-white pictures of the post office with horses instead of cars, children standing shoulder to shoulder with no smiles, landscapes with no houses. "Oh wow, those are new," says Gia.

The warmth of the inn wraps Gia with a welcoming embrace as she exits the foyer and reaches the check-in desk. A free-standing, roll-top desk painted with layers of high-gloss black sits at the bottom of a tall wooden staircase. The stairs separate the kitchen from the inn's spacious dining family room combination.

Jack, sound asleep, leans back in a chair at the desk with his hands folded on top of his round stomach. His shiny bald head balances against the stair's reddish-brown banister. Jack's blue-and-red plaid nylon pants are hoisted well over the top of his gut and held up with an aged brown leather belt. His traditional cotton, white crew-neck t-shirt matches Marguerite's and is not only as tight as usual but is also tucked neatly into his pants.

He isn't wearing his top false teeth, and his upper lip sucks inside his protruding lower jaw. His six remaining lower front teeth jut out over his top lip, and his grunting snores vibrate through his nose. He reminds Gia of a giant, cuddly bulldog.

Gia touches his arm with her palm. Her touch shakes him awake, and he jumps to a standing position. The floor and Jack's thick neck jiggle with his sudden movement; Jack's breathing causes a wind on Gia's forehead and forces his unsupported top lip in and out. He licks his dry lips, which appears to be difficult without his top teeth.

His face lights up at the sight of Gia. Jack smiles a gummy grin and hurries out from behind the desk. He lifts Gia from the floor into a hug while wrapping his arms around her shoulders, roping Gia's arms to her sides. Gia giggles.

"Jesus, it's good to see you, dear," says Jack. He returns Gia's feet to the floor and releases his hug. He cups her shoulders in his big hands and kisses her cheek.

Gia places her hand on his forearm and kisses him back. "Oh, Jack, I've missed you. How are you?"

"Good. Good. Things are good. Where are Gail and Ella?" He looks past Gia outside to the car.

"Gaillynn stayed home this year. I have a new kitten, and she offered to babysit, but Ella's already in the kitchen with your lovely wife."

"Ah, yes, of course." He whistles through his floppy upper lip. "Please, you must join them. I'll park your car and take your luggage up to your regular room. You just settle on in and enjoy your stay, dear." He rushes out to the car to valet it around to the side of the inn. He doesn't fit and has to push the seat backward. Gia chuckles at him and heads for the kitchen.

Gia also stops at the memory board and searches through the years in photographs. She finds the Polaroid of herself sitting with a group of other guests on the patio on a warmer than average winter night in 2012. She inhales the mouthwatering smell of the kitchen and scans the hundreds of photos of guests who have become family. Some faces are familiar, and many are not.

A photo of Gaillynn smiling a broad, happy smile catches Gia's attention next. Gaillynn, sandwiched between Marguerite and Jack, wraps her arms around their necks—each of them is holding a cocktail. Her sweet and heartbroken Gaillynn is happy in this photo. It seems so rare to see her content since Robbie's death.

Gia's heartache returns.

The death of Robbie was my doing, and I'm too ashamed to tell Gaillynn the truth. Someday, when I'm ready, when the time is right, I will tell her.

Marguerite touches Gia on the shoulder. "Are you okay, dear?" Marguerite smooths the loose pieces of Gia's hair back from her face. Gia doesn't respond but musters a sad smile and hugs Marguerite. They embrace for a long while; Gia tightens her grip, not wanting to let Marguerite go. Gia takes a deep breath and pushes her regrets back inside their crypt.

Marguerite holds both of Gia's hands in hers and smiles an understanding smile—Marguerite's eyes disappear. Gia can smell cigarette smoke on Marguerite's breath. Yellow and brown stains color the vertical stress lines in the woman's teeth—perfectly aligned but have worn edges flat from years of gum chewing or gritting her teeth that appear chiseled and square.

"My sweet Gia, you look beautiful but sad. Come, come. Help us cook."

Gia glances back at the memory wall—another photo draws her in. It's the three of them: Gaillynn, Ella as a toddler, and herself. Their hips are squished together on a small love seat on the inn's screened-in porch on the backside of the house; it was Ella's third birthday. The photo seems overexposed and light.

Their skin is yellow as if a golden light shines over them. Gia has never noticed this before. She scans the wall for more photos of the three of them together and sees the same overexposed effect in each one—brightness beaming from their physical forms.

Marguerite pulls Gia away.

Gia retrieves her apron and joins Ella and Marguerite at the stainless-steel cooking table in the center of the kitchen; however, she's a little hesitant to get her hands dirty. Instead, she watches Ella, who is already at work drowning thick slices of fresh-baked, white bread into a mixture of eggs, whole cream, and melted butter in an extra-large, stainless-steel bowl. Ella plops the saturated piece of bread onto a mound of sweet-smelling brown sugar and chopped pecan granola mix. She flips the bread to blanket the entire bit.

Marguerite melts a square of butter on the hot steel stove. Ella places the slice of coated bread into the sizzling butter filling the kitchen with its mouth-watering smell.

"Oh my goodness, that smells divine," Gia says.

"That, my dear, is an understatement," says Marguerite. "This is breakfast goddess-liness with a splash of perfection and love. Just wait until you have some of the finished product tomorrow."

"Whose dairy products?" asks Ella.

"Ella, you know I only use Mitchel's Dairy Farm. Boy, oh boy, you are a teenager now, aren't you?"

"I was just checking, 'cause if it's not Mitchel's, I'm not eating it."

"Me neither," says Marguerite with a wink. "We finally got rid of all the others. Mitchel's farm is the only name on dairy in this entire town. I'm telling you, we boycotted everyone else. Those big companies don't even try anymore."

"Okay then, am I going to have to fight your other guests for this breakfast?" asks Ella while she holds up her fists and dances like a boxer. Gia smiles at Ella. Seeing her cooking and acting silly helps her forget about her regrets.

"Ha, no, my dear, you get first dibs. You're the birthday girl. Plus, I always make about four baking dishes too many. That's okay; Jack will eat it." They all laugh and shake their heads.

"Now, don't you two ladies worry about Gaillynn. She is going to take care of that kitty, and you two are here with me. You're all mine." Gia and Ella look at each other and laugh. "You three women are like a triangle; stronger together and never truly separated when apart. I can see it, damn it, I can feel it. When you are together, you radiate happiness and strength. Your bond is like none other I have ever seen. It's your familial energy; your connection is electric." Marguerite lingers a smile upon Ella.

"I miss Mom. I wish she had come," says Ella.

"For Gaillynn to miss this weekend, there must have been a good enough reason. I know she loves it here, and I know that cat would have been fine alone. She has her reasons, and we must trust her," says Marguerite.

Ella snaps a quick look at her grandmother. She squeezes her eyebrows together. *Of course*, she thinks. *Something has been troubling my mother. She's up to something. But what?*

"Ella," says Marguerite, "Why haven't you finished high school yet? That brilliant mind of yours is beyond high school already." Marguerite flips a piece of French toast on the stove.

"Mom wants me to have normal high school experiences. So she doesn't want me to start too young."

"Ah, yes. Of course." Marguerite looks at Gia as if they share a secret. "That has always been very important to Gaillynn. Normalcy," Marguerite articulates the world with slow precision. "You ladies should be proud to be way more interesting than normal. Hasn't Gail figured that out yet?"

Ella and Gia laugh.

"You'd think so," says Ella.

"You should tell your mother that you want to skip eighth grade at least. There's fourteen-year-old freshman all the time," suggests Marguerite.

"Exactly," Ella says with excitement. "I'm going to do that, Marguerite, thank you. Brilliant idea. Eighth grade is an absolute drag. It's so boring. I'm so far beyond my classmates academically that it's hard for me to even hang out with them sometimes, you know?"

"See, I knew it." Marguerite's eyes disappear into a proud smile. Gia gives in, washes her hands, and joins in on the cooking fun. She lifts a piece of the soft white bread and submerges it into the wet mixture. Gia lifts the bread, heavy with dairy products, and presses it onto the mound of brown sugar, oats, and chopped pecan mixture. She cradles it in her hands and waits until Marguerite has a bubbling pond of butter for her to place it in.

"Marguerite, let's send a picture to Mom." Ella wipes her hands on her apron and pulls her cell phone from her back pocket. She holds it above their heads; Marguerite wraps her thin, muscular arm around Ella's waist and readies for the shot. "Let's blow her a kiss," instructs Ella. They hold a hand under their puckered lips and blow. Ella clicks the button on the side of the phone and captures their happy faces. "Oh, I love it," she says. She sends the picture to Gaillynn then returns her phone to the back pocket of her blue jeans.

The women spend the afternoon cooking hundreds of pieces of French toast. Once the bread is ready, they line up the cooked pieces to cool, then move to the giant mixer. Marguerite fills the six-quart mixing bowl with eight squares of cream cheese. On top of them, she pours in a triple-shot of pure vanilla extract and tops it with four heaping cups of white sugar.

"Okay, Ella, dear, mix away," instructs Marguerite.

Ella flips the mixer's on-switch and places her hands around the bowl as it hums and turns the ingredients. After a few minutes, the contents have become smooth and fluffy. Ella clicks the mixer off, releases the bowl, and spoons out the filling from the blades. Ella carries the heavy bowl to the cooled, golden-brown French toast.

Marguerite has already lined half a dozen glass baking dishes with the French toast. Ella and Gia get busy spreading a thick layer of the cream cheese mixture across the layers of toast. Marguerite follows with a spoonful of chopped peaches then tops their masterpiece with another slice of French toast. They cover the glass pans with aluminum foil then line them up in the walk-in cooler.

"We will let the toast rest until morning when they will be heated and served with a hearty birthday girl breakfast," Marguerite says.

"What time are you starting the bacon and the cobbler in the morning, Auntie Marguerite? I would love to help." Ella lifts an extra piece of crunchy French toast to her mouth and takes a bite. She rubs her tummy and nods her head to Marguerite. "Delicious," she mutters through a mouth full.

"Ella, you can come on down at four-thirty am; I'll be here. Jack might still be sleeping, so I would love the help, my dear. Now you two go rest, and I'll see you for lobster dinner at six pm sharp." Marguerite wipes her hands on her apron, winks at the women, and heads to the cooler.

"Oh, yum, lobster." Ella dances and claps her hands in front of her face squishing what's left of the bread. She shoves it into her mouth, and her cheeks puff out as she chews.

Gia and Ella untie their aprons and return them to the apron rack. Gia wraps an arm around Ella's shoulder and steps up on her tiptoes. "Are you taller than me now?"

Ella looks at the top of her grandmother's head. "Yup."

"So, no hot chocolate because it's too sugary, but you just stuffed a whole piece of that French toast into your mouth like a starved animal." Gia tickles Ella's armpit.

Ella giggles. "Stop, Grammy. Forrest's doesn't make their hot chocolate with love."

The women exit the kitchen; Jack spots Ella and gallops toward her bouncing the floor under his weight. Ella frees herself from her grandmother's arm and runs to Jack. She jumps as high as she can, and he catches her in a hug. He swings her around, knocking over a red-and-white lobster buoy on display, decorated with vines of dried bittersweet and pine cones in the corner with Ella's feet.

Gia rushes over to clean up the mess while Jack ignores the crashing decorations. He holds Ella in his arms and presses his palm against the back of her head. Ella rests her head on his shoulder and breaths in his man scent.

"I've missed you, Queen Ella. Welcome back, my dear," he says through his loose top lip.

"I've missed you too, Jack." He kisses her on the cheek and puts her down. He pats the top of her head.

"You ladies go rest. Lobster dinner is at six." He points to the stairs and motions them to go to their room.

◆

Eden's Garden is a late seventeen hundred antique home turned inn. It is operated and owned by Marguerite and Jack Mendalion; they refuse to refer to Eden's Garden as a bed-and-breakfast. "It is so much more," Jack says. "We prepare three hearty meals each day for our guests. The hefty cost of a night's stay includes all food and drinks."

Jack often boasts, "We provide the perfect Maine experience, and our service and friendliness are beyond exceptional."

The inn's interior design is classic nautical decor. Its walls, covered with wallpaper with yellow roses in full bloom, are bright and cheerful. Like Locket Manor, the inn collects remembrances, antiques, and relics of earlier, more difficult times—memories of their family's history and culture.

Clear glass bottles covered in barnacles from a past life in the ocean line wooden shelves hovering over the lace-paneled windows. Picture frames constructed of retired barn boards outline oil paintings illustrating the sea's many temperaments occupy each room throughout the inn.

The transformed stern from a wooden lobster boat is now a bar in Eden's Garden's lounge. A red-and-green stripe against the yellowed white paint outlines the repurposed ship and stops abruptly where the bar's creator cut the craft in half. A sheet of thick glass covers the flat stern, and through it, her name is visible: Comfort. A driftwood chandelier hangs above Comfort and brightens the bar. Recycled painter's ladders support a wall full of various liquors.

◆

CHAPTER NINE

Gaillynn stumbles through the door and into the Union Station pub. She staggers, weaves to the right, redirects, and heads to the bar. Gaillynn presses her bosom over the sticky countertop and spills her cleavage for everyone to see. With a wider than average flirty smile at the bartender, she orders a shot of tequila. Cooper and his friends immediately notice Gaillynn. She downs the tequila, then squeezes a lime between her teeth and sucks on it hard.

"Whooo!" Gaillynn hoots and raises the shot glass over her head. "I'll have another one of those, please."

The bartender considers her request with a raised eyebrow—after all, she already seems pretty drunk. Gaillynn scans the crowd around her. Her eyes meet Cooper's. She gives him a stare, lifts one of her cheeks into a half-smile, then waves a forgiving wave at him. His eyes widen with delight, and he puffs out his chest toward her.

The bartender lays down another shot and lime wedge and announces to Gaillynn, "This is the last one." He focuses on the lipstick smudged across her face—this solidifies his decision to stop serving her. He raises his eyebrows and turns away from her.

She pretends to almost fall off of her stilettos as she whines, "Why?" She clutches the edge of the bar catching herself from a sure plummet to the floor just in time, then pours the second shot into her mouth. Gaillynn sucks on the sour lime wedge, swallows hard, plops herself down on a barstool, and pretends to cry. Gaillynn's behavior interests Cooper. It is the in with Gaillynn he's looking for, and with a quick hop, he dashes toward her.

Gaillynn hides her head in the crease of her elbow and convulses her body in pretend sobs. She can see his feet; he stands next to her wearing those damn boots. Gaillynn's mouth waters with nausea rising in her throat.

What a stupid piece of shit, she thinks.

"Hi, Gaillynn. Are you okay?"

"No. No, I'm not. My daughter is gone for the weekend, and I'm all alone." She lifts her head and looks at Cooper. She squints her eyes and wobbles her head. She pretends to struggle to focus on his face. Her eyes light up. "Cooper? Is that really you?"

"Yes, Gail. I'm here. What's wrong? Why are you crying?"

"I'm always alone. Why am I always alone? Do I deserve this? Doesn't anyone love me?" Gaillynn drops her head back down and pretends to cry. Cooper pulls a nearby barstool close to hers and sits next to her. He massages her shoulder and whispers into her ear.

"I love you. I have always loved you. You don't have to be alone."

She sticks her finger into her mouth and fishes out some saliva and rubs spit around her eyes. She smudges her makeup, so it looks like she's crying. She lifts her head and faces Cooper. "I don't?"

"No. You don't. I can take care of you. Don't cry, Gaillynn."

Gaillynn wraps her arms around his neck and leans in close to his face. "Cooper, will you take me home?"

"Yes." He stands up at her request causing her arms to break free of the grasp behind his neck. He sits back down and regrets his show of eagerness. "Yes, of course, Gaillynn. Whenever you are ready to go," he says.

"I wanna go now. I don't feel so good. Will you drive my car?"

"You drove here? Jesus, Gaillynn, you're lucky you didn't kill yourself. I'll drive you home; where are your keys?"

"Oh shit, I left them in the car. Oops," she slurs through a giggle. He wraps his long arm under hers and attempts to help Gaillynn to her feet. She drops all of her body weight into his arms and plunges her hand into his pocket. He is surprised by her weight but steadies her with ease. She pulls his cell phone from his pocket like a slippery sloth and places it on the barstool. He guides her outside and to her car, without his cell phone.

"You know, Cooper, you are so cute. Why do you have to be a dick? If you weren't such a dick in high school, I totally would have gone out with you," Gaillynn lies.

"I'm not a dick anymore."

"I know you're not. Cooper, I have an idea; let's go to my house."

"I thought we already were? My God, you are hammered." He laughs.

Cooper steadies Gaillynn's wobbling body into the passenger seat of the Mercedes; then, he hustles over to the driver's side. The keys are in the ignition right where she left them. Gaillynn leans her head on his shoulder, and they drive in silence toward her house. She squints one of her eyes open to watch him. Gaillynn can hear his heavy breathing. He holds the steering wheel with two hands, and he leans his body forward with impatience.

Gaillynn's blood boils with angst. She, too, is impatient and craves her revenge.

They reach Locket Manor; Cooper accelerates along the driveway, causing the rumble of the cobblestones under the car's tires to become a rapid buzz. He forces the fast-moving vehicle to a quick stop in front of the house. Cooper flicks open the car door and rushes over to help Gaillynn, who has managed to get one foot out of the car and appears to have passed out from trying. He jiggles her hip, and she opens her eyes.

"Cooper. You're here." She pulls the keys from the ignition without him noticing then lets him help her out of the car.

The trip up the porch stairs. Gaillynn giggles and says, "Shhhhh, don't wake the neighbors." He looks around at not one single neighboring house in view. Cooper releases a low, demonical laugh.

Gaillynn rolls her eyes.

Once inside, Gaillynn turns to face him, takes his arms, wraps them around her waist, and kisses him. He pulls her closer and tries to continue their kiss. She pulls away and commands, "Come with me." Gaillynn pulls him by the hand.

Cooper inspects each enormous room and cranes his neck to see into the living room, searching for the clock. It is dark, so he can't tell if it is still there or not. The blanket worked.

She leads him to the kitchen, where she swings open the extra-large refrigerator door and retrieves two beers fingering both bottlenecks in one hand. Cooper continues to investigate the room; Gaillynn jerks him forward by pulling his arm. She leads Cooper out of the kitchen and up the stairs. He searches for the clock as they travel through the estate and into her bedroom.

Gaillynn pushes him onto her bed; she identifies which beer has the torn label and hands it to him. They twist open the screw top beers and take a long drink.

"Cheers to you, Cooper. For getting me home," she says, then swallows some beer, "And for loving me." They click the glass containers together and take another long drink. "Now, you give me something to toast," she instructs.

"Okay, um, cheers to you for being so damn drunk."

"Bottoms up to that," she says. He guzzles the rest of his beer. Gaillynn pretends to finish her's as well and sets it down on the bedside table. She watches and waits for signs of the drug she slipped into his bear. He leans back, making himself comfortable on Gaillynn's bed. Cooper studies every inch of her.

"Why don't you come over here, Gail? Come sit on my lap," he says.

Nausea rises in her throat. "If we are going to do it, I want to be in charge," orders Gaillynn.

"Okay. You're in charge."

Gaillynn turns away from Cooper and performs a seductive dance across the room. She circles her hips at an exaggerated circumference. Once she reaches the safe, Gaillynn leans her upper body into the gold wheel and thrusts her buttocks toward him.

"Yeah," he whispers.

Gaillynn spins around and examines his face. He appears to be reeling with excitement that his body is too weak to express; however, he's not quite ready. He needs more time for the drugs to affect his enormous size.

To delay, Gaillynn reaches her hand down under the hem of her silk dress and caresses her leg, making sure to take her time. Cooper is delighted. Her hand reaches her crotch, and she rubs the matching red underwear between her legs. Gaillynn slips her fingers inside her panties and pretends to arouse herself. She turns around and lifts her dress to reveal her tiny red thong hidden between her legs. Cooper is mesmerized by her beauty and swaying hips.

"Damn, Gail. You're fucking hot."

Gaillynn clutches the gold spindled wheel on the safe, turns it counterclockwise, and then pulls open the thick door to reveal its contents inside. All the while, Cooper's eyes remain fixed on the small patch of red silk between Gaillynn's legs.

She rubs her hand over the seat of the chair she placed inside the safe. "You sit here, Cooper."

He attempts to blink the haze from his blurred vision. "What? Why? Come over here, Gail. On the bed like a normal person."

Gaillynn freezes—she didn't consider Cooper may refuse to sit inside the safe. Her eyes dart from the bed to the chair inside the safe. "It's the only way I can get off. I have to ride you on a chair. In a dark space," she makes up as she goes.

"Okay, fuck, whatever you say. You're in charge." He wobbles over to the safe. He leans in and hits his forehead on the metal. Gaillynn catches his arm and guides him into place. He sits on the plastic that is covering the chair inside. Eager to satisfy Gaillynn, he attempts to undo his pants. He pulls at the button on his jeans without success. "Jesus, how much have I had to drink?"

"Just one beer and six Rohypnol, my prince charming." She grabs his face and pulls it close to hers. "Cooper, I want you, so please don't argue with me; I want you to be quiet and let me take care of you." He smiles and relents.

"What's Ro-hipp-nul?" he slurs.

Gaillynn lifts a leg and straddles it over Cooper's lap. He leans forward and tries to kiss her. Cooper is clumsy and attempts to find the thong she teased him with, but his hands are a fumbling mess. Gaillynn pushes Cooper's face away from hers. She grabs his hands from under her dress and presses his arms back behind him. She kisses his neck to distract him from her retrieving a pull-tie hidden inside her bra under her breasts. Gaillynn wraps and tightens the white pull-tie around his wrists. She remains on his lap and whispers in his ear. "You fucking fuck. You will no longer threaten my family."

"What?" His speech is slow and quiet. He has become exhausted from the sedative Gaillynn planted in his beer. "I haven't threatened your family. I just want that fucking stone," he confesses. "I think it wants me, though. I think it loves me," he slurs with a childish chuckle. His head rolls back, and his eyes close. He passes out.

"The stone loves everyone, you idiot. And it's using you as its tool for whatever fucked up reason. I know what you are capable of to get our stone, you piece of shit. You killed Robbie trying to get close to me; you lied and said you thought he was raping me. You sneak around my house all hours of the night. I've had to look at your ugly face over and over again, haunting my video surveillance. I can't delete it fast enough." Cooper is unconscious, but Gaillynn continues her rant just the same. "I will stop this story from spreading to another generation of Chandler men. It dies with you, you son-of-a-bitch." She lifts her legs from his lap and kicks off her high heels.

Cooper's legs are long and stretch far beyond the length of the garment bags that Gaillynn situated inside the safe earlier that day. "Oh shit. Frig, of course, he's taller than the fur coats." She lifts each of his legs, bends them at the knee, and pushes them in toward his body. She wiggles the plastic around his now cramped position and seals the large garment bag closed like a giant Ziplock bag.

She reaches under her bed, pulls out the food saver vacuum, plugs it in, and connects it to the garment bag. She flips on the switch, and with a quiet hum, the vacuum begins sucking all of the air out of the thick plastic bag: the plastic crinkles and collapses. Gaillynn becomes fixated on the buzz and the slow removal of the air inside the bag. She watches how it changes him. His once perfectly fitting clothes appear taught, and the removal of air has disfigured his body. Gaillynn listens to the vacuum's purr. Its hum is satisfying, and Cooper's noiselessness is vindicating. The plastic crinkles as it's pulled tight, and after a few minutes, the machine's purring turns to a moan. The lack of air inside the garment bag puts a strain on the vacuum's small but hard-working motor.

She clicks the vacuum off, then seals the garment bag's opening with the vacuum unit's unique heat-seal feature. She repeats the same routine with the second garment bag already in place under the first. Cooper's body is too drugged to know Gaillynn is suffocating him and that he will never regain consciousness. Cooper's life quietly leaves his body.

Through the clear plastic, Gaillynn takes particular notice of how tight it is around his skin. It distorts his face to the point of being unrecognizable, almost as if he is mummified. The pull the removal of air caused on the bag parted his lips, and it appears he is frozen mid-attempt to gasp for air. His long legs and bent knees appear he has crouched into a fetal position.

"I knew this would be way too easy." She looks up to the heavens. "Yes, Grammy Ginny, I took care of it. So don't worry anymore. God, I'm never going to be done dealing with stupid. I'm dealing with dead stupid right now. It will never end.

"Well, I'm sure your dead ass is going to stink." Gaillynn moves out of the safe and pulls three tubes of clear caulking and a metal caulking gun from under her bed. She affixes a headlamp to her forehead, turns it on, and steps inside the safe with the lifeless, vacuum-sealed Cooper. "Airtight? Maybe one-hundred-years-ago, but I'm sure you're not anymore. But I'll make sure you are." She pats the side of the safe like it's an old friend.

Gaillynn squeezes the caulking into every corner and seam inside the walls of the thick iron safe. She hopes to seal the potential smell of her murder inside. Once her task is complete, Gaillynn closes the safe, turns the gold wheel to engage the locking mechanism, and proceeds to seal the seams around the door from the outside. She locks the safe for the last time by turning the dial on the combination lock. To ensure that her mother, who also knows the combination, could never open it, she beats the dial with a sledgehammer until it pops off.

Gaillynn situates herself in her bed and fixes her eyes on the safe. After a few hours of waiting and anticipating a struggle from the suffocating man inside, nothing happens. Gaillynn becomes bored. "Well, Coop, this has been exciting," she says. She removes her headlamp and places it on the bedside table, and without changing out of her red dress, she lies down and fluffs her pillow under her head.

---◆---

CHAPTER TEN

Ella and her grandmother climb the wooden stairs toward their room at Eden's Garden as instructed by Jack. At the top of the stairs is a small landing circled by five guest rooms. Ella opens the unlocked door of room number three and rushes into the bedroom.

"Home away from home." Ella jumps over their luggage already in the room, twirls into a belly flop on her favorite bed, and kicks off her shoes. "Let's take a nap, Grammy."

"I would love that," answers Gia. They climb under the burgundy bedspreads adorning a pink rose pattern without changing out of their day clothes. Each woman fluffs a pillow under their heads.

"Grammy, what is Mom doing this weekend?"

"As far as I know, nothing, sweetheart. Babysitting Dondy."

Gia's guilt floods out of its storage crypt and into her mind again. *It is odd that Gaillynn was so willing to stay home this year. Dondy would have been okay with his litter box and automatic feeder. Could it have something to do with Cooper being out of jail?*

Ella's breathing becomes heavy; Gia lifts her head to check on her granddaughter. Ella appears so peaceful and comfortable in the soft bed. Ella's body twitches as she falls to sleep.

Gia's mind busies itself worrying about Gaillynn. She thinks of

Robbie, and of course, her daughter's pain, and how Cooper killed him fourteen years ago. *It was my fault,* she thinks. *If only I hadn't tried to intervene. If only I hadn't tried to outsmart the stone and send him back to the mill that night.*

Gia's guilt wrenches at her heart as she lay in the stillness of room number three in one of her favorite places on Earth. Her stomach develops its familiar ache—Ella's birthday marks another year of her cowardliness. Another year of not telling Gaillynn the truth has passed. Gia's breathing deepens, and she recalls the first time she met Cooper.

◆

Gia's mind flashes back, like a dream, to that quiet Wednesday afternoon during Gaillynn's junior year of high school. Gaillynn was at cello practice, and Gia was in the kitchen doing chores when the doorbell chimed. She hurried to the door and swung it open with a curious smile. A burst of ocean-scented wind pushed against the door, slamming it wide open and out of her hand.

"Hello, Mrs. Amirah. My name is Cooper C. Blethen. I am friends with your daughter Gaillynn." He stuck out his hand. Gia returned the gesture and shook his hand.

"Hello, Cooper. How very nice to meet you. Are you also a junior in high school like my Gaillynn?"

"Yes, ma'am, I am. I'm in Gaillynn's statistics and chemistry class. Your daughter is brilliant."

"I know she is. I can't keep up with her. Oh, please come in. Excuse me; we don't get many visitors. Please come in." She stepped aside and invited Cooper in. As he entered, Cooper scanned the large home. The wind pulled the door closed behind him. Gia jumped.

Gia led him to the living room. The arousal in Cooper's eyes heightened at the rare pieces of art and history. Gia was curious, so she studied him. The hair on her arms stood up. She rubbed the worry away.

As soon as they entered the living room, he immediately noticed the clock on the opposite wall; he stepped toward it. He moved his body close to the clock, and he leaned in with his nose to smell it. He dropped his head back to scan the tall clock from the top, then down to the floor. He caressed the wood carvings and fingered the seams of the clock's edges.

"Now that is cool," he said, pointing to the stone. "What kind of jewel is that in your clock?"

Gia knew she couldn't tell him anything. She became nervous and tongue-tied. Lying did not come easily for her. Her insecure attempts were never successful. Unlike Gaillynn, who could rattle off an impromptu deceitful narrative like it was her super-power. She decided to ignore his question and changed the subject.

"Cooper Blethen," Gia said. "I think I've heard of your mother. Yes, Attorney Blethen, right? Her office is in that gorgeous brick mill on Harbor Creek, isn't it?"

"Yes. That is my mother, Jessica." He shook his head. "Mrs. Amirah, I am here about Gaillynn."

"I'm sorry, Cooper, she is not here." *But you already know that,* she thought.

"I know she isn't. I came to talk to you."

"Me? About what? Is everything okay?" Gia turned to investigate the position of the stone, fearing something terrible was happening. Like usual, the pendulum swung the stone, keeping time—it appeared that nothing was going on. A feeling, a warning of betrayal, darted through her chest. Gia ignored it.

"Oh yes, very okay. You see, I like your daughter, I mean, really like her, and I just wanted to ask you for your blessing."

"My blessing? For what, my dear?" *No*, she said to herself.

"Your blessing for me to ask Gaillynn to dinner. I will be a perfect gentleman, and I will not keep her out past her curfew. I promise," Cooper said.

"Oh, well, my, you are so sweet. Yes, of course, I give you my blessing. Yes, absolutely. Thank you. Thank you for coming to me. Coming to me first is truly gentlemanly." Gia raised her chest and clasped her hands, pointing her elbows, and shrugged off the warning signs she wasn't adept at recognizing

Cooper clapped one single clap and leaned toward Gia to give her a tight and unexpected hug. "Thank you. Really. Thank you. Your permission means a lot to me," he said while still embracing Gia.

"You are very welcome," Gia squeaked as his tighter than necessary embrace limited her lungs. A weft of ice-cold air passed under Gia's nose. The last time she felt the cold air was when her late husband threatened to harm her with a physical attack. *It must be getting cold outside*, she thought.

"Thank you. Okay, I will leave now." Cooper turned to leave but held his gaze on the stone in the enormous clock one more time.

"Wow, that is so cool," he whispered.

The stone brightened, and the pendulum's swing turned to a sway. Gia received a calming message—an invisible transmission for her to remain calm—and the stone displayed a sensation of love for Cooper. "Oh," she said. "Okay."

◆

Gia rolls onto her back and fixes her eyes at the ceiling. The inn's bed is much smaller than hers at home, but she enjoys the closeness of sleeping near Ella. She closes her eyes and covers them with her hands. *How could I have been so naive? Gaillynn told me I couldn't trust him, but instead of listening to her, I let the stone trick me into thinking he was decent, and I ignored my intuition. Even worse than that, I pushed her to accept his romantic advances,* she thinks.

◆

Gia remembers when Gaillynn returned home from her cello lesson that day. Gaillynn carried her school bag over her shoulder and headed directly to the kitchen. Gaillynn was hidden inside the refrigerator searching for something to eat when Gia approached her from behind.

"I had a visitor today," she said with excitement. "He was a very handsome visitor."

"What? Who on earth visited you and is handsome?" Gaillynn closed the refrigerator, leaned against the counter, and crunched her teeth into a juicy green apple.

"Cooper Blethen," Gia announced.

"You're kidding me, right?" Gaillynn's jaw dropped open, exposing chewed apple.

"No. I am not kidding. Cooper is so sweet and, oh my goodness, he is going to ask you to dinner. He asked for my permission. I thought he was so charming."

"Mom, no. Please no. Tell me you did not encourage him."

"Of course I did. Are you crazy? You should say yes."

"Never. Mom! I can't believe you fell for his bullshit." Gaillynn threw the uneaten apple into the garbage and stormed out of the kitchen.

Gia followed Gaillynn. "Why, honey? What is the matter? I think he is a very nice catch. Don't pass up a good thing, honey. He's cute, and he thinks you're pretty amazing and smart. He even likes all of our antiques. He wanted to ask you out for dinner and promised to have you home before your curfew."

"I don't have a curfew, Mom."

"I know, but he doesn't know that. I just thought that was a very considerate gesture."

"He is full of shit, Mom. He has gone out with every girl in the junior and senior class and most underclassmen. All he wants is for me to say yes. That is all that matters to him. He can't handle the fact that I have said no like a million times."

"Oh. I don't remember you mentioning Cooper before. What if you gave him a chance? You never know, honey."

"Oh my God, Mom, you are so dumb sometimes. He is a lying piece of shit."

"I am not dumb, Gaillynn. I know a good man when I see one. You don't have to find the bad in everyone, you know. I have always looked out for you the best way I could, and I have always been right here." Gia knew Gaillynn was right, but she was too ashamed to admit it. Gia turned away from Gaillynn to hide her tears.

"I'm sorry, Mom. I know. Listen, I love you so much, but I worry that sometimes you are a bit naive to people like him—like Dad. You have to trust me, Mom." Gaillynn hugged her mother.

"Gaillynn, honey, he comes from a great family. His mother is very successful, and I know he is something special."

Gaillynn pulled away with a huff. Trying to escape her mother, Gaillynn chose the usual left side of the double spiraling stairs to her bedroom. Her mother followed at her heels. "Oh my God. Mom. Stop." She slammed the door to her bedroom, almost nipping Gia's nose.

◆

Gia lifts her head to check on Ella. Her granddaughter's mouth is relaxed and open, and her hair covers most of her face. Her breathing remains heavy, and she exhales a restful, sound-asleep snort. Gia lays back on the pillow and releases a long sigh.

◆

Gia recalls Gaillynn's junior and senior years of high school and how fast they passed. Cooper visited Gia on occasion. He tried everything to win over Gaillynn but only had luck winning over Gia.

The stone seemed to fancy him too, so she thought.

◆

Gia misses the stone—she sensed the loss of the stone's closeness as soon as she left Locket Manor, and her energy was quick to deplete. Because of her age, the distance between her and the stone would affect her faster than Ella. "I will be back on Sunday," she reminds herself.

◆

Gia's mind continues to dwell on Gaillynn. The night of Gaillynn's senior Homecoming comes into focus like a projector playing a real of evidence against her. Gia recalls Gaillynn kissing her goodbye, dashing out of the house, and down the street to catch a ride to Homecoming with her girlfriends.

"You look beautiful, honey. Have a great time," Gia said to Gaillynn.

With a night ahead all to herself, Gia planted herself in the recliner situated next to the stone. She clicked the power button on the remote control to the large television and continued her knitting project well into the evening. Soon, she began dozing off. The beautiful sound of the doorbell ringing woke her. She staggered and yawned her way to the front door to find Cooper in a black tuxedo with a red rose pinned to his chest.

"Hello, Cooper, how come you're not at the dance?" She blinked her dry eyes, yawned, and motioned him to come inside. He stepped inside, and she could tell he was distraught by the look on his face. "Come sit down, Cooper."

She led him into the living room and clicked the television off. The beautiful clock stood poised in front of him—he sat on the yellow settee across from it. He remained silent and glared at the stone. He appeared hypnotized by its beauty. Gia hears voices calling to him. She wondered if he was aware of the sounds too. The beautiful singers crooned in her ears, muffling out all other noises around her. It reminded her of a tribal chant in an ancient language—voices of women. Their words were firm, potent, and instructive.

"Cooper?" Gia became concerned with his quietness. "Are you alright?"

Her words broke his focus on the stone, and he turned to Gia. His serious expression was beginning to worry her.

"Mrs. Amirah, you know how I feel about Gaillynn."

"Yes, dear. I know how you feel."

"I am worried about her, to be honest. I want what is best for her, and I want to protect her and love her." He turned and studied the glorious light beaming from the stone. "You know I would."

"Yes, dear, I believe you would. Cooper, has something happened?"

"I don't think Gaillynn realizes what kind of person I am. I am not like the kid I pretend to be at school. I do all that to get my mom and dad's attention, or maybe to punish them, I don't know." He turned away from the clock back to Gia. "My dad is always on me to be more, to be better, to be stronger. But deep down, I'm not like that. All I want is to love her." He rested his hands on his knees. "That is a beautiful clock," he added and returned his eyes to the stone.

"Cooper, Gaillynn doesn't care about all of that popularity stuff.

She wants kindness and honesty. She wants someone she loves and can trust. Cooper, you have to stop with the attitude at school. That is the only way. I know you are a kind person deep down and can be a great man, one that any woman would be lucky to be with."

Gia tried to comfort Cooper by rubbing his forearm, but the moving clock drew her attention away from him. The stone and pendulum swung far to the right and fixed itself there. The color of the stone brightened the room with magnificent gold and clarity of pure happiness. Something extraordinary was happening to Gaillynn right at that moment: Robbie. But Gia didn't know about Robbie.

Cooper also noticed the swing. His eyes widened, and he pointed his finger at the stone. "I think there is something wrong with your clock," Cooper said. He stepped toward the clock and squinted his eyes at the beaming rock.

Gia had an idea. She knew that there would need to be an equal pull of sadness to offset the incredible, happy energy the stone was receiving. Something good was happening to Gaillynn at that very moment, and Gia knew there would be a debt to settle with the stone.

Gia decided to give Cooper the heads up on the stone's backswing to comfort Gaillynn during the fall. "It's a brilliant idea." Gia giggled a proud trill at her delight in thinking of it. *If Cooper is there for Gaillynn through the hard times, she will see the honest Cooper.* As this idea settled into her brain, becoming a reality, the stone and pendulum dropped and leveled to the left.

"Already? Oh no. Cooper, do you know where Gaillynn is?"

"Yes, ma'am, I do. She is with Robbie Stetson," he exclaimed with relief. His eagerness to interrupt the couple at the mill had been pulsing inside his head. "They left the dance. I followed them in my car. I saw Robbie take her to a building behind the mill. The mill is closed, and there is no one else there. I didn't know what to do, so I came right here to talk to you because I was worried."

"No. No. Something bad is happening right now. You have to go to Gaillynn. I will be right behind you. Go, go, go. Now, Cooper."

Cooper ran to his car. His tires squealed and smoked as he sped away back to the mill.

Gia leaps to the phone, planning to call the police but found a folded note addressed to, "Mom." She opened it so fast she almost tore the paper. She read Gaillynn's words.

'Dear Mom,

I need to tell you that I lied to you tonight. I went to the dance with Robbie Stetson. We have been dating most of my senior year, and I have kept it from you. I didn't want you to try and talk me out of it or pursued me to be with Cooper. I know you like Cooper, and for some reason, you think the stone does too. We cannot trust Cooper; I feel his evil when I am around him. I chose Robbie, and I was hoping you could accept it. I am going to the dance tonight with Robbie. I plan to marry him someday. We love each other. Please understand. Love, Gaillynn'

"Oh, no," said Gia. "What have I done? What have I done? My God, what have I done? My idea caused the return swing. Helping Cooper get close to Gaillynn settles her debt of happiness, and indeed death will be the stone's only accepted currency."

◆

"It doesn't make any sense," Gia whispers into the darkness at the inn where Ella sleeps.

Ella mumbles an incomprehensible string of words—she is still asleep; Ella's voice jolts Gia out of the memory of the night she helped Cooper kill Ella's father. *And poor little Ella, what will she think of me? I sent Cooper to Gaillynn and told him something terrible happened, but my idea caused the return swing. It was all my fault.* Gia catches the tear that has escaped onto her nose—she wipes the wetness on the soft pillow under her head.

Gia wonders if the voices were speaking to Cooper that dreadful night. *He did appear to be in a trance—hypnotized by the color and humming of agents in his ears. Maybe they were talking to me?* She thinks.

Gia pushes away the thoughts—they are too traumatic to bear. She retreats this moment in time to the secret door buried in her mind, and Gia closes her eyes to join Ella in an afternoon nap. A desperate desire to rid herself of this guilt pangs at her ribcage. "I want to enjoy this weekend at Eden's Garden. The only way I know how-to is by ignoring the familiar pain of regret I suffer from every day."

Gia's mind fogs into sleepiness and her thoughts travel to the familiar sounds of Gaillynn playing her cello; the music lullabies her and puts her at ease. Relaxation overcomes her with a dreamlike trance. The music waltzes throughout Locket Manor and Gia welcomes this familiar and beautiful sound coming from Gaillynn's cello—she drifts into a tranquil rest.

Gia's sleep deepens. She can see a cello leaned against Gaillynn's body as if the two are one. Their bodies move together with the rhythm of Gaillynn's emotions that pour out of her instrument. Each melody is a ballad of her soul—always rich and emotional, but most often a cry of heartbreak.

Gia's dream journeys to one of the many nights she spent storytelling in Ella's childhood bedroom. She sees a mound of soft, colorful blankets where she and Ella sink their heads into fluffy pillows and cuddle way, way past bedtime. Gia spoons her knees perfectly, snug around Ella. Gia traces her granddaughter's ear with her fingertip, then tickles her way down her neck, back up, and through her brown curly hair. The two sing the Itsy Bitsy Spider song to the rhythm of the melody Gaillynn is playing on her cello.

Their singing is awkward as they attempt to match the lyrics to the melancholy riff. Ella squirms with delight and sucks her thumb with lips curled into a smile.

Ella removes her thumb out of her mouth long enough to say, "Grammy Gia, tell me the story about the clock."

"Oh, Ella, that is a long story," Gia replies.

Ella cranes her head over her shoulder to make direct eye contact with her grandmother and declares, "I'm not tired." Then she adds, "It's my favorite story, Grammy," as if her grandmother didn't already know.

"Okay, honey, where do you want me to start?"

"With Glinda, the clockmaker." Ella puts her thumb back in her mouth, snuggles into her pillow, and prepares for the story that makes her so happy and so proud to be an Amirah girl. "And don't forget about the part that Great-Grammy Gloria always knew when something was wrong."

"Okay, sweetie, I won't forget; here we go. Long, long ago, in the year 1692, in a small village at the base of England's largest mountain range lived your ancestor, Glinda Elaine Amirah…"

Gaillynn's music continues to dance through Gia's sleeping mind. Tears forming in her closed eyes escape and drain onto the pillow. The cello's cries drown out the dream of the familiar story Ella begged to hear. Instead, the cello tells stories of the lost lovers of generations of Amirah women widowed by the power of the stone, all of them knowing that loving meant losing.

The cello chords vibrate tales of the cold-hearted act of purchasing enormous life insurance policies for their husbands, knowing they would die after a short romance. Strings of eerie notes dance through Gia's subconscious, describing the ghosts of their ancestors and all of the husbands with no chance to survive. The sound of the vibrations leaping off the strings intensify and pound inside her ears. They announce a triumphant and conclusive symbol of their love for the stone and this life they are cursed with and willing to suffer for its gifts.

The ground outside of Locket Manor begins to rumble. The cello becomes silent. The grass uproots and mounds of dirt bubble up, exposing gurgling lava from below. Cooper is there; he screams—his body gets sucked into the hole. His flesh melts from his bones. "Help." His head bobs above Earth's molten core. "Help me. Help me. Hell..." The dirt pulls itself back into the hole and covers him. The grass realigns.

"Hell?" says Gia, still within a dream—an awakening. "Heaven and Hell are right here—Earth is the higher power. Hell is below the ground in which we walk. Heaven, rather than galaxies away, is right here. Right here within her protective ozone. Our shelter."

Ella shakes her sleeping grandmother's shoulder. "Grammy, are you okay?"

Gia's dream halts; she blinks open her eyes. More tears escape. Ella wipes the water from her grandmother's cheeks with her fingers.

"Grammy, you're crying. What's the matter?"

"I had a dream, honey. I am okay."

"What was it about, Grammy?" Ella retrieves a tissue for her grandmother and joins her on her bed.

"It was about the stone and you when you were a little girl."

"The stone? Me? Then why were you crying?"

"Well, sweetie, I am often torn between the stone's potent energy that sustains us, the glory of all of the wealth and beauty in our home, and the lives lost that earned it. Through it all, we must go on." She places her hand on Ella's cheek. "The power of the stone has already taken your father, but your very life depends on being near it."

"My life for his. Like a trade. He was a sacrifice." Ella looks down at her hands and closes her eyes.

"Ella, no. His death was not your fault. It..." Gia hesitates. *It was my fault*, she thinks, but she can't admit it. A tight squeeze pains her heart. "No, Ella. Don't you ever think it was your fault." She pulls Ella to her chest and wraps her in a tight hug. "I'm so confused about the meaning of it all. I have a nagging suspicion that the stone is more than just a life source that we need to be near and more than a curse that needs to be balanced. I have had dreams about a bright blue and gold light emanating everywhere and the sound of women's voices all messy and unclear. It feels like they are trying to tell me something."

"Me too, Grammy. I've had that same dream. I've always had that dream. Like for as long as I can remember."

Their bodies jump at a knock on the door. Marguerite peeks her head inside the room. "Are you ready for your lobster feed?"

Gia and Ella respond by standing up. They hold hands out of the room and hug down the stairs toward the dining room.

The inn's rectangular, wooden dining room table is piled high with dark-red steamed lobsters, matted gray clams, shining black mussels, giant orange crabs, bright yellow corn on the cob, and baskets of fresh from the oven butter-biscuits. Other guests have already gathered around the table set for twelve. Jack is circling the group wrapping plastic bibs around their necks and assisting them with pulling up their sleeves. He now wears his top denture, and he smiles, showing his bright white teeth.

Ella stops partway down the stairs, pulls her cell phone from her back pocket, and snaps a picture of the table heaping with food.

The other guests already gathered around the table are tourists who have never eaten lobster before. They sit in front of the pile of seafood, confused about where or how to begin. The biscuits seem the easiest, so they all grab one and put it on their otherwise empty plates.

In front of each person is everything they will need for the hearty feast: a wooden mallet with a matching square of wood for pounding the crab and lobster claws, a thin stainless-steel meat-picker, a tub of hot clam broth, and a bowl of melted butter.

Neglecting to wrap a plastic bib around their necks, Ella and Gia find empty chairs. They each grab a lobster and a crab. They scoop up as many steamed clams and mussels as their palms can hold and pile them on their plates. They top the mound of food with an ear of corn. Ella breathes in the steaming salty smell and opens her first clam.

The other guests copy Gia and Ella. They retrieve their food exactly as Gia and Ella did, then wait for the next move.

Marguerite wraps the heel of a loaf of bread around a stick of butter and uses it to roll the salty topping around the hot corncob on Ella's down-east feast. Marguerite then circles the table, buttering up everyone's corn. Whenever she comes upon an empty drink glass, she yells the refill order to the bartender mixing drinks behind Comfort.

"Another Bud Light, Joe."

Joe is tall and thin with jet-black, spiked hair. He rolls up the sleeves of his black button-up shirt, revealing an uninterrupted pattern of tattoos covering both of his arms. He tucks his shirt into his pleated black pants. Not his typical, most comfortable attire, but perfect for his shift at Eden's Garden. An empty tip jar rests on the rim of Comfort, and he twirls on his heels as he retrieves the bottled beer for Marguerite's order.

Jack sits across the table with the tourists to guide them through opening a clam, cleaning off the neck, rinsing the belly with a shake in hot clam broth, followed by a dunk into the warm butter, and then into his mouth. They copy and cheer each time a piece of seafood makes it into their mouths. Once they progress to the crabs, the noise in the room rises. Constant thumping of the mallets and the tourists' shrills of surprise from the splattering juice adds an ingredient of joy to the dinner.

Gia and Ella enjoy watching the tourists and laugh at the seafood-eating rookies. They dine with more elegant seafood etiquette and suck every ounce of salty juice from each lobster claw. Ella savors the salty-sweet lobster meat and rolls her eyes back with the pleasure of each bite.

This type of dinner requires time and patience; however, the food disappears. The wait staff was busy clearing the thick shells and splattered mess of dinner's delights off the table to prepare for dessert. Ella rubs a wedge of lemon on her hands to remove the smell of lobster and wipes them on a clean napkin.

Jack arrives with warm slices of blueberry pie for everyone. Marguerite follows behind with freshly brewed coffee and fills large glass mugs to their rim. Jack sets a tall glass of milk beside Ella instead of the coffee, and he pats her shoulder. She places her hand on his. "Thank you for remembering, Jack."

Once the guests finish their homemade blueberry pie and coffee, the kitchen crew dives into the task of the messy dinner's clean-up. Jack and Marguerite join Ella and her grandmother in the guest living room. Ella sits near the fireplace; the warmth reminds her of the stone. She wiggles her bare feet toward the heat from the fire. She is happy, content, and at home.

Ella wraps Jack and Marguerite with an imagined hug as they enter the room. She can see the return of love in their eyes. *I can be myself with Jack and Marguerite. It's like they know we are different, and they love us anyway,* she thinks.

Marguerite goes to Gia and smooths Gia's hair. Marguerite lifts a handful of hair and examines it. "Our water is so hard on your hair, Gia; your color is coming out already. Look, your gray is showing; it wasn't when you got here. Your gray comes out every year but not usually this quick." Marguerite's eyes disappear into her smile.

Ella knows her grandmother has not taken a shower, nor does her grandmother color her hair. Gia shows signs of being away from the stone more quickly than Ella, but this was much faster than usual. Ella's eyes meet her grandmother's, and she mouths, "Are you okay?"

Gia gives Ella a wink and a nod. "I know, right, any more showers, and I'll be completely gray." Everyone, except Ella, giggles.

"Jack and I remember the first year you came here with your mom and grandmother, Ella. You weren't even one yet, but boy were you talkative," begins Marguerite.

"What do you mean talkative? I was a baby," says Ella.

"I know you were, but you gurgled and trilled your own words that none of us understood but seemed to make perfect sense to you. And you would sing. It was like you were singing a beautiful, foreign language. That is when I knew you were a genius."

"Oh, you knew first, did you, Marguerite?" asks Gia with a grin.

"Yup. I knew it. I could feel it. There is something special about this child, and the older she gets, the closer she is to realizing just how special." Marguerite beams with pride.

Ella knows the song Marguerite is referring to; it is a humming of the women's voices from a dream that she has always had. It recurs often, and though it makes her wonder, it also brings her happiness and peace. The humming from her dreams has become a regular part of her everyday life. She closes her eyes and replays the song in her mind. Ella hums out loud.

Gia sits up straight—she recognizes it too. Ella's melody is the same as her dream, and now she realizes it's the same Ella has hummed and trilled since she was an infant. Gia looks at Marguerite with wide eyes. Marguerite wears a smug smile.

"That's the song," says Marguerite.

Gia begins humming along with Ella—their voices harmonize beautifully together; they sing the song of their family stone, their precious ore, and as they do, their skin begins to beam a brightness into the room. The fire in the fireplace becomes more intense. The entire house gets hotter—beads of sweat appear on Jack's forehead and top lip.

The humming distracts the bartender—Joe stops his cleaning to listen. The two women's voices are heavenly and mesmerizing. The guests leave their private rooms to seek the energy that is arousing them to find themselves in the inn's living room, hypnotized by the rich harmony of Ella and Gia's humming, which is now gaining volume.

The number of voices sounds to be many more than just their two. Each person becomes enlightened with a feeling of purpose and strength like they have never felt before. And now, once strangers are connected.

After three or four minutes, Ella and Gia end their charming and haunting serenade. The room erupts with clapping and happy laughter. The bartender sits at the piano and begins playing a boisterous song. The inn's guests spend the remainder of the evening dancing with each other amongst the love in the air.

PART TWO

◆

TIME

KEEPER

◆

Chapter Eleven

Early Saturday morning Gaillynn changes out of her red dress and into her button-up blue pajamas. However, for the first time in fourteen years she doesn't fasten all of the buttons. Gaillynn leaves the last two near her neck, unbuttoned feeling like she can now breath a bit more freely. Silence rises from the safe. Cooper is dead and forever her bedroom companion.

She pats the side of the cold metal. "Right where I can keep an eye on you."

With her cell phone in hand, she tiptoes down the left side of the broad and slopping stairs—a balcony over the entry room and its marbled floor. Gaillynn steps off the stairs onto the cool marble toward the living room for her morning dose of love and energy from the stone. She presses her body close to the front of the clock and visits with her coveted ore. While she and the stone share an embrace through a nonphysical connection, she phones the home of Cooper's mother and stepfather, where he has lived before and since getting out of jail. As she hoped, no one answers, and the call goes to voicemail.

"Hey, Cooper, it's Gaillynn. I just wanted to thank you for driving me home last night. I was really drunk. I am sure the boys were happy to see you back at Union Station when you returned. Oh

God, I just realized you must have walked back—geez, I'm sorry. I hope you had a drink for me. Anyway, I just wanted you to know that I accept your apology for Robbie. I guess I finally understand it was a total freak mistake. Thank you again. See you around. Oh, I don't know your cell number, so can you call me?"

◆

At that exact moment on the same Saturday morning, while having coffee and breakfast at the round table in their kitchen, Jessica Blethen and her new husband, Roger, sip warm mugs of coffee and read the Gazette newspaper in silence.

A flat-faced computer tablet leans on its tripod on the serving table to their backs. The tablet's face brightens when Gaillynn's call comes in. A list of family phone lines emerge, and the one named *Home Phone* blinks in rhythm with the sound of an antique phone ringing. Instead of getting up or lowering his newspaper, Roger orders the computer to: "Screen Call." His voice command allows the tablet's digital answering machine to pick up. They listen to the message in real-time as Gaillynn leaves it.

Jessica and Roger drop their papers to their laps and listen. Jessica's eyes water at hearing Gaillynn's words of forgiveness. Evidence of an almost imperceptible smile brightens her face. Jessica's anger at her son and late husband, Hank, who betrayed her belief in them as good and decent human beings, softens. She has been so disappointed with them. Their lives became media targets in the years following Robbie's death. And she will never recover from her husband's obscure sacrificial suicide. Her chest lifts in response to a deep breath then lowers with its release.

Jessica's eyes land on her second husband's round face. Her stomach heaves with disgust. She crumples the paper in her hands and smashes it to the table. She pushes against the floor with her feet, and her chair screeches backward. She stands. Jessica grimaces a scowl toward Roger. She darts to the bathroom and locks the door behind her.

Roger follows behind and knocks on the door. "Jessica, what's wrong with you?"

"Roger, get out of my house."

"What the fuck, Jessica? Why?"

"Roger, I can't stand to look at your money-sucking face for another minute. I want you out."

"Let's talk about this."

"No. Get out of my house, Roger."

"Are you listening to yourself? You're one crazy bitch." Rogers pounds his fist on the bathroom door. Jessica jumps.

Jessica sticks her finger into her throat and hurls the contents of her stomach into the toilet. She attempts to rid herself of years of a feigned existence—her fictitious display of having moved on and being okay. The truth is she has allowed a rotten constellation prize to take residence in her soul. Settling for Roger, the loss of her husband, her son committing murder—all have corroded her faith in human decency and love.

"GET OUT." Tears drip down her nose and into the toilet.

"I'm not going anywhere, you stupid bitch." Roger kicks the door with his foot. He huffs spit onto the door, returns to the breakfast table, and raises the Gazette in front of his face.

◆

Gaillynn is satisfied that her plan is now complete. Her message to Cooper was the final piece to this puzzle. She rests the cell phone on the settee next to the clock, rubs her eyes, then hugs her waist. The stone reaches for her. She steps closer to the clock and absorbs the stone's love. Gold swirls within the blue gem.

Neuro-stimulants filter through the air from the glowing ore to Gaillynn's body. Warmth and an all-powerful sensation delight her insides. She never once considers that she may have done something terrible or vile. She knows it was necessary and executed this task with absolute control.

Gaillynn traces the carvings of magnificent roses whittled by her ancestor, Glinda, who constructed the clock more than two hundred years before. An energized sensation funnels through her limbs. She looks to her palms and basks in the feeling—the strength of all Amirah women channels through her. She has ensured their survival; Ella will be safe, and Cooper will never steal the stone.

Gaillynn wraps her arms around the clock and hugs its entire immense shape. She runs her hands down the back of the wood frame, caressing it with love. Her fingers bounce over a raised panel on the left side. It moves—Gaillynn has never noticed this before.

She dashes upstairs to retrieve the headlamp she wore the night before and situates it on her forehead. She jumps down the stairs and clicks it on to investigate. Gaillynn squeezes between the wall and the clock focusing the light from her forehead on the secret compartment. With the tips of her fingers, she presses the raised panel—it pops open.

Gaillynn traces the inside of the dark crypt with her fingertips and finds a book bound and tied closed with aged leather. She caresses the leather cover and raises it to her nose. She sucks in the musty aroma of dust and age.

"A diary?" Gaillynn flips through hundreds of pages filled with faded, beautiful penmanship on worn pages. Dates as far back as 1738 begin each entry, and to Gaillynn's surprise, the last entry, dated 2009, is in her mother's handwriting. She walks to the kitchen while fanning through pages. She is eager to read this discovery, so instead of waiting for the coffee to percolate, she retrieves hot water and a teabag and returns to her bedroom.

Gaillynn climbs into her luxurious sleigh bed with the steaming cup of tea; she opens to page one of the ancestral diary that she discovered in the clock. She eyes the safe and acknowledges Cooper's presence. She begins to read.

◆

Amirah Family Journal—Time Keeper
May 1738

I am grateful for my captain and his crew. They have assisted with bravery in transporting my husband, myself, and our possessions to the shore of this new land. Our journey has been long and trying. The manic moods of the sea ravaged us with equal doses of serenity and terror. There were moments of such calmness I worried we would be lost adrift, headed nowhere, and other times I was convinced the ocean was trying to toss us out of itself.

We lost three horses from dehydration, and we almost had to eat the last of our swine to survive ourselves. Some good fortune—the fishing proved plentiful. The harsh truth of this quest for new land and a new beginning was ugly, shocking and has undoubtedly made me question my motives. But now, as I write, and as I gaze through heavy rain, upon the most beautiful land I have ever seen, I remember why we embarked on this long journey—my mother.

The months of sailing with heavy cargo made my husband worry. He wanted to lighten our load to speed up our journey, but he would part with nothing, nothing except my clock. He suggested that we push the clock overboard into the deep ocean. He tried many times, and I restrained him. I sense anger growing in him, bitter hate for the clock and the stone. All of our fortune and all of our belongings are precious to him, but not the clock. Like a jealous lover, he scowls and spits at it whenever he is near. My husband has changed.

I found him sweet initially; I thought maybe he could be a man I would learn to love. His lean figure, no taller than I, thinning hair, and pale complexion, all that I did my best to find attractive and somehow endearing, has now become sickening to me. I force the contents of my stomach down with every encounter, every kiss, and I cannot breathe when he talks.

He has pressured me for sex, and I cannot bear it. I resist him—I excuse my refusals with lack of hygiene, stating that I must bathe in fresh water first. His desire for sex is foul. His requests are not loving nor decently affectionate; he is brutal and gruesome. But, alas, the stone's most valuable contribution to my physical being is strength— surprising at first but exhilarating, to say the least, as I fear not for my physical safety.

I am stronger than him; I refuse his advances with ease and confidence. I struggle to feel thankful that he has assisted in getting me here, in one piece and alive. I could have done it without him, but my mother wouldn't allow it.

◆

Gaillynn pulls her eyes from the diary and giggles with delight. She hugs the book to her chest, then dips her tea bag up and down in the steaming liquid. She takes a large gulp, slips under the covers, and adds another pillow to the mound behind her head. She continues reading.

◆

I refused to take his surname, as I believe it is befitting of the woman to carry on the family name, and he refused to take mine for the sake of his ego. Wives and mothers not only live longer than their husbands, but a mother allows conception and fosters the growth of a child in her womb.

A mother nurtures her children, her grandchildren, and her husband to evolve into their best selves. She is the matriarch, the queen, and her name should be the surname.

I regret there is an unintelligent persuasion of culture that frowns on women conducting themselves comparably to men and a woman's birthright name to follow. And as all are children of the same Earth, it should be an analogous acceptance of behavior and desire.

My brief departure from my journaling of our voyage is a mere expression of my frustration in our societal normalities; few dare resist. I shall wander my pen back to our current state of affairs.

Our money will serve us well as we build a new life away from my mother's cursed past. She will surely die, maybe already has, without the stone. And as I write the stories I promised to tell in this blank book, I wonder if my version would suit her? Would she favor how I choose to create this new life?

I am dissatisfied that she would not accompany us. She was fully aware that she would become ill and die without the stone to sustain her; regardless, at only fifty-four, my mother was ready for the end of our family curse. She found Henry, convinced his family to betroth him to me, rather than me to him, and commanded me to begin a new life—one without a curse. And as it was her wish, I will do my best; however, I fear there is no escaping our curse.

This day, we are in the final trek of our pilgrimage; we sail along the coast. The rain beats loudly upon the ship and what I behold, mere moments away from feeling under my feet, is brand new and breathtaking.

This land has weathered the sea and won. It pushes back against the angry waves and is more determined to survive than any other land I have seen. There are trees so tall at the edge of its mountainous earth that I imagine they are the posts to a gateway created by God. An *immense illustration of his power and the enduring test of our very own obstinacy. Are we worthy to enter?*

Perhaps God is this land. And the beauty is evidence of a higher power. An almighty being that has given us life and allows us to continue to spoil its sacred skins. The edge of the earth is aggressive and jagged; the crisp, cold ocean is clean and filled with life—home—our faithful God.

Finally, our foreman greeted us in a small rowboat. He was indifferent to the soaking rain and agitated waves attempting to deter him from us. He tied his craft to the ladder and climbed onto our vessel. His body was large and soaked with rain. His hand swallowed my husband's, and they proceeded to discuss business and plans. They bent over boxes full of our possessions, and he pointed out ideas on the blueprints he brought on board.

I smile at my husband's error of assuming the supervisor's role in constructing our future home. My ship captain's eyes shifted uncomfortably from my husband to me as I watched in amusement. All building decisions are mine, and the payment for his labor and building supplies would be addressed by me and me alone.

Instead of making a scene and demanding leadership over the project, I chose to prove my authority with implicit endorsements and allowed the men to converse. I rather enjoyed watching this large man.

The moment he boarded our ship, our eyes met, and right away, my cheeks reddened, and my body temperature rose. His presence pleased me. These feelings for our foreman are curious and delightful.

He is quite possibly the most beautiful man I have ever seen, the exact opposite of the bastard who was betrothed to me just one year ago. He is over six feet tall with broad, round shoulders and thick legs. His skin, browned and weathered from the sun, begs for my touch, and his wavy dark hair was a complete watery mess. His hands are rough and large, and his smile: genuine and shy. I did not care if he could see my heart pounding out of my chest or that he noticed how long I stared.

His name is Jacob Mallett. After he exited and while we sought our final port, I sat in front of my vanity mirror, cramped inside the tiny bedroom of the ship, yearning to see him again.

Seven months of bathing in the ocean and the lack of proper clothes-washing has been difficult. My fair skin has become golden and freckled; tresses of tangled curls fall uncontrolled to my lower back. My attempts to unweave them are unsuccessful, and I cannot feel the bristles of my hairbrush near my scalp, regardless of how hard I press. These past seven months have been strangling for my hygiene and sanity.

◆

Gaillynn realizes she has not showered, brushed her teeth, nor checked on Dondy. Suffocating a man in her bedroom's safe has been strangling for her hygiene. She leans forward to check her reflection in the large mirror over her dresser. Her thick hair is curly, and the makeup from the night before darkens underneath her eyes. She licks her pointer fingers and attempts to rub the war paint away. She gives up and sits back to continue reading.

◆

June 3, 1738

I am confident my husband is changed. The clearing of our land and the forthcoming construction of our new home has made him agitated. We have sufficient funds, at least eleven chests full of money and gold, but he wants to sell the clock. He has lied to me about how much we have spent, and he says we are now broke. I know the truth. He is bitter, dishonest, and angry. I fear he cannot tolerate the intensity of the stone.

For an insecure man like Henry, the stone will reveal all of his weaknesses. I have seen this power of the stone—it can tell the truth about a person. Its presence among the last three generations of women in our family, including me, has allowed us to survive and thrive; however, many men have proved their stamina and shortcomings.

Again, I digress—women force themselves into complacency. We tend to nurture the evil in men unknowingly. We see insecurities in them, and we submit ourselves to build up their fragile egos. We want to take care of our spouses, our lovers, our families, mother them; therefore, we give men what they need to feel worthy. We have perfidiously drowned ourselves to be less than them, even though it eats at our souls and screams inside of our ears that it is not correct.

Women are giving in to men because we know they cannot bear their truths. They want to dominate us, control us, and own us simply because they are afraid. Why has our mothering taken on such an enabling of bad behavior? These errors must come to an end for all of us.

The stone tells me that there are men who provoke war, men who cause and allow famine, and some who refuse to nurture the strengths of others; instead, men reject and condemn others to mask their weaknesses. But not all men—not fearless, loving, and secure men. I, like the stone, have grown tired of fearful men. Women will reign as queens, and the constructive nature of women's fury will save our Earth and her people.

The stone warns me that women have allowed our world to become threatened by weak men with power-hungry egos and that chaos will continue until there is balance—until there is intolerance of men who cause pain. We will be vital in our physical and soulful being, and the stone will require an equilibrium among us until it is time for us to reign as queens.

My husband behaves like a child having a tantrum. I will not tol-

erate his risking my loss of the stone, and I will put an end to this if I must. I have no fear.

However, I, too, am changed. I am alone with the stone. All of its power is focused on me and me alone. Our connection linked our minds. The three of us shared the stone's potency—mother, grandmother, and myself. I have also changed with beginning anew but not alone—it is me and the jewel in the clock.

It is odd that an artifact, a literal piece of earth, has such a connection to me. I don't understand; however, I accept this with questions but no desire to seek answers. Do we question love, our nature, or our instincts? No. The stone is love; it is part of my nature to the core of who I am. It simply is.

◆

Gaillynn folds the diary closed and reaches for her cell phone. She types "Jacob Mallett" into the search bar. A page from Wikipedia comes up first. "Passamaquoddy Tribe native Jacob Mallett and brothers Thomas and Harold migrated along the coast of Maine and settled in what is now known as Stonington. The aftermath of the Seven Years' War drove them there, where they settled and became master carpenters, building the likes of homes still copied today."

Gaillynn rests her phone on the bed beside her and returns her eyes to the diary.

◆

This morning I sent my husband hiking the coast to the next town searching for a runaway horse. While he was gone, I visited the workers clearing our land, and I encountered Jacob Mallett.

"Hello, Mrs. Amirah," said Jacob. "Are we causing too much noise this morning?"

"No. No, not at all. I love the smell of the cut trees," I responded.

"Mr. Mallett, have you had your breakfast?"

"Please, call me Jacob. Yes, Mrs. Amirah, I have."

"Would you at least like some coffee? I am brewing a fresh pot in the cabin; it should be about ready. And please, you can call me Gwendolyn."

"Gwendolyn. Yes. Of course. I would love a fresh cup of your coffee." We strolled back to the cabin. "I understand your husband has a buyer for your clock. He has asked me to move it upon the buyer's arrival. Do you know when that might be, Mrs. Amirah—uh, Gwendolyn?"

I paused just as we were about to enter the cabin. "Henry has sold my clock? My grandmother made that clock, and Henry cannot sell it."

"My mistake, ma'am, I'm sorry. I must have misunderstood."

I put my hand on Jacob's forearm and pulled him into the cabin. I pulled him so close that I could smell the outdoors on him and his intoxicating breath as his face bent toward mine. "Please, Jacob, don't help my husband sell my clock."

"Yes, Gwendolyn," he whispered. Jacob poured his eyes into mine; I lowered my eyes to his chest, and I studied its roundness along with his bulging body under his shirt. I fingered the button near his neck. He moved his eyes to my chest, which heaved with desire. He began breathing so heavily I thought it was panting. "Mrs. Amirah," he whispered.

"Yes?" I could see a pulsating glow of gold behind him. Like a compass, the pendulum swung far to the right, and it beamed. The stone shared my happiness, and the stone's joy affected Jacob as well. In an attempt to ignore the thought of the reciprocal swing left and what kind of heartache I would feel, I closed my eyes. No, not Jacob.

"What is happening?" Jacob asked. "I feel I have lost restraint of my good mind and may be about to lose control of myself." Jacob's face revealed fear of what he was feeling for me.

Outside, the wind picked up. The leaves sang a unified song of glory *in the canopy above. "Timber," rang through the air. A large tree fell near the cabin. The sudden crash and danger of its closeness to the house broke our connection. He took a deep breath and turned to leave.*

"Wait," I said. I wanted to repay Jacob for his honesty, repay him with my touch, my body. He could see it in my eyes. He caressed my cheek with his muscular hand. I pressed my mouth to his palm and kissed it. I covered his hand with mine and guided it down my chin, to my neck, and my chest. I pushed his fingers under the edge of my dress and forced his hand to expose my breast. I inhaled a sharp breath of desire. He wrapped his other arm around my waist, lifted me off of the ground, and pulled me against his sturdy and robust waist. I felt his desire hardened against me, and I ached to pull him inside of me.

He mouthed my nipple until a man called to him from outside. He released me. He pulled my dress back up over my breast and kissed my quivering lips. He turned and left.

◆

Gaillynn's body jerks at a sudden call from the other side of Locket Manor. A deep, thundering vibration from the Kendal wing's library has disrupted her reading. She lifts her eyes and peers out of the window to make sure it's not a storm—the first thing she does every time she hears this noise. As usual, there is no storm. Instead, the sun's journey to the center of the sky is still underway. Orange and pink mix with bright blue above the ocean with no rain clouds in sight. Again the noise from Kendal's wing calls to her.

"Hmph," she mutters. She resists going to the moan from her home—it's a quest for her embrace. And yet, its haunting familiarity is what scares her the most. Fear in recognition. Recognition of a feeling so embedded in her core that it is frightening—uncontrolled fury.

Gaillynn closes her eyes for a moment. She is dissatisfied her reading has been interrupted. This moment between Gwendolyn and Jacob reached a part of her that she has kept hidden for fourteen years. She relaxes her shoulders and lets go of her irritation. Gaillynn returns her eyes to the diary.

$$\spadesuit$$

Chapter Twelve

Saturday Morning at Eden's Garden

A musical harp alarm lights up Ella's cell phone at precisely 4:22 am. She taps off the notice and creeps into the bathroom to pee and brush her teeth before she tiptoes down the noisy wooden stairs. She can hear Jack snoring from the couch in the living room. An empty wine bottle and his dentures rest on the table next to him. His top lip flutters with each gurgling exhale. Ella smiles.

Quietness fills the early morning air until she reaches the kitchen, where a radio blasts a local station playing oldies. Marguerite faces an open window, and she doesn't hear Ella enter. Marguerite smokes a cigarette and sways her hips to the song that she sings with the radio. Ella steps up next to her. "Good morning, Auntie Marguerite."

Marguerite directs the smoke from her lungs out of the open window and away from Ella. She waves at the clouds in the air with her hand. Marguerite squishes her cigarette into a coffee-can ashtray then hugs Ella.

"Good morning, my little sweetheart," says Marguerite in a scratchy voice. "Last night was so fun, Ella. This place hasn't danced all night like that in years. Jack was so exhausted I couldn't even get him to bed. I hope his awful snoring didn't keep you awake, dear."

"Oh, no, not at all. I slept great." Ella pulls her hair back from her face and ties it into a ponytail. "I had fun too."

"Let's start the bacon. That'll wake everyone up," Marguerite says. She turns the dial on the iron stove, and the grill begins snapping and popping. The two women line the stovetop with strips of uncooked bacon. Before long, the bacon begins to sizzle and dance over the heat.

While the bacon browns, Ella washes her hands. "Do you want me to cut the fresh fruit for the fruit cups?"

"Be my guest, sweetie; that's the hardest job. We also have extra blueberries we didn't use in the pies in the walk-in fridge. Let's eat those up today too."

Ella retrieves the blueberries and sets them aside. She begins cutting the first of three round watermelons with a large knife, followed by strawberries, oranges, and pineapples. She fills dozens of glass bowls with various fruit and tops each with a fistful of the picked blueberries while tossing an occasional sample into her mouth.

"Ella, when you finish with the fruit, can you put the pans of peach cobbler French toast into the ovens? The stoves should be pre-heated by then. I'll start all four of the large coffee pots," says Marguerite.

"You got it," says Ella.

The inn's waitstaff arrives. Ella finishes the fruit, places the French toast into the ovens, then dashes up to room number three to retrieve her grandmother. "Grammy?" Gia is already gone.

Ella searches the living room for her grandmother. Jack is also missing from the couch, along with his teeth and the empty wine bottle. He now circles the dining room, tidying it up for breakfast.

The long dining room table is, once again, set for twelve people. Jack smiles a toothy smile at Ella. "Good morning, Queen Ella." He hugs her and lifts her a few inches off the floor.

Ella squeezes back. "Jack, you need a shower." She doesn't want to let go. "Have you seen my grammy?"

"Yes, dear," Jack says. "She's in the garden."

"Of course."

Ella pushes open the squeaky back door to the garden that overlooks the quiet bay. "Hi Grammy Gia," she calls. Ella tiptoes through the lawn. Pieces of green grass tickle her feet. She wiggles her toes and wraps her arm around her grandmother.

"Good morning, Ella. How did you sleep? I didn't even hear you get up."

"Good." Ella rests her head on her grandmother's shoulder. "Last night, that song. Is that the song you hear in your dream, Grammy?"

"Yes. That's the song you have heard that song since you were a baby?"

"Yes, and not only in my dreams. I hear that song all the time. I think I always have. I hum it all the time. I guess I never realized it."

"It's coming from the stone, isn't it?" Gia kisses the top of Ella's head.

"It's coming from women, and it feels like the stone is their messenger," says Ella.

"Yes. I see what you mean."

A squeak from the back door causes them to turn. "Breakfast is ready, ladies," calls Marguerite.

"Coming," replies Ella. "Grammy, would you like to walk the beach later today?"

"I would love that, Ella."

"Let's go eat, Grammy. I can't wait to try that French toast."

"Me too, honey." They dash inside and join the inn's other guests for an abundant family-style breakfast. The special peach-cobbler breakfast dish is an unanimous hit, and Jack piles four servings onto his plate.

◆

After breakfast, Gia and Ella walk to the beach. They travel barefoot on the cold sand inside the quiet bay. The ocean wraps their feet with tiny welcoming hugs of water that gently caress their toes and ankles. Ella picks up a dirty plastic bag that she found in the sand and fills the bag with other pieces of litter as she spots them. She spots a plastic bottle cap. She examines it closely. "It looks brand new, but you know this could've been in the ocean for years, and it would still look the same." She huffs and puts it in the bag.

"I know, honey. I'm sorry," says Gia.

Gia shuffles along in the sand to a thick piece of driftwood that landed on the beach years ago; she sits down to face the sea's horizon. Ella joins her. They lean their heads against each other and wrap their fingers together to hold hands. The women hum the song from their dreams and close their eyes.

Gia and Ella are unaware of the sand dancing around their feet that has become aroused. A swirl appears in the ocean in front of them, and a small whirlpool forms. Earth is embracing them and is joyous at their presence.

Gia and Ella continue their song; the repeating melody engulfs their bodies with warmth, love, and emotional strength. Their minds travel, together, to a land filled with vibrant and lush gardens and earth the color of their stone. Within their minds, they have the sensation that their bodies become wrapped with the vitality of this golden-blue land, and they're one with it.

Ella squeezes her grandmother's hand. Their eyes remain closed, and they continue on this path of discovery between them. Voices join in with their humming. A mass of women's voices chant along and harmonize a message they cannot decipher; a vision forms in their minds: thousands upon thousands of women appear with their arms entwined at their elbows while each palm an identical stone to theirs in a belt wrapped around each of their waists.

In this shared vision, the women have the skin of gold that reflects a blue iridescence—like the stone, and require little clothing due to the atmosphere's heat. The increased temperature surrounds Ella and Gia's physical beings, turning their skin red and moist with sweat.

The women within their minds sing their song and sway back and forth. They are united. Their queen arises into view, and she stands at a golden-mirrored podium. The queen wears a crown whose golden color swirls with life. Two stones are levitating in front of her. One of the floating stones is identical as the one inside Locket Manor, now confined in a beautiful clock. *Could this be our stone?* Ella wonders.

The queen's long, brown curly hair blows in the wind produced by the stones before her. A moon reflects brightly behind her against varying shades of blue. She mouths words, but Gia and Ella cannot hear her. This queen appears to be praying to the stones while another woman holds her hand. They embrace for a kiss.

Gia and Ella pass out. They fall backward and off the wooden log onto the soft, white sand behind them. Exhaustion has overcome their minds and bodies, and they remain on the quiet beach, asleep for hours.

The ocean's horizon engulfs the sun, and darkness fills the sky. The inn's squeaky back door opens.

"Queen Ella? Gia?" calls Jack. "Ella," he yells.

Ella wakes with a jerk. "Where am I?" A half-moon reflects off the smooth water. Gently gushing waves on the sand in front of her remind her where she is. Ella shakes her grandmother, who wakes with the same confusion.

Gia blinks. She rubs her hands together to rid them of sand then hugs Ella. "My God, Ella."

"Gia? Ella? Are you two okay?" Jack stumbles across the sand to them. He extends his long arms toward them and lifts them to their feet.

"Ella and I must have fallen asleep. I'm sorry, Jack. We didn't mean to scare you."

"Marguerite wasn't worried at all; she said you both were fine, and I didn't need to worry, but my Jesus girls, you have been gone for hours." His words run together and his breath smells of wine and garlic. "Are you hungry? You missed lunch. We have baked scallops and fiddleheads for dinner."

"I'm starving," says Ella, and they trudge through the soft sand toward the back door of the inn.

"No shoes, ladies?" asks Jack. "Of course," he says, answering himself.

◆

Marguerite pours Gia a half glass of red wine. "Thank you," says Gia. She swallows the entire contents of the cup and holds it up to Marguerite for a refill.

"Grammy!" Ella says. "You never drink wine."

"I need it, honey." Gia takes a large gulp from her refilled glass. She recalls the vision she shared with Ella on the beach with confusion. The face of the queen appears in her mind—her resemblance to Ella is alarming. Marguerite stands close by just in case Gia needs more. Gia holds up her hand. "I'm good, thank you."

Jack fills Ella's plate with large, seared scallops and dark-green sautéed fiddleheads. The young ferns' spiral shape always brings Ella joy, and she finds their earthy, rich flavor delicious.

"Is there any vinegar on the table?" Jack passes the small glass vinegar carafe to Ella. "Thank you." She drips some onto the fiddleheads, then takes one into her mouth. "Mmmmm."

The two women eat everything on their plates then ask for more. Ella yawns and all of a sudden, neither of them can keep their eyes open. The exhaustion of the quest their minds journeyed earlier at the beach has returned.

"I think I need to go to bed," says Gia. She finishes the last few swallows of the red wine in her glass.

"Me too, Grammy."

"Awww, no dancing and singing tonight?" asks one of the other guests as he lifts his brown beer bottle to the air.

"Sorry guys, we are exhausted," says Gia.

Marguerite stands to give Ella a long goodnight hug. "I'll do breakfast myself tomorrow; you sleep in, dear."

"Okay, Auntie Marguerite. I love you."

"And I love you, Ella."

Jack approaches and hugs Ella next. She breathes in his clean, now showered odor and the comforting smell of his aftershave and deodorant. Ella wraps herself into his round belly and closes her eyes. "You're the only man I have to hug, Jack. Hug me a little longer?"

"Of course."

Once Ella has her fill of Jack's loving embrace, Gia and Ella climb the creaking stairs to their room number three, and without changing into pajamas or brushing their teeth, they pass out on top of their covers.

CHAPTER THIRTEEN

The night Gaillynn gave her virginity to Robbie was the last time she felt a comparable passion to Gwendolyn's seductive encounter with Jacob. She and Robbie couldn't get enough of each other—just like Gwendolyn and Jacob. Gaillynn misses Robbie's piney wood scent and the way she felt when she was near him. Her eyes tear, and she sniffles. Gaillynn rubs her face and examines the safe, then continues to read.

◆

June 12, 1738

Upon the return of my husband from his trek to find the lost horse, I am suffering. I cannot control my desire for Jacob, and Henry is in my way. I must do something and soon. I cannot bear to live another moment with Henry in this cabin.

The stone is also restless. Its energy is euphoric that I sense I am powerful and this path that has led me to Jacob has a more significant meaning than I will ever understand. Henry must go. I cannot expect anyone else to make that happen; no one except me. Like my mother, I will persevere and protect the stone and myself at all costs. I will wait for the next thick fog when the men don't work due to poor visibility. That is the day Henry will cease to be a threat.

◆

Gaillynn lifts her head and raises her eyes to the safe—she imagines she is looking directly at Cooper's distorted face through the plastic. "I suspect I know exactly where this story is going, and it makes me feel part of something bigger than I have ever considered before," she says to him.

She rests her head back and lifts her eyes to the chandelier. Tiny fractions of light bounce between the amber and clear crystals like mirrors. "For the first time, I see our curse with a new perspective. Protecting my family and the stone is a charge I now understand. It is my heroic purpose. My mother's purpose is the ability to heal and see our destiny. Ella's brilliant mind will figure this all out— she is the seeker of answers. Why have I desired to be more normal like my friends? I am a comrade with Gwendolyn." Gaillynn winks at Cooper inside the safe. She returns to the diary.

◆

June 14, 1738

I stepped out on the porch yesterday and saw that the fog had blanketed the earth and saturated Earth's skin with dew. The men would not be working. I stepped back inside our temporary cabin and faced Henry. The stone and I decided that today was the day. Today would be Henry's last.

I took the cup of coffee from his hand and set it on the table. I touched his lips with my finger, and I moved my hand down to his shirt and began unbuttoning it. He smiled.

"*Finally,*" he said. "Not once this entire trip, and look at what I've done for you, Gwendolyn." I didn't respond.

I undressed my husband and then myself. I faced him and moved to him. He plunged his hand between my legs with force. Out of pure instinct, I grabbed his neck with my right hand.

"Ah, you like that, Gwendolyn, don't you?"

I wanted to strangle him. And I could have, but I had a plan. Instead, I released my grasp of his neck and removed his hand from between my legs. I weaved his fingers in mine and led him outside.

He complied. We walked away from the cabin toward the planned location of our future master bedroom—for now, it is still dirt. The air was so thick with fog that I couldn't see beyond the tips of my fingers intertwined with his. His eyes pierced my skin as he stared wantonly at my breasts that jiggled and swayed as I walked.

I guided him through the many mounds of debarked hardwood trees intended for the lumber to build our home. The smell of fresh-cut wood and pine invigorated my heightened senses.

The fog's wetness drenched my bare skin like an intoxicating potion readying me. Both of our naked bodies became blanketed in Mother Nature's ghosts and our toes sunk into her cold dirt. Our journey ended at a specific pile of logs taller than both of us.

"Henry, my love, lie down here. This spot will someday be our bedroom. Think of the things we will do here."

He lay down as I had asked. "Yes," he said.

The moisture in the air soaked our skin. It cloaked us in a salty embrace, and I sensed that nature was on my side. I stood over him and straddled his face. I planted one foot on each side of his head. His eyes, desperate and wanting, sought to defile my femininity. He longed to satisfy his urge to overpower me, subdue me, and this was his weakness. As my womanliness was not obedience, this day, it was my weapon.

He reached for his hardening manliness and moaned with delight and studied the prize between my legs. The thought of entering me excited him, but not for love's sake, for his own masculinity's sake.

I leaned forward, steadying myself against the pile of large cut trees. I lifted my knee. Henry groaned. I stomped as hard as I could on his neck with my foot. With all of my physical power and the entire weight of my body, my heel dug into his throat. The ground below his spine hugged my heal. His arms and legs flailed at the impact; he clutched at his crushed throat.

I forced multiple trees off the mound of logs to smash onto his face and torso; I trapped him. He was too small, skinny, weak, and injured to free himself. I stood over his body and waited until he became still.

My naked body absorbed the fog's moisture. It aroused my skin and stimulated my desire for Jacob. I stood there, over him—the victor, and pressed my hips forward. Beads of water soaked through the hair between my legs, and the cool wetness lapped at my skin. My chest heaved as I made love with the air and my hands while the ocean pounded the cliffs around me. Though hidden in the fog, the crashing waves applauded my climax and Henry's death.

I retrieved his clothes from the cabin and forced them onto his trapped body before the fog lifted. I left him there to be discovered later, hopefully by one of the workers. I returned to the cabin, bathed, and dressed.

Later that day, the sun burned through the fog. Before long, loggers, the sound of falling trees, and the smell of fresh-cut wood filled the property.

Jacob arrived at my cabin. His eyes turned down, and his chin dropped to his chest. He asked me to sit down, so I did. He knelt before me. His expression pleased me; his blindness of the truth aroused me. He took my hands into his and explained, "I have terrible news, dear Gwendolyn. Henry has been crushed by fallen logs. He is dead."

I forced a tear and welcomed a long embrace from Jacob. I breathed in his smell and squeezed his waist. My hands explored the roundness *of his back and the curvature of his spine just above his buttocks. He did not pull away. I leaned my body close to him and pressed my hips against his. I pressed my face toward him, and he let me kiss him. He wrapped his forearm under my legs, and he carried me to my bed. He let the weight of his body press against mine, and he ripped the corset from my waist. His hand reached behind me, and he slipped his fingers between my legs.*

◆

Gaillynn lifts her eyes from the diary, and a smile spreads across her face. "Oh my," she says. She places the book face down on her chest and takes a deep breath. "Whoa."

She moves the book to her bedside table and stretches her arms up to the ceiling. She looks at her watch: 9:05 am Saturday. Another thirty-six hours until my mother and Ella would be home, she thought. Feeling hungry, she climbs out of bed and heads to the kitchen.

"Here kitty, kitty, kitty, kitty," she calls to Dondy. Gaillynn shakes some dry cat food into the kitten's dish and replaces the water in the white bowl with fresh water from the faucet. "Here, kitty, kitty, kitty. Here, Dondy. You hungry?" Gaillynn searches for the cat in the halls of her mother's wing of the house. She peers into her mother's tidy bedroom—no Dondy.

Gaillynn climbs the stairs to the third floor and heads to the library. The purring cat greets her with its tail pointing to the ceiling; Dondy rubs face and body along his favorite bookshelf while strutting back and forth.

"Right where Mom said you would be."

Dondy's fluffy gray and white hair gives him the appearance of a tiny gray lion, and his handsome white whiskers are long and beautiful. Gaillynn reaches for the young cat and picks him up.

Claw marks in the wood of the bottom bookshelf catch her eye. "Dondy, you shit," she whispers while wrapping him in a hug to her chest. She carries him out of the room and attempts to close the door behind them.

The door resists—something pulls against Gaillynn. Gaillynn tightens her grip. A blast of air tears at the heavy wood attached to the crystal doorknob in her hand. Thunder rumbles inside the library, startling Dondy. His claws react and sting Gaillynn's chest. *Not again. What do you want from me?* she thinks.

"What the hell? I hate this library." Gaillynn lets go of the doorknob. The door swings open, and the sound of rushing air silences. She scans the now quiet library. "Just the wind or a loose window frame? I hope so, buddy. This room gives me the creeps."

But something about it reminds me of myself. Gaillynn cuddles the kitty, closes the door to the library without trouble this time, returns to the kitchen, and places him in front of his food.

Gaillynn presses the power button on the coffee and espresso machine. She examines the world outside the window while she listens to the gurgling percolator. The wind blows colored leaves from the trees over white patches of snow deposited from the stormy encounter when Cooper surprised Gaillynn with his first visit. Otherwise, the outside world appears quiet and normal. "Normal," she says. "As normal as sleeping with a corpse the rest of my life." She rubs her hand along Dondy's back.

"Cooper will remain hidden in my bedroom, forever."

Gaillynn slices a cinnamon-raisin bagel and drops it into a large silver toaster. She checks her cell phone for messages from Ella.

There are a few unread text messages. Gaillynn opens them to find a selfie of Ella and Marguerite wearing kitchen aprons and blowing kisses to the camera, followed by a picture of the dining room table at Eden's Garden covered with seafood.

Gaillynn closes the texts and opens the friend-finder app on her wristwatch to confirm Ella is still far away from Locket Manor. Ella's smiling face appears on her arm with a chime, and below it: Eden's Garden, Mount Desert, 97 miles away.

The golden-brown bagel pops up in the toaster. The smell of cinnamon and fresh coffee causes Gaillynn's mouth to water; she blankets the hot bagel with a thick layer of cream cheese, pours herself a cup of black coffee and exits the kitchen to return to her bedroom.

On her way, she veers off into the living room for a quick visit with the stone. Gaillynn sips her coffee and focuses on the beacon of love. She lingers in this moment of shared satisfaction that Cooper is dead. She smiles and winks at the stone.

"Here, kitty, kitty." Dondy obeys, gallops behind Gaiilynn up the winding stairs that balcony over the entry room, through the hall, and into her bedroom. Gaillynn places her breakfast on a metal tray on her bed. She slides her legs under the blankets. Dondy cuddles in around Gaillynn's knees and purrs himself to sleep.

Gaillynn is pleased to have such a fantastic read to occupy her while she waits out the death of Cooper for the weekend. Although she assumes he is already dead, she wants to be sure.

She crunches into the warm bagel and begins to read.

◆

June 24, 1738

Jacob buried Henry today. I watched him dig the grave; we were silent. His body moved with such power, and he was focused and intent on his task. I craved him, my mouth watered for his lips, and I remembered how we had become one the night before. Simply laying my eyes on him gives me such pleasure. My body becomes overwhelmed with desire, and I struggle to control myself from touching him and taking him back to my bed. We must bury Henry; I will maintain my passions at least until then.

Finally, with the insertion of Henry into the ground and the heavy earth on top of him, I am relieved.

Jacob carried me to the cabin, and I kissed his dirt and sweat-covered face. I inhaled his hot scent, and I caressed the sweat that made his skin soft and slippery under his shirt. He laid me down and undressed me. Our eyes spoke a secret language of lust to each other; we were sick with passion. I couldn't talk; I held my breath. I needed to feel him, melt into him, become part of him. And I could see he needed to be inside me, to become one with me. The brightness of the day revealed it all, and we submitted to the hunger and the love between us.

I ordered a gravestone for Henry from a local mason. Jacob has agreed to assist with the delivery upon its completion.

◆

September 29, 1738

I am detecting an intense semblance of satisfaction from the stone. It is more lucent than I have ever seen—it sways weightlessly though wrapped in heavy chains and affixed to a long iron pendulum. The stone is content for the time being, but I fear there is still something I'm missing. It calls to me during the day, humming happiness in my ears and sadness at night.

My dreams are vivid and much more frequent. And there is one that recurs—the stone reminds me that Jacob will die; however, I do not see the cause of his death. I am standing in the center of a small graveyard. There is a large linked and rusted chain draped between thick granite posts fencing the graves within. Vines of green ivy cloak the graves, masking their words. I see a grave with Jacob's name. It is surrounded by dozens more with names too blurry for me to read.

Jacob. My love.

If the legend of the stone is true, then he will die a terrible death. The idea of it horrifies me—I cannot imagine myself without him. Our bodies cannot get close enough, and the coldness I will feel when he is lost frightens me. I crave him; I ache for him; my soul cries for him.

It is unusual that he has been in the presence of the stone for so long and has remained unchanged. He is still the trusted man that the stone guided me here to find—the man whose destiny is to help me begin our new life, the life of an Amirah woman, life without a curse.

The stone becomes vibrant blue in his presence. Jacob says that he can feel a sensation of love in the stone's presence, like purpose and destiny. He does not understand. He tries to convince me that the clock is alive. I disregard his comments to keep the secret. Maybe this life will be different, and perhaps he will not succumb to the need of the stone to equilibrate all good with evil. Perhaps Henry was enough. I pray.

◆

Gaillynn licks remnants of the cream cheese from her fingers and gulps the last of her black coffee. She scratches Dondy's forehead; he stretches out his body and kneads his claws into the bedspread. She pulls the book back up to her chest and continues.

◆

October 8, 1738

Our baby girl grows inside me, and with her life, the stone has become more energized. Its swing is heavier, more deliberate, and extreme.

I feel as if there is a reason for this, a purpose. Something that

I know, something that I understand but cannot explain. Perhaps a plan? Or another piece of our cursed puzzle?

Amirah Manor is beginning to look like a giant wooden skeleton. We have a well now. Our vegetable garden has been extremely fruitful and continues to be even this late into the fall. We are producing so many vegetables that I am sending the workers home with baskets full daily. Also, our livestock is multiplying with frequent pregnancies and multiple offspring. I have hired as many hands as I can to tend to the rich abundance we are so lucky to have.

I hear the workers talking. They refer to me as Mrs. Widow. It sickens me that they think of me as grieving. Widow—it is such a sad and lonely word as if I am helpless and depressed. No, I am not a widow. I am kindred to the spirit and will of the black widow spider. Like the black widow, I dictate my destiny. I ensure mine and our child's survival—a nerve in all of the Amirah women I have known or heard stories of my entire life. When a man, like Henry, becomes an enemy, we will ensure our survival in exchange for his.

However, this undesirable charade I must sustain. It will serve me well. I prefer the workers assume that I am innocent and powerless to the comings of life's unfortunate events rather than a murderer and the keeper of a witch's stone or, God forbid, magic. The mayor would hang me. And I prefer they assume this baby belongs to Henry.

Mine and Jacob's love remains a secret for now.

◆

Dondy leaps off the bed, creating a loud thump on the floor. Gaillynn is startled, and her body jumps. "Fuck." She eyes the safe. Dondy struts across the floor with his tail pointed at the ceiling and out of the room. Gaillynn exhales, "Phew." She fluffs the pillow behind her head and continues.

◆

December 3, 1738

The air has become brisk; I prefer to stay inside except for an occasional barefoot walk in the cold snow while my sweet Jacob leads the workers along in the construction of our home. Progress is slow but perfect. He becomes uneasy with my bare red feet—even though they melt clear through the snow with each step, he worries. So when I wear my boots outside, it is for him.

My dreams continue to be lucid and meaningful. Just this last night, I had the clearest vision of the future of this incomplete dwelling. It was as if I saw our legacy, a vision of what Amirah Manor will become.

In the dream, I am looking at a framed newsprint hanging on a wall. It read: "America's Most Cursed Historic Home, Locket Manor, is an enormous, lavish estate on the southernmost tip of the state's rocky coast in the majestic town of Stonington. Home to generations of Amirah women and their families, the mansion was built in 1738 and named Locket Manor in honor of the hundreds of tragic memories locked inside along with countless grim details of lives lost, borne, and burdened by this family, all protected by its grand architecture. Locket Manor's beautiful esthetic is sadly overshadowed by decades of tragedy.

"Secluded by acres of forest, Locket Manor was designed and erected by the brilliant minds of only the best artisans and craftsmen of its time. A trophy construction of The Mallett Brothers, legendary builders of historic homes, Locket Manor's heavenly view of the ocean competes only with its structural beauty."

September 1, 2021, Edition, is written in the lower-left corner—a date I cannot begin to understand. Am I to believe the curse is not broken and remains centuries beyond this life with Jacob? Is the destiny of the Amirah women already written and doomed for sadness?

And then, in my dream, I remember becoming lightheaded, almost dizzy, as if I was floating—I explored the estate. It appears a perfect image of how I plan it will be.

The exterior is bright white, with hundreds of expansive windows serving as our primary source of light, but I see exquisite, sparkling fixtures hanging from the ceilings within glowing with light and beauty.

Then I am outside again, and I drop my head back to scan upward toward the sky at large white pillars reaching stories high that support the overhanging metal roof.

Then I am far away at an iron gate—a breathtaking ornament intended to protect the home. The entrance has remained open for so long that it had become overgrown with thick vines of Bittersweet.

I float down the lengthy cobblestone driveway and return to the grand estate, which from a distance appears a castle. It stands three stories high with three separate wings; one wing is above a stable, I think, something with six bays with large doors for the horses and carriages. I am looking inside one of the bays, and I see a beautiful beige horse neighing and scraping its hooves on a rigid white surface. Adjacent to the horse is a machine of sorts—a large red, rectangular carriage with wheels and glass.

Again, back inside, and as I soar along, I am counting bedrooms. I can hear myself counting: eleven bedrooms, nine and a half bathrooms, three full kitchens with shining metal hardware.

I explore dumbwaiters in each wing—they traveled through cryptic passages from the stone cellar to the spacious attic.

Oh, and how beautiful it was inside, nothing less than an exquisite representation of Queen Anne-style architecture and extreme wealth. The interior, decorated with liberal Victorian details, is adorned with priceless paintings, mirrors, and iron candelabras. The ceilings appeared to be eighteen feet from the floor and are a decorative tin of artisan gold with a whitewash finish; the oversized sparkling fixtures glowed from their center. Large oriental rugs colored the floors through-out—even the ones I have brought from my mother were there.

In the large entry room, double spiraling staircases, one on each side of the room, with black iron railings and spindles winding skyward to meet the balcony of hallways leading to the second and third-floor bed-rooms. Two libraries, filled with books and history, display hundreds of treasures accumulated by generations of Amirah as if our home were a museum dedicated to our ancestors—dedicated to our secrets.

I'm back outside Locket Manor, which I will now forever call it, and I see imperishable gardens. Deep, red roses bloomed while white snow-flakes fell from a low cloud directly above them—an isolated winter cloud. Tall lupine of every color metastasized into the stone patio and pushed up through the walking stones reached for the hot sun. Bright daisies filled the grounds and swayed in the slightest breeze while white flowering hydrangea, laced with pink, fill in the garden's edges. Cherry trees blossomed sweet-smelling buds, and apple trees bore large fruit. Bees and butterflies busied through the pollen-rich sanctuary.

An enormous wisteria tree climbed the backside of the house and around the East wing. This side of the house faced the ocean—just like I planned, to take advantage of most of the day's sun. The giant wisteria tangled its way around whatever it could. Vines climbed three-quarters of the grand estate and bore thousands of lavender flowers.

Beyond the breathtaking gardens rolled endless acres of sublime green grass, which abruptly ended at the jagged edge of the earth where land meets the ocean—a beautiful but dangerous and sudden drop into the pounding waves. The rain poured down on the grass and sea—an-other localized change in weather.

I sense this was not a dream but a premonition of our future reality.

Just as I planned, we will be surrounded by beauty and separated from distant neighbors—protected by distance and our secrets safe from *discovery, but we will never be safe from the stone. Who will harness its power to serve our happiness rather than simply our strength?*

◆

Gaillynn lifts her head from the diary and scans her bedroom with raised eyebrows. An enlightened awareness of her home's architecture and treasures of past generations replaces previous oblivion; now, she looks at them with a fresh appreciation. Locket Manor is described on these pages of an ancient ancestral diary precisely as it is for her at this very moment—a fortress.

Gaillynn has become tired, and though she is eager to continue, she can't. She lays the open book on her chest and falls asleep.

◆

Chapter Fourteen

Gaillynn wakes hours later. She eyes the window—it is pitch black outside. She retrieves the headlamp on her bedside table, straps it to her head, and clicks it on. Gaillynn arches her head toward the safe and traces the edges with the light on her forehead. She listens for noise and breathes through her nose in search of any stench in the air. The dead Cooper remains silent and odorless. She focuses her headlamp on the pages of the book and finds her place.

◆

February 24, 1739

My belly grows round, and the snow piles deep. I am alone and tending to a flickering fire. I rejoice in this tranquility. Jacob pushes the men on through the bitter cold as we hope to be in Locket Manor by late spring, but likely not before our baby is born.

I promised my mother I would write our story—hers, her mother's, and mine. History, so engraved in me that I must carry it on; I must document our lives to ensure future Amirah do not forget our life and lessons. I will start with my grandmother, Glinda, and in the simple words of my mother's bedtime story, I will write about her discovery of the stone and how she built the clock.

◆

Gaillynn extends a hand to the sky like a student raising her hand in a classroom. "Ah-ha! This diary is where Mom learned that story," Gaillynn says out loud. "I have heard this story hundreds of times. Now, Mom even tells Ella. Humph. I don't need to read it right now; I want to know about Jacob." She has an idea. "His grave must be in our graveyard."

Gaillynn sets the diary aside and goes to the window overlooking the backyard, ocean, and the family graveyard. I could have put Cooper there. "Hell, no," she reminds herself. "Our family graveyard is far too precious for the corpse of Cooper, and likely the first place police would look for a dead body."

Gaillynn had not visited the graveyard since she was a child, so she decides it is time to visit. She tiptoes down the winding stairs and outside. She inhales the smell of the ocean through her nose and strolls through the cold, wet grass toward the cemetery.

With little help from her dimming headlamp, she inspects each grave, looking for Jacob Mallett. The coolness of the mist and dewy ground on her bare feet tickle her skin. She inhales the humid scent of saltwater and visualizes the waves crashing against the coast hidden below in the dense fog.

Though the fog is thick and she cannot see past her feet, Gaillynn knows precisely where the edge of the earth plummets to the sea. Gaillynn visualizes the ocean's appearance by the sound of it. In her mind's eye, she can see the water's powerful and beautiful heavy blows against the rocks. The ocean's strength invigorates her with its persistent attack withdrawing and smashing itself again and again. Gaillynn mimics the water's push and pulls by swaying her hips; in her mind, she can see the clear blue water turn white with every assault to the coast, only to remove all of its defeat back into itself and rage on again.

Jacob's memorial is large and rectangular with worn inscriptions. The letters of his name are difficult to read, but she is confident she's found him. She kneels beside his tomb and caresses the cold stone.

The stone reads, "Here lies my beloved Jacob Mallett. 1717–1763."

"Whoa, he lived long. Well, he lived longer than most of the men," Gaillynn says to the darkness. "My God, I talk to myself a lot."

"I've hidden from the outside world, life beyond Locket Manor has become irrelevant; therefore, I turn to the spirits of the women before me, to my home, the earth, my belongings—my only allies." She twirls. Her feet dig into the cold dirt.

Gaillynn pulls in a long breath through her nose. An owl hoots at her. Its message is profound and croons sincerity; its masterful vocal serenade is airy and deep yet rarely heard. Gaillynn becomes overwhelmed with sadness—a sob escapes her throat. The crickets around her, repeating their nighttime serenade, attempt to comfort her. "I don't think the stone causes all of the horrible things we have blamed on it. I am starting to wonder if, perhaps, it has been trying to warn us."

Gaillynn returns to her bedroom to read one last entry in the diary before she will attempt sleep. She scans the dated entries, through the birth of Jacob's and Gwendolyn's daughter, Geneve, and searches for the date of Jacob's death hoping to find something that makes sense. "How could Jacob have lived so long? If the stone requires death as its debt, he wouldn't have." And then she finds it.

◆

January 23, 1763

I believe it is cancer that will take my Jacob from us. We celebrated his forty-sixth birthday, and I fear it will be his last. My heart aches, and my body weakens with each day that he does. I feel his pain and illness; I breathe his shallow breaths, and my head pounds with his anguish. I am losing him. The stone's rhythm is slow and sad. I sense that the stone loves him too. Jacob's life was not taken by the stone—on the contrary. He was essential to our survival and key to the future of our legacy. The stone needed him as much as Geneve and I did, and together we mourn our loss.

It began with a hoarse cough, a nagging in his throat. And then his neck became swollen, and he lost his appetite. His body, once round and sculpted with muscle, is now thin and frail. He moans from the pain that has spread throughout his body.

Geneva lies with him all day long. She reads to him and has put her education on hold for these last moments with her daddy. I join them often—we wrap our arms around him and listen to his heart thump in his bony chest. He cannot speak, but we know what he is trying to say—we are one unit of love at its finest.

And now, as the sun is setting, it begins to rain; a heavy rain with drops so large and numerous it blurs the air and soaks the earth. Geneve kisses her daddy goodnight and leaves us alone. Tonight is his last night; I feel him drifting away. My tears drip on his hand in mine.

I speak to him, "One more time, my sweet Jacob, I want to feel your skin against mine, I don't want you to leave this world feeling ill nor weak; instead, I want you to feel our passion, our love, I want you to touch me. I am with you, my love, just as you have been with me these past twenty-three years.

"You are the only man that I have ever, or will ever, love."

The stone embraced us with warmth, which supplied Jacob with enough energy to make love to me one last time. After months of not being able to speak, he whispered, "I love you." And as he left our world, he was without pain; however, his death is my punishment; this is the stone's retribution for my joy. Here it is; although, I am aware of the stone's pain at his death. I do not understand. The stone's anguish mimics mine, and together we cry. The earth cries. For a full seven days after his death, the sky poured her tears.

I cannot continue writing. I will hide this journal within the clock for a future author who has the strength to continue the documentation of our family biography.

Signed, Gwendolyn Lynn Amirah.

◆

Gaillynn drops the diary to her lap and wipes the tears from her cheeks. She presses the bed sheet to her face, bends forward, and sobs into her hands. "I loved Robbie this way," she says to the darkness. "Since his death, I haven't allowed myself to remember that. I have become bitter and withdrawn, devastated to the point of hatred for all life outside of my home." Gaillynn hugs her pillow and cries herself to sleep.

◆

Gaillynn wakes a few hours later; she tiptoes to the bathroom to pee. She splashes cold water on her swollen eyes and brushes her teeth. She heads down the stairs and, with a weak and tearful voice, calls to Dondy.

"Here, kitty, kitty, kitty." Tears empty down her face. She takes a deep breath and tries to compose herself. Gaillynn wonders how Ella's weekend has been going and realizes she hasn't checked on her with the locator app in about twelve hours.

She chooses espresso for this early Sunday morning, and while the espresso machine steams and hisses, she taps the locator app on her wristwatch—Ella's smiling face chimes up on the map—ninety-seven miles away, Eden's Garden, Mount Desert. Gaillynn cries through a smile. "I miss you, Ella. My sweet girl. I'm sorry that I was so eager to get you and Mom out of the house two days ago." Gaillynn thinks back on the slow exit of her mother's car and the blinker flashing in what felt like slow motion. She imagines Ella's weekend has been perfect and excellent, as it always is at Eden's Garden.

I've got a couple of hours left before they return, she thinks. Dondy appears. He rubs his body back and forth along Gaillynn's bare legs. She reaches down and picks him up. "I'm going to write my story in the diary," she says to Dondy. Gaillynn retrieves a pen from the counter and puts it behind one of her ears. She scratches Dondy's neck and carries him and her espresso to her bedroom.

They settle into her bed, and Gaillynn readies the pen in her hand. The entry, written by her mother, dated 2008, delays her writing. She squints her eyelids and considers reading it. Ella was three when Mom wrote this. *I can't read Mom's right now. This weekend has already given me enough burdens.*

◆

Chapter Fifteen

Marguerite knocks on the door of room number three waking Gia and Ella. "Come in," says Gia in a gruff sleepy voice without lifting her head.

"Jesus, you sleepy-heads need to get up." Marguerite enters the room, puts her hands on Ella's back, and gives her a firm shake. "You missed breakfast, and you're about to miss lunch."

"What" Ella lifts her head. She picks up her cell phone and looks at the time. "Oh my God. It's 2:30."

Gia stirs. "No way." She yawns. "It can't be."

"Come downstairs and eat before it's too late. I've got crab cakes, crab rolls, fried clams, and shrimp. It's almost gone. Get up, my lazy girls." Marguerite whisks out of the room, leaving the door wide open.

Lunch's wonderful smell wafts in. Ella leaps up and out of bed to follow Marguerite downstairs.

Jack address Ella from the dining room, "Queen Ella, Jesus dear, you feeling okay?"

Gia moves with resistance, climbs out of bed, and stretches her stiff neck. She presses her right ear to her shoulder, circles her chin to her chest, and rounds her head to the left shoulder. "Ugh." She climbs down the stairs while grasping the railing with two hands. She lumbers across the floor and sits down at the last empty chair next to Ella.

"Is there any coffee?"

The other inn's guests at the table quiet their conversations at the sight of Gia. Jack, Marguerite, and Ella's eyes widen. Ella swallows hard. The aged and tattered appearance of her grandmother sends a tingle of fear up her spine.

Marguerite approaches Gia. "You look awful."

"I'm sure I do. Coffee?" Gia's hair has turned bright white, and her skin is dry with deep wrinkles. Her green eyes have become so pale they appear almost yellow.

"We should get going," announces Ella. She stuffs an entire crab cake in her mouth, places a crab roll on a small plate, and heads for the room.

"Where do you think you are going with that?" says her grandmother. "Ella, you sit down here and eat with us. I'm fine, plus I haven't finished my coffee."

Ella freezes at Gia's command and sits back down. She takes large bites of the crab roll that puffs out her cheeks as she chews.

"Ella is right. You should pack up and hit the road. Take your coffee to your room, dear." Marguerite's concerned expression causes Ella more worry. Ella downs a glass of water and runs up the stairs.

"I'll get you a tall coffee mug for the road, Gia dear. You look like you need it." Marguerite hurries to the kitchen to get a travel mug for Gia.

The women toss all of their belongings into their bags and hurry down the stairs. Jack loads the luggage into the trunk. Marguerite hands Gia a large metal coffee mug with a clear plastic lid.

"Strong and black. Get more along the way if you need it." Marguerite wraps her arms around Gia and hugs her goodbye. "I'll see you next year, my sweet."

"I'm going to go pee real quick," announces Ella. She runs into the inn's foyer. She stops at the tall wall filled with framed photos. "This is new."

A photo near the ceiling has caught her eye. The glass over the image is smoky with age. The black and white picture behind it is a woman wearing a white dress with a shotgun strapped over her shoulder. Her curly hair is dark brown and piled high on top of her head. The woman's eyes are cold and menacing.

"That looks like my mom," she mutters out loud. Then Ella gasps. "That's Locket Manor." Ella pulls her cell phone from her back pocket and takes a photo of the picture on the wall. Forgetting she has to pee, she returns to the car.

"Are you ready, Ella?" asks her grandmother.

Ella ignores her grandmother and goes directly to Marguerite. Ella wraps Marguerite's hands into hers. "Have you ever been to my house?"

"No, dear. I have not. Why do you ask?"

"There is a picture of it on your wall."

Gia straightens.

"Really? Show me." Ella pulls Marguerite toward the house. Jack and Gia follow. Ella points to the picture—Gia covers her mouth.

"That looks an awful lot like Gaillynn," says Gia.

Jack is tall enough to reach the photo. He lifts it from its wall anchor and wipes the dust from the glass with his white apron.

"Yup, that's Locket Manor," says Gia.

"I found that picture in my mother's belongings years ago," explains Marguerite. "I just thought it was beautiful and eerie all at the same time, so I hung it in the inn. That's your house?"

"Yes. But who is that woman?" asks Ella.

"I have no idea. Jack, take the picture out of the frame," says Marguerite. He spins the rusted framing nails with his fingertips and removes the wood, softened with age that has been holding the photo in place behind the glass. On the backside of the image is faded, cursive handwriting: "Geneve Amirah," he reads. "Holy shit," whispers Jack.

"My mother spoke of a Geneve Amirah. Geneve saved my great-grandmother's life, somehow. I don't remember the whole story."

An unusual heaviness in the air squeezes Gia's lungs, and she breaks out in a full-body sweat. Fog moves toward her from the still ocean, and suddenly, clouds cover the low afternoon sun—a threatening storm circles above them. Gia craves the cooling wind force and the sound of crashing waves from home.

"We've got to get home," announces Gia. An expression on Marguerite's face sends shivers over her sweaty skin. "Have you realized something, Marguerite?" *A connection to the photo or the Amirah family?* Gia thinks.

"Marguerite, I don't know what this means, but it's a pretty odd coincidence, don't you think?" Asks Gia.

Marguerite doesn't respond. Her face has become white, and all she can do is nod. Jack helps Marguerite walk inside, and Gia and Ella speed out of the driveway toward home.

Gia and Ella spend the drive home speculating over the photo and their vision shared on the beach. Ella studies the photo she took with her cell phone. She zooms in on the woman's face and examines all of her features.

"That picture is of one of our relatives, Grammy. We must be related to Marguerite and Jack. What else could this mean?"

Gia remains silent, but thoughts dart and collide in her mind:

the diary, Gwendolyn and Jacob, her vision of the queen with Ella's face. Was it the future Ella they saw? Gia focuses from the road to Ella and compares her features to the woman in their vision. Ella looks up at her. Gia whips her eyes back to the road.

"What, Grammy?"

Gia swallows. "In our vision, on the beach, did that queen remind you of anyone?"

"Yeah. The queen looked like us but from the future. And, Earth appeared to have evolved into a hot, humid land. There is no glow like our stone now. Did you see the glow? From the people too?"

"Um, yes. I saw that. But, the queen didn't remind you of anyone?"

"Yes, she reminded me of us. I already said that, Grammy."

After an hour of driving with a windstorm at their tail, the two eager-to-be-home travelers pull into the driveway of Locket Manor. They hesitate to exit the car. Instead, sit a moment longer in the parked vehicle inside the six-car garage. Gia's preoccupation with the photo of Geneve and Ella as queen almost made her forget Ella's last birthday present until now.

Gia shakes her head. She reaches over Ella's lap and retrieves a wrapped present from the glove compartment. "I have something special for you, Ella." She hands the birthday gift to her granddaughter.

"Oh, Grammy, a present?"

"This is just something that reminded me of you. I hope you like it."

Ella tears at the multi-colored balloon wrapping paper revealing a black cardboard jewelry box. She lifts the cover. A gold rope chain with a pendant covered in diamonds sparkles up at her. She turns the charm toward the last few rays of the setting sun coming in through the open garage door. Dozens of diamonds swirl in a circling pattern, like a fiddlehead, spiral to the center to surround one larger blueish-gold gem.

"Wow, it's almost the same color as the stone," Ella says. "I love it, Grammy; it's beautiful." She studies the crystals and decides the necklace is a symbol of everything that happened on this trip to Eden's Garden. She pulls the chain over her head and rubs it with both hands. "I can't wait to show Mom."

The women exit the car, and the heavy wooden garage door closes behind them. Ella hurries inside, expecting her mother is waiting in the kitchen, eager for their return.

"Mom, we are home." The house is quiet. Dondy greets them. He rubs against Ella's legs, his purr vibrating her skin. Ella bends down to pat him. "Where's Mom, little guy?"

They climb the stairs to Gaillynn's bedroom. Gia feels the energy of the stone anesthetizing her toward recovery. The trauma of being absent from the stone for the weekend lifts. Her white hair disappears, and the brilliant brown mahogany color returns. Her skin smooths and brightens, and her lips plump back into shape—the deep wrinkles cutting into her skin smooth and disappear. Jade green replaces her yellowed eyes. Gia takes a deep recovery breath and smiles.

Gia also tries to release the painful knife lodged in the pit of her stomach for years. "Lessons," she whispers to console herself.

"Mom, we are home! Mom, are you here?" Ella calls.

"I'm upstairs." Gaillynn stashes the diary and pen under her pillow, jumps out of bed, and tries to flatten her tangled hair. Gia and Ella are already up the stairs. They enter her bedroom.

"Oh honey, are you sick? Have you been in bed all weekend?" Gia asks.

"Yes, I had a pain in my neck, but it finally went away. I think I just missed you two, that's all. Let's go have some tea, and you can tell me all about your weekend." Gaillynn ushers them out of her room. Her eyes linger on the safe as they exit, and the three women descend the tall staircase.

"Pretty necklace, honey. Is that from Grammy?"

"Yes, she just gave it to me in the car before we came in. Isn't it pretty?" Ella smiles at her grandmother. "Grammy, you look better."

"I feel better."

Chapter Sixteen

As the teabags steep in mugs of hot water, Gaillynn warms the peach-cobbler French toast that Marguerite wrapped and sent home for her in the microwave. The women eyeball each other with suspicion.

"What did you do this weekend, Mom?"

"I babysat Dondy. And read." Gaillynn looks at her mother with one eyebrow raised. The microwave beeps—she withdraws the fragrant French toast. Gaillynn sets her plate down at the small round table that overlooks Locket Manor's West garden. Gia and Ella make eye contact, and Ella mouths to her grandmother, "Tell mom what happened."

"What?" Gia says to Ella.

"What?" Gaillynn looks up from her food.

"Grammy!"

"Ella, what is going on with you two? Do you have something to tell me?"

"I don't know. Do you have something to tell us?" Ella asks.

"No. Why? What could I have to tell?"

"Maybe the real reason you stayed home this weekend? Marguerite thought it was very odd and that you must have had a good reason," explains Ella.

"I did. Dondy."

"Gail, there is something you need to know. Ella and I had a moment on the beach. We were in tune with these women…" She hesitates. "They seemed to be from the future or something; I don't know how to explain it. We became united with them."

Gaillynn coughs. "From the future? Mom, have you been drinking?"

"Yes, she has, but that's beside the point. It's true, Mom," says Ella. "We saw our stone. If you would sit with us and the stone, I bet we could make the connection again."

"It was probably the stone playing games with you," Gaillynn says. Gaillynn fills her mouth with another large bite and talks through her food, "So you're telling me that this weekend, you two became enlightened with women from the future that had our stone? That's all? Anything else?"

"Yes," adds Ella. "Great-great-grammy Ginny let her refused love hear the story of the stone."

"You don't say?" says Gaillynn.

"Yup. And it is possible that one of the relatives of this guy, Christopher Chandler, may still live in Stonington."

"Really? That's possible. I'm not so sure about the women from the future, though." Gaillynn takes her empty plate to the sink and rinses it off. "That was so yummy."

"We want to try and find them if we can. Did you know that Ginny didn't let herself love Christopher Chandler, and that was her equal sadness? She just said no to him and married someone else. Great-great-grandfather Hendrick. Do you know the one who they named our wing after? How could she do that? My God, she tortured herself."

"She saved his life, honey. As far as I can tell, she made the biggest sacrifice she could have made for the man she loved. And she didn't become a widow until much later."

"But she didn't love Great-great Grampy. And yes, she did eventually become a widow, Mom. And it's not like Great-great Grampy had an easy life. He had the worst luck ever. He was always getting hurt, and when he died, it was not of natural causes," Ella argues.

Gaillynn laughs and nods her head. "Well, it is true, driving the lawnmower off the edge of the lawn into the ocean after too many rum punches isn't a natural or common way to die." They giggle through guilty smiles.

"But, Mom and Ella, it is strange that you bring up the Chandlers because I realized over the weekend that we do know the Chandler family. I went to high school with the last one. Mom, do you remember Cooper C. Blethen?" Gia's face loses all color.

"The C stands for his daddy's last name—Chandler. It was hyphenated."

Gaillynn and her mother stare at each other in silence. Thousands of questions and answers rush through Gia's head at this discovery. *The boy she pushed Gaillynn to date is a Chandler? The boy who killed Robbie is a Chandler? Does Cooper know about the stone? He must.*

Ella's eyes dart from her mother to her grandmother and back and forth. "Hello? Do you guys want to explain who he is? Did you date him, Mom?"

"No. No. God no. He went to high school with me; he was no one I was interested in dating. He was very manipulative and took advantage of naive, trusting women. He tricked them into getting what he wanted. But don't worry, our secret is safe." Gaillynn holds the stare with her mother. She raises an eyebrow, gives her mother a discrete wink, then looks away.

Ella taps her computer. It blinks to life. With her stylus, she scribbles lines through the notes she wrote in regards to the Chandler mystery. "Hmph. Well, that one's solved," she says. "Oh, Mom, I think we are related to Jack and Marguerite."

"Of course we are related; they are like family, honey. They always have been."

"No, I mean like really related. I found a picture of a woman named Geneve Amirah standing in front of Locket Manor. Here, I'll show you. She looks just like you, Mom, when you get that look." Ella opens the photo on her cell phone.

The French toast rises in Gaillynn's stomach. She snatches Ella's phone from her hands. "Whoa. That is Locket Manor."

"Mom!"

"Sorry."

Ella attempts to get her phone back from her mother. Gaillynn turns her back to Ella and lifts her elbows.

"They didn't know who she was at first. Marguerite said she found it in her mother's things and thought it was cool, so she hung it up. Jack took it out of the frame, and her name was on the back. Geneve Amirah. Give me my phone, mom," says Ella.

Gaillynn takes a deep breath. "No way," she says in a whisper. She looks at her mother with a raised eyebrow.

Gia is surprised by the look and cocks her head. "What?"

Gaillynn pulls the phone close, enlarges the photo, and studies Geneve. The daughter of Gwendolyn and Jacob is right there in front of my eyes. Her heart pounds—she can see it bouncing through her pajamas. She taps the print option on Ella's phone, and the wireless printer in the library engages with the received command.

"Well, we certainly could be related to the woman in the photo,"

Gaillynn says, then passes the phone back to Ella. "They could have picked that print up at a yard sale, honey. Who knows?"

"No, Mom. Marguerite said her mother spoke of a Geneve Amirah—she saved her great-great-great grandmother's life."

"That doesn't mean we are blood-related, though, honey."

"I guess you're right," Ella says. She huffs. She scribbles more notes out of her computer pad and tosses her stylus on the table. With the hope of one successful pitch to her mother, Ella brings up high school. "Hey, Mom? I want to go to high school. There are fourteen-year-old freshmen all of the time."

"Sorry, honey. No. I am not going to allow you to grow up too fast. I lost your father in high school. Living a normal life is the only way I know how to protect you, Ella. Please don't rush your life."

Ella huffs. "You ruin all of my plans. You ruin everything. I wish we didn't have to come home." She thrusts her computer under her armpit and stomps out of the kitchen. Ella pounds her feet with each step the entire lengthy distance to the stairs, through the lasting climb up them, then continues stomping overhead as she travels the stretch of hallway to her bedroom.

Ella's elongated parade of frustration quiets for Gaillynn and Gia the further away she gets from the kitchen. Ella ends her show of anger with a slammed door. She is so far away by then, all Gaillynn and Gia hear is a muffled thump.

Gaillynn and Gia remain at the table but don't speak. Gaillynn contemplates Ella's request to go to high school. *I should have said yes. Ella is not like me. Maybe I should let her—I'll tell her she can go tomorrow.*

Gia palms her teacup and presses her eyebrows together, and thinks. *Is Cooper a Chandler? My God, what have I done?*

Gaillynn stands. "Mom, I'm going to my room. I have something I want to finish."

"Oh, okay. I have to unpack," Gia responds without looking up.

"Good night, Mom."

"Good night, Gail."

The two women go their separate ways. Gia picks up Dondy and carries him upstairs to her bedroom, where she unpacks her bag. She wrestles with two secrets—her involvement with Robbie's death and now also her knowledge of Ella's future self. She prepares for bed with gritted teeth and a pounding heart.

Gaillynn, now in her bedroom, pulls the diary out from under her pillow and continues her writing.

◆

Later that night, Gaillynn visits her mother's bedroom. She places her hand on her mother's hip and wiggles Gia awake.

"Here you go, Mom," Gaillynn whispers. She tucks the diary under her mother's palm. In place of her sleepiness, Gia's eyes widen at the sight of the leather book. "It's time for you to read my story," Gaillynn announces, then turns to leave.

Gia jolts to a sitting position and turns on the lamp next to her bed. She presses the book to her chest. "Gail." Gaillynn turns back to her mother. "You read it?" Gia asks.

"Yes."

"All of it?"

"The important parts. You know, the parts about me."

"Honey. Oh no. I'm so sorry. I didn't want you to find out this way."

"Find out what, Mom? That you sent Cooper there that night? Didn't you worry about me, Mom? What if he killed me?"

"No. No, I never worried about you. Not at all. I knew you

would be okay; I always know you will be okay. You are the strongest, bravest person there is. I never once worried about you."

Gaillynn's lips part, and her chin drops. "Should I be mad at that? Or is this a distorted compliment?" She shakes her head. "I'm pissed. Do you know? I'm pissed. But Mom, it's not your fault Robbie is dead. It's Cooper's. If it didn't happen that night, it would have happened at some point."

"How do you know?"

"I just do. If you trust me, Mom, believe me. It would have." Gaillynn turns again to leave.

"Gail? If Cooper knew about the stone, he could easily have stolen it back in high school when visiting me. Why did he wait for you? I don't understand. Is it possible he didn't know about the stone?" asks Gia.

"Mom, of course, he knew about the stone. When will you realize how strong you are? The stone has bestowed many gifts on us, and one of them is physical strength, and I would rather not think that you would have allowed him to steal it. Robbie's death was the stone's doing, Mom. All of it. There is a prophecy unfolding, and I would like you to get caught up, so read mine."

Gia eyes a bookmark sticking out from between the pages of the diary. She opens the cover and discovers the printed photo of Geneve Amirah marking Gaillynn's story inside. Gaillynn turns to leave her mother's bedroom.

"Gail."

"Hmm?" she huffs. "What, Mom?"

"This is a photo of Geneve, and maybe the only one."

"I know." Gaillynn's irritation at her mother quiets, and she sits on the corner of her mother's bed. "That photo at Eden's Garden belongs to us, Mom. She looks just like us; it's so strange."

"But like a ghost. I'm sorry, but Geneve does not look happy in this photo. She looks scary and crazy. It makes me worry about what we don't know about her."

"I disagree. Geneve appears to be a strong woman dealing with some crazy shit. If she looks so much like me, when I get that look, whatever the hell that means, then I'm thinking she is protecting her family and the stone. In whatever way she must."

"Oh." Gia studies the photo. "Yes, you are right."

"I'd rather call that look on her face 'heroic warrior.' If she's crazy, it's because of this insane life we all have to live. And with that shotgun on her arm, I think she is pretty capable."

"You're right."

"Her story isn't in the diary. About one hundred and thirty years are missing between Gwendolyn and Ginny. We need to know Geneve's story, Mom," says Gaillynn.

"There's more, Gail. The vision I shared with Ella was of her."

"Of Ella?"

"Yes. Ella wore a crown, like a queen. It was the future."

"Why do you think it was Ella, Mom?"

"It was her."

"Huh. That's weird; We can talk more tomorrow. Read my story, please. I love you, Mom."

"I love you too, Gaillynn."

Gaillynn leaves and closes her mother's bedroom door. Dondy repositions himself near Gia's pillow and wraps his body into itself.

Gia reclines against her soft mattress. Gaillynn's words, "It wasn't your fault," repeat in her mind. She takes a deep breath and exhales slow. "It wasn't your fault." Relief and calmness, like a tranquilizer, replace the sharp knife in her stomach.

She holds the diary above her face with both hands, takes a deep breath, and summons the courage to read Gaillynn's story.

She piles two pillows behind her neck and opens the soft leather-bound diary. With the help of Geneve's photo, she finds the entry written by Gaillynn and begins to read.

◆

October 17, 2025

My name is Gaillynn Shea Amirah.

I suspect the powerful stone linked to my family and me is magic, or we share its same maker—Earth. The stone, a beautiful ore, and the atmosphere around me, my mother, and my daughter reacts to us. The stone gives us physical strength, my mother can see things that are happening or that will happen, and she can heal our minor ailments. My daughter is brilliant and will find our purpose. Me? I am its warrior, protector, and guardsman against its enemies.

My earliest childhood memories are of my parents spending their days in the bedroom. Young and lustful, they only left the Hendrick wing to make food in the second-floor kitchen. I remember my parents' laughter during those days. They shared happiness until the day they didn't.

My father's temper and the abrupt switch with which it would appear was like a tornado hitting shore without warning.

The air would fill with an evil heart, and my mother's body would overflow with adrenaline. Though she never instigated his rage, she also didn't possess the ability to calm him. He provoked fear in her. Endowed with the strength of the stone, yet she cowered to him.

My child-euphoric moments of nursing were constantly interrupted by his vile presence. Yes, I can remember—though I was a baby and shouldn't be able to remember, I do. The memories are clear and vivid— he was jealous of me and my close connection to my mother. He envied her love for me, so my presence challenged her devotion to him. He claimed her affection first, allowed little for me, and only if my mother filled his quota of her adoration.

My father felt no love for me—hell, he was incapable of love. And his once gentle touch with my mother transformed—he became desperate and abusive. He forced intimacy on her, and he demanded constant praise. I wanted to escape.

As soon as I could walk, it became impossible for my mother to keep me confined to the Hendrick wing, and she would often lose me in the house. I could, one hundred percent of the time, be found with my grandmother, Gloria. Where ever Gloria was in the enormous estate, I could locate her. Her energy drew me to the quiet and her love. I could call to her with my thoughts when I needed to be free of the torment between my parents. She would respond with telepathic messages and maps to find her.

Though I was young, I was very well aware that I craved the touch of my grandmother's skin. Like the stone and my mother, our connection was magnetic and crucial for my well-being and growth—my grandmother's lap was my favorite place to escape my father.

His yelling would echo through the house, and my ears would buzz with resonating trauma from the sheer volume of it; my grandmother would shield me with walks outside, always barefoot. Some of my favorite memories are moments with my Grammy; she carried me on her back. I cupped my hands around the skin of her neck or just underneath the collar of her shirt.

If I were lucky enough to have my mother and grandmother together, I would instinctively hold both of their hands to unite the bond between us. Our moods would soar, and our bodies would beam with pure health and happiness.

◆

Gia wipes her tearing eyes with her palm and smooths the photo of Geneve into the crease between the pages. She folds the blankets off of her legs and goes to her bathroom for a tissue. Gia blows her nose and returns to her bed with the entire box of tissues. She absorbs the tears from the corners of her eyes with the soft white cloth then lifts the book to continue.

◆

As a child, I was adventurous, independent, and I preferred to be outside and barefoot. With no other siblings, I thirsted for friends and the normality I saw outside of Locket Manor. Lucky for me, my home was a short walk to a welcoming neighborhood full of kids. I found comfort with my friends and their ordinary families who were not cursed and didn't have to bear the tremendous weight of an unimaginable secret or the madness of a deranged father.

My grandmother told me that my most exquisite and endearing personality trait was fearlessness. She said I was born with a force uncommon in most women she knew, especially the opposite of my mother. She told me that I was clever and determined and had a knack for always finding a way to figure things out or get things done. All true—I tire easily of excuses, cowardliness, dishonesty, and disrespect.

My grandmother also told me that as an infant, I would growl at my maniacal father if he misbehaved. Dad particularly disliked when I was nursing. He expressed disgust and scolded my mother at the act of nursing. He convinced Mom she had done something wrong—as if her bond with me was unnatural and repulsive.

My grandmother described my intolerance of him as an inborn ferocity. I would stop nursing, set my eyes on him, and examine his mood. If he came too close to my mother or me, I would growl.

My grandmother said it startled him every time. I was not afraid of him and very protective of my mother.

At a very young age, I developed a "tell," as my grandmother called it. When I sensed something was off and in need of correction, my body language warned my mother and grandmother that I was ready to act. My golden-green eyes would darken to deep jade green, just like the stone does when it needs correction. I would drop my head down to my right shoulder, chin to my chest with a slight tilt to the right. My eyes would pierce, and I would exhale a forceful huff. They learned that an impulsive behavior would follow this tell to set the situation right.

Maybe a trait I learned from the stone or adopted by the exact opposite behavior from my mother. I'm not exactly sure, but there it is.

I love my mother but hate how vulnerable she is—she trusts everyone. Mom gives everyone the benefit of the doubt and tries to find the silver linings of most evils, including the abuse from my father.

His name was Toby, and he thought he ruled my mother and her life. Down to when she went to the bathroom or what she had to drink with dinner. Dad punished any decision she made that did not benefit him. I hated him. And when my mother would do nothing, say nothing, it became my job to react. I threw things at him, stomped on his toes, dumped his drink on the floor, and even pulled his hair.

◆

Gia chokes on a sob and sits up to compose herself. Dondy has become aware of her crying, and he sits in front of her, purring. He presses his head against her hands. Gia pulls him to her lap for a tight hug. The hug is not exactly what the cat had in mind, and he wiggles himself free. Gia removes a fresh tissue from the box and absorbs the wetness from her face. She continues to read the heart-wrenching truths written by Gaillynn.

◆

Thank God for Andie. She became my best friend and the only person I ever considered telling about the stone. However, I never did. Even so, it felt like she was on my side, somehow. I find it very strange that after the first time we spoke on the playground just before my seventh birthday, I had a dream that I still remember to this day.

In it, I am watching the pendulum in the clock swing from side to side. A golden-blue haze blurs its swinging path. Back and forth. I can hear the humming of unfamiliar female voices chanting words I don't understand.

Wind blows my hair just like the wind from the swing set at school, but in my dream, the wind is coming from the swing of the clock's pendulum. The clock is twice as tall as it is in reality, and it is unnaturally bending toward me. Like it is made of heavy rubber and is going to squish me.

I push on the clock to keep it from squishing me, and I grow tall enough to straighten the clock back up. The wind continues to blow at me with force, and I lean toward its power with my fists on my waist. The force lifts my hair from my face and pushes it behind my back, resembling the cape of a superhero.

Fragments of gold and blue light absorb into my body, multiplying my strength. A tiny form of my father steps out from behind the clock. He holds my mother by the foot, dangling her like a mouse in the air by its tail. My mother's hands and feet are flailing for help. I yell to her: "Mom, you are stronger than him."

And then I woke up.

I remember being overcome with an uncontrollable hostility for my father after that dream. My anger erupted in my stomach, and I pounded a fist into my pillow.

I tried, without success, to relax back to sleep. My thoughts wandered to memories of my grandmother, Gloria. Gloria was brave, and she believed in me. When Gloria was my age, she refused to look at the clock or let the stone influence her life. Gloria didn't want the clock's need to balance its energy when something extraordinary would happen to affect how she lived her life. I wanted to be free of that burden, just like my grandmother. I didn't want the stone to dictate how I lived.

So that night, while I struggled to remain calm, I decided that I would never be afraid. I would not be afraid of the stone or the inevitable pain and tragedy. I would not allow it to dictate my happiness or decisions. I would not let my father hurt my mother any longer. After all, my choices were limited, I wouldn't survive without the stone, so I chose to be brave, clever, and impulsive like my grandmother, Gloria.

I vowed to live my life with a decided and intentional obliviousness to the clock and accept the good and bad from that dream forward. I would remain loyal to the secrets and steadfast at protecting my family; however, I convinced myself that I was just like my friends and their families. Everyone suffered from good and evil in life. In my six-year-old mind, the only difference was that I knew an equal negative would follow a positive. A debt I would willingly enforce should it be required of me, without question.

◆

Gia places the diary on her lap and takes a deep breath. "I'm more of a coward than I thought. Gaillynn is right. I didn't react when Toby was abusive. I didn't respond because I believed his behavior was my punishment from the stone for the love I felt for Gaillynn. I thought my debt to the stone was the horror with Toby—like it was payment for my debt for Gaillynn. The strongest love I had ever felt. The torture had always been worth it. But now I realize Toby's behavior affected Gaillynn. Toby was cruel to both of us." Regret rears its familiar and hostile heat in her chest. Gia draws from Gaillynn's courage and lifts the book in front of her face to continue reading Gaillynn's words.

◆

And then, on my seventh birthday, I killed my father.

◆

Chapter Seventeen

Gia sits up straight and blinks her eyes to be sure of their clarity. She re-reads the last line, this time out loud: "And then, on my seventh birthday, I killed my father." Gia hugs the book to her chest.

"No, Gail, that was not you. That was an accident. No." Gia rehashes the memories of his death. There was a moment. A brief moment that she feared Gaillynn was involved. Just a small but intense fraction of time when a flicker of the idea did appear in her mind, but she never allowed herself to consider its possibility. Not ever again, until right now.

"Gail?" She straightens the book and finds her place.

◆

I could hear my father in the other room. He was speaking in that awful, loud, and accusing tone to my mother. And, of course, she had been sucked into his twisted, narcissistic vortex of blame and redirecting. She took his words to heart and tried to apologize as if she had done something wrong, something so bad that she deserved his wrath.

He wanted to know why she was making such a big deal of my seventh birthday. He accused her of trying to impress someone, another man. My God, my mother didn't even know any other men. He was insane. Still, she cringed; she begged and pleaded and assured her love for him was true and the deepest she had ever felt for any man.

I tiptoed, on bare feet, into the room while they argued. I stood behind Dad and listened. My blood boiled, and my body stiffened. The thick odor of alcohol vaporized out of his breath and turned my stomach. Adrenaline rushed through my mother's veins, causing their blue plumpness to show through her skin. Her feverish attempts at controlling her anger reddened her face. She chose her words with a creative ambition to calm him.

The wind threw sticks and leaves at the window from outside. Clouds darkened the sky, and the tall trees shook in a furious wind.

He clutched my mother's neck with both hands, and I'm telling you, I know my mother could have easily pushed him away. He squeezed her throat so tight that his knuckles turned white. He snarled and spat as he spoke.

"I'll fucking kill you if this is for another man. You didn't do this for my birthday, Gia. She's turning seven, you fucking idiot, wake the fuck up."

I growled. My father was crazy, possessed, and irrational, and my mother allowed it. She has always been stronger than him, but she never knew it.

Not until she saw me.

Once my mother saw the look of intolerance on my face, she panicked. The following huff of disgust released from my lungs told my mother that I would act. She jumped up so quickly that Toby fell off of her like a rag-doll. He stumbled to the floor and landed at my feet. Dad looked up at me. His eyebrows unfurled, redirecting themselves from anger to shame. Maybe he was regretful but too proud to admit it, or perhaps he was just an ass; either way, he bolted with an entire bottle of whiskey and went to pout by the ocean.

My foolish, unsuspecting mother left me alone while she went to pick up my birthday cake. The cake that my asshole father could have picked up, at the very least, for her hours ago. Instead, he made her day more difficult. I had had it.

As soon as my mother left, I exited Hendrick's wing. I climbed into the dumbwaiter hidden under the ladder of spiraling stairs. I pressed the glowing yellow button for the attic. Once at the top of Locket Manor, I danced through the clutter, skipped around boxes, and pirouetted over dusty paintings.

On the outside wall, facing the ocean, is a half-circle window so large that my petite seven-year-old body was equal in size to just one of the dozens of panes. Its frame, constructed of pure copper, had greened from the weather but would reflect the sun with blinding brilliance when shined.

I pushed the heavy window forward and opened it as far as it would go. I squeezed out of the attic and onto a small terrace. None of us came up here much, but it was to look for shooting stars on clear nights or witness the ocean's anger during storms when we did.

I propped open the window with the large metal lever hidden below the window frame made specifically for this purpose. A pair of binoculars hung inside on a hook; I retrieved them, all the while not taking my eyes off Toby.

Dad was sitting far away near the ocean. He looked so tiny, trivial, weak, and deplorable. I peered through the binoculars and focused in on him—Dad was drinking the whiskey fast. He had already drunk one-quarter of the bottle's contents. "Keep drinking, you piece of shit," I said.

The wind had calmed, and the sky cleared. I could hear the

waves smash against the rocks beneath the cliffs at the edge of our lawn. A seagull sent a long and approving "keow," from far away.

I looked at my watch—thirty minutes before my mother would be on her way back from the store with my birthday cake. I continued watching my father take large, repeated gulps from the whiskey bottle. Soon it was half-gone.

He set the bottle to his side. It fell over and spilled out and sank into the grass. A wisp of exhilarated wind wafted over my face. His body slumped back; the weight of his head and arms became too much for his early morning intoxication.

"Yes!" I said.

I explored the attic patio and discovered the forgotten Dulcinea statue standing in the corner. The stone carvings illustrated a masterful rendition of her slender body, wrapped in drapery, and her elegant hands holding tiny flowers. She certainly weighed more than I did. Dulcinea, a courageous and proud woman on this patio all by herself, was, and will always be, my kin.

Giant green ferns in clay pots thrown and fired in the pottery kiln in the basement by my grandmother, Gloria, lined the patio's edge. I peered over the edge of the patio railing to the garden below—I spotted a similar Dulcinea statue down there. I smiled at her.

I climbed back inside the attic and made my way to the dumbwaiter. I pressed the glowing number one. During the slow ride down, I solidified my plan. I squinted my eyes with hate and pulled my chin to my chest. I peered up over my eyebrows as if staring Toby, Dad, directly into his eyes.

My father, a man I lived with, only had meanness inside of him as far as I knew. A man I had listened to fight, yell at, accuse, and belittle my mother as long as I could remember—since my birth. And now, he'd almost strangled her and threatened to kill her. The volcano inside me boiled; the heat from the molten lava rose in my face, and I began breathing like an angry bull.

Out of the dumbwaiter and back outside, I walked toward him. Once at his side, I listened to him breathing. I stood there waiting for some sort of movement or awareness that I stood over him. He was still.

"Dad." His eyes blinked open. He licked his dry lips and sat up. Too weak to deal with the brightness of the sun, he covered his eyes with his palm.

"Hey, Gail, what's up?" His voice was hoarse and scratchy.

"Do you know why Mom is up on the attic patio with the electrician? They went up there like half an hour ago, and I have not seen them since. He told Mom he liked her dress, and he was all smiley. I guess he is nice, but it just seems kinda weird." I twirled a long piece of grass between my fingers and tied a bow with it.

My dad jumped to his feet, kicked the whiskey bottle, and staggered toward the house. He swayed right and left across the lawn then tripped up all three flights of stairs. I followed behind.

Once we reached the attic, he forced his body through the window's small opening and outside onto the patio. I slid through and headed for the Dulcinea statue. My strength did seem impossible for me being so young, but to be honest, it felt incredible. I carried the statue with no trouble to him. He searched for evidence of Mom and the electrician.

"Look," I yelled. I pointed my finger toward the ocean where he and I had just been on the grass moments before. He stepped to the edge and squinted his eyes. Dad leaned forward against the rail. I climbed up onto the bench to his left, and I swung the beautiful statue of Dulcinea over his head. I struck him hard.

The force of the blow against the back of his skull knocked him off balance. His body tumbled over the edge. His arms flailed in an unsuccessful attempt to catch himself.

As he somersaulted through the air, his eyes met mine. For a brief moment before reaching the stone patio below him, our eyes locked. I hope he saw my hate and my relief in hurting him. He hit the ground while staring into the eyes of his killer—his daughter—me.

The impact was heavy, and his bones crunched against the ground. The statue continued to fall behind him and landed on his face.

I descended the layers of Locket Manor by climbing down the limbs of the wisteria tree. I confirmed his death with a swift kick to his ribs. I smiled at the similar Dulcinea statue situated in the garden near where he landed. This statue was a different version of Dulcinea than the one I used to hit him. This Dulcinea sat on a bench. I thought it appropriate that she could finally relax. "Have a seat, my dear," I whispered to her.

I know my grandmother, Gloria, saw. I know she was in the library of the adjacent wing from where I pushed my father to his death. I saw her in the window; I saw her step back and cover her mouth when I hit him. I knew she was there, reading in the sunny attic library, until she heard me yell, "Look." That is what drew her to the window to investigate. She saw the whole thing. I had just killed Toby.

I could see my grandmother pace the library. I could hear her thoughts. She struggled with what she saw, and she tried to make sense of it. She believed that I must have had a good reason. "Toby was a fucking asshole after all, but why? Oh, Gail. My God, Gail. Why?" I heard her think.

My gram paced the room a few more times, realized she was

still holding the book she had been reading, and threw it on the floor. She fell to her knees and pulled her hair back out of her face, and squeezed her hands into tight fists. She let out a scream which she tried to keep quiet and to herself. She planted her elbows on the floor, and she cradled her head with her arms. She rocked back and forth. "I've got to get away from this stone," she said, and I heard her.

◆

Gia covered her mouth with her hand. "All of this time, I was so mad at myself for sending Cooper back to the mill that night; Gail-lynn has dealt with this. Her secret is much worse. And my God, Gaillynn's solution was to kill her father at age seven" Gia's regret, now changed, clung to a different mistake. "I should've protected you better. My brave girl." Through her tears, Gia read on.

◆

When my mother returned from the store, Grammy Gloria didn't say a word. She played right along with me. It was amazing.

Mom ran past the ambulance and police cars and inside with the cake to find Grammy holding me on her lap and cradling me while I wept. I remember my mother was carrying a pink-frosted birthday cake with yellow roses made from true love. In calligraphy-style cursive writing, it read, "Happy 7th Birthday, Gail."

"Mom, Dad fell off of the attic patio, he was carrying the statue, and they fell, and now he is dead," I said through counterfeit sobs.

My mother's jaw dropped. Her arms went limp, and the birthday cake smashed to the floor.

In my defense, I have to say that he robbed Locket Manor of our safety and happiness. I knew he was toxic and dangerous, and my blood boiled when he was near. My eyes would become hazed with a black shadow blurring his face. To this day, I cannot remember what he looked like. I realize now that I premeditated his murder, but our survival depended on me taking care of this. I had had enough.

I know my grandmother was horrified because she moved to the Florida Keys a few months later and let herself die in a boat. I will never forgive her for leaving me. It was the most selfish thing she could have done. I needed her, and my mom needed her. When she left, I lost part of myself.

I have never been able to speak to anyone through my mind again. I wonder if it was simply an enlightened awareness you hear of children having because they are young and innocent? I guess I lost my innocence that day. But you know, after reading this book, I realize I am not so different than the rest of the people in it.

Years past and I grew up—the stone nourished me into the person I am today. People say that my beauty mimics the generations of Amirah women before me; of course, I can't take any of the credit. All of us bear similar features that set us apart from others. Our beauty also is enhanced by the effects of the stone. You know, glowing, flawless skin, full naturally rosy, red lips; we all have dark wavy hair that is wild and exotic, long eyelashes and beautiful green eyes, blah, blah, blah, who the hell cares. I hate hearing about our beauty and how we remain young long after we grow old.

More importantly and similar to my childhood self, I remained genuine, kind, strong-minded, intelligent, and resourceful. I became poised and well-spoken and worked very hard in school.

I spent my junior and senior high school years being pursued aggressively by an obsessive and ego-blinded boy named Cooper Chandler Blethen. His popularity was well known and built by his Prince Charming-like looks and a boastful and indignant personality.

I misunderstood his advances. I thought that he pursued me. Now I know the truth.

◆

Gia exhales through her fingers. She stops reading. "It's all so much to believe. Have I always known, unconsciously, that Gaillynn killed Toby?"

Gia takes another deep breath and continues to read Gaillynn's words.

◆

Cooper Chandler visited me one week ago. He was after the stone, and that is why he killed Robbie. I killed him too, and he is vacuum sealed inside the safe in my bedroom. Here are the details:

◆

Gia finishes reading the account of Gaillynn's second murder. First, her father, and now Cooper decays in a cold metal tomb in Gaillynn's bedroom. He's just fifty feet or so from the graveyard behind Locket Manor but not worthy of its dirt. *Perhaps he could have shared Toby's coffin?* Gia shrugs her shoulders and decides she must accept Gaillynn's behavior—a born protector. He took Robbie from Gaillynn and Ella—he deserves worse.

Gia feels different. Something inside of her has changed. She sits up straighter in her bed, smiles, and dries the last of her tears. This entire weekend has granted her the insight she has been missing. The time she spent with Ella at Eden's Garden, and now the reinforcement of her belief in Gaillynn's tenacity, above the regret of tolerating the abuse Gaillynn endured, above it all, Gia experiences a brand new and wonderful thing—an acknowledgment of her strength.

A charge tingles up her spine.

"If Gaillynn, born of my blood, can do what is necessary without regret, no second-guessing and always without fear, then so can I—this wonderful journal of lessons from all of us. Our history is documented by the authors of our ancestry and lineage, only here, in this book.

"Time Keeper," she whispers.

"My charge to heal the minor ailments of this family—their tired minds and stiff necks, has a larger purpose. Now I must recover my broken heart. I will stand with Gaillynn for Ella—the future Queen of Earth. Yes."

Clarity mixes with more confusion. "What is the destiny of the Amirah family? The stone? Our world?" Gia slinks back under the covers and lays down.

She squeezes her waist to hug herself. "I love this sense of purpose and commitment to the stone and my family. My strength has always been there, the power Gaillynn sees in me. I will embrace it. I will not smother the abilities bestowed on me by the beacon of our life source—the stone.

"I am certain there is more to learn about the stone and why it is here with us," she whispers. Gia removes the diary from her arms and places it on her nightstand. She pats the outside cover, closes her eyes, and attempts to find sleep.

◆

Chapter Eighteen

The early morning sun begins to reveal itself over the ocean's horizon, and the doorbell at Locket Manor bongs. The noise wakes the sleeping house; all three women stumble to the door. Gaillynn swings it open with a huff. Two police officers stand before her—the brisk morning air barges into Locket Manor.

"Good morning, ladies. We have some questions for Gaillynn Amirah."

"That's me. What's up?"

"Oh, you babysat Dondy, huh, Mom?" Ella whispers, her eyebrows pressed together.

"Are you still mad at me, sweet girl?" Gaillynn takes the robe Ella is pushing toward her and wraps it around herself. Ella ignores Gaillynn's question.

"Can we come in and speak with you in private?"

"Umm, okay. Come in. I'll make coffee. Why so early?"

"We are looking for someone, and we think you may have been the last one to see him." They enter the house and follow Gaillynn. She ties the bathrobe around her waist and yawns.

"Okay, well, I haven't been out of my house since Friday, so I haven't seen anyone lately," Gaillynn points to the stairs. "Mom, Ella, you can go back to bed."

Gaillynn leads the police officers through the house and into the first-floor kitchen. The officers admire the home as they travel through.

Gaillynn shoos Dondy off of the broad marble island, and she motions the police officers to take a seat. Matching white counter-tops shine with high gloss, and a wall of windows reveals the ocean as far as the eye can see. The orange sun peeks halfway up beyond it.

She presses the button on the coffee and espresso maker, and it begins to hum and steam. The rich smell of coffee fills the air.

Gaillynn's beauty is one of her many weapons. It rivals her wit, which makes her a deadly opponent, and she is well aware of her effect on men.

The police officers, still standing, smile as they watch her busy around her kitchen gathering sugar and cream and three large cof-fee mugs. "Sit down, please." They remove their uniform hats and sit down on her command.

Ella peers around the corner. Maybe her mother was up to something while they were gone. She dashes off to her room for her computer pad and stylus. She tiptoes toward the kitchen and hides around the corner where she is out of sight but can hear ev-ery word.

Ella taps the black screen, which lights up, revealing her elec-tronic notepad in legal-sized yellow. Ella deletes the crossed-out notes from the previous night's conversation with her mother and readies her stylus. "I knew that something'd been up with you, Mom." She leans against a wall and lowers her body to the floor. "We were gone for two days, Mom; what the heck went on?" Ella whispers to herself.

"It's about Friday night, actually," admits one of the officers with a nervous smile. "Did you go to Union Station Pub this past Friday night?"

Ella writes: "Union Station Pub."

"Yes, I did. My God, I'm sorry, I got pretty drunk."

Ella huffs from the hall. Gaillynn and the two police officers turn their heads and see no one. Deciding to ignore it, Gaillynn continues, "So my mom and I usually take my daughter to this bed and breakfast every year for her birthday, and this was her four-teenth birthday, but we got a new cat, so I stayed home to babysit, and they left on Friday. I missed them. I know that sounds pathetic, but I was lonely. Locket Manor is a big house, and I was all alone." The officers shake their heads.

Gaillynn leans over the counter toward the officers; she unnec-essarily stirs her black coffee with a spoon. She then slips the spoon in her mouth and sucks it, dips it into their steaming cups, and stirs each one. Her robe drops open and reveals the soft skin and the roundness of her full breasts exposed by her partially unbut-toned pajama top. The officers shift in their seats.

"Umm, so how did you get home that night?" one stutters through the question.

"Cooper Blethen drove me." Ella's eyes pop open. She adds his name to what she decides is a list of evidence. Cooper Chandler Blethen.

"And then what happened?" asks the same officer.

"Ugh, this is embarrassing. Cooper kissed me. And, I let him. And then things got somewhat hot and heavy, but we kept our clothes on, but he smelled so good, and I was so drunk, and then I thought I was going to throw up, so we stopped, and I told him he had to leave, and he left.

"When I woke up in the morning and saw my car in the drive-way and remembered what happened, I couldn't believe I made him walk back to the bar or home or where ever he went. I was hoping he would call me back. After everything that happened in high school, I feel like I understand why he did what he did. It was an accident, and he has apologized to me so many times."

"Have you heard from him since Friday night?"

"No. As I said, I was hoping Cooper would call me, and we could try again sober. Why? What's going on?"

"He hasn't gone home yet since that night," one of the officers adds.

"What do you mean he hasn't gone home yet? Is he missing?" Gaillynn stands up and holds a hand to her almost bare chest. She adds a gasp for a dramatic effect.

"His mother and stepfather have reported him missing, and they said you left a voicemail message at their home phone number Saturday morning."

"Yes. Yes. I did. I wanted to thank Cooper for driving me and my car home. But we, well. He left. I realized he must have walked. Or maybe he called a cab? Did you try that?"

"Yes, there is only one cab company in town, and they didn't get any calls that night. However, it appears he made it back to the bar because we found his cell phone there."

"He was with friends. I remember seeing him with a big group of guys from high school. Any luck with them?"

"No, also no luck with them. None of Cooper's friends saw him again after he left with you. We have to ask you, Ms. Amirah, are you still upset with Cooper because of Robbie's death?"

Ella's mouth drops open. Her eyes fill with tears. She writes her thoughts down on her computer. Cooper Chandler killed my father?

Ella recalls the version of the story she has been told repeatedly by her mother: *My father died from an attack at the mill where he worked. He was there with my mother when he asked her to marry him, and someone broke in.*

"What do you think? Of course, I was upset. He killed Robbie, the father of my daughter. I was furious. For a long time." Gaillynn embraces her heartbreak and summons honest tears for Robbie. She begins to cry. "Cooper was a stupid kid, with an ego too big for him to handle. He wanted to be the tough guy, and he thought Robbie was raping me. I understand that now. We are older now, and he has apologized many times. He served his time. And he gave me a ride home, took care of me when I was drunk, and he was delightful about it." Gaillynn wipes the tears from her eyes and sniffs her running nose.

Ella scribbles out the question and rewrites, "Cooper Chandler killed my father," followed by "Last Chandler missing." Tears empty down her cheeks and drip onto the screen.

One of the police officers pushes a receipt from Davis's security toward her. "This is a pretty hefty security system you purchased and had installed just one week ago—the day Cooper got out of prison. Was it turned on Friday night?"

"No, it wasn't. I have no idea how that system works. It was a waste of money," says Gaillynn.

"Then why did you get it?"

"My mother. She thinks someone is going to steal her Van Gogh's View of Aries painting. She was worried someone would come while she was away this year for my daughter's birthday. Please don't tell her it wasn't on while she was gone; she will never trust me again." Gaillynn presses her fingers under her eyes.

"Okay, Ms. Amirah, thank you, we are sorry to upset you. We have no other questions for now. The detectives at the station may want your statement at some point. Would you be willing to do that?"

"Yes. Of course. Anything."

Ella stomps into the room with her computer and stylus; her cheeks are wet with tears. Ella huffs at her mother and pounds a heel into the floor. "You forgive him? He killed my father, and you forgive him? You kissed him?" She steps toward her mother. "I hate you."

"Oh no, honey, I will always be mad at him."

Ella turns her back to her mother and addresses the police officers. "What does he look like? What was he wearing?"

"Leave those kinds of questions for us, young lady," one of the officers replies as he stands up and replaces his hat to his head.

"I can help you. Just tell me everything you know about Cooper Chandler, and we can work together," Ella suggests.

"So, do you plan on becoming a detective someday or something?" asks one of the officers.

The question pushes Gaillynn over the edge. She has reached her limit on remaining calm. "Why would you ask Robbie's daughter such a stupid question? Because of you, she just overheard who murdered her father, and you think she wants to help because she wants to be a detective when she grows up?" Gaillynn emerges from behind the counter and points to the front door. "Get out of my house."

The officers realize how insensitive the comment was and obey Gaillynn. They turn and begin walking out of the kitchen. "We're so sorry, Ms. Amirah."

Gaillynn wipes the tears from her eyes and waves at her daughter behind the backs of the officers. She mouths the words, "Upstairs now," and points toward the stairs. Ella ignores her mother and continues her interrogation.

"What kind of car does he drive? Does he have a job? Does he have a girlfriend?"

"That's a great question." The two police officers look at each other, and one asks the other, "Does he have a girlfriend?"

Ella's eyes light up. She wipes the tears from her face. "Maybe he is with her, and she is so mad that he drove my mom home that she won't let him leave her sight." Ella walks out of the kitchen while she scratches notes into her computer. In all caps, she writes: "MOM IS HIDING SOMETHING!"

The police officers leave, and Gaillynn locks the door behind them.

"Grammy!" Ella yells, then turns to Gaillynn. "Mom, we need to talk."

"There is nothing to talk about; everything's fine, my sweet girl. It's all under control."

Gia rushes down the stairs.

Ella throws an I-told-you-so look to her grandmother. "What is under control, Mom? Seriously. What happened this weekend?"

"Let's make breakfast." Gaillynn wraps her arms around the shoulders of her mother and daughter and guides them into the kitchen. Ella breaks her shoulders free of her mother's embrace. She sits on the window seat overlooking the ocean.

Gaillynn lifts the cup of black coffee to her mouth. The scent of fresh coffee and suspicion fills the air.

"Get ready for school, Ella. You're going to high school," announces Gaillynn.

Ella lifts her head; her anger dissipates. Ella goes to her mother and hugs her.

"I'm sorry about your dad, sweetie." Gaillynn returns the hug.

"I'm still mad about Cooper, Mom. But I have to get ready for my first day of high school. Will you call them and warn them that I am coming?"

"Of course."

Ella leaps out of the kitchen.

PART THREE

◆

Legend

of

Queens

$$\blacklozenge$$

Chapter Nineteen

Mr. Qu scribbles his short name across the chalkboard in extra-large print for his new student. It is Ella's first biology class of her high school career. Though high school classes began two months ago for everyone else, today is Ella's start date.

Mr. Qu sputters through a spirited explanation of the syllabus for Ella's benefit. "We will continue our study of cell biology, reproduction, genetics, evolution, oh, and the wonderful laws of genetics, and the principles of chromosomal inheritance, and what makes us all different." His excitement, exploding from his whiny voice, muffled through his nasal cavity with a strong Cantonese accent, makes it difficult for Ella to understand what he's saying.

She stops scribbling on her notebook, looks up at Mr. Qu, giggles, and tries to make sense of his ramblings. She catches the word "inheritance," and raises her hand right away.

"Oh my goodness. A question from our new student already. Yes, yes, please go ahead, ask your question," sputters Mr. Qu with enthusiasm.

Ella hesitates. She realizes she must be careful with her words. She studies the shine of Mr. Qu's combed hair pressed flat with the majority pushed to one side, the equal luster of his oily skin, and the roundness of his large pores. His trendy, wide-rimmed black glasses seem a little at odds with his nerdy science teacher esthetic.

In less than ten seconds, Ella considers how best to gain knowledge of the stone while not giving away her secret. She realizes that no one in this room knows her, and she could quickly come off as a know-it-all. The eyes of her new peers study her with judgment. She craves answers and hopes high school will provide them.

She takes a deep breath, swallows her eagerness for fear of being ridiculed, then speaks. "Mr. Qu, you mentioned inheritance and how we are all different. What about how we can be the same? Like in families. What makes some traits so strong? Is there energy to cells that can determine which ones become inherited beyond random chromosomal pairing?"

Quick breaths draw in around her. As far as her classmates could remember, the energy of cells and heredity had not come up in earlier years' science classes.

"That," he says with emphasis, "is a good question. An intriguing question. What a scientific mind you have. We will put all of the pieces together, and it will make sense to you by the time you take your midterms."

Ella's body slouches. *How can I wait that long to learn how the stone connects to us? Why and how are we linked? Why do we only have female children? It just seems like something is missing, and no one has ever pressed to solve this mystery. It has all just become tradition.*

"Legacy," she says out loud by mistake.

Mr. Qu hears her. He pushes his glasses up and asks, "Legacy?"

"Oh, umm, I was just thinking of a poem I could write about heredity. I could call it Legacy," she lies.

"Interesting. I would like to read that."

◆

Ella's first day of high school passes with incredible slowness. She makes her way through it with high anxiety but without being bullied or ridiculed for being the town's genius or the town's richest genius, nor for her choice of first-day clothing—a difficult decision. She chose casual and comfortable. Black leggings, new Nike running sneakers with a gold swoosh, the necklace her grandmother gave her for her birthday hidden beneath her favorite yellow sweatshirt.

When Ella returns home that day, her mother greets her at the already open door. Gaillynn wraps her in a hug. Ella, unprepared for the embrace, does not return her mother's affection.

"How did it go? Was it as awesome as you'd hoped?"

Ella pushes past her mother into the living room, drops her heavy backpack on the floor, and slumps into the recliner. Ella rests her head back and closes her eyes.

"That bad?" asks her mother.

"No, not terrible; I'm just exhausted from being on edge. And the police woke us up so early. I expected—" Ella stops to take a deep breath. "I waited for something terrible to happen since I got my way. You know, a bad for something good." Ella's eyes meet her mother's. She can see the love and concern in her mother's stare. At this moment, it annoys her, and Ella doesn't feel up to acknowledging her mother's compassion. Ella moves her eyes away from her mother and settles them on the stone, which sways as the enormous clock keeps time.

"The stone doesn't react to normal things like high school, sweetie. Just powerful things like love."

Ella's grandmother sits on the floor in her meditation pose in front of the stone. Gia's breathing is loud and deep. Her arms are outstretched to each side with her hands resting on her knees; her palms face the ceiling, and she touches her thumbs to her middle fingers. Her ankles cross in a childlike crisscross position.

This position of Gia has become a familiar sight for Ella. Today, though Ella is very tired and doesn't feel the same level of enthusiasm as her grandmother, she decides to join her on the floor. She had fantasized that going back to the basics—Science 101 would answer all of her questions. Instead, it was a complete disappointment, except for finding her new favorite teacher, Mr. Qu.

Ella recalls the wall of advanced science books she spent the last four years reading. She also whizzed through doctorate classes offered online through the University of Maine. She knew everything—cell DNA, genetics, cell reproduction, geoscience, gemology, and mineralogy. Ella found no answers. Her last shred of hope was that her high school science teacher would surprise her.

"I'm making cookies to celebrate your first day of high school. Your favorite—chocolate chip with white chips and M&Ms. I hope you will eat some; they're a special treat made with love. And you deserve it, honey," Gaillynn announces, then leaves Ella and her grandmother to themselves on the living room floor.

"Mom. Why are you acting so nice to me? I'm too tired to be angry at you anymore." Ella huffs. She adds, "I'm in high school now, Mom. Cookies? Really?"

In the kitchen, Gaillynn rolls her eyes, knowing Ella won't be able to resist and that her expressions of a moody teenager only show how much little girl is still present.

Ella wiggles into the same pose as her grandmother, and their knees touch. The stone brightens, reacting to the closeness of more than one Amirah woman, and enhanced by the connection between their bodies. The stone embraces Gia and Ella with warmth. Golden inclusions within the stone's body swirl with activity.

Ella smiles. This comforting connection with the stone makes her so happy. Her soul is becomes nourished, and her imagination is excited. Her immune system is flourishing, and her enlightenment becomes more robust, and her body healthier. She concentrates on these feelings, then turns her focus to what she can hear.

The hum—the hum she has always heard and the same she and her grandmother heard together at the beach at Eden's Garden.

Their minds are linked. The caroling of many women's voices soothes them. As the hum becomes more pronounced instead of blackness behind their closed eyes comes a blueish gold brightness. It is the color of the emotions and feelings they are experiencing: pure ecstasy. They settle into this grand connection to something so wonderful, yet they want more.

The intoning begins to change to a rhythm, like words, but not words. Yet, somehow they become clear; Ella and Gia understand. A story of survival and death unfolds—thirst, hunger, and torture. The stone needs something.

The stone pulls at Ella.

What is torturing the stone? The stone thirsts for something, the same thing she desires. But what is it? And the deaths caused by the stone have been warnings. All an attempt to get closer to its purpose. But what is the goal of the stone? Ella thinks.

The stone's desire for what it craves engulfs their minds and bodies. A black fog clouds their intuitive vision—an insurmountable thirst. Their mouths become dry, and their chests fill with a painful longing so sorrowful their hearts ache.

Ella's hand lifts toward the stone—an involuntary movement. Her fingers tremble as they get closer and closer. She touches the front of the clock. Her fingertips bounce against the glass between her and the stone. Ella's eyes pop open. She realizes her hand has traveled toward the stone without her control. She eyes her grandmother, whose eyes remain closed. Ella returns to her original pose and seals her eyelids closed.

Ella concentrates on this feeling of longing: *the stone is sick* because *it needs something, and so are we.* Ella struggles to understand. The stone makes them feel so fantastic; it keeps them healthy, strong, and happy, but she now understands a profound sadness.

"Alone." Ella opens her eyes to meet her grandmother's. "Grammy, what did you just hear?"

"Humming. Humming of thousands of voices. The women's voices, from the beach." Gia's eyes are wide. "They've come back to us."

"They're back, Grammy." Tears drip down their faces. They hug and hold each other, wrapping their trembling bodies around each other's.

"Ella, did it sound like the humming was trying to tell you something?"

"Yes. It was telling me that the stone needs something, as do we. Kind of like there is more intended for us in this life. Is that what you heard?"

"Yes, that too, but they showed me our planet, its oceans, forests, mother animals with their babies, the soil, and then a feeling of suffocation. Like the mothers are suffocating. The women's hum was soothing but was telling me something horrible. Like there is a problem to fix, and the time draws near. I saw the queen again. She was standing alone on a jagged piece of earth in the middle of the ocean with waves crashing over her feet. Did you see her, Ella?"

"No, I didn't. But I saw the ocean below me. I could feel the cold water washing over my feet, and I felt powerful and all-knowing. I felt like I was part of a larger being. I was part of Earth." Ella becomes emotional and begins to cry. They hug. "I think there is a problem to solve, Grammy."

"Ella, you were what I was seeing. You are the future queen."

"Me? I'm the queen?"

"I have seen her before—you. Marguerite is right. You have a destiny for something greater."

"Grammy, I don't know about any of that. It seems impossible."

"And this stone isn't impossible?" she says while pointing at their coveted ore.

"I know."

"Ella, I need to go to my Zen garden for a little while. I want to think about this for a bit. I love you, sweetie." Gia stands up and heads to her garden sanctuary.

Ella's desire to touch the stone continues. She studies her hands with doubt. She shakes her head, tiptoes to the clock, and opens the glass door. She stops the slow swing of the pendulum and wiggles on the chains holding the stone in place. The chains are tight, but the stone moves a little. With some prying, Ella relieves the ore of its shackles.

Gaillynn begins talking to Ella from in the kitchen, but Ella is oblivious to what she is saying. Ella wraps her hands around the stone and becomes enthralled by its effect on her.

Her entire body tingles with weightlessness and delight. Ella's direct contact with the stone warms her with love so pure it is like the stone is injecting her with a drug. Ella's muscles fortify, and she now hovers about two inches from the floor. She has unknowingly become resistant to injury and more potent with strength beyond human. The stone's brilliance brightens the room: Ella and the stone share equal arousal in touching each other.

Ella is unaware of what is happening to her physical being by holding the stone. Her skin gleams a polished glow, and her acne clears; her hair blooms and lengthens into shining thick curls. The most glorious change of all is that touching the stone bestows Ella with an energized contentment and abilities that she has yet to discover.

A sudden, banging knock on the front door of Locket Manor causes Ella to drop the stone. Her levitation ceases and her feet stomp to the floor.

The hypnotic connection has broken. Ella reaches for the stone, but before her hands make contact, the stone emits a loud sound that shakes the entire home. Louder than a crack of thunder—more the sound of a sudden shift within the earth's crust. A tiny piece of the stone splits off.

Ella inhales. "Oh no." She retrieves the decorative serving tray from the ottoman and places the stone and the fractured piece on the tray—Ella bolts out of the living room with the stone on the serving tray.

Gaillynn walks toward the door and passes Ella in the entry room. A shadow of a large-bodied caller on the other side blocks the sunlight.

"Ella!" Gaillynn's voice is firm and piercing. Then she whispers, "What on earth are you doing with the stone? And what was that noise?"

"I don't know. It wasn't me. I'm studying the stone. For science," answers Ella.

Ella hurries up the tall stairs, down the hall, into her bedroom, and slams the door. She places the serving tray and its contents on her bed, and she jumps up. She studies the brilliance of the stone—its color, its heavier-than-expected weight, and how holding it made her feel so powerful.

◆

Gaillynn opens the front door to find Roger Blethen standing on her porch.

"Hello, Mr. Blethen. This is an unexpected visit. How can I help you?" Gaillynn asks.

"Gaillynn, can I speak with you about the last time you saw Cooper? I know you have spoken to the police, but I am curious about what could have happened to him and thought maybe you and I could talk. You know, maybe figure this out."

Gaillynn inhales the spicy scent of dishonesty. She eyes his thumbs pressed inside the pockets of his tight blue jeans. Her ears perk at the sound of treason. The falseness in his monotone voice reveals his game. Gaillynn welcomes him into her home.

"Oh, I know, Mr. Blethen, I cannot believe he is still missing. Have they found any new leads? Please come in, and we can talk. Would you like coffee?" Gaillynn attempts to lead him to the kitchen, but he doesn't follow. He goes into the living room instead.

He is looking for something. Gaillynn watches him.

"Why did you all of a sudden decide to forgive Cooper?" he asks.

Gaillynn leans into one of her hips and crosses her arms. He searches the room. His boldness causes her fists to clench. "We are both older now, and he served his time. He seemed genuinely sorry. Did he speak with you about what happened?"

"What happened? To what are you referring?"

"The night he beat Robbie to death," she says.

"No, he didn't ever discuss Robbie with me. I mean, he didn't know me very well. He was in prison when I married his mother." Roger turns to Gaillynn. He studies her from head to toe. Her beauty awakens a fear in him, and because of this fear, Roger becomes angry. He focuses on her messy hair—this helps him regain control.

"I have in my possession proof of your secret." Roger takes a deep breath and a seat on the settee in front of the tall clock.

"My secret? And what is that, Roger?" Gaillynn asks as she moves to sit beside him. The hair on her arms stands up.

"The secret that that clock has a stone that has power." He points at the clock and the empty chains without the stone.

◆

In her bedroom, Ella retrieves a magnifying glass from her desk and examines every stone angle. "You are so heavy," she says. "Your irregular round shape resembles a giant uncut precious gem. Like a rare blue diamond with luminescence and boldness in color. If a gem cutter polished you just so, I imagine you would become a blinding jewel." Ella lays back onto her pillows with the stone on her tummy.

"I feel so different. Touching you has changed me." She pulls her necklace out from under her sweatshirt and runs her fingers around the diamonds. "Wait until Grammy touches you."

The necklace feels different. Ella inspects the pendant. "Oh no," Ella exclaims in a pronounced whisper. "The center gem is gone." She spies the small fractured piece of the family stone and has an idea.

◆

Downstairs, Gaillynn becomes aware that Ella has exited her bedroom and now descends the stairs. Gaillynn stands up to shield Roger's view of Ella passing the living room. Gaillynn explains, "Oh, that clock is just one of many antiques that have been passed down to me from our family over the years."

Then in almost a whisper, she asks, "What do you mean by stone? I would love to have a stone that has power. Like a super-power?" Gaillynn smiles at the perfect timing of Ella's stone removal, and she taps her lips with her pointer finger. *Jessica Blethen's second hus-*

band seeks the stone. Somehow she had not contained the story with Cooper in his resting vault. "Jesus." Roger tilts his head.

◆

Ella rushes past her mother and a man she doesn't recognize in the living room. She can hear that they are talking, and when she passes, she catches a glimpse of them both gazing at the clock, and this man is pointing a long finger toward it. Ella stops to listen. She hears her mother explaining that it is just one of the many antiques passed down to her. Relieved, Ella continues into the library to her mother's antique oak desk. She searches for the chair so she can sit down, but it is gone. She pulls the bronze handle and fishes through the typical junk drawer contents until she finds the super glue.

Ella sprints past the living room and leaps up the stairs back to her bedroom.

Ella drips glue onto the center of the pendant of the necklace from her grandmother and replaces the missing stone with the fractured piece of her family ore. Her fingers stick to the quick-drying glue—she peels it off with a wince and an "Oops."

Without replacing the glue's cover, she tosses it onto the tray and lays down on her bed. She fixes her eyes at the large glass chandelier high above her head, twinkling through the sheer lace netting surrounding the tall pencil posts of her bed. She presses the gem to her chest. This tiny piece, this close to her skin, also makes her different. Just like holding the entire stone in her hands, she feels better, stronger, healthier, and the sensation of longing diminishes.

A heavy blanket of the stone's love wraps around her body. She closes her eyes, and the stone commands her to drift into a deep sleep.

◆

Downstairs, Roger is confused. "Wait, doesn't it have a stone the color unlike any other? Where the hell is it?" asks Roger.

"Are you talking about that old urban legend about the clock measuring, predicting, good and evil? Good Lord, Roger, you don't believe that, do you? That was just a made-up story told to the children in our family. I guess it got around. It was a good story.

"You know, like the scary story everyone has heard with the hand tapping on the windshield of the car when the girlfriend is hiding in the back, and the boyfriend went to get gas."

"No. Don't give me that shit. I don't trust you, and I think you had something to do with Cooper's disappearance and, I'm betting, his murder." Roger stands up and moves toward Gaillynn. He puffs out his chest, widens his arms, and he leans over her.

Gaillynn puts a hand to his chest and pushes him away from her.

"That is crazy. Cooper is one of the biggest people I know—how could I have done anything to him he didn't want me to?"

Gaillynn's blood boils, and she becomes impatient. Ella is home. She needs to get Roger out of this house.

"I hear Jessica wants nothing to do with you, Roger. How does that feel? Is that what this is all about? Is this a pathetic and desperate attempt to find a reason for her to take you back?"

Roger faces Gaillynn and pulls his hand back like he is going to strike her. He restrains himself. Gaillynn is thrilled to have manifested a rage within him. The thrill of a battle rushes through her.

"Roger, why don't I call the police and have them join our conversation?" Gaillynn reaches for her phone.

"No." Roger lurches at her and grabs her wrist. Gaillynn stares at his hand wrapped around her arm. He is holding on so tight that his skin is a mixture of white and red. "This is between you and me.

I don't know who you think you are, but you will not get away with this. I will make sure of it. Why don't you just tell me the truth?"

Her eyes brighten at his attempt to intimidate her. His want of the stone has turned to desire, a thirst he yearns to quench. Gaillynn has identified a weakness: greed. Her strategy unfolds in her mind. *Another man is seeking power by way of manipulation; how perfect. This is a sport I excel at.*

She places her free hand on his, still grasping her arm. She caresses his skin. "Okay, Roger, let's talk. I think I know what can help us both. But not right now. My mother and daughter are here, and I don't want them to hear anything. Come back tomorrow at ten in the morning for coffee, and we will talk. We can work all of this out."

He releases his grasp of her wrist. He smiles and pulls on his tight white Oxford shirt, smoothing it down over his protruding belly. His breathing is heavy and stressed. Gaillynn tilts her head.

"Roger, are you okay?" She smiles. The stone's magic is gripping his airway.

Roger ignores her question. He is surprised by his sudden fatigue and tightness in his chest; he wipes the sweat from his forehead. "Tuesday at ten. See you tomorrow then." He turns and leaves the house.

Chapter Twenty

Gaillynn races upstairs to Ella's room and is relieved to see the door is closed. She goes in and sits next to Ella on her bed. She pushes Ella's hair out of her sleeping face and kisses her forehead. Ella's body temperature feels much warmer than usual. Gaillynn puts her hand on Ella's forehead with concern.

"Ella, wake up." Her mother shakes her awake. Ella's eyes squint open. "Please don't take the stone out of the clock. Why did you do that?"

"Who was that guy?" Ella redirects.

"Actually, well, he knew Cooper Blethen. Do you remember the man that I went to high school with? The one that went missing?"

"Yeah, you mean Cooper Chandler. So, why was he here?"

"He was just passing by and stopped in to ask about the night I saw Cooper at Union Station," she says.

"And you don't think that is odd?"

"No. Ella, it's no big deal, sweet girl. When people lose someone they love, it can be hard to stop talking or asking about them. That's all," she explains.

"Mom, I just think it's weird that he is here and not the mother. I think he is up to something."

"Come downstairs and put the stone back."

"Mom, you carry the stone. Hold it in your hands. See how it makes you feel. I'm serious; you have to. Mom, here." Ella forces the stone into her mother's hands, and in fear of dropping it, Gaillynn grabs onto it with both hands. The stone blankets her with tranquility and clarity. She becomes enchanted with the stone's brilliant intoxication.

"Whoa," Gaillynn whispers.

Gia saunters in. "Hey Gail, are you two coming down for dinner?" Gia freezes at the sight of the stone in Gaillynn's hands.

"Hold this, Mom," Gaillynn instructs, then forces the stone into Gia's hands.

"Why? Oh. Oh my. What is happening?" asks Gia.

"Okay, listen, I know you are going to be mad, but I needed to find out how and why the stone connects to us, and science class isn't going to help me, and Grammy and I heard the humming of women's voices today, and we felt like the stone was trying to tell us something, so I took it out of the clock to study it myself, and, well, when that guy knocked on the door, I kind of dropped it."

"What?" Gaillynn and Gia say in unison.

"It's okay, the stone is fine, but, well, a tiny piece flaked off, and I glued it to my necklace, and I feel just like you do, Gram, right now. And all it took was this little tiny piece."

"Ella, I don't know what wearing that will do to you. I think you have a temperature. We have never done this before. What if it is too much and harmful to us?" Gaillynn says.

"Mom, seriously, does it feel dangerous? It feels good. Doesn't it?" Ella says.

Gia cradles the stone in one arm like she is holding a baby and pats the stone's belly with her other. "Yes," says Gia. "It feels terrific." She hugs the bundle to her chest and smiles.

Gaillynn interrupts, "Okay, put the stone back in the clock and let's have dinner. We can talk about it while we eat."

◆

At the dinner table, the women are silent. The stone, secured in its prison inside the clock, presses far to the right—a persistent fixation North indicating happiness and a reach for its women.

Ella smiles while eating. The food on her plate is nearly gone, yet her mother and grandmother toss mounds of mashed potatoes around with their forks.

Gia elbows Gaillynn and points to Ella. They tilt their heads to the side and study her. Ella's skin glows, her hair shines and floats weightlessly into the air.

"What?" Ella asks.

"Go look in the mirror," orders her mother.

"Why, what's wrong?"

"Oh nothing," answers her grandmother with a chuckle, "You're just glowing."

"And you smell like brown sugar! Do you smell that, Mom?" Gaillynn asks.

"I smell maple syrup," answers Gia.

Ella goes to the ancient, gold-framed mirror opposite the dining room's table. "Mom just made cookies. Oh. Wow. Awesome!" Ella caresses her new, fuller, longer hair and touches her face where her acne was noticeable before. "It's gone."

The women race to the living room. Gaillynn frees the stone and presses it into Ella's hands. "Okay, do whatever you did before and see if you can get another piece."

"Two more pieces," corrects Gia.

"Okay, I was right here in front of the clock. See that small dent on the floor? I dropped it there." Ella drops the stone. They lower themselves to the floor. Nothing fractured off the gem. Ella picks it up again, raises it slightly higher, and drops it again. Nothing. "Well, I did reach my hands toward it when it made that loud cracking noise."

"That's what that noise was?" Asks Gaillynn.

Ella opens her palms toward the stone but doesn't touch it.

Gaillynn and Gia copy her. Locket Manor's foundation shakes and the sound of an ice glacier cracking against the Earth produces three specks of the stone.

"Woo-hoo," they cheer. Gaillynn sweeps them into her hand.

"I have necklaces we can use upstairs in my bedroom," announces Gaillynn. They go to her bedroom.

Gaillynn and Gia skirt around the safe that holds Cooper at an exaggerated distance. Gaillynn retrieves a small jewelry box from her dresser and empties it on her bed. She fishes out two gold necklaces. Gaillynn plucks a ruby out of one of them and a pearl out of the other. She places the ruby, the pearl, and the extra stone fragment into a white ring box, stows them inside the square jewelry box and returns it to her dresser.

"How did you stick it in there?" asks Gaillynn pointing to the necklace around Ella's neck.

"Superglue. It's in my room. I'll go get it." Ella bolts to her room for the glue. "Oh no," Ella hollers.

"What?" her mother yells back.

Ella returns with the open glue. "It's dry."

"Is there any more?" asks her mother.

"No, that was the last one."

"My God, child. When will you learn to put the caps back on things?"

"We have to get more," says Gia.

◆

The three women insert themselves into Gaillynn's red Mercedes. Gaillynn backs out of the garage before they are seatbelted and buzzes over the cobblestones. She whips the car out of the driveway, causing their headlights to shine on the face of a passing motorist.

"Oh hey, that was my science teacher. Mr. Qu. Does he live on our street?"

"Your science teacher is Leonard Qu?"

"Yeah, why?"

Gaillynn looks at her mother with wide eyes. "I went to high school with him. He was an exchange student from Hong Kong. He lived with the Blethen's."

"You mean the Chandlers," clarifies Ella.

CHAPTER TWENTY-ONE

Gaillynn drives to Harvey's Hardware & General Store.

"I'll be right back." She slams the car door harder than necessary.

"I'm not sitting here." Ella exits the car leaving Gia alone. Gia watches Ella chase after Gaillynn. The car is too quiet, and the air inside is too still. Gia gets out and hustles in behind them.

In an aisle adjacent to the glue, Andie focuses on the hundreds of swatches of gray paint. She is distracted by an intense warmth and the sweet smell of brown sugar. "Gaillynn?" she whispers to herself. The familiar heat and body odor of her best friend whisks through the air. She follows the smell with her nose to the ceiling. Andie overhears whispering coming from the next aisle over.

"Mom, you only need one tube. Why are you buying so many?"

"Ella, you cannot trust superglue. It never works the first time and, as you have proven, leave the cap off once, and it's toast." Gaillynn fills both hands with packages of superglue, attempting to ignore her preoccupation with Roger Blethen and Leonard Qu. Her quest to silence their secrets is incomplete.

Gia approaches and whispers, "Gail, my God; we don't need that much. The pieces are tiny."

"Shut up, Mom. I told you two to stay in the car. Jesus Christ, come on, let's go."

"Do you have to swear, Mom?"

"Yes. I do. Is that okay with you? Go out to the car. Now."

Ella huffs. She presses the stone on her necklace between her fingers and exits the store. She climbs into the back seat of the car and crosses her arms. Gia follows and returns to the passenger seat in the front.

Andie steps out from the aisle of paint cans and stands behind Gaillynn, who waits to pay.

"Gail?" she says.

Gaillynn turns with a huff and with the dozens of superglue packages in her arms. "Andie," Gaillynn remembers hanging upon her the day Cooper visited, and she knows she is about to be rude again, but she has no choice. *God, I'm a terrible friend.*

Gaillynn turns her back to Andie and throws the glue on the counter. "Can you hurry, please? I'm in a huge rush," Gaillynn says to the clerk at the checkout counter.

Andie puts her hand on Gaillynn's shoulder. "Gail, is everything okay?"

"Wonderful." Gaillynn fishes out a fifty-dollar bill from her jeans pocket, throws it on the counter, and flashes a quick, guilty smile at Andie.

"It doesn't seem wonderful, Gail. Can I help?"

Gaillynn grabs the bag of glue and turns to leave without waiting for her change. "Nope. Everything's fine. Thanks, Andie. Nice to see you." Gaillynn walks so quickly out of the store that her hips twitch from side to side.

◆

Gaillynn, Ella, and Gia return from their brief outing with more tubes of superglue than they will ever need.

"I still don't understand why you bought so much glue, Mom. It only takes a drop," Ella complains as they enter Locket Mano then climb the stairs to Gaillynn's bedroom.

"Ella, I don't trust superglue. Sometimes you can't get it out, sometimes it all comes out at once. It's a nightmare." They dump the bag of glue on Gaillynn's bed and open the first tube. It works perfectly.

"See, Mom?" Ella smiles and crosses her arms.

"Hold a necklace, know-it-all," says Gaillynn with a smile.

Ella holds a necklace while Gaillynn glues one piece of the stone to it, then the other. Ella wraps one around each of their necks.

The tiny pieces of stone glimmer and glow with happiness, and so do the women. All three of them lie on Gaillynn's king-sized bed. Ella kicks her feet up in the air and rests them on one of the tall corner posts. Gaillynn leans back against the mound of pillows at the elaborate headboard, and Gia rests her head on Gaillynn's thigh. Each presses her palm against their newly-charmed necklaces.

All three Amirah women touch the stone and unknowingly touch each other. This connection has been the stone's ultimate goal—to bridge each in the most powerful way—the intended way. United and their skin glow; the air fills with the most beautiful scent of sugar, honey, molasses, and maple.

◆

Leonard Qu drives his car through the open iron gates and onto the cobblestone driveway. Locket Manor grows more considerable as he approaches, reminding him of castles he's seen only in textbooks.

With rumors of such an evil curse, he imagines this castle named Locket Manor was forged with dungeons to hide its demons and is likely the only place he wouldn't be surprised to discover the corpses of dragons.

A golden glow radiates out of a large window on the third floor and brightens as he nears. Leonard is overcome with a glorious feeling that he is doing the right thing. He places his right hand over his heart, takes a deep breath, and continues toward the estate.

As he ascends the grand staircase to the front door, he senses sadness. The beauty here is the price they have paid for the loss. It's not a gift. It's a trade. A wager—a gamble they couldn't help but make.

And then, an emotion so heavy his knees shake, wraps around his shoulders. "Hell, what is happening?" He cannot describe it, but he understands; something on the tip of his tongue—a feeling so strong and vivid.

"Alone," he whispers. "Gail?" he says. He shakes off the feeling and lets fear return to pound through his heart and out of his chest. He presses the gold doorbell button on the right of a sturdy wooden door. Again. And again. He scans the grounds and twitches with insecurity.

The three women are in a trance; they don't move. The doorbell rings a third time, finally Gaillynn hears it. She wiggles the other two. The doorbell rings yet again. They hide the necklaces under their shirts and head downstairs together.

"Ella put this back in the clock." Gaillynn hands Ella the stone. Ella replaces it inside the tall clock as instructed. Wrapping the stone in its chains causes a dim in brightness.

Ella smiles at it. "Don't worry. I won't let you stay here long." Gaillynn's gasp at the front door startles Ella.

"Leonard Qu? What the hell are you doing here?"

"Gaillynn, I must talk with you. It's imperative!" His words are quick, and his body fidgets. He peers around the yard and behind himself as if looking for something or someone.

"Why, what is this about?" says Gaillynn.

Leonard surveys the driveway one more time then focuses on Gaillynn with desperation in his movements. His eyes dart from Gaillynn to Gia and Ella. He holds his chest, breathes irregularly, and bends forward over his knees.

"Okay, get in here, Lenny. What the hell is going on?"

"You are all in danger," he announces. "There is someone after the stone. I have come to warn you."

"Oh. Is that right? Have you come to warn us? And you are not after the stone?" Gaillynn asks.

"No. No, I am not. I swear I am not."

"I don't believe you." Gaillynn clutches Leonard's arm.

Feeling her newfound courage, Gia takes his other arm and says, "Yes, I don't believe you either."

Ella and Gaillynn turn to Gia.

"Grammy!"

"What has come over you, Mom? Let go of him; I've got him."

"I'm helping," Gia insists and doesn't let go.

They pull Leonard toward the basement door. He doesn't resist or struggle against them.

"Mom! Mom, stop! Where are you taking him?" Ella asks.

"I am tired of this shit. I've had too much of this today, and Lenny will not have this stone. If I'm wrong, Lenny, I'm sorry. But I cannot take the chance." She forces Leonard down the steep basement stairs faster than he was expecting. He trips at her heels. Gia and Ella are close behind.

"Mom, what are you doing? Stop this, let him go. Mr. Qu, what are you talking about?"

"You may be shocked to find out that I have known about your stone since Cooper went to jail. It is why he killed Robbie." Leonard inhales, "Shoot." His eyebrows push together, and begins to tear up. "Ella, I'm so sorry."

Gaillynn pushes Leonard down into an old wooden chair in the center of the cold, dark basement. She pulls a string above his head, and a dim light flickers above him.

"How do you know about the stone, Lenny?" Gaillynn places her hands on the wooden armrests of his chair and leans her face close to his. She can see the sweat dripping down his nose along with his sliding glasses. She pushes his glasses back up high on his nose and asks again, "How the hell do you know about the stone, Lenny?"

"Gaillynn, you have to trust me. You're in danger. Please hide and hide the stone. Your daughter is not safe here."

Gaillynn moves to the far wall to a panel for the security system. With the touch of a button, a large screen brightens into focus, revealing the front gateway. She enters a code, and they watch the iron gates rip through the years of vine growth and close with a heavy clang.

Gaillynn clicks through each of the different views of the house and sees nothing unusual. She initiates an order to lock all windows and doors and activates the hundreds of cameras and motion detectors inside and out.

"I'm very capable of protecting my daughter, Lenny. Why don't you explain yourself?"

"Someone knows about you and the stone. I fear this person wants to steal it or hurt you or Ella. Or worse, all of you." Lenny begins to cry. The women watch him. Tiny tweets of sadness escape his chest. His breathing remains erratic. Gaillynn giggles. She attempts to hide her fondness for Leonard and reclaims her hardened exterior.

Gaillynn doesn't sense insincerity. She doesn't care. *You are right, Lenny,* she thinks. *Roger Blethen is after the stone. Two men in Locket Manor in one day.* "Huh," she says.

"What, Mom?"

"Nothing, sweet girl."

Ella's head whips to her grandmother. Gia catches on.

"Gail, is there something you're not telling us?"

Gaillynn doesn't respond. She hopes her next move will distract Ella and Gia's curiosity. She retrieves two coils of colorful rope that she bought years ago with intentions to make a swing for Ella and wraps Leonard's body, wrists, and ankles to the chair.

Gaillynn removes one of the four tubes of superglue stowed in her pocket and unscrews the cap. She rips Leonard's glasses from his face and throws them to the floor. Ella picks them up with a huff, wipes them against her shirt, folds them, and sets the glasses on the workbench to her left.

"Mom! What are you going to do with that glue?"

"It all depends on how honest Lenny here is. Lenny, tell me how you know about the stone?" She points the superglue at Leonard's eye. He squeezes his eyes shut and screeches a high-pitched squeal.

"Cooper," he says without hesitation.

"Bullshit. Cooper didn't tell you. I don't believe you." A low growl escapes Gaillynn's throat. She holds his head with her free hand and goes for his eye with the superglue again.

"I took his journal. I read it." Leonard's eyes remain squeezed. "After he got arrested, I went through his room. I found it inside his desk. I read it. He didn't actually tell me. I read about it." Leonard peeks out of his left eye and sees Ella beside him with crossed arms. She attempts to deter her mother by reaching for her the glue. Gaillynn shakes her off.

Leonard squeezes his eyes tighter to ward off a potential glue assault. "His father, Hank, told him the story when he was a kid. It was a bedtime story, and Cooper believed it, even though his dad insisted the story was made it up, but Cooper was obsessed. He wanted the stone for its power. That is why Cooper killed Robbie. And Gaillynn, he wasn't sorry at all. He knew Robbie wasn't raping you. He just wanted to get close to you to get near the stone."

Gaillynn relaxes her grip on his head and drops her hands to her sides. Ella turns from her mother to face him; Leonard has their full attention.

"Cooper was obsessed with your beauty too. He wanted you and the stone as possessions. Cooper assumed the stone was worth millions. He's greedy and heartless, and I hate him. But now Roger Blethen has the journal, and I don't know him very well, but I don't trust him. He seems like a lunatic. You know, volatile." Leonard continues to squeeze his eyes shut. The room is silent.

"Do you believe me, Gail?" His chest heaves, and then Leonard holds his breath. The room is still. He opens one eye at a time and discovers the three women frozen by his words.

"See, Mom, you can trust him. He's known for over fourteen years."

"Okay. Let me think," says Gaillynn. She wants to trust him and realizes that at least part of his story is genuine because Roger Blethen visited her earlier in the day. "I can handle Roger." *But I'm not sure how to deal with Leonard.* Her mind and heart conflict. *He is trying to help me—a man. A man has never wanted to help before.*

Gaillynn's heart flutters. Relief threatens to replace her anxiety. She's not sure letting go of her worry is the best decision right now. "Let's go upstairs."

Ella reaches for the ropes to untie Leonard. Gaillynn touches Ella's arm. "No, Ella. I have to make sure. Leave him. Just for now," instructs Gaillynn. "Please, both of you, come upstairs."

Ella discerns that this is not a time to disobey or question her mother. She lets go of the ropes and follows them up the stairs.

◆

Gaillynn closes and locks the door at the top of the basement stairs. Leonard is all alone and tied in the basement. He wiggles his body under the tight ropes. Leonard's vision is blurry without his glasses. He squints along the perimeter of the room, searching for his glasses, and identifies their familiar shape on a wooden bench nearby.

Leonard struggles to make out his surroundings. A gold wheel identifies a large safe to his right. There are hundreds of boxes of belongings with labels: Christmas, Easter, Halloween, Donate. The face of a demon with red eyes shows through a clear plastic bin. He lets out another high-pitched squeal.

Leonard avoids eye contact with the red-eyed demon and scans the ceiling. Dust sprinkles into his eyes as footsteps pass above him. He blinks away the splintering particles and listens to muffled, unclear voices from the women above him.

◆

Gaillynn, Ella, and Gia gather in the entry room of Locket Manor between the spiral stairs, the grand piano, and the front door. Gia sits at the piano on its wooden bench and twiddles her fingers.

"I knew it the moment you said he's your science teacher and the way our headlights revealed the panic in his eyes. I knew he knew. I trust no one right now, and Lenny is no different," explains Gaillynn.

"Mom, what are you going to do with him?"

"I don't know yet."

"Well, you can't keep him tied up in the basement, and you surely can't put superglue in his eyes. My God, Mom, give that to me," demands Ella. She unfolds her mother's fingers and takes the glue.

"Ella, this is my responsibility, and I will do whatever it takes to keep our secret from getting out."

"Mr. Qu is so nice, though, Mom. I am sure he won't tell anyone about the stone. Maybe he can help us. He's a scientist."

"Nope. Not even Lenny. The sweet exchange student from high school who made me laugh and whom I strangely found cute in a nerdy, super smart, totally trustworthy kind of way. Nope. I don't even trust him."

"Well, you certainly can't kill him too," exclaims Gia. The women go silent. Gaillynn presses her forehead toward her. Gia slumps.

"What? So now we are murderers too?" Ella storms off to the living room, pounding her heels against the floor as she walks. She returns with her fists on her hips and a heaving chest. Ella frowns at her mother.

The antique piano bench under Gia gives way and slams to the wooden floor. Gaillynn and Ella rush to Gia and help her up.

"Let's go talk about all of this somewhere more comfortable," says Gaillynn. She wraps an arm under her mother's and leads her up the stairs.

"Gail, I didn't break a hip, honey. I can walk. I'm fine. It's the piano bench you should be worried about." Gaillynn giggles and continues to hug her mother.

◆

Leonard thinks Ella's angry footsteps pounding the floor are Roger Blethen's, then the piano bench collapsing on the wooden floor sounded like a gunshot. He panics and bounces his body and the chair to free himself. "Gaillynn!" he hollers. The dim light above his head burns out, surrounding him with cold darkness. He screeches another high-pitched trill.

Leonard breathes in the chilled scent of the musty historical home. "I'm trapped. I can't help them." His chest heaves with panicked breathing. Leonard squeezes his biceps and pulls his wrists against the ropes. They don't loosen. Leonard closes his eyes, puckers his lips, and inhales large deep breaths through his mouth. Silence rings in his ears; he whimpers.

The women above him have become silent. Leonard shivers; his heart pounds in his throat. Leonard jerks his body up and down and bounces the chair toward the stairs. He stops and listens once he is close enough to see a small amount of light glowing under the door. More silence. "Gaillynn?"

◆

The women, arm in arm, make their way to Gaillynn's bedroom and arrange themselves into a circle on Gaillynn's large bed.

"Ella, I want you to go to school tomorrow as you normally would. I will talk to Lenny in the morning, and I am sure we can work something out." Gaillynn gives her mother a stern look over Ella's head as if to say, "Shut up, Mom!"

"Mom?" asks Ella. "Did we kill someone?"

"Honey, that is something your grandmother should not have brought up. But trust me, it is not something for you to worry about, sweet girl, and I will tell you all about it someday."

"Oh my God, Mom. It's Cooper, isn't it? Isn't it? You killed Cooper. Oh my God. Mom! Mom, tell me. Did you do it? Please say yes." Ella, on her hands and knees, climbs across the bed to her mother and hugs her mother's waist.

Gaillynn and Gia's eyes meet. Surprise raises their eyebrows.

"I mean, I was so mad at you when I heard you tell the cops that you forgave Cooper for the death of my dad. And that you kissed him. I was like, that is not like my mother, and because of that jerk, I will never know my father. Thank you, Mom."

Gaillynn embraces Ella and kisses her head. "Please don't thank me. I'm sorry for all of this, sweetheart. I'm sorry Cooper killed your father and that there is now another threat in your life. I promise everything will work out. The stone has a plan for us."

Gia pulls herself closer and hugs Gaillynn from behind.

The effects of their unity, while the stone touches their skin, endows them with more paramount and magical strengths than they would ever imagine and have yet to discover. Their skin glows and radiates pure gold and energy. The stone in the clock glows more profoundly than it ever has. Their energy force brightens the rooms throughout the home, and the glare escapes the windows and beams outside.

"I'm not sleeping alone tonight. Not with Mr. Qu tied up in our basement and someone supposedly after the stone. We should all sleep in Mom's bed," suggests Ella.

"I agree," adds Gia.

"I guess so," Gaillynn says, still hugging Ella.

"I love you, Mom," says Ella.

Gaillynn squeezes Ella and kisses her head again. "I love you too, honey."

They separate long enough to ready themselves for bed. The women return in their pajamas and with fresh, minty mouths. Their bodies contact each other as they sleep, and the stone particles around their necks cause a magical reaction. Things around them begin to change.

The gardens grow lusher and more colorful than ever. Locket Manor shines with architectural perfection—its chipped paint smooths. The two hundred years of green oxidation on the copper roves, gutters, windows, and exterior light fixtures gleam with brilliance. The cancerous rust in the iron gates at the end of the driveway clears away, and the windows sparkle with pristine clarity. The wonderful aroma of maple and sugar, which is the usual scent of their bodies, enhances and pours from their skin and escapes the confines of Locket Manor.

Chapter Twenty-Two

That night, in Gia's dream, she stands on the edge of the attic terrace and peers down at the spot where her husband, Toby, fell to his death. She scans the deck around her and finds the sitting statue of Dulcinea surrounded by ferns. "How did you get up here, Dulcinea?"

At the sound of her daughter's laugh, she turns to see Gaillynn and Ella spreading a checkered picnic blanket on the grass at the edge of the lawn near the ocean. The sun is bright, the flowers in the garden are in radiant bloom, and the falling apple blossoms blow by in the wind.

Gia's arms are heavy; her biceps burn with heat. Gia looks to them to discover she is carrying a baby boy. He is holding a silver rattle made with a speck of their family ore on one end and a round rattle on the other. He mouths the stone as he coos, and his skin radiates golden blue.

Gia and the baby float to the picnic blanket and join Ella and Gaillynn in a circle. Gia rests the baby boy in the center of them. Gaillynn reaches into a square picnic basket full of food. She is wearing a silk dress with a bright floral pattern, and she wears glossy red lipstick. In a long side-braid, Gaillynn's hair trellises over her shoulder and follows the shape of her torso. Gaillynn pours crystal clear water that reflects off the sun into three round glass mugs. Gaillynn then pulls the baby boy to her chest to breastfeed him.

◆

Gia wakes from her dream with a jolt. She attempts to open her eyes, but a bright golden light makes it difficult. Her eyes have difficulty adjusting. She squints toward the window and discovers it is still night.

The light is coming from their bodies. Gia sits up. She looks to her arms where she cradled the baby boy in her dream. Reality creeps back into focus. The current situation is not so sweet. "Gaillynn has a hostage in their basement, and I expect that she will kill him by sun-up."

"Time Keeper," she whispers. She creeps down the stairs to the living room and retrieves the leather diary from the back of the clock. She sits on the settee and rubs the piece of stone around her neck. Gia cradles the book of their stories in her lap like she did the baby boy just minutes ago in her dream.

She opens the book to the next blank page following Gaillynn's entry and writes the current story happening in their lives. After an hour or so, Gia tires; she returns the diary to the clock and joins her daughter and granddaughter back in Gaillynn's bed.

◆

Leonard drifts in and out of exhausted but uncomfortable sleep. He hears a single set of footsteps above him. He tries to yell, "Gaillynn," but his voice is low and scratchy with dryness. His mind flashes back and forth between his current predicament with Gaillynn and high school fourteen years before. He remembers when his concern, and his love, for Gaillynn began.

◆

It was senior year, only days before the Homecoming dance.

Leonard, part of Cooper's entourage, followed Cooper to Gaillynn's locker. He was invisible behind Cooper's tall frame but witnessed Cooper ask Gaillynn about the dance and her decline. Cooper slammed Gaillynn's locker and strutted toward Andie.

Leonard followed Cooper, passing Gaillynn. "Hi Gaillynn," Leonard said. His stare lingered at her green eyes, her wide smile, and broad teeth. *She's so beautiful,* he thought.

"I've heard he is after your dowry," giggled Leonard as he tried to make a joke.

"Hi, Lenny," she replied. Gaillynn's smile led Leonard to believe that she found him to be the sweet exchange student matched with a monster. "If you only knew how funny that is, Lenny," she said. Her laugh made butterflies dance in his stomach.

He recalls later that same evening, after hours of scouring the internet for blogs of well-known scientists in hopes of finding an internship when he took a bathroom break. Cooper, as usual, had locked Leonard's door to the shared lavatory. He skipped around to Cooper's bedroom and tiptoed in. Cooper was nowhere around.

He sat at Cooper's desk and explored Cooper's computer. On the screen was an online news site titled "Curse at Locket Manor." He clicked the back icon to review Cooper's search history and found a similar article, "Amirah Woman Widowed Again." He hit the back arrow again, this time a digital copy of their high school paper, "Gaillynn Amirah Named Lacrosse Rookie of the Year at Stonington High." Leonard heard Cooper stomping up the stairs. He returned Cooper's most recent search to the screen, snuck into the bathroom, and closed the door. Leonard felt saddened that Gaillynn's family was the focus of such intense media coverage.

Leonard returned to his computer and began his research on

Gaillynn. He learned a long tragic history of husbands lost to terrible deaths—and they did seem cursed with bad luck in love.

He read of the family fortune coming from life insurance policies. Journalists speculated that because of the curse, the Amirah women preemptively purchased significant life insurance policies. They were called selfish, murderous widows, and greedy. Leonard became angered at the cruel perspective and accusatory writers profiting off assumptions and speculative accusations for their financial gain.

The joke he told Gaillynn at her locker became even more ironic. Leonard laughed out loud. "Maybe she should let Cooper marry her; then he would die," Leonard said to himself in Cantonese and roared with laughter.

"Shut up, Qu!" Cooper yelled from his bedroom.

Leonard held up his middle finger at Cooper and pressed it against the wall between them. He folded his computer closed, and as he settled into bed for the night, he concluded, "This mystery of Gaillynn's family's past is fascinating, and I vow to find the truth and help her in any way I can."

◆

Bound by ropes so tight that his wrists bleed, Leonard pledges to keep that promise. He understands why Gaillynn is fierce in her distrust of men. Leonard assures himself that he will have the chance to tell her everything. Everything he has discovered will help her. Years of his research and discovery, more incredible and fascinating than he could have ever imagined.

Leonard's fingers and toes have become numb; he wiggles them to keep his circulation moving. A cricket accompanies him, hidden in the darkness. The insect plays a non-empathetic song. Music from the Homecoming dance—the night Cooper killed Robbie comes to his mind. His hate for Cooper swirls in his chest as he remembers. "This is why I am here, Gaillynn."

◆

Mrs. Blethen yelped up the stairs, "It's time to go, Lenny." Leonard finished tying the merlot-colored bow-tie that matched his merlot tuxedo; he checked his smooth black hair in the bathroom mirror and winked at himself.

The Homecoming dance was inside the school gymnasium; Leonard sipped punch from a small plastic cup; he wiggled his body to the music. Leonard smiled and said hello to anyone who passed him. A group of girls joined him. They danced in their small circle.

"Lenny, you look so handsome," said a girl wearing a dark-blue, sequined, mermaid-style dress. "You look like a giant valentine."

"Ooh-la-la, beautiful girl. Can you be my sexy valentine candy?" Leonard took her hand, twirled her with grace, then caught her by the waist in a quick dip toward the floor, all while not spilling the red punch in his other hand.

The circle of girls cheered and clapped. Leonard took the hand of each of the girls standing around him and led them to the dance floor, where they stayed for most of the night.

Leonard kept a watchful eye on Cooper. It worried him how he glared at Gaillynn and Robbie dancing on the edge of the dance floor. Even though Cooper came to the event with Andie, he was obsessed with Gaillynn. Cooper ignored Andie for most of the night and didn't converse with her, even when they danced.

Gaillynn and Robbie collected their things, appeared to be saying goodbye to their friends, and left. Cooper followed. "Oh shit," Leonard said in Cantonese. He trailed Cooper out to his car.

The shining black Camaro lurched backward out of its parking space, nearly hitting Leonard. The car bounced to a stop. Cooper stuck his head out of his open window and yelled: "Get the hell out of my way, Qu."

"Hey, Cooper, where are you headed? How come Andie isn't with you? Your date?"

"She's fine. I'll be back. I'm just going to get some beer."

"Oh cool, can I come?"

"Hell no, Qu. Get away from my car." Cooper pressed his foot on the accelerator, and the moving car forced Leonard to step aside. Leonard returned to the high school's gymnasium and asked Andie to dance. With a relieved smile at Lenny, she accepted.

Later that night, as the sweaty dancers exited the school and descended the long steps to the parking lots, loud voices with an edge of panic and distress echoed toward the school. Leonard approached to see what was going on.

One of the girls who left the dance early had returned in her pajamas with terrible news. "My parents own a police scanner, and they heard there was a possible break-in at the Mill. When the police got there, they found Gaillynn and Robbie, and Cooper Blethen," she said. "Cooper thought Robbie was raping Gaillynn, and Cooper attacked him. An ambulance took Robbie to the hospital. He was unconscious, and the paramedics were saying that his pulse was very faint and very slow. He was hardly breathing."

The crowd of students dashed for their cars and rushed to Stonington's only hospital. Teenagers wearing tuxedos and gowns filled the hospital's reception area.

A group of girls hovered in close to Gaillynn and hugged her as she sobbed. Gaillynn wore her Homecoming gown, which hung from her body due to the untied ribbons. Andie wrapped her jacket around Gaillynn's arms, and Gaillynn leaned her head on Andie's shoulder. Andie held her best friend with both arms.

The curse of the Amirah women proved itself true once again: Robbie died.

Cooper was allowed bail and spent the three days before his hearing at home.

◆

Leonard's mind raced, and his eyes dart back and forth under his closed eyelids. His breaths are heavy, and he presses against the ropes that confine him. A creak in the basement stairs makes him jump; the pointed brightness of a flashlight darts around the room. Leonard holds his breath, then blurts, "Roger, you don't have to do this. Leave this family alone."

Someone directs the flashlight into Leonard's face. Leonard squints in retreat, screeches another high-pitched trill, and bounces his chair away.

Gaillynn laughs. "Lenny, it's me. I'm not going to hurt you."

"Oh, thank God. Gail, is everyone okay?"

"Why do you ask?"

"I heard Roger earlier and a gunshot."

"What? Lenny, no, listen. I need to know something."

"Anything. Can you please untie me?"

"No, I'm sorry. I can't. I just can't. I want to trust you, but if anything happens to Ella—"

"I get it. It's okay. Keep me here as long as you need to, Gaillynn. I understand."

Gaillynn tilts her head in surprise. "You're okay with this?"

"Totally. It's okay. But I can help you if you let me."

"Lenny, if you knew Cooper killed Robbie on purpose, how come you didn't go to the police?"

"Gail, it was a nightmare. I didn't know what to do. I was afraid your secret stone would become the target, and according to Cooper's journal, it would have killed all of you if you lost it. That's why you still live with your mother at age thirty-two."

Gaillynn chuckles. "Yup, I have to live with my mother forever."

"You have space here." Leonard smiles back.

"I can't imagine living with that creep for four years." Gaillynn sits down on the cement floor in front of Leonard and wraps her arms around her knees.

"Mrs. Blethen tutored him," offered Lenny. "That's how he got off with such a light sentence."

"How do you mean?"

"I heard her. She said, 'In public, you need to hold your breath until your face and eyes turn bright red. Walk hunched with your shoulders slumped forward with your chin to your chest and drag your feet. Make zero eye contact with anyone, and you must say I'm sorry over and over and over again to anyone who asks you a question.'

"On the day of his hearing, Cooper acted precisely as his mother taught him. I watched him from the window. Three police officers escorted him from the house through a shitload of media into the back seat of a police car. He did exactly as his mother trained him. He dropped his head down and watched his feet as he shuffled along. He held his breath for as long as he could, then when Cooper finally inhaled, it appeared he was getting choked up. He made no eye contact but mumbled, 'I'm sorry' to any reporter that stuck a microphone in his face.

"After Cooper and his parents went to the courthouse, I was alone. I went into Cooper's bedroom and searched around. His computer was off, and I knew that Cooper's dad had been in there earlier that day, clearing his son's browsing history.

"I pulled open Cooper's top desk drawer. Inside I found a couple of porn magazines." Leonard raised his eyebrows. "I pushed them to the side to search underneath. I found a black-and-white checkered composition notebook. It looked as if Cooper had heavily used it. Unusual, since I never once saw Cooper doing homework.

"So, I investigated. There was a rough drawing of a grandfather clock inside the cover—dozens of drawings of a large gem or diamond shape surrounded by dollar signs. I flipped through more scribbled pages to one of a repeating name written on it: 'Gaillynn Amirah,' over and over and over, hundreds of times. I turned the page again and saw what appeared to be a story. It was titled 'Ginny Amirah's Bedtime Story: True.'"

"Oh shit," Gaillynn says.

"I read Cooper's story many times. I tried to make sense of it. Cooper believed the story, and it led him to commit murder. There were so many tears for Robbie's death; the town could have drowned in its sadness." Leonard sniffs his running nose and blinks away the tears.

"And if that wasn't enough, Cooper's father, Hank, was found dead from suicide the very next day. Hank was a good man. He felt so bad for all of this."

"I know, Lenny. I'm sorry. What have you been doing since high school? Where have you been?"

"Researching your stone."

"You're kidding me. Did you find anything?"

"I'd say I did. High school was over, and I was desperate for an internship for summers between my upcoming years at Harvard. I prayed my computer would find something. Like it knew just what I was looking for and would populate my search with the most pertinent links. I logged into my favorite chat room, What's New in Science and Discovery's live discussion, and typed in some keywords with the hopes someone knew something.

"I kept it secret, though. I asked, 'Hey nerds, has anyone heard of a rare stone or gem that is gold and blue? I think discovery could have been in England, the Hills, or the Midlands.'

"I waited impatiently for responses. Then all at once, they started pouring in from unknown sources linked in with the chat.

'Sapphire.'

'Hematite.'

'Labradorite.'

'Blue-gold stone India.'

'Fool's gold.'

"I had already considered all of those. So, I added, 'What about discoveries in the last few decades?'

"Then I got something. A chat buddy of mine responded, 'Hello L.Q., glad to see you're back in the chat. I know of a group headed to Black Mountain; they said they found fragments of glowing rock. It's blue gold and extremely weighty. No known elements have been identified like this before. You should check it out; they are building a team and need help carrying the equipment. They don't pay very well, but I know you've been looking for an internship—this could be your chance. Reach out to Reece Mathews at the GeoMatters Institute. Over and out, L.Q., come back and chat soon. ShftR.'"

Gaillynn jumps from her reclined position to upright with excitement.

"I immediately searched for the GeoMatters Institute, found its website, then searched the list of researchers and scientists. I found her, Reece Mathews. I composed an email inquiring about her research at Black Mountain and offered my unpaid help in return for a research assistant internship. The very next day, she responded with an invitation for me to join the expedition leaving in three days.

"The team trekked to an area hidden between two mountain

ranges where strange specs of a gold-blue compound were discovered during a standard soil test by some local scientists. They could not identify it, so they mailed samples to the GeoMatters Institute, which also had no luck.

"The area where scientists found the flecks of color was extraordinarily fertile and marked with a beautiful dark-green moss that grew in a perfect, large circle, with unusual tiny red flowers that resembled the shape of roses. The same patch of dark-green moss with small red flowers grew in a similarly shaped ring in a nearby cave.

"Soil tests also indicated evidence of volcanic residue stemming from very deep within the earth—deeper than any other discovered. That means older, too. Your stone came from or very near the Earth's core.

"The team set up camp near the two discovery locations. They constructed a large plastic tent to house their mobile lab. Power blocks and giant batteries, replenished daily with the sun's energy, supplied the electricity and power we needed for life in the field.

"Their archeologists removed the thick moss and dark layers of rich dirt in tiny increments. They uncovered what they later identified as human bones. It was so exciting, but it took so long.

"After seven days, they uncovered a skull, ribcage, pelvic bone, hands, and feet. The archaeologists found no long bones. We spent the last month of summer scouring the area in search of the missing bones of the arms and legs of the female skeleton.

"I went back every summer. Through all nine years of college, I spent summers back at Black Mountain with the research team. We never found the missing bones. By the last summer, we had identified the woman discovered as one of the earliest Neanderthal human women to have lived. They were able to decipher from her pelvic bones that she had had at least one child. Evidence suggested that her bones experienced an incredible amount of rapid healing and straightening when she was about eighteen years old.

"Within the bone and periosteum samples studied were an unusual amount of chondroblasts and osteoblasts that are essential to the healing of bone. However, due to the age of the bones, no bone marrow remained, which narrowed our testing.

"Her bones were significantly denser than any human bone ever studied. Her teeth had healed areas of decay and were much whiter, with zero evidence of alveolar bone loss due to periodontal disease that the scientists would have expected. She was exceptionally well preserved and exceedingly healthy for someone from that primitive time.

"All of us were baffled and couldn't explain these findings. Our team expanded our interest to nearby streams where other early Neanderthal families may have gathered in search of more answers. To our surprise, we found an area with signs of another family not far from the first.

"We discovered a third dark-green circle of beautiful moss-covered with specs of tiny red flowers near a shallow cave. I watched with disbelief as a large gold stone from the center of the darkened moss was unearthed. We were mesmerized by its beauty—intense blue and gold glowing and swirling—and its weightiness. It matched the particles discovered at the first location, but this was a complete stone, measuring eight inches in diameter.

"It looked exactly the way Cooper described the stone in your clock in his notebook." Leonard becomes excited as he tells the story to Gaillynn. His speech becomes mixed with Cantonese and English. "Holy shit. It's true. That son of a bitch was after that stone. I knew I needed to get back to Stonington before he got out of jail, but first, I needed more proof."

"Lenny, calm down. I can't understand you."

"Sorry."

Gaillynn giggles at Leonard. Beyond the details about her stone, she enjoys his story, and listening to him makes her happy.

"The scientists of GeoMatters placed an immediate gag order on all interns, scientists, researchers, and archeologists there. The gem was a discovery, and they knew nothing of its composition or its effect on nature or humans.

"So, by this point, I was convinced that Cooper was right about the stone; I was even more worried about you. I left the group of scientists, and I said nothing of my secret knowledge of a sister stone oceans away.

"But I didn't stop there. I spent two years looking for authentication and a connection to the Amirah family before returning to Stonington. I scoured thousands of records searching for the woman Cooper described as the clock-maker in his notebook: Glinda Amirah. She also proved to be real. Records revealed a woman with that exact name lived in Lancashire, just a few hours' hike from the discovery, during the mid to late sixteen hundreds. I also found payroll and tax records for her, having worked for J. J. Kyffin, Clock Maker.

"Armed with proof and doctorates earned in genealogy, bio-chemistry, geology, and astronomy, I headed back to Stonington, Maine.

"My alma mater welcomed me in with open arms and a teaching position at the high school. I know I'm overqualified for the position, but my main objective is protecting you, Gaillynn, and your family."

"Lenny, protecting us isn't your job. I can protect us. You spent the last fourteen years studying the stone and trying to find answers for us?"

"There's more, Gaillynn. Because of this discovery, the scientific community has learned more about our planet than we ever imagined."

"Like what?" Gaillynn extends her legs onto the cool floor and crosses her ankles. She leans back on her palms and smiles at Lenny.

"Our planet, Earth." He hesitates. "It's a living and breathing mass."

Gaillynn huffs. "What?"

"Okay, think of Earth as an animal. Her plants are her lungs. Individual plant species are like the alveoli of the bronchial passageways in a human. Her immune system is the ocean. The ocean helps circulate her air, and the saltwater cleanses and purifies many of our toxins. The rain washes mineral ions into the sea to fuel the astringent effect."

"I can imagine all of that, it sort of makes sense. But alive?"

"Your stone has something gold in it, right?"

"Yes."

"That gold is part of Earth's core. That's what made it so hard to identify. We cut the stone to study its compounds. It is one of the hardest diamonds ever known. It contains vital, living DNA. In fact, the bones we found at the site have matching DNA in high concentrations. I suspect you do too.

"The plants surrounding the discovery sites were not of this era. They contain the same DNA as the core material. We hypothesize that the stones rose from so far below the Earth's crust that they brought the cells of the plants from an earlier day on Earth with them. Gail, the stones traveled from the core. They are not stones; they are blue diamonds with profound imperfections. The imperfections are fractions of Earth's molten core."

Gaillynn pushes her eyebrows up. "Whoa."

"Blue diamonds are scarce. Your blue diamond is an entirely different kind of diamond with a composition of vital DNA and cells.

Blue diamonds are of the deepest found, but none ever revealed evidence of being from the core. The Earth's core is its circulatory system. Volcanoes are like an out pouched vesicle that bursts." Lenny uses his hands tied at the wrists to help explain as he talks.

Gaillynn watches his fingers. She says, "I have always felt like the stone communicated with us. Alive, you say? Okay, so if all of this is true, how did we get Earth's DNA and not you? Or anyone else?"

"I don't know, Gail."

Gaillynn leans forward, rubs her wrists, and yawns. "We'll talk more tomorrow, Lenny. Goodnight."

"Good night, Gaillynn."

Chapter Twenty-Three

The sun rises, Ella wakes to her mother's instructions to get up and ready for school. "No, Mom, I need to stay home. Mr. Qu is in our basement, and I don't trust you with him."

"What, honey? I didn't say anything." The pillow muffles Gaillynn's voice.

"Yes, you did. You just told me to get up and get ready for school," explains Ella.

"No, I didn't. I was thinking about it. But I didn't say it. You heard it?" Gaillynn pushes her face up.

Ella perks up to sitting. "I heard it plain as day, Mom." Her sleepy eyes widen. "I could hear what you were thinking?" They stare at each other without saying a word with their mouths.

"You just said: Yes, Mom. I heard it. But you didn't say it with your mouth; you said it in your mind. Didn't you?" asks Gaillynn.

Ella wiggles with excitement. Again her mother is silent. Gaillynn thinks, *Holy, fucking, fuck shit.*

"Mom!"

"Oh my God, you did hear me," exclaims Gaillynn. "Let's try your grammy. She isn't awake yet. You talk to her, Ella honey. Tell her something."

Ella concentrates.

"Ella, quiet down; you don't have to yell; I'm right here. I can hear you." Gia squirms in her sleepy state. Ella and her mother smile at each other.

"Try again, honey, but not so loud this time," Gaillynn thinks to Ella.

"Okay, this time, I will think: whisper." She concentrates on her grandmother again.

"Oh gosh, honey, we can't make peach-stuffed French toast today. Leonard Qu is tied up, and in danger of your mother, so I don't think we will have time. I'm trying to get up. Okay, okay, I'm up." Gia sits up and rubs her eyes, then stretches to the ceiling. Ella focuses on her and sends her another unspoken message:

"I've been speaking to you through my mind, and you have been hearing me without me saying anything out loud. Grammy, think something you want to say to me. Tell me something with your mind so I can hear you."

Gia looks at them both. "I'm confused," she says. They look back at her with eagerness. Gia's eyes dart back and forth between them.

"Come on, Mom, give it a try," Gaillynn thinks to her.

Gia swallows hard and struggles to think of something to say. Then she looks at Ella and tries to send her a message. "Your hair is a mess." Ella and her mother both laugh out loud. They both heard Gia's thoughts.

"Wow. I guess we can have three-way conversations too. Just don't think about a secret, or I'll hear you," chimes in Gaillynn. By saying this, she causes herself to think of her secret upstairs in the safe. She slaps her palm to her forehead.

"The safe, Mom? OH MY GOD!"

"Oh, stop it, baby girl, go get ready for school. Let's go make breakfast, Mom."

◆

Lenny wakes in his chair in the basement to the smell of bacon and maple syrup. His mouth waters with thirst and hunger. His neck aches from sleeping upright all night, and he stretches it to the side. He wiggles his hands and feet, and the tightness of the rope against his raw skin makes him wince.

"How can they cook bacon at a time like this?" Leonard jumps in his chair.

◆

Ella enters the kitchen; her eyebrows are squished together and her lower lip sticks out. "Okay, Mom, I'm ready for school, but I don't understand what I'm supposed to say about Mr. Qu."

"You don't need to say anything about Mr. Qu. He will just not show up today, and you know nothing about it. Do you understand how important this is, Ella?" Gaillynn places a steaming piece of French toast sprinkled with diced peaches and a dollop of cream cheese in front of Ella.

"Yes! Of course, I know how important this is. I'm freaking out here."

Ella hears her mother think, "Calm down, sweetheart." Ella relaxes and tries to eat. She bends over her plate, careful not to get drips of maple syrup on her clothes.

"I can't eat, Mom. I'm going to throw up." Unable to finish her breakfast, she puts her plate in the sink and scrapes the leftovers into the garbage disposal. She looks down at the floor, imagining Mr. Qu still tied in the basement.

"Mom, promise me you won't kill Mr. Qu."

"I promise. I won't kill Lenny."

Ella kisses her mother and grandmother goodbye and heads to the front door. She opens it as slowly as possible, hoping she will give her mother enough time to change her mind and let her stay home from school. The cold air hits Ella's face, and she steps outside, turning to make one last plea to her mother.

"Go," commands Gaillynn.

Ella shuffles toward the end of the driveway where the bus is waiting for her. She turns to look back at the house over and over again. The bus driver taps the horn. Ella doesn't want to leave, and going to school with Mr. Qu tied up in her basement seems so wrong.

She trusts her mother and shares her confident, independent state of mind, but this is bigger than just her mother; and her mother needs help. The iron gate opens as Ella nears. She climbs with reluctance into the school bus.

As she enters the quiet school bus, she realizes her newfound ability to hear what other people are thinking doesn't only work on her mother and grandmother. She wraps her hands over her ears in hopes she can stop listening to all the worry, panic, fear, and insecurity pouring out of the students' minds on the bus.

Ella has enough to worry about.

◆

Leonard takes a deep breath and wiggles his cold fingers and toes. He rolls his head forward from shoulder to chest to shoulder for a painful stretch of his tight muscles. The light of this new day revives his dedication to Gaillynn and protecting her truths.

He waits for Gaillynn's return to his side in the basement. And waits. He practices versions of his speech admitting his love for her over and over. He shakes the fogginess from his mind and attempts to remain clear-headed and focused. He closes his drying eyes and licks his parched lips. He falls back to sleep.

A few hours pass. Leonard opens his eyes. The rising height of the sun illuminates Locket Manor's basement. The demon mask that scared him the night before appears tame and childlike. He huffs a laugh. Footsteps above him and the mumbled voice of Gaillynn vibrate through the ceiling. He points his eyes up the stairs and catches a glimpse of shadow footsteps passing by. "Gaillynn. Talk with me. I have things to tell you. Gaillynn!"

The soreness around his wrists has become piercing with rawness. Wiggling his hands is becoming more difficult, but he continues. He strains against the rope and closes his eyes.

Leonard's eyes flash open to the sound of Gaillynn rushing down the basement steps. Dozens of large ceiling lights flicker to life. He squints at their brightness. Leonard identifies the tiny lightbulb above him that fizzled out the night before abandoning him in the dark. A relic of a former age of Amirah women—however, effective at scaring him to death.

Gaillynn goes to Leonard. She kneels in front of him and places her hands on his knees. "Lenny, I'm sorry about this. I hope you are telling the truth, but you must understand I have to protect this family."

"Gail, I understand more than you know. I have so much more to tell you."

"I can't listen. Not right now. Roger will be here soon. He, well, how can I put this? He's not going to get the stone. I need you to stay here just a bit longer, Lenny and don't make a sound. No matter what you hear."

"I can help you. Gail, untie me. Please. He's dangerous."

"So am I."

Splashes of blood on the floor and the saturated red rope around Leonard's tied wrists pierces Gaillynn with shame. She takes a deep breath, closes her eyes, and reminds herself, "I have had limited choices, none of which were good. I must be sure I can trust Lenny." She exhales and stands up.

She and Leonard lock eyes. She identifies a caring and determined assuredness in Leonard's face. It surprises her. He wiggles against the ropes. He presses his eyebrows together and winces with anger at the pain.

"Gail, Roger has Cooper's journal. He knows about the stone."

"It doesn't matter, Lenny."

"Yes, it does. It was my fault Roger found it. I'm sorry I was careless."

"What do you mean? How did he find it?"

Leonard wiggles against his restraints. "I was tired from class planning. I wanted to take a shower. As soon as I got in the shower, I heard a persistent knock at my door. I ignored it, but the knock recurred. Over and over. I yelled over the sound of the water, 'I'm in the shower.'

"I took the quickest shower I could muster, wrapped a towel around my waist and another over my shoulders, and went to the door.

"Who's there?" I said.

"Hey Leonard, it's Roger Blethen. I, umm, I just stopped by to welcome you back to town."

"I'm just getting out of the shower. Can you come back later?" Leonard Explains. "I opened the door a crack; my eyes land on Roger's chest. He's a big man Gail.

"Roger pushed himself in against the door. His wide shoulders and protruding elbows threatened the space around him. He turned to me with his hands fixed in the pockets of his tight jeans. Roger planted his larger than average work-booted feet, wide and steady under the immense girth of his frame. He was scary."

"He's not scary, Lenny. Just get to the point." Gaillynn lifts her watch into view.

"I escaped to my bedroom and got dressed as fast as I could. It was hard; I wasn't all the way dry, and my clothes kept sticking."

"Lenny, the point."

"I heard the rattle of Roger opening the refrigerator door, followed by the glass-clicking sound of him getting a beer bottle. My mind raced. What could you want to discuss, Roger? Maybe Cooper was fully aware that Robbie wasn't raping Gaillynn, and he was trying to get Robbie out of his way so he could get close to Gaillynn.

"Or, maybe Roger would ask: so did he kill Robbie on purpose, or was that just a bonus to his final plan of getting the stone? Or, are you aware of the screwed-up way Hank committed suicide the night following Cooper's arrest? Or, could it possibly be that he is worried that Cooper is still missing and wants to find him because he loves him so much and his mother is bedridden with grief that he is gone? No. None of that."

Gaillynn rolls her eyes and turns to leave him.

"Gail, when I went out to talk to him, he was gone. All that remained was a partially consumed beer on the coffee table. Then, that night, I searched for the first draft of the freshman biology syllabus in the pile of paper on my coffee table. I sorted through the entire stack—I realized Cooper's notebook was missing.

"I swept through all of the pages on the table, knocking them to the floor. Roger took it. My body felt weak and heavy, as if I would pass out. How could I have been so careless?"

Gaillynn ignores his question, climbs the stairs, and locks the basement door behind her.

Leonard stops pulling against the ropes for a second. Slippery blood coats his skin, providing a small amount of relief from the pain. He has made some progress, and the knots have loosened slightly, but he needs a break. He drops his chin forward and closes his eyes.

He takes a deep breath, holds it in, and pulls his hands against the knot around his wrists. The slippery blood allows a small part of his palm to escape, but the pain is intense. Leonard exhales, then takes tiny breaths in and out as he readies himself to try again.

The greasy blood lubricates his trapped hands. He holds his breath, puffs out his chest, and pulls—Leonard makes more progress. He breathes heavy and quick, fighting against the agony as if the pain is his skillful opponent. One he cannot let win.

---◆---

CHAPTER TWENTY-FOUR

It is nearly ten o'clock, and Gaillynn waits for her present adversary, Roger Blethen, to arrive for their planned meeting. She is ready. Ella is at school, she sent her mother outside to her Zen garden, and Gaillynn ordered her prisoner in the basement into silence. She prepared two mugs of coffee and a plate of cookies, and now she waits.

A buzz from the closed gate at the end of the driveway alerts her of Roger's arrival. Gaillynn walks to the front door. To the right of the door is the main panel to the home's security system. Gaillynn views the monitor and sees Roger alone in a box-shaped car. He hangs his arm out of the window, and his eyes peer up at the camera. For a moment, it reminds her of the cold and callous eyes of Cooper. She has a vivid flashback of his hypnotic stare into the living room through the window for hours at a time. Then she remembers his vacuum-sealed face and wide-open, distorted mouth. She relaxes.

Gaillynn commands the gate to retract. Roger enters the property and parks his car near the gurgling fountain.

She opens the heavy front door. Roger exits his car and, with caution, climbs the numerous stairs, his eyes fixed on Gaillynn's the entire time. Roger reaches her; she smiles at him. Roger raises an eyebrow and does not smile back. Instead, he huffs and pushes past her and into Locket Manor.

How dare he have the confidence of the victor in this situation? Gaillynn thinks.

Neither one says a word. Gaillynn closes and locks the door behind him, then turns to the security panel's keyboard and types in the code to close the gate. She spies a notebook under his arm. She motions for him to follow her to the living room. "Coffee?" she asks.

"No." His smirk annoys her. He smiles as if he has the upper hand—he knows not to trust her and drink the coffee, which is not poisoned and is an excellent cup of coffee. Gaillynn rolls her eyes.

Roger protrudes his chest and directs his elbows outward. He is large, primarily muscular, but also obese. Roger wears tight blue jeans and steel-toed work boots that add inches to his already six-foot-two frame. He scans the house, huffs, and shakes his head. "Blood money," he whispers. "Thieving bitches." Gaillynn huffs and rolls her eyes again.

"What is it that you said, Roger? I'm sorry, I thought I heard you say something?"

"I have information that I'm sure you want to keep secret." He pulls the notebook from under his arm and tosses it on the coffee table. He sits in her mother's recliner. To his surprise, the stone is in the clock were the day before it was not. It is beautiful. It confirms his intense desire to acquire it, a need, an immeasurable quest he must fulfill.

Roger stands up and steps toward the clock, stone glowing brilliantly. Gaillynn watches him, studies him. If he moves too fast, if he goes for the stone, she is ready. A bulge of a gun under the back of his tight white Oxford catches her eye.

She becomes aware of a visibly dark aura around him. Something she has seen before, around her father and Cooper. Something familiar that she now can see with clarity. It seems so evident today. She touches the stone in the necklace around her neck. All have been much clearer since the ore that she now knows is a diamond touches her skin.

Gaillynn identifies a dark shadow surrounding him against the light of the stone. The stone reveals the nature of his true self: darkness, void of light, empty of goodness.

She remembers the first time she noticed the darkness surrounding her father; he pounded his elbow into the ribs of her mother's chest to stop her from picking up Gaillynn to console Gaillynn's crying. The dark shape took on the figure of a demon pulling at his limbs like a puppet master.

It is the same darkness she saw around Cooper the night he beat Robbie to death. It surrounded him as he swung and pounded on the man she loved, as Robbie's head bounced off his foot. The stone was warning her, even back then, but she misunderstood.

Gaillynn always thought it was a blur in her eyes caused by fury.

Roger kneels at eye level with the stone and caresses the glass in the clock's door as if he were touching the stone itself. Gaillynn can hear Roger's thoughts. He is already addicted to its power and hypnotized by its beauty; he has become fixated on possessing it. He is sure that the journal is a powerful piece of ammunition rolled in his weak artillery.

He first wanted money to keep quiet, but now he wants it all: the money, the stone, and her life. Gaillynn becomes irritated and angry. The loss of the stone would surely kill her family.

Gaillynn wraps her palm around Roger's shoulder and squeezes, lifting him to a standing position. His eyes widen. "How did you do that?"

Gaillynn doesn't answer—she doesn't know. Gaillynn presses her open fists on his chest and caresses him. She can feel his heart pounding faster than it can tolerate. He slaps her hands away.

"Don't put your hands on me, woman. I know your game. You're just a spoiled girl in a woman's body. You're nothing but a greedy slut." He steps toward Gaillynn and towers his giant frame over her. "All you women are the same. Weak, needy, and emotional without a man. You think sex is your greatest weapon. Fecund the cunt and your widow's stone."

Gaillynn pushes him across the room and up against the wall. She holds him by the throat, and his feet dangle and kick against the air. "No. Sex is not our weapon. It's your weakness. If it didn't work, we wouldn't use it against you—men." Gaillynn's eyes darken. "You're disgusting."

Gaillynn's chest rattles with deep growls. Spit seethes through her teeth. "Assuming you know anything about me based on my gender alone is ignorant conjecture, vile, monstrous, and selfish. You are filth, and I will be happy to rid the world of your foulness."

Gaillynn pulls her cheeks into a smile. Ella would be so proud of me for saying those things, she thinks. Rogers's feet flounder in the air—one kicks Gaillynn in the knee. She looks down; her eyes pop.

"Whoa," she whispers. "I'm doing this?" Shock cools her anger, but only for a moment. The familiar click followed by the squeaking rumble of the dumbwaiter rising from the basement restores her fury. Her eyes dart from Roger to the entryway. She releases him. He bolts for the stone, and she reaches for the plastic bag and rope she has hidden under the seat cushion of the settee. She clutches the plastic and the end of the rope and is moving toward him. Roger struggles to open the clock. Gaillynn eyes the gun hidden down the back of his trousers. She reaches for his gun.

Roger smashes his hand through the glass door, and with bloodied knuckles, he grabs for the stone. Before he can remove the stone and before Gaillynn can take the gun, Leonard stumbles out of the dumbwaiter shaft. He blinks his eyes against the brightness and runs at Roger. Leonard pounds his shoulder into Roger's ribs. The two men tumble away from the stone.

Leonard continues to blink and squint in futility at adjusting to the light. The brightening glow of the stone makes it even more difficult. The two men struggle on the floor.

Gaillynn's prisoner from the basement has sabotaged her plan—she thrusts the rope and plastic to the floor with a huff. A golden aura surrounds Leonard revealing his true nature—Gaillynn gasps. The exact hue covers Ella and her mother.

But Roger, Gaillynn thinks.

Her first thought is to flee with the stone and leave them to kill each other. She frees the stone from its chains and holds it to her chest. Her heart aches for Leonard, and she watches how he fights for her.

She pushes her compassion for him away. *Ella must remain safe.* Gaillynn dashes away from them and up the two flights of stairs to her bedroom. She locks the door.

Roger knees Lenny in the stomach and crawls away from him. He reaches around to his back and pulls the gun from his belt.

Without hesitation, he aims and fires a shot at Leonard. Leonard flails in pain, rolls to his stomach, and becomes motionless.

The thunder of the gun's blast echoes through the halls of Locket Manor. Gaillynn sucks in a quick breath. "Shit."

◆

Outside in her zen garden, Gia sits cross-legged in the sand. She jumps to her feet at the noise of the gunshot. The air around her chills and storm clouds gather like smoke filling the sky. Gia studies the house and waits for more sounds. "Shit."

She runs through the gardens, up onto the back porch, and swings open the stubborn back door with such ease and force it bangs against the inside wall punching a hole in the plaster. She races toward the living room and bounds directly into Roger's chest. He is holding a gun. She kicks it out of his hand—it skids across the marble floor.

Gia hears his thoughts. He is after Gaillynn, who has the stone, and Roger just shot Leonard. Gia's face whips toward the living room, and she sees Leonard lying on the floor. Her hair floats in the still air, and her eyes glow a golden green. Her strength overflows, and she has embraced her all-powerful being.

Roger is becoming asphyxiated by his greed and the dark shadow engulfing his physical body. Gia turns to him and studies the dark figure hovering around him. Struggling to breathe, he realizes the woman he has just encountered could quickly get to the gun before him. She floats toward him with glowing eyes. He pretends to concede, holds his hands under his nose into a praying position, and bows to her. He shuffles past and follows Gaillynn up the stairs.

"He's coming," Gia thinks to Gaillynn.

"I know, Mom. Please take care of Lenny."

Roger's chest heaves against an invisible weight, and he fights the suffocation overcoming him. The stone is squeezing at his heart and tightening his lungs. The restriction depletes his muscles of strength—the stone pulses with happiness in Gaillynn's hands.

Gia rushes to Leonard's side. She places her hands on his chest and begins praying to the stone. Swirls of golden-blue energy seeping from her hands enter Leonard.

◆

Gaillynn dashes into her bathroom and locks the door. She searches the bathroom for a barricade. A chiffonier to her right will do the trick.

Roger climbs the stairs. With each step, two large breaths. He clasps the metal rails and pulls his body up each step but cannot hear signs of Gaillynn over his desperate breathing. He searches the maze of rooms, bathrooms, kitchens, game rooms, libraries, and endless hallways. A gray cat hisses at him from a library. It arches its back and walks toward Roger, showing all of his teeth.

Roger bends forward and presses his palms against his knees to support his upper body weight. "What is happening?" he whispers. His fight for oxygen feels inconsequential to his desire for the stone. So close to suffocation, but yet he continues—fueled by greed. Dondy has reached him and swats at his pant leg. Roger scoops the cat up and rolls it down the hall. Dondy screeches a loud meow, lands on his feet, and gallops away.

Roger opens doors and searches empty rooms and finds nothing. Until a doorknob that won't turn—a locked door. He hears a faint noise from inside. He steps back and lunges his heavy body at the door. He heaves for air and uses his near-dead weight over and over again until the lock gives way—he falls inside Gaillynn's bedroom.

He scans the room from his position on the floor; the enormous safe containing Cooper's lifeless body is to his right. He climbs to his feet, wiggles the safe's gold wheel, and pulls at it.

Maybe there's money inside, he thinks. He eyes the missing combination lock. He kicks the safe with a huff and moves on.

He reaches another locked door. Gaillynn is on the other side in her bathroom, where she has barricaded herself inside with a ten-drawer chiffonier pressed against the door.

"Just give me a minute, Roger." Gaillynn squishes the stone inside her bra for safekeeping while she searches the bathroom cabinets for a weapon. *Maybe I am strong enough to kill him with my own hands?* she wonders. She looks at her hands and remembers how easily she lifted the beast, Roger, off the ground just moments before in the living room. "Ew. No, thank you. That would be like smooshing a worm with your fingers. Gross."

She makes eye contact with herself in the bathroom's fully mirrored wall. Her reflection reveals something unusual—energy echoes back at her—energy radiating from her skin. In the mirror, it looks like a blurred and electrical outline of her form. She peers down at her body—it is normal. Gaillynn looks back at the mirror and again sees her power resonating in her reflection.

"Whoa."

Roger thrusts his body against the bathroom door, and the noise breaks her moment of self-adoration. Gaillynn pulls open drawers under the marble countertops and digs through endless products, lotions, bath crystals, cleansers, and cleaning products. She finds a pink razor, holds it up as if it could help her, and real- izes it barely cuts the hair in her armpits. She throws it to the floor and continues searching.

She finds a decently sized syringe given to her by her dental hy- gienist, who instructed her to fill it with Chlorhexidine and squirt it into her healing wisdom teeth extraction sites about ten years ago. She healed from the surgery so fast she never needed it. She searches for something to fill the syringe.

"The cleaning products," she remembers out loud.

Gaillynn locates a small bottle of bleach, unscrews the cap, puts the tip of the syringe into the caustic chemical, and pulls back on the plunger. The needle fills with the viscous, yellowish liquid.

Roger bangs on the bathroom door with his fists. "Gaillynn, open the fucking door." She doesn't respond.

He repeats, hefty lunges into the door. The chest of drawers shakes; outside, large ocean waves crash against the cliffside with each of Roger's blows. His persistence pays off, and with one final attack, he breaks through. The chiffonier tips over and crashes to the unforgiving marble floor.

His gluttony, exhaustion, and the stone are working to suffocate him; however, his heavy black aura pushes him to continue as a master puppeteer. He is slow and weak. He presses the door open: a desperate grumble escapes his throat, and the chiffonier slides across the floor. He lunges himself through.

Gaillynn whacks his temple with a heavy, marble toothbrush holder. His body becomes limp, and he falls to the floor. His face smashes against the marble tile—a pool of blood pours from his broken nose, spreading across the polished white stone. He rolls to his back, revealing his flattened nose and his missing front teeth. He groans and attempts to curl himself forward to sit up. He is too weak.

Gaillynn grasps the syringe filled with bleach; she identifies his carotid vein pulsing in his neck. She sits on his ribcage and presses her knees against his biceps, trapping him on the floor. Gaillynn sinks the syringe's point into the blueish red skin over the throbbing carotid vein and injects the bleach. She withdraws her weapon, then pulls back the syringe's plunger to fill it with air and injects the air into the same spot on his neck. She repeats the injections of air five more times.

A mini-tornado twirls toward the house. It steps up off the ocean and onto the lawn. It circles Locket Manor, whipping debris against its exterior.

Roger's breathing becomes labored, and with Gaillynn's weight on his chest, he can only manage tiny quick breaths in and out. His eyes bulged wide with panic. He groans and struggles against Gaillynn.

The bleach and the air travel through his veins and arteries. A bolt of lightning cracks against the sky and lands on the ocean opposite Locket Manor. Gaillynn's unique homemade armament causes his heart to become stressed. He reels in pain, extreme distress, and cardiac arrest takes hold. His lungs are unable to function, and his gasps for air become urgent and torturous. His brain goes into an irreversible seizure. His body twitches and convulses. His head bounces against the marble floor, causing even more damage to his skull.

Gaillynn continues to sit on him through his seizure and imagines she is riding a bucking bull. She even puts her hand over her head like she has seen men at the rodeo on television. The waves retreat, and the ocean calms.

Roger is still.

Gaillynn puts her fingers on his wrist in search of a pulse. Nothing. She stands up and, to ensure he's dead, delivers a swift kick to his ribs.

"Lenny," she remembers out loud. And then Gaillyhnn hears her mother's thoughts:

"Gaillynn, we need you."

Gaillynn jumps down the stairs three at a time to the living room to find her mother pressing towels over the gunshot wound to Leonard's chest. Gaillynn continues to listen to her mother's thoughts, "I can't heal him alone. His injury is much too severe; he needs all of us to save him."

Gaillynn pulls the stone from under her shirt. She wraps a

hand over the jewel and presses her other fingers around the piece in her necklace. She listens for a message of instructions.

Her mother yells, "Go get Ella, Gaillynn."

Gaillynn jumps. "Sorry." She places the stone on Leonard's chest and runs to her car.

Chapter Twenty-Five

Gaillynn presses her toes into the accelerator. Rubber squeals out of her driveway, and at a frantic pace, she navigates to Stonington High School. She arrives. The red Mercedes comes to an abrupt stop at the front door of the school. She whips the car into park and pushes the car door open so hard and fast it bounces back at her. She catches it before it whacks her in the shin and she jumps out.

Gaillynn leaps up the stairs and goes straight to the attendance secretary, who is staring at her computer and oblivious to Gaillynn's presence. Gaillynn can hear her silent reading of a chicken-pot-pie recipe.

"Ella Amirah has a doctor's appointment. I forgot to tell her about it, and you need to dismiss her right away."

"I'm ready, Mom. You didn't forget to tell me. Let's go." Ella stands behind Gaillynn.

Gaillynn exhales with relief and explains silently, "Lenny needs us all and fast."

The attendance secretary looks up at them and smiles. "No problem."

"Okay, Mom, let's go," Ella insists. They speed-walk out of school with their elbows wrapped together. With her thoughts,

Ella speaks to her mother, "I knew you were coming. I could hear you, and I already know what has happened. I've been dying here. I should've stayed home, Mom."

"Hell no," Gaillynn responds in silence. "Your grandmother is at home nursing a gunshot wound to Lenny's chest."

"I know. What the heck, Mom, you promised me."

"No, no, no, honey. It was not me; it was Roger Blethen, Cooper's stepfather. Roger found out about the stone because it appears Cooper kept a journal. Lenny knew Roger was a threat, and he was trying to warn us. Lenny broke himself free of the ropes in the basement and attacked Roger. He tried to protect us. I'm sorry I assumed the worst of him."

Their eyes embrace a moment at the silent communication between them. They enter the Mercedes, and Gaillynn bounces the car over the sidewalk and heads home toward Locket Manor. They voice their continued conversation through their thoughts.

"You don't trust anyone, Mom. But honestly, I understand. You have kept us all safe, and I know that's a tremendous job."

They hold hands for the entire ride home, and Ella recites a silent prayer to the stone that Leonard will make it. They park the Mercedes outside of the garage to save time and run up the front steps and into the house.

The women's minds are one and don't need to speak a word. It is clear what they have to do next. The stone is funneling nonverbal instructions through them.

Their intensified connection to the stone since wearing one tiny piece on a necklace has made things so much more apparent. The link has answered all of their questions. They know that the stone and the women are more potent when in contact with the other.

The stone thirsted and hungered for their contact and has been so desperate and alone hanging in the clock. It created turmoil, pain, death, and horrible tragedies so the Amirah women would hold it. The stone hoped grief would give the women a reason to touch it so that the stone could console them. It has called to them, all of them, over the centuries of its time. It wanted to be one with its humans. A piece of Earth united with her children.

◆

Andie enters Locket Manor's driveway through the gate that Gaillynn forgot to close. The car moves fast and rumbles over the cobble-stones; she parks next to Gaillynn's Mercedes, exits her vehicle, but halts after only a few steps. Andie scans the atmosphere around Locket Manor. If air typically had weight, it currently did not. The pull of gravity under her feet is gone. Instead, she floats and feels a push toward Locket Manor. She, too, is weightless. Her body drifts toward the house. Twigs, leaves, flower petals, acorns, and pine cones float around her and bounce off her. Once she reaches the stone steps, gravity returns. She leaps up the stairs and into Locket Manor.

"Gaillynn?" Andie calls. "Where are you?" She turns her head from right to left, scanning the large room. Noises are coming from the living room, so she dashes toward them.

"Andie? You cannot be here right now," says Gaillynn.

"Oh hell, yes, I can. I saw you and Ella racing through town just now, and I could tell by the look on your faces that something was wrong. But first, what is going on outside?" She points behind her.

"It's Earth. Hell, I can't explain. Andie, you have to leave. I can't protect you."

"No, I'm not leaving. No more pushing me away, Gaillynn; you aren't allowed to do that anymore. I'm not putting up with your shitty friendship. I'm here, and I'm not going away. And since when do I need your protection? I can take care of my damn self."

Andie looks at Ella. An immediate love squeezes her chest at the sight of Gaillynn and Robbie's daughter.

Ella can hear Andie's unconditional love and commitment to Gaillynn, and now, herself. Ella returns a loving but worried grin at Andie.

Gia holds a blood-soaked towel to Lenny's chest. "The bullet missed his heart, but the bullet penetrated one of his lungs, and it is filling with blood." Blood drips out of the corners of his mouth and sprays across his chest every time he coughs. He is weak and close to death.

Gaillynn leaves the group and dashes out of the room. "Mom, where are you going?" Ella says out loud.

"I have a hunch that we need the piece of stone in my jewelry box," she says with her thoughts.

"She is right," says Gia.

Gaillynn retrieves the fragment of stone from her jewelry box.

Andie has become silent and frightened by all of the blood in the room.

Gaillynn returns. Gia, Gaillynn, and Ella circle Lenny and sit on the floor. Gaillynn drops the last, tiny chip of stone into the bullet hole in Leonard's chest. She then places the large diamond on top of Lenny's wound. They each place a hand on the stone, clasp their other hands around each other in any way they can, to escalate Gia's healing power. They close their eyes and begin to hum.

Andie blinks away from her state of shock and takes a moment to survey the situation. "Gail, is that Lenny?" Gaillynn doesn't answer. "What caused all of that blood? Who shot Lenny? I'm calling 911."

Gaillynn fists Andie's ankle and connects her to the stone's power. The omnipotent authority of the Amirah Diamond funnels through Andie's body. Andie gains instant understanding; she now is part of the force funneling through them. The stone's love and its healing power bring tears to Andie's eyes. "Whoa." Andie sits down and joins the circle; she has no previous stone experience, nor biological connection with its elements, her love for Gaillynn and her family bridges the gap.

The women's skin and the stone begin to glow with a golden intensity. The tiny piece of stone inside Lenny's chest dissolves into him and becomes part of him. The brightness of his aura returns—the same fantastic shade of gold as the Amirah women's aura. The stone is becoming part of him, and it is healing him.

Gia's propensity for healing, a virtue bestowed on her by the stone, becomes more powerful now and saves his life.

The women's eyes remain closed; they channel a message from the stone through themselves and each other. Their unity, their bond, and their strength will make everything right.

It is so clear how wrong they have been. The lost loves, the sadness, the loneliness was all because they needed to touch the stone. Its sole purpose was to heal, to love, to thrive, and to save them all.

Another car pulls into the driveway. It accelerates toward Locket Manor and skids to a stop. Two car doors slam, followed by heavy footsteps. Marguerite and Jack rush inside. Marguerite holds the framed photo of Geneve Amirah. Gaillynn's eyes fill with tears.

"Is this a bad time?" says Marguerite.

A loud sob escapes Gaillynn's throat. The room is filling with love and her family. Marguerite does not explain their visit, nor does she demand one of the group. She motions for Jack to sit down. She leans the framed photo of Geneve against Leonard on the floor.

Jack and Marguerite join the healing circle. With them, they bring the smell of cooked seafood permeating their skin. Gaillynn lets out a low chuckle.

Jack and Marguerite pile a hand on top of the group that embraces the stone. Everyone closes their eyes. Ella touches Marguerite's leg and unites her on their journey with the stone. Gaillynn does the same with Jack.

This moment is the what the stone has been questing for—when the stone tells them its story. The stone's magic unites them on a journey within their minds and through time, so they will understand. They see a woman wearing a crown. It is Ella, but older; and the story she tells within the group's shared vision explains everything.

◆
Chapter Twenty-Six

Queen Ella speaks to them. "Don't be afraid. It is me, Ella. Mom, you have made great sacrifices to protect us. And Grammy, you are have found your strength. A force you may find hard to believe has tested you—our home, our mother—Earth. She is all-powerful. Our stone is her gift, a fragment of her soul—her heart. Through it, she has shown us nature's way—beautiful and loving, but cruel.

"All of us are Mother Earth's children: humans, animals, beasts, and insects. We are pulling away from her. Her people no longer walk barefoot on her, swim in her oceans, or lay on her grass. She needs to be in contact with her children—as the stone does us. We are not the cause of her ruin; we are the remedy.

"Mother Earth is a living part of her children, and without a close, touching connection, she and her children are alone. Each is weak, tired, sick, and suffocating. Roads have been built over Earth, covering her beautiful skin. We built tall buildings allowing her children to live further from her than ever before. They drive in fast cars that spit out toxins, and all of her creatures breathe it in. Humankind hunts and kills her precious animals for sport and fights about gods and love."

Listening to her future self releases a stream of tears down Ella's cheeks.

"Today, you learn what you need to do—the answer of the stone and our purpose: we need to share the stone and cultivate a new race of warriors and healers to save Mother Earth and her people.

"The stone has shown us how to find gentle people with the auras that match our own and how to see the flat, colorless auras that are killing us all. And most importantly, how to stop them. Let me tell you a story."

Future Queen Ella's dark, curling hair, glistening in the light of the full moon behind her, cascades far below her waist and hips. Her locks flow and dance in the air from a subtle wind. A crown of metallic blue and gold pulls the loose curls back away from her splendid and radiant face, becoming an angelic halo around Ella's face. Her skin glows, reflecting the land and the light of her soul from within—her aura; Ella's ruby-red lips purse with stress, and her golden-green eyes water with sadness.

The tears pour from her eyes and waterfall from her cheeks onto her chest and trickle-down her body. Colorful leaves in the form of spades and hearts caress her ankles and bare feet. She holds a golden staff in her right hand, and she attempts to poise herself by straightening the delicate, beaded, haltered corset around her torso. She caresses the blue-gold metallic stone fastened around her waist.

◆

"Earth has become a hot and humid planet with fertile soil rich with exotic and colorful vegetation. The female inhabitants of Earth are the matriarchs of the galaxy and embrace all other planets and life with guidance. We thrive in the warm climate and espouse all beings and worlds with love. The air smells sweet, like honey and maple, as do our people."

Queen Ella looks out over a carved stone podium to meet the curious eyes of her people—a fierce tribe of women who love and protect each other with profound dedication. They defend and shelter each other without hesitance and quest only for what is right for their world and each other.

"Women have been in the power of Earth for centuries, and since their rule, there has been no war. No casualties from the greediness of men, no thirst for power, no poverty, abuse, or rape. The very stone Earth is composed of is connected to the core of her people's DNA. Its compounds are part of each of them. Without our land, our stones, our earth, our bodies would wither and die.

"Mother Earth is a living, breathing part of us. The land is in tune with each of us, and together we have cultivated a happy world.

"My queens, I stand before you today with the sad news of our planet. The beautiful Mother Earth once suffered, and by this, her children suffered. There was a time when she lost her power to sustain them. Her children abused her resources, and she became very sick. As a result, Mother Earth could not keep them nourished—their happiness failed, their health failed, just like their Mother Earth's, and worse, continued war appeared imminent.

"Earth's children no longer grazed upon her with bare feet. Many of them did not touch Mother Earth at all. They stopped drenching their skin in her oceans and her lakes, avoided her mountains and dirt. They stopped caressing her grass, flowers, and beasts; her children cut her flesh, smothered her derma, and suffocated her.

"Her children starved Mother Earth of their embrace, and they pulled away from her more and more. Her children stopped loving each other, and as a result, there was so much pain that all they could do was hate. They exalted themselves over all others, and their spoils became gluttonous and toxic.

"They conjured false logic to support war and intolerance. Furthermore, Earth's children's divided beliefs became targets of their hate—they argued about gods and love.

"Her people were not the disease. They were the cure. Mother Earth was starved and would have died if we did not gift our ancestors with her fertility of today." Queen Ella caresses one of Earth's stones fixed to a belt made of gold and diamonds pressing the stone tight to the skin on her waist. She wraps the palm of her hand over the jewel.

Queen Ella's skin pulses a kinetic vibration that travels through each person before her. A wave of love embraces them.

"The selfishness of power-hungry men rose over our mother. Earth and her women allowed men to smoother them. The women of Earth knew a better way but became complacent, and in hopes of healing the dark side of men, they conceded to them.

"Women granted immoral and villainous men power. The power they did not deserve and could not master permitting the rape of our world, their bodies, their happiness, and risked the lives of their children.

"I have been charged with ensuring our past queens receive our gift. In doing so, I set forth the destiny of my mother, father, and grandmother, and in it, a man murders my father the night of my conception." Queen Ella covers her face and weeps. "The Earth as we know it now will provide a small piece of itself. We must raise it from her core and provide a glimpse to the future so that all women will know their rightful place in power.

"We covet ourselves as we covet the Earth, and only for fairness and tranquility. Once we learned this, only then did the land that sustains us begin to eat away at the darkness."

There is unanimous approval from the millions of women gathered to listen to Queen Ella. Cheering and clapping fill the air with hopeful energy.

"So it is destined that we will send two stones from today's Earth back to the beginning of our time. We will pull vital gems from Earth's core and gift them to the strongest of our ancestors. We will put them in her hands and entrust them to her guardianship.

"Let us call upon our combined abilities to locate that ancestor who shall receive the gift of our power and our insight. I pray it does not destroy her, and let us hope that she listens to the stones and does what they instruct her to do. Let us begin. It is time."

A woman at Ella's side retrieves two stones from a large wagon made of steel adorned with diamonds. Her beauty is as all queens', equal in measure but unique in her way. Her hair is yellow, wavy, and wild. Her skin radiates gold with metallic blue waves that resemble the surf pattern in the sea or like ripples in a puddle.

She bows forward and hands the stones to Queen Ella. The two women embrace and part with a kiss on the lips. Each stone is large enough to fit in the palm of her hands; Ella places them on the stone podium in front of her.

The mass wrap arms around each other's elbow and places the palms of their hands on their stones around their waists. All queens, different in physique, complexion, color, and familial genetic code, are children of Mother Earth. They are thousands of mothers.

Some with large bellies don beautiful marks of pregnancy: exquisite designs formed from their skin stretching as the life inside them flourishes. Colored paint and diamonds adorn their skin to decorate the patterns, shown off with pride even after birthing is over. These are their beauty marks of motherhood: empyrean and goddess-like.

Others cannot bear children are the mothers to those who are motherless—a mission equally as rewarding and necessary. The symbol of motherhood, embossed on their loving arms, is an artful design branding their triumphs just like the marks on the pregnant bellies of carriers.

All mothers swaddle newborns and toddlers, boys and girls, with soft fabrics to their bosoms. A speck of blue-diamond earth, bound in gold, is pierced into the ears of each baby.

The women unite in body and mind, and collectively their minds travel to a place and time on Mother Earth before the wars, before corruption, before civilized times, to a time of Neanderthals.

Their traveling minds' find her, a Neanderthal mother. But not just any Neanderthal mother—she is a Neanderthal Amirah woman in the very early stages of her first pregnancy.

Through their connected minds the see: a large, leathered-skinned man is confronting the woman. He is her mate. He is aggressive and forces her down to the rocky ground. He is smelling her skin and her hair and down to the base of her stomach. He can sense something is different. She isn't fertile anymore—she is pregnant.

He becomes enraged, hits her stomach, and kicks her legs. He persists in his dominance by attempting to rape her. He pulls her tangled, dirty hair and tries to press her legs apart.

The Amirah mother fights him. She pulls her knees to her chest and kicks at his face. She pushes him off of her with her feet, but he is persistent; he comes back. She rips out his hair and scratches at his eyes. He doesn't stop.

The mother puts her mouth to his cheek, bites him, and tears off part of his flesh. He jumps back for a moment but comes back at her again. The Amirah mother spits the devoured piece of his face to the dirt, and before he reaches her, she stretches her hand toward the nearest rock pulling it into her palm. She whacks it into his temple—he falls to the ground. She continues to pound his face and skull with the rock until the father of her unborn baby is motionless and unrecognized. She stands up, drops the boulder on his chest, then arches her thick neck and roars to the sky.

"This Neanderthal Amirah mother is the one to receive our gifts," Queen Ella says. The two stones become airborne and soar from the podium. Their movement is so fast that they pull a stream of debris behind them and journey posthaste. The stones navigate a miraculous voyage and glow with fire and heat as they travel through Earth's atmosphere, opposite the planet's spinning. The stones' journey is so fast they take themselves back in time to earlier life near Earth's core.

"We will call her, Restore," announces Queen Ella.

Her name is chanted over and over by the crowd, "Restore. Restore. Restore..."

A grumbling vibration coming from the ground startles Restore. Dirt rises below her feet and pushes up from far below the surface. She gasps, grunts, and points toward the ground's movement with her firm hand and bent fingers. She growls a warning at the rising dirt; it doesn't waver. She grunts a low, "Urge," scurries out of sight, and hides behind a tree.

The stones erupt from the ground near her with a ferocious explosion soaring into the sky carrying molten lava then imbed themselves deep into the ground upon landing.

Steam rises from the earth. Restore approaches with caution walking on her hands and feet. She presses her nose to the ground—something new. She puts her ear to the soil. To her surprise, an unusual hum of women's voices. Restore halts all grunting, and she listens. Tears build in her eyes and stream down her dirty cheeks. A unique feeling has come over her: joy.

Restore plunges her fingers into the dirt and digs into the location of impact. The earth feels warm on her skin, and a sweet smell fills her nose. She becomes protective of her discovery and looks around as she covets the area with her elbows pointed out in defense. The dead body of her mate remains motionless; still, she growls at him.

Restore cups heaps of dirt with her hands that she pulls to the side. Her fingernails become lifted with packed gravel underneath them, her blood mixes with the soil. The reflection beaming from the stones through the thinning ground brightens against Restore's face. She wraps both of her palms around one of the diamonds only to receive a painful surprise. The stone, still encased in lava, burns and sears her palms.

Restore jumps back and licks her wounds. Her scalded hands heal immediately, heightening Restore's curiosity, but fear forces her to step back. Too painful to touch, she curls up on the dirt near her excavation. Her body absorbs the delightful heat coming from the ground. She falls asleep, and the stones begin their magic.

The stones' nurturing energy begin seeping into the pregnant woman's body and her unborn child.

When Restore wakes, she is startled to find strangers at her home cave; her sweet odor and warmth drew them to her in the night. Her eyelids flutter. Restore's once dark-brown eyes are now the same color green as Queen Ella's.

The newcomers mull around her. They suck in air pungent with her smell. Their bodies sway from bent knee to knee, and their fingers drag the ground below.

Something is flickering near the stones eruption site. It is yellow and orange, and smoke rises from its motion. Restore reaches out and touches it. It, too, burns her. She licks her wound and hisses at the fire. She finds a stick and pokes at it—it catches fire. She finds another log, and another, and another—each one catches fire. Soon she has created a raging beastly fire. She growls at it. The fire fills the air with heat and beauty. Restore pats the ground near it, a sign of peace and welcome. She decides it has not come to fight.

She lifts the man-beast—her mate, she killed the night before and throws him on this new, hot discovery. As the fire boils his skin and cooks his body, the group becomes delighted with the smell of it. They are drawn to it with an unusual feeling in their stomachs and drool they cannot control drips from their mouths.

Once they can touch the corpse without being burned themselves, they eat him. This newly formed tribe of Neanderthal men and women accept each other and consummate their bond with a meal.

While the others are busy pulling the last bits of flesh from the bones of their breakfast, Restore retrieves the stones that came to her in the night. She reaches through the loose dirt and pokes at them with caution. They are cold.

Restore hides the diamonds inside her cave. She cleans the jewels with her spit and dirty fingers. They feel good in her hands. She changes. Her skin radiates a golden yellow, her teeth whitened, and her body heals all of its past ailments and injuries. She stands straighter and smells of honey and maple.

The scent in the air evokes desire in the male Neanderthals eating outside. They drop their cooked body parts and crawl toward Restore's cave with their noses in the air. The women in the eating circle abandon their food and point their noses toward the sky; the women smell her too, and they realize that Restore is pregnant.

The women pick up heavy logs and beat the men into submission. The men back off, and Restore remains safe.

Restore hides the stones from the others. She keeps them in her bed. Her body and her growing baby absorb their power while she sleeps night after night. Her belly grows significant and triumphant marks of stretched skin color her abdomen.

The men of the group become submissive and take orders from the women as they learned it earns them a favor and a chance to mate from time to time. The more cooperative, loving, and helpful male occupants in the group become favorites. The other men grow jealous and try to lure the favored men away and kill or wound them to improve their place and a chance for mating in the group.

The women become protective leaders and serve the group with compassion. Restore begins to trust them and decides to show them one of her stones. She keeps one stone a secret, and in her bed made of sticks and grass, and places the other with the rocks around their fire—to keep it too hot for them to touch.

Little does she realize that the intense heat from the fire causes the stone's composition to become excited. The inclusions of Earth's core material releases powerful hormones into the air inside the steam and smoke. These particles become embedded in the cooked meat, breathed in from the air, and absorbed by her growing baby.

She continues to sleep with one of the stones and uses the other stone for cooking throughout the development of her fetus. The particles from the stone became part of the baby girl's cellular composition. It changes her DNA structure. Her genetic makeup now houses the mysterious compounds also found in the diamond— Mother Earth is now part of her.

"This unique DNA makeup passes on to generation after generation of Amirah women. Since then, only women have been born in this family, not a single boy, with the Earth's cellular com-position—a gift sent from your future with a purpose to restore Mother Earth and her people, to regain their lives, and the promise of a healthy planet and people that will thrive and live to their full-est," Queen Ella explains to the group around Leonard.

"Restore touched the stone in her bed at night while she slept—it was not enough. After many years, Restore became irritable and angry most of the time. The pull of the stone and its constant call to her made her feel crazy. She beat and killed her entire tribe for getting too close to her, her child, or the diamonds. Soon, Restore and her daughter were alone.

"Restore, old and senile, cast her daughter out of the cave and away. Restore's life went on, alone. Soon, lonely and mad, Restore died of old age and illness as she lay beside a small flickering fire. Her eyes fixed open in her death, staring at the diamond in the fire pit.

"Her daughter, who never went far away, came out from hiding in the nearby trees to her mother's side. She had grown tall, slender, and muscular. She had remained close but out of sight for years. She survived by staying near the stone—it called to her and kept her close—and by eating her mother's leftover scraps of wild meat at night.

"She would lay with the stone in the fire pit in the darkness, alone, and caress it with her hands while her mother slept in the cave. She would keep the fire alive and keep watch for danger with-out her mother's permission or knowledge—the beginning of the Amirah women's keen survival skills."

In the groups shared vision they see Restore's daughter kneel next to her dead mother and grunt. She nudges her mother's body with her forearm, then puts her face close to hers and inhales her scent. Restore doesn't respond. Her daughter drops down to sit on the ground, presses her back against Restore's back, and runs her fingers through the dirt.

The second diamond calls to her from her mother's bed inside the cave—an identical diamond under the mattress made of twigs, leaves, and moss. She wraps her hands around it and pulls the diamond to her chest—happiness and warmth wrap her body.

She leaves her dead mother and the other diamond in the fire pit. She walks into the woods, never to return.

Chapter Twenty-Seven

Gaillynn inhales, and with a light, airy whisper, she says, "Earth is our mother." Each person in the circle on the floor around Leonard, opens their eyes, their minds are still one, and without speaking, they receive a universal understanding amongst them—the solution to their curse. "If we preach the stone's purpose, Earth's purpose, and connect it to our bodies, there will be tranquility. No more equal measure of evil, death, nor horror for the Amirah women. Unless the nature of our mother deems it necessary."

Leonard wakes. His eyes flash open, and his chest rises and falls. He, too, has heard the stories from the stone. He traveled the same journey as the women and Jack through time. He puts his hands on his chest over the bullet wound, and he feels no pain. Gia healed him. The bullet lies on the floor beneath him.

His skin is bright, and his aura reveals itself and is evident to the group watching his every move. It's a full-body halo the color of goodness—golden blue. Gaillynn notices something more: a surprising attraction to him. Her cheeks flush, and desire rises in her body. Something she hasn't felt for anyone since Robbie.

Gaillynn studies him. His straight hair has become full and wavy, his skin is clear, his chin has a deep dimple, and his cheekbones and jawline have become chiseled and sharp. His lips are plump, and his teeth shine a bright white. His dark-brown eyes have turned deep emerald green, and his muscles are bulky. *Is this how Lenny has always looked, and I am just now noticing, or is he changed?* Gaillynn asks herself.

His eyes meet Gaillynn's, and they gaze at each other with infatuation.

Ella rolls her eyes. "Mom!"

Lenny sits up. Ella catches the stone as it rolls off of his chest. The group rests, share smiles, and relieved heavy breathing.

"Hello, Andie," says Leonard. His voice is quiet and weak. Andie lifts her palm and gives him half a wave and a wink. He reaches a hand toward Marguerite. "Hello, I'm Lenny Qu."

Marguerite shakes his hand. "Marguerite."

Jack reaches toward him and shakes Leonards's hand. "Hello Lenny, I'm Jack." They share cordial smiles and nods as if these introductions are a crazed standard final step to sharing a mind-trip to the future where Ella is Queen and then saving Leonard's life.

"I knew it was you in my vision, Ella. My granddaughter will be queen." Gia puts her hands to her heart. "I'm so proud of you, honey."

Ella shakes her head.

Leonard turns to the clock. He studies the etchings on the front and crawls on his hands and knees to get a closer look. He touches the rose carvings hand etched by Glinda and caresses the curves.

"This is bone," he says. "I have located the missing bones from the body found at the original dig site. These are the bones of your ancestor. She has been with you, all of you, all along; she was possibly the first." They gather close to the clock to touch the carved flowers.

"It's not wood?" Ella asks.

"No," answers Lenny

"I have something to tell you," says Marguerite.

Marguerite begins, "My name is Greta Lynn Amirah. My mother used to call me my Greta. After a while, it just became Marguerite."

The group goes silent.

"My great-great-great-grandmother was Geneve Amirah."

"How old are you, then?" asks Gaillynn.

"One-hundred and fifty-six. I think."

"How? You live so far from the stone. You saw how sick I got being away from it for two days when we visited Eden's Garden," says Gia.

"I can explain. Geneve had twins—two girls. Their powers were great and obvious from birth. Their unity caused an electrical charge around them. Things levitated, their skin beamed gold, and intense weather followed them. Many men accused Geneve of being a witch. People tried to kill the babies. She decided to separate them so their powers would quiet. She placed a speck of the stone onto my great grandmother's tongue. Then nursed her so she would swallow it. She took the baby by horseback to an orphanage and left her at their door."

Ella squeals. "We're related!"

Jack's face is white. "You never told me."

"Jack, honey, I'm sorry. You would have thought I was crazy. After what we have all seen today, I knew you would have to believe me now."

"Have you been married before?" Jack asks with hesitation.

"Um, yes. Yes, I have. You are my seventh husband." Marguerite's eyes dart from her hands to Jack and back and forth again.

Gaillynn breaks the silent tension among them. "Who wants coffee?"

"I do," says Ella. She jumps up.

"I do," says Leonard.

"Me too," says Andie.

Gia wraps Marguerite in a tight hug. "I love you." She joins the group in the kitchen, leaving Jack and Marguerite alone to talk.

◆

Later that evening, in the pitch black of midnight, Lenny, Ella, Gia, Andie, Marguerite, and Jack carry Roger Blethen's dead body wrapped in a blanket to Roger's car parked next to the fountain. Their strength doesn't require as many hands to help, but they are unite in the effort regardless.

"How the heck to do you open the trunk?" mumbles Leonard from the driver's seat. "Oh," he says. The trunk pops open. They lay Roger in, and the car bounces under Roger's weight.

Gaillynn, inside her bathroom, is kneeling on the floor with her face pressed close to Roger's blood. Her rear-end points to the ceiling as she pulls back on the plunger within the same syringe she used to kill Roger to suck up what's left of his wet blood pooled on the floor. Once complete, she squeezes the thick red liquid into a Ziplock bag labeled in red marker by Ella: "Plastic will be the death of us all." Again and again, she withdraws blood from the floor until no more wet blood remains.

Gaillynn scoops up his fractured teeth with her gloved hands and plops them into the plastic bag, then scrubs the dried smears off the floor with bleach. She fills a large black trash bag with dozens of blood and bleach-soaked white towels.

Once Gaillynn's chore is complete, she tosses the plastic bag down over the stairs to the basement and joins the group outside. Armed with cleaning products, Gaillynn also carries Roger's blood out of the house to Roger's car.

All seven of them squish into Roger's four-door Volvo sedan.

Leonard drives the makeshift hearse to the cliff that overlooks Rockefeller Bay. The ride is silent and dark, and the headlights remain off. Once they arrive, Leonard, Jack, and Marguerite lift his body from his temporary coffin and carry him to the edge of the cliff.

The crashing waves below work effectively to muffle the sounds of their presence on the cliff. The air is filled with a salty scent and is cool enough that their breath puffs white as they move about the night.

Leonard breaks the silence, "Hank Chandler Blethen took his own life at this exact spot. The legendary Amirah curse has taken two husbands from Jessica Blethen. And what of her son, Cooper?" Leonard shivers.

Gaillynn and Gia make eye contact.

"Roger called it a widow's stone," says Gaillynn.

Leonard's eyes meet Gaillynn's. Worry presses his eyebrows together. The memory of the group's enlightenment of the stone's purpose and his love for Gaillynn settles his thumping anxiety.

The group holds Roger's dead body in their arms, they eye each other, and with their thoughts and nods, agree to toss him over the cliff's edge. Roger's body falls toward the jagged rocks exposed by an extremely low tide. They watch his falling body until its impact. Gaillynn leans over the edge of the cliffs and dumps the Ziplock bag of blood and teeth out into the ocean to accompany Roger in the cold water. Gaillynn reseals and stored the bag in her pocket, planning to add it to the collection of evidence in her basement.

They leave the keys in the ignition, wipe all areas their prints could have been laid with Gaillynn's cleaning products, then remove the blanket covering the trunk where Roger's dead body rested.

They walk barefoot through the woods along the path laid by

a younger Gaillynn that leads back to Locket Manor. Marguerite whistles an eerie but inspiring toon the entire return hike. Once the group of seven reaches Locket Manor, they begin removing all evidence of Roger's visit and murder. Except for Marguerite's whistling, the house is quiet. They work until dawn, then gather in the basement to burn the blanket, the towels, the plastic bag from Gaillynn's pocket, and cleaning supplies in the ceramic kiln.

The orange flames burning all clues of Roger Blethen's murder hypnotizes the—no one speaks. Gaillynn places Cooper's black-and-white checkered notebook on top of the burning evidence. The edges brown, then it too becomes hot orange coal: the fire hisses and pops. Exhaustion settles over the group.

"I'm going to bed," announces Ella with a yawn. Gaillynn kisses her forehead and hugs her. Andie takes Ella's hand and kisses Gaillynn on the cheek; Andie leaves the group with Ella.

Gia kisses Gaillynn on the cheek next and follows Ella and Andie. Marguerite takes Jack's hand and motions for him to follow. "Goodnight," Marguerite whispers.

Gaillynn and Leonard remain. The heat of the kiln radiates against their skin. He takes her hand in his; Gaillynn welcomes his fingers within hers. His touch tingles through her arm and into her heart. She squeezes his palm in hers and pulls him close. She kisses him.

Gaillynn thinks about Robbie as she kisses Leonard. The energy from the stone rises within her, and her eyes well with tears. She cries through Leonard's lips and presses her body close to his. He responds and wraps his arms around her waist, pressing tight against Gaillynn. He moves a hand to her face and wipes her tears. Leonard traces her wet neck with his fingertips. Gaillynn drops her head back and releases a quiet moan.

The past fourteen years of holding it together come undone in the basement with Leonard. She thought she would never feel this way for another man, nor that she would allow it.

The heat from the fire burning in the kiln beside them and their desires oil their bodies with sweat. They undress each other with eagerness and intertwine their naked bodies on the cement floor. A passion rises between them so powerful that only the protective walls of Locket Manor can contain it.

◆

Chapter Twenty-Eight

Gaillynn and Lenny hold hands walking into the high school gymnasium. They pass under a wide sign that reads "Science Fair." Gaillynn wears a navy-blue pin-striped pantsuit over a white buttoned-up collared shirt and a deep burgundy-red tie—products of Louis Vuitton's Women's Valor collection and Gaillynn's recent shopping spree. Her hair is pulled back into a tight ponytail, and her makeup done in natural colors is flawless. Her patent-leather white high heels click the floor as she walks beside Lenny.

A group of high school boys begins a rough game of two-on-two on the far side of the basketball court, ignoring the science students lining the outside walls of the gymnasium with their science-inspired presentations. The science students overlook the impromptu basketball game. They busy themselves with rehearsing their lines or putting the final touches on their exhibits.

"Hey, Mr. Qu, can you help me?" asks a boy a few tables down from Ella's.

"Hi, Mom."

"Whoa, Ella, this is extremely well done," Gaillynn says.

"Thanks. Is Grammy coming?"

"Yup, she's here. Do you need any help setting up?"

"Nope, I'm all set."

"Any other good contenders for first place?"

"Well, Nathan did a pretty good job on solar energy, but nothing new. I don't care who wins, Mom. This is about bettering our planet, not a blue ribbon," replies Ella.

"Um, okay. I'll go walkthrough and spy on the other scientists anyway, and I'll let you know who your competition is."

"Ha, okay, Mom."

Andie approaches and gives Ella a long hug.

"Andie, let's go check out her competition," Gaillynn says.

"Oh, sounds scandalous. Can we sabotage?" Gaillynn wraps her arm around Andie's waist, and they begin their circle.

"Mom, please don't cause any trouble."

"You leave the parenting to me and the troublemaking to Andie and me." They laugh.

Gia makes her way in, waves at Ella, and joins Gaillynn and Andie for the rounds.

Ella presses the power button on a small white speaker hidden among her presentation. She bends over and whispers a command, "Play 'Paradise Remix Tilted,' by Kristine and the Queens." A symphony of harmonized voices coral through the gymnasium. A deep thumping base anesthetizes Ella's overactive brain.

Since she can hear all thoughts of everyone in the room, music helps streamline most people's thoughts to focus on the music. Sometimes it takes the surrounding thought processes on a dreamlike journey that Ella enjoys more than the average stressed-out high school student's brain activity.

Andie and Gaillynn screech with giddy younger selves high-school-best-friends enthusiasm at the sound of the music.

"It's your theme song, Gaillynn," Andie says.

"It's just as much yours as it is mine, toots." Gaillynn turns to Andie, and she takes both of her hands into hers. They pull back and swing their hips then twirl their arms around each other's shoulders, and with their faces pointed at each other's they sing:

"'I am actually good, can't help it if we're tilted.'"

Gaillynn, Andie, and Gia dance as they circle the room. Gaillynn eyeballs all of the other high school die-hard science students as if she is sizing up her own competition. She makes her way back to Ella's display. "So keep this on the down-low, but every other pitch is trivial and so middle school. You'll get first for sure."

"It's okay if I don't, Mom. I still plan to use this design to restore the Ozone."

"Okay, smarty pants. I'm totally behind those brains of yours; you just tell us what to do." Gaillynn, Gia, and Andie find an empty spot in the bleachers to wait out the hour or so until the science fair will begin.

◆

Kristine and the Queens, set on repeat, energizes joyful moods for everyone in the gymnasium filling with parents, students, and siblings. Lenny visits each table of his students to help with any of their final needs. Gaillynn smiles at the site of Leonard and Ella working. "God, they are adorable."

Gia waves at Marguerite and Jack when they enter, and she pats the two saved seats beside her. They climb a few rows up, shaking the bleachers under Jack's weight and hug hello.

The judges assemble with their clipboards and make their way through the crowd to the first table. Ella lowers the music in the room. Each presenter is allowed ten minutes to explain their science project before the judges score the table and move on.

After two other presentations, they approach Ella's table and introduce themselves. Ella wears a baby-blue pantsuit with a white rigid-collared shirt underneath—a vintage Chanel relic found in her mother's closet. Her hair is tied back in a tight ballet bun, and the only makeup she wears is mascara and lip gloss. Ella scans the eyes of her judges and senses they are ready to listen. She instructs the speaker to stop playing music, and she begins.

"We all know the Ozone layer is a layer of gases attracted to our planet. It provides us with protection from the sun's radiation. Without it, we will die. We all know that, right?" says Ella. The judges nod in agreement.

She continues, "We also know that this layer is getting thinner because of chemicals called chlorofluorocarbons. Most of these chemicals are produced by refrigerants and plastics. And although it is natural for the compounds of the ozone layer to break down, it is also natural for them to repair themselves. Like the cycle of dead skin cells sloughing off and replacing themselves.

"With so many chlorofluorocarbons in our atmosphere, the repair of the ozone compounds has become impossible. Therefore, the ozone layer is getting very thin. Similar to the over-exfoliation of skin cells. If the cells can't replenish themselves quickly enough, you end up with an open wound.

"There isn't an actual hole in our Ozone yet. But, there are fragile areas at the polar caps. Our atmosphere is in danger. So I'm presenting my two-fold solution.

"Here, you see a large glass ball—this glass ball represents our ozone layer." Ella taps the glass with her fingernail. "Inside the glass dome is us." She points to a small round painted planet Earth.

"Also inside this glass is the air we breathe and destroy. I have represented the Ozone layer with this glass ball, and to illustrate my point, please imagine that if we destroy the air within our atmosphere too much, this glass, the Ozone, will break. We will have no protection from the sun's radiation, and we will all die.

"The first step is that I have created an air filtration system that will remove the chlorofluorocarbons, the methane, and excess carbon dioxide in our air. We can remove the pollution from the air within our Ozone. The second step of this plan, and the only way for the solution to work forever, is to stop producing the excessive harmful carbon molecules that will destroy us and our planet.

"We need to step back more than two hundred years in our evolution of the food industry and start again with the knowledge we have now. Furthermore, we will save our Earth with her resources—the sun, the wind, the water, and us, humans—this is what we need to save the world."

A crowd has formed around Ella, and the judges are wide-eyed and impressed.

"For the world to recover, I have created a to-do list for everyone involved. And that is every single living, breathing human being on this planet." She hands each of the judges a thick stack of bound papers with the words *Mother Earth Initiative* on a cover sheet.

Ella turns to her glass ball and blows on a small prototype of her air filtration unit. With the wind from her lungs, the turbines churn, and with the movement, it creates an energy source to continue and provide wind to circulate the air around the small earth inside the glass dome.

"Have you tested the air quality after filtration, and have you, in fact, removed the harmful carbons?" one of the judges asks.

"Yes, I have."

They judges whisper to one another. Another asks, "How is it filtering the air?"

"This fan comprises an amalgamation of compressed compounds that bind to the harmful molecules and render them inert.

These inert molecules are captured in a collection container and stored until we find a use for them. However, these inert compounds could also build up and cause unknown harmful situations we are not yet aware of, so the world has to stop producing the toxins altogether."

"That is such a bold suggestion. How can we just stop? Have you a solution?" asks a third judge.

"Your question poses the ultimate barrier to the success of the initiative—fear. Fear of change. I just handed you almost two inches of paper detailing every single solution. I had to use paper because you wouldn't allow us to submit a digital file instead."

Gaillynn claps and Ella continues.

"Death is bold, don't you think? Are you willing to offer your life over it? Are you defending what is wrong because it is a big job to change?" Ella doesn't allow time for the judge to answer.

"There should be no options nor opinions to ensure our planet's survival; there should only be orders and obedience. An inconvenience like not using plastic is small in comparison to the long-term devastating effects. The inconvenience of not producing vehicles that run on carbon fuel is also trivial. Get over it, woman up, and sacrifice. Inconvenience is not a valid argument." The embarrassed judge writes on her clipboard in dissatisfaction with Ella's frankness.

"Amen, Ella," Gaillynn says from the crowd. Gaillynn, Gia, Andie, Marguerite, and Jack clap and cheer for Ella's display of brilliance.

◆

Lenny and Gaillynn hold hands and walk hip to hip behind Ella and Gia to the Mercedes. Gaillynn taps her wristwatch, and the trunk pops open for Ella, who places her science-fair gadgets and revolutionary air filtration unit into the car. Ella wears a third-place ribbon around her neck.

The group piles into the car and joins the traffic jam exiting the school.

"So, now that we know we have been anointed with destiny to extricate our planet and her people from the pending annihilation caused by our thoughtless desecration, what is on my to-do list, my sweet love?" Gaillynn asks Ella as she winks at her through the rearview mirror. Gaillynn and Gia are in front of the Mercedes, and Ella and Leonard sit behind them.

Gaillynn turns to her mother, sitting on the passenger side of the car, and gives her a proud smile. Gia smiles back, and as they wait for Ella's response, Gia raises a tissue to her nose to catch a sneeze.

"Nothing for you to do, Mom. But Grammy has to seduce the richest man in the world and get him to back my initiative."

Sitting in the back seat beside Ella, Leonard lifts his eyes from Ella's initiative, nods at Ella, and chuckles.

"Mom?" Gaillynn asks into the rearview mirror.

"Me?" Gia turns to Gaillynn with her fingers and tissue still squished up her nose.

"I'm serious, you guys."

"How about something more realistic like Ella Amirah for President," says Gaillynn.

"President? Oh gosh, no. I'm going to be Earth's queen. Remember?"

"I remember," Gia says through her tissue.

Happy laughter and teasing fill the six-minute ride home. However, it comes to an abrupt stop in the driveway. Ella's and Gia's bodies lunge forward against their seatbelts.

"What the heck, Mom?"

Lenny's body bounces forward, but he is unfazed and remains oblivious, due to Ella's initiative that he has been trying to read all the way home. He is utterly enthralled.

Gaillynn leans forward over the steering wheel—she is focused up at Locket Manor.

"What, Mom?" Ella and Gia also lean forward and lookup. "What are you looking at?" Gaillynn remains silent. "Mom, are you okay? I can't hear your thoughts."

"How many chimneys do you see?" Gaillynn asks. Gia begins to count.

"There are eight, Mom." Ella already knows without counting. She begins making the same realization her mother has.

"Yup, I count eight," says Gia.

"How many fireplaces do we have?" asks Gaillynn.

"Seven," Ella says in a cheerful tone. "There is a chimney over Kendal library, but there is no fireplace in that area, and the furnace is nowhere near. Mom, what happened to the eighth fireplace?"

"I don't know, but I'm going to find out." Gia and Ella follow Gaillynn through the halls of Locket Manor into Kendal wing's library. Dondy greets them at the library's entry and welcomes them by rubbing against their legs. The three women stand side by side in front of a wall of books. The familiar coolness in the room sends shivers up Gaillynn's ankles.

"I've always hated this room. It's there, behind those books," says Gaillynn. "That space is too deep for a bookshelf alone. There is something behind it, and there is no good reason anyone would have covered up this fireplace. This room is the draftiest room in the whole house."

The women set aside their copies of Ella's *Mother Earth Initiative* and begin removing books and piling them on the floor around them. Ella climbs the rolling library ladder for the books near the ceiling and passes them to her grandmother. Gaillynn kicks off her high heels, removes her suit coat, and rolls up her crisp white Louis Vuitton sleeves.

◆

Leonard, still reading in the car, realizes the women are gone. He gets out and heads to the house. Leonard searches for them in the living room. He eyes the clock out of habit and sees the gray rock from the garden that Ella wrapped in the heavy chains, that now swings along with the pendulum. Gaillynn replaced the front after Roger's smashing attempt to steal the stone with glass from the hardware store.

Leonard could listen, and he would hear their thoughts to locate the women; however, his preoccupation with Ella's astute remedy has complete control of his mind. Next, he searches the empty kitchen, the backyard—no one. He knocks on Ella's bedroom door, and it squeaks open. The blue-and-gold family ore rests on her bed beside her pillow and teddy bear; but, no women.

Leonard tries the Hendrick library first—it's empty. He reads as he walks and makes his way up the stairs and through the halls of Kendal's wing to Kendal's library.

"Found you. What are you doing?" He approaches Gaillynn and wipes the dusty sweat from her forehead, and kisses her on the lips. "You smell delicious," he says in his mind.

"God, you two." Ella covers her ears as if it will help drown out the thoughts between Gaillynn and Leonard. "I wish hearing people's thoughts could work like Wi-Fi, and I could turn it off sometimes."

Gaillynn chuckles and turns back to the wall of books. "I don't know what we are doing. I just have this feeling there is something behind this bookcase."

"It's built into the house, Gail," he says.

"Not originally, though." She explores the now-empty shelves with her fingertips.

"What are you looking for—a secret lever or something, Mom? This isn't Indiana Jones."

"You're right. Don't touch anything; I'll be right back." Gaillynn leaves them.

As instructed, they don't touch a thing. Instead, each with a copy of Ella's work, they settle into the reading chairs. Dondy meows and digs his claws into the empty bookcase. He circles the legs of the preoccupied readers, then jumps up onto Gia's lap and demands scratches to his head.

"Ella, I have read your initiative once already; it's brilliant. However, I need to reread it; there is so much to absorb," says Leonard. "Once this gets out, and it will because it needs to, it's going to make the people killing this planet pissed. But," he said with emphasis, "all the people who will save the Earth will embrace this. Just be ready for a storm."

"I expect as much."

"There's always been a storm," says Gia from behind the white document in front of her face. "What do you mean by 'vitiating, without exception, profanation and gross defilement of indigenous resources in addition to the obliteration of the sewage of our existence?'"

"Gram, there are twenty-five pages dedicated to clarifying that, but it essentially means stopping anything that is causing pollution that is overwhelming the world and stopping overusing and depleting our natural resources."

"You are one intelligent woman, Ella. There are going to be many raging wealthy, gluttonous fools," giggles Gia.

"I have solutions for them all; it's in there."

"I particularly like Index Q, where you defend this digital age as the answer to our overuse of paper and trees, our natural air purifiers," adds Leonard.

Gaillynn returns, donning a pair of black leather work gloves with several various-sized crowbars and a rubber mallet in her arms.

Leonard jumps up to help. "Don't touch anything, Lenny; I don't want anyone to get smash-happy," she points to each of them one at a time. "I'm going to take this apart piece by piece, very carefully." Leonard shrugs, returns to his chair and continues reading.

Gaillynn climbs the rolling ladder and begins with the wide crown molding at the ceiling. She pounds the crowbar between the top and the wood and loosens its grip. She pulls it off, and it drops to the floor. She pulls the rolling ladder along as she makes her way down the wall, separating the trim-work and peeling away the layers of paint that glued it all together.

She moves to the molding along the floorboards; once removed, she begins pounding her crowbar between the wall and the book-case. She moves from ceiling to floor over and over again, pressing the boards out little by little.

Gia asks, "Ella, who is Dr. Abheck Noblemyer?"

"He is a doctor of psychology and a master of human behavior research. He blames modern humans' deterioration and dysfunction on the fixation of bad in the media and news. He postulates that we would be a better behaving world with the simple act of hearing only good news. For example, when we are told stories of other human beings being evil or violent, we innately connect that to ourselves. We experience the trauma and hopelessness and become it; we become damaged by it secondhand, and as a nation, we become insecure."

"That's what your blog, Good News, is for? No wonder Fox wants to pick it up," says Gia.

"What do you mean they want to pick it up? Since when?" asks Ella.

"Oh sorry, they called yesterday on the house phone. You were at school." Gia hides behind the document.

"Grammy!"

A loud rumble shakes the floor. A spilling mass of something has avalanched from behind the bookcase.

"Guys," says Gaillynn. The bookshelf is now pulled open and away from the wall. It reveals what it was constructed to conceal.

Ella gasps and covers her eyes. Gia goes to her and wraps Ella in a tight, protective hug.

Leonard moves to Gaillynn and catches her before she falls. "Holy hell," he says. Leonard lifts and carries the limp Gaillynn to one of the reading chairs and places her in it. He wipes the sweat from her forehead. "Take deep breaths, Gail honey; I'm right here."

Ella approaches the fireplace relic that the giant bookcase has covered. She fans the cobwebs away with her white document and kneels to the hearth. Human skeletal bones intertwined with rusted chains pool on the floor; Gaillynn discovered a crypt with dozens of bodies inside the walls of Locket Manor.

Moving the bookcase disrupted their resting place allowing the bones that filled the entire chimney flue and fireplace to empty onto the floor. Dust and cobwebs become aerosolized and float through the room.

"It looks like these bodies were dumped down the chimney from the roof," says Ella. Leonard leaves Gaillynn to investigate.

"How?" asks Gia.

"By climbing," answers Leonard. "All it would take is a strong woman and a massive wisteria tree." The women look at each other, then out the window at the wisteria leaves covering it. "And by doing that, the smell would've gone right out the top of the house, like a pipe. The third-floor library, likely the least used room in the house. A perfect hiding place for dead bodies. Who are they?"

"I have no idea," says Gaillynn.

"Dondy knew it, didn't he?" asks Gia. Dondy jumps off of her lap and creeps toward the bones with his body pressed to the floor.

"I've heard noises from this room my entire life. I think these people's ghosts are in this room," says Gaillynn. "It sounds like thunder sometimes or rattling."

"It's just the air trying to escape out of the chimney, Mom. I've heard it."

"I've heard it," adds Gia. "I hope it's just air."

"I don't think air trying to escape out of the chimney would be so loud. I think Locket Manor is haunted."

"Okay, Mom," Ella whispers and rolls her eyes. Ella's attention draws to something hidden within the bones. She picks through the pile with her fingertips, placing each bone to the side with a delicate touch. She uncovers a leather-bound book covered in dust. One of the skeletons clutches the book in its hand bones. Ella pulls open the clasped fingers and retrieves the book.

Gaillynn jumps to her feet. She grabs the diary from Ella's hands.

"Mom!"

Gaillynn opens the soft leather cover to the first page and reads: "The Year 1771 Geneve Elaine Amirah."